A Bed In Sheol

by

Sam D. Pakan

ATHANATOS
PUBLISHING GROUP

A Bed in Sheol
   by Sam D. Pakan

ISBN: 978-1-64594-222-1

Copyright 2024, Sam D. Pakan. All Rights Reserved.

Published by Athanatos Publishing Group.
                                        www.athanatos.net

Also available in hard cover: ISBN: 978-1-64594-220-7
And as an E-Book: ISBN 978-1-64594-223-8

To Gigi

Acknowledgements

Every sentence I write and every paragraph I review, I strive to see through your eyes, Dorothy J. Clark. I've never doubted that you have the firmest grasp I've ever encountered on the principles *showing* a story. Thank you, always, for your guidance, tutelage, and patience.

Curtis Shelburne, copy editor and friend, I am indebted to you for the gentle questions that I learned to welcome. My obsessiveness with style was balanced both by your insights and your familiarity with every divergence of opinion in the world of grammar. I doubt I'll ever be confident about a manuscript that doesn't bear your stamp of approval. May *The Chicago Manual of Style* be with you, my friend.

I salute my friends and military experts, Kyle Marks and Alan Mann. Your availability, even under incessant questioning, was indispensable. And thank you, Alan, for leading me to Charles (Ed) Neely who greatly simplified the task of gathering information on the procedures and practices of the Judge Advocate General's Corps.

So, while I'm confessing my deficiencies as a researcher, I must acknowledge E. David Dolak for connecting me with a professional researcher, David Abernathy, who uncovered in a few minutes what I'd spent weeks trying to find. Who knew that a shortwave radar transponder, the Rebecca/Eureka as I was to learn, didn't need to be reinvented for this novel?

Finally, I offer eternal gratitude to Terry, my good friend, who called frequently or rode by on his bicycle to ask if I'd finished this book. I so miss our visits, Terry! Also, a big thank you to Ben who insisted that I keep things in perspective by remembering that I'm not Shakespeare. Then there's Barbara, who admonished me to take better care of Dancer, this time, and Roger, who never failed to ask how much longer it was going to take. If the four of you can find this book in a small shop along the golden streets, I hope you like it. If you can't, I'll bring extra copies when I come.

PART ONE

Chapter I

*Bruges, Belgium
October 1943*

Land flowed out before him, hills swelling above a dry creek bed. Cottonwood and shinnery leaves mounded around roots blown free of soil, and grass crested in the wind as blood drained from a glacial sun. Dancer dropped his head, leaned toward him, the horse's mane a liquid black, the eyes heedless of the icy tentacles that lashed his friend to the earth. Nicole moved close and rested her head against Dancer's neck, her presence stirring a fever in David's breast.

Something shifted, and he opened his eyes to a blur of motion, white and frigid.

"Can you stand, Lieutenant?"

"I don'..." The words rasped across his swollen tongue and goaded him from the dimming peace. He urged himself upward, then fell back.

"It would appear you cannot just yet."

The voice moved behind him, and he flinched to avoid another Wehrmacht boot. Lightning flashed behind his eyes, and pain shot down his neck. "Lord, now lettes' thou thy servant—"

"The Nunc Dimittis, is it not, Lieutenant? An inappropriate prayer, I should think. You are quite safe now."

Schneider. David drew crystalline air and tilted his head to ease the pain. His arms heaved upward, air gusted from his lungs, and his boots scraped across the bitter white.

"My apologies, Lieutenant, but I am unable to carry you." The German's lisp warmed his brow. "Prepare yourself. I must now drag you into the car."

David pushed the pain away and conjured the gentle sweep of Nicole's hair across his cheek. Arms slid around his chest and hove him into a velvet warmth, the cushioned seat a momentary reprieve. He forced his eyes wide and stared at the canvas top quivering in the breeze.

"You should drink this, Lieutenant. You've lost a quite a lot of blood."

A bottle appeared from beneath Schneider's coat and rested warmly against his lips. Water filled his mouth, singeing his gums, and setting his loosened teeth ablaze. He tried to swallow, but something obstructed his greed, and the bottle moved away.

"You may have more, but you must first rinse the blood from your mouth. Roll to your side and spit." The leutnant chuckled. "You needn't worry that I will require you to clean it. This time."

David turned, the rawness of his neck catching him midway, and pulled himself to the edge of the seat. He spat the viscous mix onto the floorboard, rolled back, and let his eyes close. The bottle touched his lips again. He shuddered at the sting but was overcome by want and drained it.

Schneider stirred above him, and a door slammed behind his head. A few breaths and a second door slammed at his feet. Springs sagged, and the engine raced an octave higher than the Saloon that had delivered him to his execution.

The car wheeled around, the world spinning beneath him, memories forming in warmer air. He squinted above the front seat and saw the edge of Heinrich's face within the brightness. Black hair fell in rare imperfection across the flawless brow.

Thoughts surfaced on stiller waters. "So, I owe you." The words were powerless against the ice thrashing beneath the fenders.

The German listed, tilting his head. "What's that?"

"You saved my life." David drew what breath he could, held it against the throbbing and paused, reluctant to release it. "What's it going to cost me?"

The leutnant straightened and jerked the Stabswagen to the left. "You were quite effective at delaying your execution. That may not have increased von Felder's fondness for you, but your survival was a remarkable achievement. And quite good fortune, I would think."

He sucked against his charged teeth. "So was your showing up. Finally."

The German grinned. "You will be in the infirmary for some time. We shall discuss the cost of my intervention there if you wish."

"You took von Felder's prey. He'll—" The effort stole his strength, and he let his head ease back against the seat. A spasm contorted his back, burrowing beneath his shoulder blades.

"The Wehrmacht is no longer your concern, Lieutenant. You are my prisoner now. The matter is settled."

So, Schneider had won his appeal. David steadied, let his gaze drift toward the window behind the leutnant's seat, and released his thanks in silence. Heinrich might not be trustworthy, but the man was still the closest thing he had to a friend in this little corner of hell. "You're the victor, Herr Leutnant. You beat the Wehrmacht." He paused, took in what air he could. "Will you still allow Nicole to leave Belgium unharmed?"

"So long as you keep your band of hellions from any further mischief, Lieutenant."

Pine and alder branches stuttered against the dizzying brightness beyond the window. David closed his eyes and pictured Nicole as she brightened the perpetual dusk of their sanctum. The little car dropped into a hole and rebounded. He bounced from the seat, the earth tilting. The azure clarity of her eyes blurred, burning coals searing his shoulders and neck. He drew hard for air. "My ribs, Heinrich. Can barely breathe."

The leutnant turned, his face betraying some concern. "Perhaps the infirmary will allow you morphine. That should make it easier."

He hadn't the patience for Luftwaffe fairy tales, would have snorted if he'd had the air. "You got the letters from my Bible?"

"Henri dispatched them before my return."

"The letter to my father, too?"

"He sent both letters, David. Try to relax."

The car skidded against a frozen rut, and fire shot through his ribs, scalding his neck and shoulders. He struggled to hold onto his thoughts, but lost his grip, closed his eyes to the dizzying brilliance, and yielded to the comfort of the dark.

Chapter II

Something pierced the sweet unknowing and turned the air electric. Jesse jolted and opened his eyes to the near dark. *Dancer?* The horse wanting oats, maybe, or nickering for David. He turned his head and saw the faint glow of the window on the wrong side of the room.

Naomi's place. He forced himself to breathe, to know it as the way things were. He would learn to sleep here for all the strangeness, the traffic and commotion, but it would never be home. It was like waking after the fall, his legs withering beneath him, weeds behind a cultivator, the truth beyond belief.

This new truth was no easier. The telegram came first, telling them David had been shot down over Belgium and was missing in action. The letter came nearly two months later. He'd scarcely restrained his hope at seeing the address on the front of the envelope written in the boy's hand. Until he read it.

He raised himself on the mattress, rolled toward the desk beside the bed, pulled his right leg over with his hand, and thought of the loss folded neatly within the drawer. David had asked for his forgiveness, had requested that he take care of the horse, to see to it that Dancer didn't go to Morgan or anyone who would take his heart and spirit with a knife. Or any other way. Jesse could find no hope of his son's return, no matter how he read the words, the boy as much as saying he wouldn't be coming home. Not alive, anyway.

He rubbed the growing tightness in his chest, had done as Naomi thought best and offered Morgan a lease-purchase on the place, but he woke with doubt crowding out breath most mornings. A man might build a business for himself, for his old age, to have something to sell. But not a ranch. A man built a ranch for his children and their children, so they could know the life he knew. If not that, then a place to produce food if the life they'd planned failed. Or the country failed them. A ranch was something sure to hold onto, a piece of eternity you could sink your fingers into. Was all that gone? All his father worked for? All he'd sweated for and bled over? All David had hungered for and loved? The sweet earth was as much a part of him as blood and bone, and he'd spent his life watching her turn her fecundity over to death, until he'd become a part of the rhythm. But he'd been severed from her pulse, torn from all things good and somehow lived. Too long, as it turned out. Not in years, maybe, but in usefulness.

The patterns on the wall took form from blackness. He heard Naomi stirring in the kitchen and took in the mingling of coffee grounds and gas burners. He hadn't questioned his sister's judgment before and shook his head at the loss. And he'd outlived his son and vowed not to allow himself to hope he hadn't.

* * *

Jesse sat in his chair outside the kitchen, watching Naomi move within the gray, so certain of her perception that she had no need for light. The fleet unfurling of her hands above the cutting board reminded him of their mother's. He hadn't known the comfort of a woman's presence for so long—the order of things, the yielding of life from the certainty of her plans, her never doubting she was right. No man could do that. He'd not lived with it since his woman died with David just a boy. Eleven then? Twelve maybe. But of an age to work—too old to waste his time on tears and mourning. The boy had learned. Eventually.

He gripped the push rings and eased the chair across the rug and onto the kitchen floor. Naomi turned, put a finger to her lips, warning him not to wake the baby, as if he were a child himself unable to discern when to speak and when to keep silent. He gritted his teeth and tried to dampen the fire in his chest.

Bacon lay on a wet towel, the eggs readied in a row. He turned toward the window and saw the trees bending in the gray. David would have had his cup poured and cooling on the table. He pushed the thought away and wheeled toward the stove to get the coffee pot. Naomi rushed from behind, lifted it above his reach, and poured the cup half full, then placed a saucer beneath it, as she insisted on doing.

"It's hot, Jesse. Don't spill it on yourself!" The whispered words suffused him with shame.

He pushed the saucer onto the cutting board, placed the cup between his legs, and tightened his grip on the push rings. The chair squeaked as he spun about the linoleum. Just once he would have liked his cup poured full, not having to ask for more, then be left waiting for her approval. He stopped, let the fire lay, and looked back.

Naomi nodded toward the parlor, wanted to talk where they weren't apt to wake Isaac or Delores, he supposed. He wheeled around the dining table and chairs. It was a finer room than he could find comfort in. Without kindling in the fireplace, it was the coldest, too. Wind whistled through the eaves, the first cold front of winter bearing hard. Such a small thing, chopping firewood, and him powerless to do even that.

Naomi faced him, pulled her sweater close, and looked down at the cup and saucer cradled in her hands. "We should make plans for Christmas, Jesse."

"It's a ways off." They'd need a tree, of course, and presents for Isaac. What else was she thinking?

"Never too early to make plans." She shifted, glanced around the room, and wet her lips. "Don't you want to go back to the ranch and check on things?"

The words carved a hollow in his chest. Truth was, he didn't want to see what Morgan had done, tried not to think of what the cows might look like. Or the mules. He didn't know if the man had gotten a stand of wheat or if the land might be blowing on a day like this. But he worried most for Dancer, wondered if Morgan had managed to corner the horse or if he bothered to leave feed since the grass had turned. He rubbed his useless legs. No question Morgan coveted that animal, no less than he would another man's wife. David had a place in that horse's heart that made him what he was, and Morgan's whip and rope would never oblige the black to offer what he gave the boy freely.

It was a confounding thing. He'd seen it happen with dogs, of course, but not a horse. Wouldn't have thought it possible. But David's love had shown him more than he would have dreamed, and Dancer's affection for his son was likely all that was left of him in this world.

"Jesse?"

He rubbed his eyes and pushed the thoughts away. "Hadn't considered going back."

Naomi's glare bored a hole in him. "Delores said she might go alone and check on things, and I thought—"

"I'll bet she did."

Naomi searched the air and looked back. "What do you mean?"

Was the woman blind? "Nothing. Think I'll refill my cup. Full this time."

Naomi stepped close. "Is there something I should know?"

He fixed her with his stare, had kept the peace as long as he could. "Plenty, as I see it. What made you think she would make the boy a good wife? Why her?"

Naomi drew the cup to her breast. "It's cold in here. Let's go back to the kitchen."

He held her stare. It wasn't her way not to meet him straight on. She'd been the one to try him on a thing since they were kids, always coming out with what she had to say and leaving no question she knew she was right.

She bumped against his legs in her eagerness to leave, so he wheeled his chair before her. "And why is it she wants me to have no part of my grandson?"

Naomi refused to meet his eyes. "Why would I know that?"

"I'm not sure, but you do, don't you?"

Her knuckles grew white where they bent around the cup, and she closed her eyes. "Have you thought that maybe he isn't..." Her words dwindled.

"Isn't what?"

"What are you two doing in there?" Delores sashayed from the stairs and through the dining room. The kitchen lights came on, and the brightness of her camisole fluttered like a flame on wood. He turned back to Naomi.

She met his eyes then looked away. "I'd best fix breakfast. Isaac's likely up."

Delores spun from the ice box. "Are we out of cream again? I detest my coffee black."

The whine set Jesse's teeth on edge. "You've grown accustomed to the finer things. Didn't take you long." He stared out the window, watching from the corner of his eye.

"I've always lived here. Grimsland, I mean. Just lived out in the sticks long as I had to." She scooted onto the edge of the table, her camisole open in front as if she were expecting Morgan to walk in. He could almost see her leaning close, inviting the man's touch, feigning an effort to conceal herself.

He released his clinched teeth. "Hear you're wanting to go back. To the sticks, I mean."

She picked up an emery board and began filing her nails. "I thought you might feel better knowing the house was taken care of."

"The house." He let the words fall, allowing the barest ripple along his jaw.

Naomi hovered about the room but stopped before Delores. "Not over the table, dear."

Delores offered a blank stare. He'd not seen her deliver a better one.

Naomi straightened, stood like granite. "Your nails, dear. Don't do them over the table. We're going to eat here."

Delores went slack, prepared a response that a knock on the door stopped cold. She slid from the table, placed her hand between her breasts, and ran for the entryway.

Naomi raised her hand. "Not without your robe, dear!"

Delores grabbed Jesse's coat from the rack and pulled it over her shoulders.

He rolled around and stopped at the dining table, Naomi's grip on his shoulder, constraining him. He fisted his hands.

"Delores Faye Dremmer? Western Union, ma'am. Would you sign here, please?"

He watched Deloris tear the envelope and stare at the telegram, mouthing words into the chill. Her eyes lowered on the page, her face paling to white.

Air surged from Jesse's lungs. He'd known the boy wasn't apt to make it home, but the certainty threatened to crush him. David's death would mean freedom for Delores, the uncontestable release of a war widow with a monthly check. But he was left with all he hadn't said, the pledges he hadn't made, a heart he'd never opened. At least not to David.

It wasn't that he hadn't tried. He'd marveled at how the boy took to his schooling and what he'd done after coming home, but he'd not said so, had never told him that he'd done well. He'd assured himself it was because he didn't want to make the boy prideful, but that seemed such a shallow worry now. And when David told him of his plans for the ranch, he'd seen right away that most would work. But he'd pointed, instead, to the failures that were apt to overtake him.

David needed his esteem. He knew it, heard it when he listened with more than his ears. But the boy had stopped talking after a while, and the gloom of those nights almost choked him. He just hadn't known how to say what needed to be said.

Deloris caught a breath, her eyes glittering as she turned and scurried across the room. She dropped the thin, yellow paper onto his lap before rushing up the stairs.

Naomi's hand tightened, her fingers pressing into his shoulder. He shrugged free, adjusted his glasses, rolled to the window, and raised the paper.

KA 4475 41 GOVT=WASHINGTON DC V ii2 6P
MRS DELORES FAYE DREMMER
273 FINDLEY DRIVE GRIMSLAND TEXAS

THE SECRETERY OF WAR WISHES ME TO INFORM YOU THAT YOUR HUSBAND SECOND LT DAVID DREMMER IS A PRISONER OF WAR OF THE GERMAN GOVERNMENT BASED ON INFORMATION RECEIVED BY PROVOST MARSHAL GENERAL STOP FURTHER INFORMATION RECEIVED WILL BE FURNISHED BY PROVOST MARSHAL GENERAL

J A ULIO THE ADJUTANT GENERAL

Chapter III

David labored against the restraints and tried to sit up. The room was afloat on sea-green light, his neck and shoulders in spasms. IV poles drifted on a pale horizon, the dingy ribbon of blue that flowed from wall to wall above the injured and infirm. He surrendered and fell back on the canvas, had still not learned to suffer well. Gerhardt would have been disappointed.

He scalded the corners with his stare, his pain immersed in trepidation. The windows he'd looked through the first few days were behind him. Now he faced three rows of beds, white sheets and gray blankets spread in disarray over groaning Wehrmacht schoolboys. He drank antiseptic air, unable to look out at the interrogation center and get a fix on Schneider's office or the fetid cellar he'd called home. The need to know what the puppeteer was up to had become an obsession, and he feared his ruse would be discovered. If that should happen, Nicole, the person he least wanted to suffer, would pay the same price as Gerhardt.

He released his breath. It was the perfect irony. Schneider had become his most trusted ally, and his defense of truth lay bound and quivering on a web of lies. The need to protect the Partisans made his broken ribs and throbbing joints seem more disloyalty than pain. His body had betrayed him, left him cinched to his cot tighter than a saddle on a spiteful colt.

Something moved to his right, and he swiveled his head, spotted von Felder's blond hair and effeminate gait. The Wehrmacht leutnant, followed by two of his sycophants, marched in his direction. He closed his eyes, worked to quiet the thunder in his chest, and waited for the man who'd tried to kill him.

"So, Lieutenant Dremmer, it appears you have survived."

The words rang behind his head. He shivered, his blood gelid and thick, and turned his eyes away from the voice. "No thanks to you." The air was electric on his loosened teeth. He focused on the faint blue line, his refusal to look at the interrogator his sole agency of protest.

Von Felder's slender hand appeared above his face and balled into a fist white with malice. "The Luftwaffe may have your body, Lieutenant, but I still own your soul."

The words deepened his shiver. He wished for the morphine Herr Doktor had refused to waste on prisoners. The two gefreiters marched beside his cot, lifted, and turned him so that he faced the long row of windows. Von Felder mumbled something throaty, and the boys raised the head of the bed so that he looked onto the grounds of the compound and the interrogation center beyond. The leutnant pulled a lamp from somewhere behind him and lifted it high.

Two men and a woman stood facing him a few yards beyond the windows, their faces pallid. The first, an old man, gray hair sticking from beneath his cap, squinted into the window. A feldwebel stood beside him, shouting in pantomime. For a moment both figures froze, then the sergeant raised his pistol, his sleeve shuddering sharply. The blast rattled glass, and the old man crumpled, his expression vacant before he sank beneath the window.

"You're insane!" The words erupted with more force than he knew was in him. He fought the fever in his neck and wrestled the bands holding him to the bed. "No more, von Felder! I'll do whatever you want." He turned away.

"Open your eyes, Lieutenant. We have gone to some effort to arrange this."

"I'll do what you want. Just let them go."

"It's too late for that. You should not have misled us. It is our duty to ascertain who might have aided you in your attempted escape."

He turned away. Von Felder groused as rough fingernails cut into his forehead and cheeks, tore at his eyelids, and pulled them wide. He fought for words. "You going to shoot every poor bastard you meet until someone admits responsibility for your fantasies?"

"Perhaps."

A woman, her gray face twisted, her eyes pleading, locking onto his, shook her head at whatever the feldwebel asked.

A pop, muffled by the pistol's nearness to her face, suspended his plea. Her head issued a crimson surge, and a fine red mist drifted toward the nearest windowpane as she sank beneath the sill.

David's stomach roiled. "Burn in hell, von Felder!"

The leutnant laughed. "I have no fear of your curse, Lieutenant.

Life is not for the weak like your friend Herr Schneider. That anything should exist afterwards is—"

"Schneider!" He turned his eyes toward the frail officer. "This is for *him*? You want him to release me to your custody?"

Von Felder put the lamp down and brushed a blond tuft from his forehead.

"You'll stop this if I convince him?" He swallowed against nausea.

The leutnant ran his hand down the side of his face, lifted a finger, and pointed toward the remaining hostage. "Please, Lieutenant, I do not wish for you to miss this."

The boy stumbled, confusion on his face. He could see it, now. Mongoloid. The woman was likely the boy's mother, innocence his only crime. The feldwebel turned, waiting for a signal.

"Please, don't—" The crack riveted his gut. He drew hard for air as the boy fell back, his forehead compressed by the impact of the bullet. Revulsion boiled up, and he made no effort to contain it. He hurled to the limits of the restraints, hands scratching his face. Vomit spewed as he tilted his head toward von Felder, dancing gracelessly away from the cot.

* * *

"Get me out of here, Herr Leutnant! Do it now! We have an agreement." David shuddered at the persistent image of the boy's face emerging within the translucence of Schneider's skin. "Or turn me over to them. I won't be responsible for any more murders."

Heinrich's chin rose in the sanitized air. "You're in no condition to travel, Lieutenant. And, as you said, how are you to honor our agreement from the grave?"

"We've dealt with that. MI6 has the letter. Your Élodie will not be subjected to retribution so long as Nicole is allowed to safely leave the country." He looked into Schneider's eyes. "And I'm in no condition to stay. Who knows how many more they'll bring?"

Heinrich stepped slowly around the cot, his cap pinned beneath his arm.

David refused to release the German's stare. "Who were they?"

The leutnant dropped his chin. "Put them out of your thoughts. Von Felder reported them guilty of collusion. They were enemies of the Reich." Schneider stared at the windows.

Rage surfaced on a shiver. "Enemies of the Reich. They were shot for being sane?"

"That's quite enough, Lieutenant." Schneider scoured the room with his eyes. "You'll be overheard." The voice drifted beneath the stillness of a dying storm.

How does one reason with people bereft of conscience? "And they were supposed to be in collusion with *me*?" He knew the answer, of course.

Schneider glared through the windows, his affirmation bound by a clinched jaw.

"When you people have murdered all the innocents, who will you lord it over then?"

The muscles along Heinrich's jaw rippled. "I will return when you are able to discuss this reasonably."

"Sure. I'll be more *reasonable* the next time you slaughter Belgians for a demonstration."

The leutnant turned to meet him, his eyes flashing. "I did not do it. And this is war, Lieutenant. You, too, have taken innocent lives."

He offered the barest pivot of his head. A painful one. "Not intentionally. We don't make a sport of murdering civilians. In fact, we put ourselves at risk to avoid it." He offered a parting jab. "And I'm beginning to believe there are no innocent Germans."

Color was returning to the translucent face, Schneider's blue uniform as out of place within the gray as his own striped shirt. "I might be able to arrange for you to be moved to my outer office, Lieutenant. Henri could look after you there. That would please you, yes?"

For all of Heinrich's sensibilities, he was more than capable of subterfuge. It could be a trap. Still— "Yes, very much. Please, Herr Leutnant, if that's possible—"

* * *

Schneider bent low, opened the bottom drawer of the filing cabinet, and extracted a pear-shaped bottle and two glasses. "Might I offer you Scotch, Lieutenant?"

"The last time I was offered Scotch, it cost me dearly." David shifted, remembered Delores' insistence at crawling beneath his tarp and the tinkling of glass as she presented him with a bottle. Only two years. It seemed a lifetime. He straightened the blanket on his cot, couldn't afford to reject the geniality. "But in the interest of international relations—"

"Of course." Heinrich poured three fingers and held it to the light. "As you might imagine, this is quite difficult to acquire within the Reich."

He caught the crystal stare and detected a shadow on the pale face. A black dollop hung over his forehead. Only the second time he'd seen Heinrich with his hair mussed. "You keep making that mistake. This is Belgium. And I hope that's your glass."

The leutnant turned, his brow contracting.

"It's a bit much for me." He glanced at the vent behind Henri's desk. Schneider always spoke with such ease here. Not in his office, though. It left little doubt where the microphones were hidden.

The leutnant poured two fingers into a second glass, handed him the lesser and held the first high. "To diminishing hostilities." Schneider downed the whiskey in two swallows.

David lifted his glass, eased the liquid onto his tongue, and held it against his swollen gums. What might Heinrich do if he learned that Henri was his only remaining contact with the Resistance? "Man wasn't created for intrigue, was he?" He watched the question narrow the brow again. "A man needs to believe he can protect those he loves."

Heinrich pondered his empty glass. "A philosopher, no less."

"Just an observer, Herr Leutnant."

Schneider poured himself another drink. "The Scots know how to make good whisky. There is beauty in doing something simple and doing it well."

"A philosopher, no less." David smiled. "And what simple things did you do well before the war, Herr Leutnant? What beauty is being denied you?"

Schneider searched the ceiling. "I am but an observer, Lieutenant." The German covered his mouth, hiding the pleasure of their badinage. "At one time, I thought— " He waved it away.

"Go ahead. What did you think?"

"I thought I would be a good husband. A good father, perhaps."

David pushed the image away and prayed the Scotch had reached its mark. "And who did you expect to be the mother of your children, Élodie or Nicole?"

Schneider returned a crystal stare. "To you, beauty means one thing only, Lieutenant. You are incapable of seeing any other. I do not look through your eyes."

He felt the spasm ease in his neck as the Scotch warmed him. "But you knew Nicole. You were in love with her."

Schneider's lip contracted, his perfect teeth glinting beneath the contempt. "Love? That's absurd." The leutnant appeared to be approaching Nirvana. "Socrates argued that love could not be good, since it is the desire to possess what is good, and one does not seek what one has."

David nodded. "If I remember correctly, he also said human nature could find no better helper than love." He paused. "His argument was that love was the desire to possess what was beautiful, and that beauty was the least definable part of what is good." He let the silence build, hoped the German might see he wasn't unarmed in this battle.

Schneider leaned over the desk and smiled. "Perhaps so. It has been some time."

He stared. "She is beautiful, isn't she, Heinrich?" He took a deeper draft of what his heart had locked away, saw her dark hair falling from her shoulders as she leaned toward him, the crescent of her face, the soft, sweet scent of her as she bent close. He sipped his Scotch, pictured her standing on the stairs, her silhouette a promise of something eternal.

Schneider rallied. "And who is to say what is beautiful, Lieutenant? To you it is one thing; to me it is another."

"Beauty is like truth; it's absolute." He waited. "I'll willingly grant you your preferences, but we both know it when we see it."

Schneider leaned back in Henri's chair. "Why do I always have the feeling we're discussing more than one thing at a time, Lieutenant?"

David raised his glass and put it to his lips.

The leutnant swiveled toward him. "And what about your wife? Delores Faye Dremmer. Faye with an *e*. Would I see in her something I recognized as beauty?"

Touché, Heinrich. The whisky burned his throat, and he couldn't restrain a cough. "There's no doubt many have found her beautiful."

"But not you? What an extraordinary thing for a husband to say."

He tried to appear unruffled. "I didn't say it. You did."

Heinrich glowed, clearly pleased with what he'd uncovered. "You will remain here until you are well enough to travel. I would think it unnecessary to tell you that there are guards in the hall. You will have

15

access to a bathroom, however. That should be more pleasant."

He met the leutnant's eyes. "All the comforts of home and no murders outside my window. What more could I ask for?"

"You will not be processed through Dulag Luft. I will expedite the usual procedure."

David eased into his pillow. Did Schneider fear he might make a better deal elsewhere?

"You will go straight to Stammlager 17 B in Krems where you will be reunited with what remains of your crew. I will follow as soon as my transfer is approved."

He attempted a nod. "So long as our agreement is honored, Herr Leutnant, and Nicole is kept safe."

Schneider smiled, looking down his nose. "Do you believe this vast organization of yours has members in Austria, Lieutenant?"

"Of course." He lifted his glass and smiled. In truth, he had no idea, but, for the moment, he had Henri's reluctant support.

Schneider shook his head. "I wish you pleasant dreams, Lieutenant. With your imagination, I am certain they are most colorful. I only wish you could share them."

He smiled. The leutnant didn't know if the Resistance reached into Germany, either. He would never have allowed him to write the letter to MI6 if he did. "Oh, you'll share my dreams, Heinrich. Wait and see."

Chapter IV

Saint Peter's heaved beneath the weight of coal smoke and death. David leaned against the wall, closed his eyes, and saw the woman again, the supplication on her face. He heard the crack of the pistol and opened his eyes to Nazis moving freely, the rapture of power etched on their faces. Women scurried against a cold wind, *babushkas* pulled tight, their heads lowered to avoid the hungry eyes of Wehrmacht troops.

Broken glass ground beneath jackboots, the sound of wind in dry grass. No one moved to sweep it up. A man, drawn and gray, watched as a young girl skirted a pair of officers, her pace nearing a run as they stopped to stare. The old man pulled his coat tight and scuttled into the shadow of a stone arch, shamed, David guessed, by impotence and rage.

The line grew. He glanced at the other prisoners who had arrived on the same lorry, two of them Brits that kept to themselves. The third, a first sergeant with pilot patches on his flight jacket, vomited feebly at the end of a bench.

Nicole had spoken of Saint Peter's Station more than once during the sweet afternoons in the cellar after he'd been shot down. So beautiful, she'd said. The flower vendors, the kiosks, the blend of coffee and coal—it had become the scent of excitement for her. But no longer.

David looked back to see if the girl had made it past the soldats. An officer hollered from up the queue. The unteroffizier he was assigned to snapped straight, turned, and motioned for the group to stand.

He bent over the sergeant, slid the duffle over his shoulder, and whispered in his ear. "Can you stand? We're moving out."

The sergeant groaned, eyelids quivering, his skin bloodless and wet.

David raised the limp left arm, grabbed a loop on the other side of his flight suit, and heaved, his knitting ribs howling in protest. One of the Tommies spotted him, moved to the opposite side, and helped him drag the sergeant along the line.

Wehrmacht troops circled, inspecting their dark sovereignty, the bleakness of the scene reflected from the eyes of civilians. The line edged toward the tracks, but the Brit stayed, helped him haul the sergeant up the stairs and into the aisle. The bull-necked unteroffizier pointed them inside a compartment for six, and the train jerked forward.

"You!" The unteroffizier pointed to the flight lieutenant helping them. "You vill stay!"

The Brit straightened. "And will I be accounted for?"

David turned to the smirking German seated opposite the American pilot. "The sergeant's in a lot of pain, Unteroffizier. May I put his feet beside you, so he doesn't have to sit up?"

"Leaf him." Heavy lips parted, some dark pleasure spreading across his face.

* * *

The countryside lay in small plots sectioned by irrigation canals with ditches at the lower ends, not unlike the one Bear told him he'd hidden in. He had no recollection of it, only the dreams. Then Nicole, the waking dream that stilled the others.

So much had happened. He was different now with a life more precious to him than any he'd known then, and her dependent on him for survival. Convincing Schneider that his lover was under surveillance by the Resistance had proven an effective ploy, the only leverage he had in keeping Nicole alive. Unless the leutnant discovered the truth. A shiver traced his spine. British intelligence would surmise the nature of the agreement from the letter. At the very least, they were aware of Nicole, now. And Élodie and Schneider.

He slouched, trying to lean back. *To sleep, perchance to dream.* The unteroffizier's eyes met his as they closed, and he was left with the image of the repulsive grin.

"You vill not sleep, Lieutenant. You vill remain avake to see vat you shvine haff done." The unteroffizier's words rattled with phlegm.

David swallowed a response, found no comfort on the straight-backed bench, and pushed himself into a corner. It was a formidable thing, her life dependent on his choices, and him incapable of saving anyone. Empty words drifted into darkness, powerless at first, until sureness came and formed a prayer that flowed from somewhere deep to somewhere deeper still, a place of more power and mystery than any he'd known a few weeks back. Finally, he knew communion and drifted into a peace that might have brought sleep but for the unteroffizier.

* * *

The sun bled out against the sky, its grief covering the trees. David turned to his captor, the German's gaze black and heavy, a reptilian roll to his head. "Where are we going?"

The unteroffizier turned, came awake by degree, his eyes rounding to viperous bulbs. "To transit camp. Ozzers vill be routed from zere to Dulag Luft. Var is over for you."

"You don't get to decide that. Neither do I. I wouldn't be here if I did."

"I am here because I vish to be." The big man's words burbled with threat.

He shook his head. "Why would anyone want to be a part of this?"

The German leaned forward. "Vy vould anyone but little girl vish to be anyvere else?"

He winced and looked away, then extended his hand to the Brit. "Second Lieutenant David Dremmer."

The Brit gripped hard and offered a slight lift of his mustache. "Flight Lieutenant Howard Lawrence, Lieutenant."

"And zis one?" The German lifted his hand toward the sergeant. "He iss dead or vaiting to be presented?"

The pilot's jaw was slack, his body conforming to the corner. David stood, reached across the bench, and slapped the cooling face as the Brit leaned over his shoulder.

"You veel seet down! Bose of you!" The unteroffizier rose and kicked the sergeant's boot. The lifeless body spilled onto the floor.

Chills coursed David's spine. "You're not going to just leave him there, are you?"

"He vill be taken out viss garbage."

The snake's trilled r set his teeth on edge. He tasted bile and looked at the unsecured Walther in the unteroffizier's holster. It would be easy. He glanced at the Brit, then shook his head. He couldn't do it without knowing Nicole was out of Belgium.

The flight lieutenant leaned forward. "And what is your name, Unteroffizier?"

"Unteroffizier Hans Biederman." The mouth broadened.

David picked up the cue. "Who's your commanding officer?"

The head swiveled. "Hauptman Reinhardt Schreider."

He pushed harder. "And where is he?"

The smile spread. "He vill return from Berlin soon. Our gruppe iss assigned to stalag system. Most shpeak English. Zat is vy you are here and not on stock train."

"And you can write POW on top and not get strafed. So, where's your family?"

The wide brow narrowed. "Munchen. You vish for revenge, yes? After var, you vill remain to rebuild Deutschland. Do you not know zeese?"

"What's your wife's name?"

"Do you vish to frighten me?" Hans offered an unconvincing chuckle. "Her name iss Hilda. My daughter's name iss Andrea. Vat do you hope for in asking zeese?"

David smiled. "We could have taken your pistol, Hans. And your life."

The Brit followed suit. "We've not slept in two days, Unteroffizier. Unless you also wish not to relax, it might be best if you allowed us to sleep."

* * *

The train rocked steadily into low mountains, pines above and valleys below covered in grass and hay meadows. Remnants of a snow melted in the shade. David looked at Biederman. How could such malice spring from this land? As surely as good existed, malevolence did as well. For evil to be born from this, a will was required, one so malignant it defied chance.

Biederman's glare drifted across the compartment, dull and angry, the train swaying to a soporific clack. David ached from lack of movement, yearned for an end of cruelty, a death to this day's life, a knitting of the raveled sleeve of care. Had Shakespeare been drafted, he might have penned a thousand more soliloquies on the subject.

"Lieutenant, you're knackered. I'll watch our captor. You sleep."

He nodded. "Thanks. If I'm not awake in three hours, rouse me. We'll trade off."

"A gleamer, Lieutenant."

The train rocked into uncertainty like Dancer's easy gait.

Chapter V

The boy was alive. Jesse gripped the telegram. Could it be? He feared believing it, couldn't survive another disappointment.

Naomi stood in the portico, crowned in reluctant light, her eyes submerged. "Oh, Jesse!"

He heaved in the dense air, raised the telegram beneath her gaze and mouthed it through again. It was beyond anything he could have dreamed. "Hope is a deceitful thing. All my life I've worked to keep it from ruining me, fought it taking root, making me crazy. A man who allows himself to hope is apt to grasp at anything that threatens it. But this…"

Naomi lowered her hands, a smile softening her certainty. "If a man with no hope fears nothing, Jesse, it's because he's already dead. But you're alive. Your son's alive, too, and neither of you can live without it."

He nodded. "But I don't know how to believe it."

"It's a gift, Jesse. Just take it."

He looked around. "Where'd Delores go?"

"Upstairs. She was relieved, I suppose. Probably didn't want us to see her crying."

He shook his head. "That's not it. This has ruined her plans. A war widow's check would have helped her get a new start."

Naomi moved closer. "A new start? Where?"

"At Morgan's Crossing."

"Why there? She hated the ranch."

"I won't be around forever. They'd go through all I've built pretty quick, but she can't see that. She just sees the good times it would pay for."

"They who?"

The coal in Jesse's gut began to flame. He stared as deep into her eyes as he dared, the blaze dampened by his shame. He'd offered Morgan the deal on the place—couldn't imagine her being wrong. "I thought David was gone. It didn't matter without him. What use was there in keeping the place without somebody to give it to? Somebody who knew its worth."

She straightened, her eyes searching for answers, her lips pressed tight.

* * *

Morgan leaned back in his chair. Hadn't had a good night's sleep in days, and that girl being gone didn't help none. A man could get used to having his needs met. Business was bad, too. Only two customers, and it was near noon. Customers, hell. Old man Griswell stopped to use the phone and May Cobb picked up her mail.

Delores said she'd come back soon as she got Jesse settled in. He'd figured all along it wouldn't happen. He pushed the rag mop to the back corner and looked over his shoulder through the front window. Hard keeping the lights on without no paying customers. 'Bout time Ben Niedermeyer come by. The old fool inherited all he had and still couldn't hold onto it. Turned a decent ranch into a dairy. Who would build a dairy this far away from town? No reason he shouldn't have a piece of what the old fool was losin'. Nobody'd ever give him nothin'.

He pulled the shoe box with his accounts in it from beneath the sack of Tennessee Red and flipped back to Ben's pad. Forgetful as he was, old Niedermeyer wouldn't remember if he'd stopped or not. He licked his pencil, and wrote in clear, legible print:

5 gallons gas –   .95
8 ozs. pinto beans –   .12
2 cokes –   .10
2 White Owl cigars –   .20
2 Hershey Bars –   .10
1 Luden's Cough Drops –   .13
Total – $1.60

Not a bad morning's take, considering he had nothing in it. He shoved the pad into the box and closed the lid. "Thank you for your business, Ben. I'm much obliged."

The door squeaked, and he slid the pad beneath the burlap, kept his back to the entrance, and tried to look busy.

"Hey, storekeep, you got anything soothing for a lonely girl?"

He turned, saw her hands slide up her legs the way she did. "Girl, if you ain't a sight for sore eyes! Had you on my mind all morning."

"Didn't miss me enough to write, though. Hadn't had a letter in weeks." Delores tilted her head and twirled her hair with her finger.

"Never know who'll gather that mail. Jesse ain't no fool. Don't figure Naomi for one, neither."

She moved close. "You too busy to shut down for a couple hours?"

He winked. "Folks is used to me closin' down to feed them cows. Maybe we can stop by the house for a while. Be kinda nice not having the old man around."

* * *

"Is that David's horse on the hill up there?"

Morgan stuffed empty sacks inside the first and threw the bundle into the truck bed. The girl had more questions than a kid at the circus. All the time she lived here, she'd not been on the Summit Place and couldn't spot an animal as fine as that black. "One and the same. He'll stay out of range till we leave. Comes down once in a while and helps hisself to some ground milo and cottonseed meal. Don't eat enough to hurt hisself, I reckon."

"Thought you made a deal with Jesse to feed him."

"What for? Don't get nothin' out of him. One of these days, though."

Delores turned in her seat and put her hand on his leg. "What is it about that horse? Everybody wants him more than anything ever."

Morgan winked. "Not anything, girl."

She twisted, glancing at the horse. "What if David comes back?"

He wished she'd stay on the subject. Another trip to the house wouldn't take much time out of his afternoon. "Like I said, he ain't back yet. Lotsa boys don't make it out of them camps, is what I hear."

"That's the Japs. They're the worst." She rubbed his leg and looked back across the swaying grass to where the horse stood, his mane flowing in the breeze. "Best leave that one be. He thinks more of that horse than anything ever."

"What's his is mine." Morgan grinned, slid his hand across her breast, and pulled her hard. She needed a reminder of who was in charge.

"I'm not enough? You gotta have that horse, too?"

"Why not? Ain't no reason I can see not to have it all."

Chapter VI

David shivered and readied himself for the first breath-catching splash of night. Darkness, expansive and starless, had taken the continent. Flight Lieutenant Lawrence moved within his lengthening shadow as Biederman led them toward queues of milling prisoners.

His right hand on his Walther, the German pointed them to an American lieutenant standing on a wooden crate, the paper on his clipboard flapping in the breeze. "Vait und your name is called." Hans turned and walked back to the train.

A torch surged yellow but quickly dissolved to gray, revealing in the fleeting brightness an assemblage of weathered wood, the remnants of some enterprise confiscated by the Nazis. The putrescence of boiling tallow, rotten vegetables, and fear weighted the turbid air. Men milled about barrel fires, warming their hands. Orders were shouted in German from a barracks stoop, but the prisoners, "kriegies" he'd heard someone call them, paid no attention.

Lawrence's name was called, and the lieutenant looked above the clipboard. "Your group is in Barracks Seven, Flight Lieutenant. You'll be leaving in the morning."

David turned and shook the extended hand. "Thank you for your help, Flight Lieutenant."

The Brit nodded and headed away from the fires.

Light drained into a velvet void, yielding all to blackness. Cold gathered around him as the crowd thinned. Another train arrived, and the milling resumed.

"Second Lieutenant David Dremmer. Barracks Nine, Lieutenant. Train and time to be announced. Stay with your group."

The yard was deep in mire. Men veered around the center to keep from sinking past their ankles. David pulled a smoldering stick from a barrel by the stoop, scraped mud from his boots and pushed through the door. A blanket of fear settled over the low hum of crowded men, most avoiding his eyes. A sergeant, wings on his jacket, returned his glance.

He nodded. "What do we do for food around here, Sergeant?"

The face darkened. "Those that could stomach it ate at the pots, sir. The rest of us ordered hot pastramis on rye."

He smiled. "You waiting for delivery, Sarge?"

The dark head nodded. "Just hoping it gets here before the ice cream, sir."

He found an empty bunk, folded down the frayed blanket covering the thin straw mattress, and hid the duffle Schneider had provided behind the frame. It held only his Bible now, a tin of potted meat, and another of condensed milk. He meandered toward the farthest pot and stood upwind. The settling cold brought a clarity that took him in less than a moment and overwhelmed him with certainty. He shuddered at the frailty of each soul condemned to live in a sea of others, all locked away, not one able to grasp anything beyond himself. Even as a child, he'd seen that life was solitary, that not even his mother could know him. In the vastness of the universe, he was and would always be alone.

He turned and headed to the barracks, hoped to dig the potted meat from the duffle and find a place to eat it. The darkness he'd felt wasn't his. His isolation had died, been blown away in a blistering wind that extracted the dread of dying alone, a swollen corpse on some hill littered with nameless corpses. He stared into the woman's eyes and felt her fear engorge the darkness around him. It was her isolation he felt. She'd known what was coming, had seen the old man shot, had called out to him, her eyes making an unambiguous plea to stop what was happening. That gesture was her last statement on earth. He followed the scene to its conclusion, saw the wilt as all expression drained, and the light in her eyes went out.

Who was she? The center of someone's world; the ordering force that made other lives complete, maybe. If so, the loss continued. And the old man's. And the boy's. None had deserved what they'd received. He drew stale air as he stepped into the barracks, his heart insisting their deaths would be charged to him.

* * *

The sun had scarcely cleared the trees when Flight Lieutenant Lawrence's train heaved away from the platform. David watched the coal smoke filtering into pines and low mountains. He turned at the sound of sliding doors. The men in his group were herded with a barrage of German into another crowded cubicle and seemed to be waiting for some symmetry to form within the chaos. They'd grown accustomed to a chain of command and were forced to comply with a system that had no concern for them. It struck him that had the men in front and sides held themselves away from the walls, they would create more space. They hadn't yet begun to think like kriegies, hadn't learned to protect themselves.

He cupped his hands. "Any officers here?"

"Lieutenant." The voice came from somewhere near the rear.

"Captain." This one came from the front of the car.

"You're it, sir."

The door rolled closed behind him, the extra planking on the walls containing the sound. The voice rose again, stronger now. "Arrange yourselves in rows, single file from the back. Leave twelve inches between your shoulders and face the front."

Men shuffled and scraped around him. He'd been one of the last to enter and stood near the center but was surprised at how much space had been created when the rows reached the door. The car shuddered, the coupling clanged, and they began to move. When they stood straight, a third of the car was empty.

"All right men, starting from the outside, turn to the man to the inside of you." The captain was visible now in the front, dark hair shooting from beneath his cap. "Pick up the straw beneath you and pass it forward." In minutes, a substantial pile lay in the vacated space. The train gained speed, and he strained to hear. "The front three rows, step forward and lie on the straw. You will be allowed a two-hour rest, then rotated."

Men stretched themselves across the straw. Those behind and near the outside leaned against the sideboards. Within minutes, prisoners at the rear were sitting, leaning back-to-back, a few nodding into a shallow sleep.

With each reshuffle, he worked himself closer to the wall, watched the gaps between the boards, the assurance of space and light freeing him from the press of flesh. By early morning, his back rested against a GI. Both had their legs spread to avoid others and to steady themselves against the swaying. He dozed, if only for seconds, until a pink sky filtered through the narrow slits and sliced the shadows. Magenta explosions warmed streams and ponds. Hills were covered in dense timber. Smooth-bottomed valleys lay rich in meadow grass, bright yellow in winter death and left in stacks. The pale green of cured hay was visible against patches of snow where cattle had scattered it. More frequently now, the bottoms lay in fallow cropland.

His eyes burned with exhaustion, but something enticed him, awaking a sleeping passion. The furrows were flooded within a cattail-cotton dream. The sun rose above mountains, the tracks leading them into wider plains with creeks and fields.

He leaned forward, staring between the sideboards. A farmer had hawed his mules a hundred yards away and rested against the traces, watching the train steam through his valley. Their passing must have seemed peaceful, the summer's bounty decaying beneath the man's feet, ready for fretful growth come spring. He offered a salute, smiled as the farmer rubbed his hands before turning back to a chain wrapped around a fallen tree.

Man was created for that. It was right and good to be occupied producing food or shelter, something more than numbers on a page, a higher calling that was all but forgotten by the world. Most of it, anyway. But in the heart of Germany, he had a brother, a man who loved the smell of earth, who knew the joy of seeing a calf he'd delivered kick and bawl after its mother. That was life, and war was an inexplicable blight.

Chapter VII

The squeal of brakes lowered in pitch until the train ground to a halt. David's thoughts floated on a symphony of unfinished passages, each independent of the one before. The clacking of the tracks had been the sole order in his universe, and he'd learned to trust the constancy, the unwavering cadence that had been with him for days. How many? Asleep yet awake, swaying through darkness, thirst, sunrise, hunger, sunset, forest, farmland.

Bearings screeched from the load of the door, and light poured into the car unobstructed and harsh. The reek of the honey pot in the back was quickly covered by the greater stench of open sewers, and his nose insinuated their entrance into a world Dante would have been helpless to describe. The thought amused him, and beneath his chuckle, near forgotten words emerged: "Abandon hope all ye who enter here."

"What's that, sir?" The question came from the man whose back pushed against his.

He shook his head. "Just thinking out loud."

The voice returned. "Is this the end of the line, you think?"

He peered through the door, saw nothing that brought certainty. "Sure smells like it."

"Where are we?"

His head wouldn't clear, but he knew that much. "Krems, Austria. Stalag 17-B."

"Oh, yeah? How'd you know that?"

"Just what I was told." He ignored the inquisitor, tried to remember the last time they'd been shuffled, whether it was light or dark.

"Think they'll give us food and water now?"

He struggled for an answer, remembered the man snoring through the night and his wondering at the ease of some to slip into oblivion. "Something to drink, yeah."

"Got a cigarette?"

He reached into his pocket, passed the pack over his shoulder. "Keep 'em."

"Thanks, Lieutenant. You sure?"

"I'm sure."

A steady mumble rose from the cars down the track. Fear emerged as questions were posed in ignorance to the unwitting. A Wehrmacht uniform moved before the door, three guards behind, one holding a machine gun, the bipod dangling.

"Aussteigen!" The oberleutnant growled but got no response. A boy, his uniform hanging from unfinished limbs, motioned for them to jump down.

David forced himself to his feet, shuffled to the door, and dropped to the ground. The impact electrified his knitting bones, and he dropped to his knees, then straightened by degree.

To his right, five or six cars disgorged kriegies, the men meandering into lines. To his left, the doors were latched. Before him, a trapezoidal building blocked his view of the camp, though he breathed the burden it placed on the glacial air.

"Attention! You are prisoners of the German Reich." A rigid feldwebel stood before them. His English was perfect, his lines rehearsed. "You are interned here for the duration of the war. After the defeat of your countries, you will remain prisoners of the Reich to rebuild what you have destroyed. Be assured you will remain prisoners of the Reich for the remainder of your lives for crimes committed against the German people.

"Here you will be assigned barracks and communicate with your German superiors through a Man of Confidence chosen as your representative by your fellow prisoners. You will obey all orders." The oberleutnant let his words settle, then growled at the gefreiter on his left.

The boy rousted them and waved his rifle toward the station. Prisoners queued before large block letters B-A-H-N-H-O-F on the odd-shaped building. At the front of the line, men were given parcels that David recognized as Red Cross packets. Kriegies drifted toward the train, pulling GI boots, trousers, and RAF blouses from their bundles.

How had clothing from two countries arrived in the same packets? He rubbed his neck and shoulders, saw a sign nailed to the building to his right, the script small and German, presumably for troops who knew only English or French. The issuance at the bottom sent a chill down his spine: "Commandant Oberst Berger, Stammlager 7-A."

Blood drained from his face, and he fought for air. Had Schneider betrayed him? "What did he do to me?"

"Whatsa' matter, Lieutenant?" The voice of his inquisitor.

He scarcely had breath for words. "They sent me to the wrong stalag."

"Yeah, me too, sir. I requested Florida."

"This isn't a joke, soldier. I have to meet someone." He pressed his lips, tried to focus.

"Well, you'll sure have to chew some Kraut's butt over that, now, won't you, sir?"

He turned to face the man. A corporal.

Beady eyes narrowed to slits. "What outfit you with, Lieutenant?"

He'd had enough. "What's your name, Corporal?"

"Stanislavsky, sir."

"It's important I get this straightened out, Stanislavsky, so pipe down."

"You sure you don't spreckem a little of that Doitch, sir?"

His blood reached an instant boil. "Shut your pie hole, Corporal! You *verstehste* that?"

"Yes sir, Lieutenant." Stanislavsky's teeth glinted.

He turned from the close-set eyes, but the corporal stepped to his side, then eased in front. "You have an appointment with the Führer, Lieutenant?"

A couple of men in line stirred, their mouths twitching at the corporal's insolence.

He wasn't Regular Army, didn't know procedure, but— "Corporal, if I have any further interference from you, I'll bring you before the camp administration and have you dealt with."

Stanislavsky grinned. "Just seem to be acting strange, sir. You sure you're one of us?"

He leaned forward, his fists clenched. "One of you? If I were one of you, I'd be dragging my knuckles and picking fleas. Give it a rest, or I'll settle it now. You got it?"

"Yes sir." The corporal turned to the man in front, the second kriegie turning back.

David glanced down the line, focused on the movement, and took slow breaths. He was completely at Schneider's mercy. There was no one to appeal to. He shielded his eyes from the sun and released a

30

desperate prayer.

He was responsible for Nicole, and rather than keeping her out of harm's way, he'd been manipulated, shifted to a place where it might be impossible to protect her. An icy blade slid up his back, and he stared into the frigid light. Someone nudged him, and he stepped toward the Kraut passing out Red Cross packets.

* * *

"Where you from, Lieutenant?"

David glared at the gaunt face, wished for the potted meat still in his duffle. "I told you, Captain, I'm from Morgan's Crossing, Texas, sixty miles east of Brighton."

"What bomb group you with?"

"381st." He waited. "Sir."

Hanson glanced at the notes in front of him. "What kind of bombs were you carrying when you were shot down?"

"We'd already dropped our load, but they were incendiaries."

"Who was your Crew Commander?"

"First Lieutenant Gerald Massing"

"Was he married or single?"

"I don't know, sir."

The captain looked up. "You don't know if your commander was married?"

He shifted in his chair. "Captain, is all this necessary? That wasn't a Pullman I came in on. I'm dead on my feet, same as everyone else that got through with a five-minute interview. All I need—" He looked at the narrow eyes and doubted anyone was home. "It was a temporary crew made up after my regular crew was shot up over Schweinfurt. There were three new crew members, including the pilot and co-pilot. I met Massing that morning."

"What was your engineer's name?"

"Lieutenant Sol Berkowitz. Separated. His wife felt he spent too much time at work."

Hanson met his glare, the eyes cold as windowpanes. "What was it you were upset about waiting in line for your packet?"

So, that was it. He clenched his fists. "I was told by my interrogator that I was being sent to Stalag 17-B. When I ended up here, it shook me, sir."

31

The captain glanced at his notes. "In Krems?"

"Yes sir. My crew was sent there weeks ago. That's what my interrogator said."

Hanson folded the paper. "Here's the drill, Lieutenant. You claim you were a belly gunner on a 17, you're ranked above your job, and you're in an infantry camp. Air Corps personnel left last month, and they went to 17-B in Krems. You're not with your crew, and you claim you were sent by a Luftwaffe interrogator. He interrogates *only* airmen, so he should deal *only* with luft stalags. As of now, 7-A has no luft section, and interrogators don't share that kind of information with kriegies. What do you think made this leutnant tell you that? He tell you about his mama and papa on the cabbage farm? His first fräulein, maybe?"

He tried to make sense of it. Air Corp prisoners had left for the camp he was supposed to be in. So, why had Schneider sent him here? "He didn't tell me about any of his fräuleins, sir."

Hanson leaned in. "There's no one here to substantiate your statements, is there?"

He fought the fog, tried to focus. "I don't know, sir. I haven't been here long enough to find out. Captain, my interrogation was unusual. I happened onto some information that could be important to the war effort, and I need to get it to the right channels."

Hanson leaned closer. "You think 17-B has the right channels and we don't?"

He was exhausted, needed this to end before he made a mistake. "That's not it, sir."

"Here's the pitch. I'm the right channel, and this is the right time. Read me in on it."

He had no idea what Stanislavsky told Junior G-man here, and he certainly couldn't tell him he'd parleyed an agreement with a German. He looked around, made a point of showing he was sharing a secret. "The place they held us in Belgium was an office building with a warehouse beneath. They had me cleaning offices and were locking me in a cellar at night." He looked at the captain's scowl. The man wasn't buying it.

"Go ahead, Dremmer."

White heat burned away the dross. "You need to hear me out, sir. Give me a chance."

Hanson extended an open palm.

"I jimmied my way into the mechanical room. It had a furnace with ducts that led to the offices. I found the one going to my interrogator's office, made a hole in it, stood on a bucket and listened. Most of what I heard was in German, but one evening I overheard a conversation between my interrogator and his aide. In French. They discussed transcripts of Air Corps radio communications. Transcripts, sir. They're monitoring air-to-air and air-to-ground transmissions. It's how they always know where we're going. It's why they're usually ready."

Hanson didn't flinch, seemed not to grasp the significance of what he was hearing.

David frowned. "Captain, the interrogation officers have access to this stuff. It's how they know so much. And what they have, they're using to break our boys, convince them that other crew members have already spilled the beans."

Hanson settled back. "If your story checks out, we'll get this information to the right people. So, what's the pitch? Was this secretary German?"

"Belgian. French-speaking, though he sounded like he'd spent some time in Paris. And it was the leutnant's aide." He looked into the captain's eyes, detected a slight thaw.

Hanson stared. "*Parlez-vous français?*"

He covered a smile. The captain's French sounded more like Jimmy Stewart than Louis Jouvet. "*Oui, un petit peu.*"

"And the lives you were worried about were fortress crews?"

He shrugged, wasn't ready to trust this guy that much. "Yes sir."

Hanson glared. "And there's the matter of rank. Why would the Air Corps put a lieutenant on a belly gun? And why did you think Stalag 17-B had better contacts than us?"

He held his tongue, took a breath. The man's ego would have to be massaged. "The rest of my crew, what's left of them, is in Krems, sir. I trust them. Since they got there first, I assumed they'd know who to contact. That's all."

Hanson eased. "And what's a lieutenant doing strapped to a belly gun?"

He shook his head. "It's a long story, sir."

"I've got the time. So do you, Dremmer. Read me in on it."

He worked the muscles in his leg. "Captain Dougan knew I wanted to fly. I'd told him often enough, I guess. In the last months stateside, we were flying for hours, and he put me in the catbird seat." He forced a smile. "It was unofficial, but I received some training. Flew lots of hours over England, too. Brought the plane in to final any number of times. Over Schweinfurt, a side gunner and the co-pilot were killed, and the captain was blinded. He ordered Berkowitz and me to fly the crew back to Ridgewell. Two men died, and I was commissioned, sir."

The captain's face was chiseled in ice.

He knuckled his thigh. "They made up a crew a couple days after we were shot up. Our guys were rattled. I was waiting to go stateside to enter pilot training. It was part of the field commission." He looked away. "I volunteered to go up one last time. Didn't want the boys to go through more than they already had. And it was supposed to be a milk run."

Hanson sprang to his feet. "Ridgewell! Wait here, Lieutenant. I'll be right back."

He looked around the library, the fatigue settling in, sipped water from a tin cup, and stared at the books stacked on the shelves. Stanislavsky! The man had called him "Lieutenant." The corporal couldn't see his bars from behind, so how did he know?

Hanson stepped through the door, a red-headed kid in tow. Something about the boy—

"Lieutenant Dremmer, this is Corporal Brinkman."

He rose, studied the face. "Haven't we met, Corporal?"

"Sure have." Brinkman's face lighted. "What are the odds, Lieutenant? Couple of rat-tat-tatters ending up here. You been keeping tabs on Molly down at Land's End for me?"

The face registered. He'd seen Brinkman filing in and out of briefings and in line for chow. "You were on the *Glory Bee*! Waist gunner, right? The Führer's boys put you on a diet?"

Brinkman laughed. "I was sick. In the lazarette a couple weeks. Crew left without me."

He grinned, elated at seeing a familiar face. "Molly's faithful to half the 381st, Brinkman. There's no reason she wouldn't be faithful to you, too."

Hanson pushed between them. "You're sure you know this man, Corporal?"

"The lieutenant's a legend, sir. No one can figure out how he fits into a belly turret."

Hanson moved beside him, stood a few inches taller. "He doesn't look that big to me."

Brinkman grinned. "You ever see one of those ball turrets, sir?

They have to shoehorn jockeys into those things."

Hanson nodded. "That will be all, Corporal. Thank you for your help."

Brinkman saluted. "Sorry to hear about your crew, sir, but glad you made it out okay. And congratulations on the commission."

He returned the salute. "Good to see you, Brinkman. Find anything to fly around here, I'd love to go up with you."

Hanson waited for the corporal to clear the door. "That bit of evidence was in your favor. If you continue to check out, we'll reconsider."

He looked through the windows, watched Brinkman walk across the yard, wished the boy could have stayed. He turned back to Hanson. "Reconsider what, sir?"

"Why Corporal Stanislavsky was interested in bringing you under suspicion."

He smiled. "May I offer a suggestion, sir?"

"You may." The captain didn't appear at all likely to believe it.

"My interrogator, Leutnant Heinrich Schneider, took a special interest in me. Thought I was a spy. I have a hunch he might be having me watched. Possibly interfered with."

"You suggesting Stanislavsky is a plant?"

"I'm not suggesting anything, but after I check out, would it hurt to check him out?"

Hanson shook his head. "You're assuming a lot."

"No sir, I'm not assuming anything. I know I'm all right. It's you that's making assumptions." He detected the barest edge of a grin on the captain's face.

"Dremmer, there's more to this than you're telling. I suggest you start talking if you don't want to spend the night here."

He nodded. "All right, sir, but if you have an intelligence officer, I want him brought in on this. I'll have to have his permission to discuss it with you."

The look was straight out of *Casablanca*. "There is a head of intelligence here, Dremmer, and you're looking at him. Who d'you think would interrogate you after your behavior?"

"My behavior, sir?" His ears grew hot. "Before I proceed, Captain, I'd like to request that Corporal Stanislavsky be disciplined for insubordination."

"Not at this time, Lieutenant. Now, what's the pitch?"

He rubbed the back of his neck, prayed for the right words. "When we were shot down in Belgium, we were helped by the Resistance. They put themselves in a lot of danger for us."

Hanson smirked. "And you feel beholden to them. Is that it?"

He leveled his gaze. "Yes sir, I do. Very much."

"Go on, Lieutenant."

"One of them was killed helping us escape." He waited. "He was a friend, a German physicist by the name of Gerhardt Stein. He nursed us back to health, arranged our escape, then made contacts to get us out of the country. And he paid for it with his life."

Hanson glanced at the table and appeared to soften. "Proceed, Lieutenant."

He stiffened. "He wasn't the only one that risked his life. There's a Belgian girl. She worked at the British embassy before the Nazis rolled in. She had to disappear, of course, but she was just the sort MI6 was looking for to organize resistance."

How could he tell this man who she was? That knowing she was in the world changed everything. "She was Stein's student while at university in Munich."

Hanson twitched. "Here?"

Heat surged into his face. "Are we in Munich, sir?"

"Moosburg, actually. Munich's right around the corner. Does that mean something?"

"It might, sir. This Leutnant Schneider was Stein's student, too, and he knew the Belgian girl. Had a vendetta against her, or maybe something else, but he seemed obsessed with finding her." He calmed, felt a tingle in his belly. Schneider *was* pulling strings. "Maybe there's a reason I'm here, sir. Maybe Schneider wants to revisit his past, isolate me or maybe—"

"Maybe what?" Hanson leaned back in the large chair. "You're not making sense."

"That could be, Captain, but a lot of lives depend on you believing me."

Chapter VIII

Nicole rolled to face the first jaundiced light filtering through her window. She'd been awake for an hour listening to Charles in the next room as he and Gaston muttered their soft French before heading to the cellar for morning prayers.

She pulled the covers close and bunched her pillow. They'd not received a directive in weeks nor any word of further arrests. Charles said nothing, but worry had etched itself into his tapered brow. His silence was meant to shield her, but it made her mad with dread. Sometimes she wished for the Boche to rush through the door and end the wait.

She slid to the edge of the bed, the meager warmth she'd hoarded through the night dissolving into morning. The shakeup had started weeks ago and reached the top of the organization. No one knew how many had been taken. Or executed.

She shivered and eyed her narrow slice of sky. The organizers had allowed only those operatives to meet who would be required to work together. She had done the same with her recruits. No doubt there would have been more arrests had they not. Most agents received directives exclusively through the BBC in a code only they and MI6 knew. The method assured new recruits they were dealing with the Resistance since each created his or her own message and listened as the BBC read it back a few days later.

She raised her head and let her dark hair fall from her shoulders. She ached for David with his poet's heart, so strong in many ways, and so much a little boy in others. She dabbed her eyes, prayed for word from him, then slid into the dark where her fears took shape.

Not knowing was the worst of it. Those at the top went only by their code names. Thomas was the exception, but he'd been arrested weeks ago. A familiar shiver pressed against her heart. The old Resistance operative could resist Gestapo torture. If anyone could.

The light outside the window urged her from her bed. Charles and

Gaston would need breakfast, and… It was incomprehensible that Gerhardt was gone. She closed her eyes, envisioned her first weeks sitting in his class, losing herself in his lectures. She'd never encountered such genius. He once lectured past the hour. After a few minutes, a student timidly raised his hand and reminded him of the time. All grace and apology, Gerhardt bid them a good day and shooed them off. She would not have interrupted, even then. His lectures left her breathless, as did his stories about his work with Max Planck, his mentor.

She stared into the frigid blue beyond her window. That was the day she first considered that she might have fallen in love with him. She lifted the worn gown, soft and warm against her cheek. It was clear now that it hadn't been so much love as admiration. Still, she was in awe when he asked her to be one of three assistants for the next term.

She pulled her frayed robe tight and stepped into the kitchen, picked up three eggs, two potatoes, and an onion. It was unlikely they could have survived without the squab. Fortunately, Gaston had become almost as adept as Charles at capturing them.

She filled a pan with water, reached for a paring knife, and picked up an onion. Diaphanous skin gathered before the blade, and the air in her lungs froze. *Élodie!* What had severed her best friend from her life—taken her in the night? Even from her brother. Was it love or the darkness of Nazi terror? They'd spent their evenings reading Thomas Mann, Rauschning, Dark and Essex, or Dorothy Thompson—anything written by a Jew or a Christian. And all *verboten*. Hans Kerrl, the Minister of Religion, had forbidden such writers and issued a statement regarding their work: "The question of the divinity of Christ is ridiculous and inessential. A new answer has arisen as to what Christ and Christianity are: Adolph Hitler." So, they read on and believed themselves dissidents.

A titter reached her throat before it was choked. That was when the lies started about Gerhardt and her. At least they were mostly lies. She washed the potatoes, dropped them in the water, and moved the pan to the burner. She would slice them thin to cover more of the plate and make the meager portions appear a meal. Charles was her greatest concern. It was unjust asking such a large man to get by on so little.

The water reached a boil, and she remembered the Gestapo appearing on campus asking questions. She shuddered and slipped the diced onion into a saucepan. They'd offered concessions to anyone having information that would help them determine if Stein were, indeed, *Deutschfeindlich*—anti-German. That had given his colleagues, jealous for years, the opportunity to rid themselves of this uppity Jew.

She and Élodie marched into the provost's office, demanding he stop the groundless investigation. How imprudent they had been. The man was almost as much a victim as Gerhardt, so brave and wise. Then that awful evening he came to shush her— She objected, assuring him she'd done it for him. Her vision blurred, and she heard again the tremor in his voice. "One can do more, my dear, if one is not proud of one's indignation. In quietness there is strength. Audacity in demanding justice reveals a focus upon oneself, not injustice.

"It is quite possible to be a slave to one's emotions. If I were not convinced this is so, that my will is a superior repository of love, I might, for a while, falsely conclude that I had fallen in love with you, too." The words left her stinging, but the ones that followed were crushing, their kindness quelling any ire that might have eased her wounds. "Nicole, I chose to love my wife fifteen years ago, and I promised to love her until one or the other of us dies. I intend to keep that promise. You, my dear, are young, exceptionally bright, and perhaps more beautiful than you have a right to be. You would do well to not waste your life on lost causes."

She breathed deep, stirred the eggs, and spooned in the minced onions she'd been browning, scooping the boiled potatoes onto plates, and wiping tears from her cheeks. The week Gerhardt had been deposed as head of the Physics Department, the little despot, Schwab, a geneticist known only for his sympathy with Nazi causes, was named chairman.

She grabbed her knife and slashed the potatoes. His appointment was nothing more than an attempt to curry favor from his friends abroad. The Nazis were openly wooing Americans, doing whatever they could to please those in power. Joseph Kennedy was entertained with galas, as was Henry Ford. Friends of known American eugenics advocates were offered posts for favors, and Schwab was foremost among them, an associate of Margaret Sanger in New York. It was enough to secure him the department chair.

She clenched her jaw, dumped eggs into a pan, and felt the hiss reach her breast. Everyone knew the little man had limited capabilities, that his work was of no consequence, and that he was a rubber stamp for the eugenics program. It was whispered among students that he orchestrated the case against Gerhardt, Dr. Stein. Still, no one challenged his appointment. Schwab's party affiliations would have made it unhealthy to oppose him despite his being given the chairmanship in a discipline he knew nothing about.

And Herr Schneider. She pressed her hands against her stomach. What was it about him? So handsome in his uniform. All the girls were in love with him. And so intelligent. Gerhardt had chosen him as another of the three student assistants he was allowed. Heinrich showed his pleasure at the appointment, couldn't keep it from his face despite Dr. Stein being a Jew.

She shivered and moved closer to the stove. There were times when no warmth brought comfort. She tucked her chin and wondered again if Heinrich's delight had been due to his love of physics, Stein's tutelage, or to her. And why had the campus Romeo singled her out? He could have had any girl he wanted. Any girl but her.

She slid the plates across the table, stepped to the silverware drawer, and shivered. The day she'd spurned his advances, told him she would not entertain his pursuit, Heinrich began seeing her friend, took her to the biergarten, the commons, every place she frequented. And Élodie was delighted by his attention. Nicole grew rigid in the swelling cold and placed flatware beside the plates. It had been a relief to be free of him until Élodie confided that he never failed to ask after her—where she was, and if she spoke of him.

She rubbed her arms as the chill reached her bones. The day Gerhardt was removed, Heinrich met her on the commons spitting accusations, his blue eyes flashing. "You've been laughing at me, you and our Jewish professor. You've taken me for a fool!"

She feigned ignorance, but she'd been aware of the rumors for weeks and couldn't imagine that Heinrich had not heard of their pushing Gerhardt out, accusing them of having an affair. She waited for him to bring it up, relished the opportunity to defend herself, but he had marched away, his chin raised in a pout. No doubt the Luftwaffe had plans for him as they made special provisions for his academic pursuits. Perhaps those plans included his leaving in the middle of the night, though it was doubtful they intended for Élodie to go with him.

She drew her arms about her, coveting the light of day, however little it penetrated her world. Everyone believed Heinrich and Élodie's leaving to be an elopement, but she had always thought something else had stirred her friend. Had Élodie followed a Luftwaffe man off to his Nazi lair? It seemed impossible, despite her infatuation.

The eggs smelled hot. Nicole pulled the pan from the stove and scraped them onto plates. Her aunt had been writing, pleading with her to come to Bruges, and it seemed the right time. She went to Élodie's apartment, looking for her sweater and found instead a stack of pamphlets calling for organized resistance. That was when she learned the truth. Henri, arriving for a visit during a break in his studies at the Sorbonne, admitted that his sister was a member of the White Rose, and that he had been supplying her with material. He was frightened, bewildered by her absence, and at her recklessness at leaving the literature stacked along the wall.

She looked around the kitchen. "So much has happened since you left, Élodie. What has Heinrich done with you?" She started at the sound of boots on the stairs and hurried to divide her egg and potatoes between their plates. The men needed food to work. She could wait.

* * *

"We hoped you might join us for prayers." Charles spoke softly, seemed almost fearful.

She forced a smile. "Not today, Charles. I needed time alone."

"There has been no report of arrests for days. Perhaps it is over." It was Gaston's way of offering comfort.

She smiled. "I certainly hope so."

Charles stared. If it had been anyone else, she might have thought his look an accusation. At last she turned to him. "What is it?"

"Your hands. They're shaking. Are you all right?"

"Of course. I'm just chilled."

She prayed, excused herself, and counted the moments until they left. She loved them both, but the fear was a vortex that sucked all into itself and left the room devoid of air.

Charles turned to look at her, his face darker in the gloom. "Won't you eat something? You're growing thin."

She tried to laugh. "I have an egg for myself, but I'm not hungry. Perhaps later."

The two men finished their meals, put on their coats, and started for the door, Gaston refusing to meet her glance. Something had been bothering him for days, something more than grief. That look was always there, worn and tattered. This was new.

"You will be careful, won't you? You'll watch out for each other?" She hoped her solicitude would cover her withdrawal.

Charles stood, his hat in his hand. "We could receive word today, perhaps an assignment. God knows we need to do something. You'll monitor the broadcast?"

She held his shadowed gaze. "Of course."

The big man nodded. "Be careful. Hide any instructions; memorize and destroy them."

Gaston turned, his skin a pasty white. "The times call for caution, Nicole. Be ready to fly to my flat and onto the roof at any sound."

"You know I will. Go on and don't worry. Please."

* * *

Nicole cleared the breakfast clutter and busied herself in the living room where Charles slept. She straightened her bed and wound the clock. Ten more minutes until the morning broadcast. She moved through the door and slipped down the common stairs.

The door above the stairway to the basement had been left ajar. She stopped, heard only the pounding of her heart. Life was so fragile, one's breath so easily quenched. She pulled the door, watched bright, diagonal lines slice the wooden stairs until they descended into darkness.

She whispered down the steps, the knot in her stomach easing. The cellar was inhabited by shadows. Nothing more. She glanced into the unfilled space where David had waited. When had that look first appeared in his eyes? It was as if her visits were a momentous thing, and he was intent on capturing them. His love was more real than any she'd known since her father died. She edged to the corner where he had lain, the tarp still folded as he left it, and the grommets worn smooth, partly by his touch.

It was time. She stole to the half window that opened onto the sidewalk, traced the imaginary line that fell from its center to the baseboard, knelt, and edged her fingernails behind it to drag it across the floor. She reached beyond the exposed pipe to the speaker Gerhardt had hidden within the wall, the braided wire matching that throughout the building, and lifted the speaker to her ear. She picked up the nail lying on the stone, inserted it into a hole in the wooden slats, and heard the familiar click of the receiver. Tubes glowed between the cracks, and a squawk erupted before the familiar voice of the BBC broadcaster rattled against her cheek.

She skimmed the wire with her fingers and felt where Gerhardt had spliced and covered them with tape. Such genius. Even Gestapo boots weren't apt to expose the receiver. Wires emerged from conduit that appeared to go upstairs, but power came from a streetlamp so the radio could not be silenced even by shutting off their electricity.

The host of *American Jazz in London* baritoned his commentary, his English jolting her from the constant Belgian French she spoke with her flat mates.

News of Stateside Interest began. "And this just in for our Yank friends. The Aussies have repulsed Jap attacks in Ramu Valley and are maintaining positions.

"Lieutenant General Mark W. Clark, Commanding General of the Allied Fifth Army in Italy, received the Distinguished Service Cross from his own commander in chief, President Franklin Roosevelt, while the president visited troops in Sicily yesterday.

"Also yesterday, Fats Waller died of pneumonia while in his Pullman berth on *The Santa Fe Super Chief* outside Union Station in Kansas City." Her breath caught, and she pressed the speaker to her ear. "He had just completed an engagement at the Zanzibar Club in Los Angeles and was returning east." Fats Waller. The jazz pianist David spoke of. He loved the man's music and would have grieved. Perhaps it was best he didn't know.

"In sports, New York Giant Bill Paschal put the finishing touches to the most closely contested race for an individual championship in National Football League history by making off with the ground-gaining title. He won with a one-yard margin." She smiled. Football. Why did the Americans call it that? All the head and shoulder bashing. What were they trying to accomplish? Football was a sport played with the feet, as she used to play at university.

Her code name, Electra, wasn't mentioned, her prayer for a word that David was safe unanswered. She pulled the nail from the wall, watched the glow fade behind cracked mortar, and replaced the baseboard, then walked to the corner where he'd slept, reciting his poem and straining to hear his voice in the words.

At the bottom of the paper he had written, "John 14." Another mark followed, but he'd run out of space, and she was unable to distinguish it. Strange that David, who could then not allow himself to believe that a loving God existed, would have included a scripture.

She mounted the stairs, took one last look into the corner where he stayed during the seven weeks that altered her heart, turned, and climbed to her apartment, singing a hymn her mother had taught her. A few of the words revisited her; the rest, she hummed.

A squeak sounded from Gaston's flat, and her heart exploded in her throat. She shut the door, ran to her room, and locked it. She would climb onto the roof if she had to. Falling would be preferable to dying at the end of a rope. Her mouth went dry. It was impossible to enter the flat without climbing the stairs—unless the intruder had found the secret entrance David, Bear, and Gerhardt used. But if the Boche had seen them, why would they have waited until now?

Footsteps moved above her, then silence. She waited, her breath emerging in short bursts. A tinkle of metal, and the door creaked open from the hall.

"Hullo?"

She lurched. "Who's there?"

"It's spring, and the plane leaves wither." She took a firm grip and opened the door. A young man stood beyond the table, his hands raised in assurance that he meant no harm.

Had their code been discovered? "Are you also a reader of Goethe?"

"You are Nicole."

"Yes."

"I am Pascal. I have come for you."

Her spine prickled. "How did you get in?"

"Through the roof. I came at early dark while your friend was visiting your flat, and I stayed in his closet to make sure I was not followed. I found no opportunity to enter his room without frightening him." Pascal shrugged. "He still has a pistol, yes?"

She shrugged, wasn't ready to divulge that. "How are we to escape?"

"Passage has been arranged to Spain."

"And Charles? Gaston? They cannot stay! Not if I leave."

He shook his head. "I've come only for you. You cannot leave together, certainly. You would be easily recognized."

"There are records. If the Boche come, Charles will be arrested. I can't do this to him."

Pascal covered his mouth. "Arrangements have been made only

for you. I am sorry."

She paced to the end of the room and turned. "When?"

"At midnight. We have a meeting scheduled. It is best if you don't know where just yet."

She straightened. "Good. They will be back this evening. They must know."

"You may take no more than you can easily carry. The journey will be strenuous." His gaze slid slowly down. "Are you fit?"

"It's been months, but I was quite athletic. Lots of hiking and football."

He raised an eyebrow. "Football?"

She nodded. "I played at the university. And I danced."

Pascal's face was stone. "Hiking is good. You should perhaps take something appropriate for a winter climb."

"I speak no Spanish. Only French, of course, and English. My German was once good but has become rusty."

"The instructions came from London. It is possible you could go on to England. Perhaps it won't be necessary for you to speak Spanish."

* * *

Nicole refolded the clothes in her drawers. There was a finality in it, and a sadness. She was packed—corduroy pants, a woolen sweater, her personals. She would wear boots and a heavy coat. She'd given Pascal her last egg, and he dozed in the corner near the landing. Charles was the greater concern. He had changed so after Gerhardt's murder.

Footsteps rose from the stairs, and she slipped in front of Pascal.

The door opened, and Charles emerged from the hall and turned, looking from Pascal to her, his face as wan as silk. "What's this?"

"This is Pascal, a brother at arms." She twisted her gown, tried to hide it in her fists, saw the fear on Charles' face. "He has a directive from MI6. For me."

"You are leaving?"

She nodded. "Pascal says Abwehr knows of me and that I must leave."

The boy's stare was set on Charles. "Not Abwehr, the Luftwaffe, though it's possible the information has been shared."

45

Her heart sank. She had wanted to spare her friend that, at least.

Charles ignored the boy and glared at her. "May I speak with you? Alone?"

"Of course." She heard Charles' shuffle before her bedroom door closed behind her.

"Your friend from university. Gerhardt's student. He's the one after you?"

She pivoted to see his eyes welling. "I would assume so, yes. Charles, I asked that you be extracted, as well. And Gaston. I don't want to leave either of you here."

"And what did he say?"

She lowered her head.

"I see."

"But you mustn't stay. You must go to someplace safe."

"And where is that? America perhaps?" He looked at his massive hands, gripping and releasing his hat. "I've grown so very fond of you. I had hoped that—"

"Charles, you know I love you. Like a brother. I don't know how I could have—"

"Like a brother. I see." It seemed an insult when he said it. "When are you leaving?"

"In a few hours." It was clear why they had been unable to talk. She had been too caught up in her loss to see his. Her throat constricted, and she moved to hold him. "Wish me well, Charles. I will not forget you."

He smelled of earth, rich and sweet. He released her and she saw tears coursing his face. "I much more than wish you well. I wish with all my heart for you to escape all this."

She blinked away the dampness. "And I wish the same for you."

"But I must know. Are you in love with the American?" His words were a whisper.

Streams flowed down his cheeks and disappeared into his beard as she fought to crush her reactions. It was unjust that she should feel revulsion at Charles, a friend who had cared so much for her.

"Nicole, you must hear me on this. It is not right. He is married."

She tightened her fists. "But his marriage is like ours, Charles. Only for appearances."

"It is not like ours. Ours was to save our lives and to fulfill our obligations. Most of all, it was to stop evil. His was a lie of convenience. We lied only to the devil."

She looked away. David's wife was half a world away. Perhaps she had simply not allowed her to be real. The means and purposes Delores may have had in arranging the marriage didn't matter. David had chosen, too, but a new fire burned in her for Charles.

The big man worried his hat brim. "Our marriage does not have to be a lie at all. We could have a real marriage. Before God."

She shuddered. "Please, Charles, don't. Not now."

"There is no other time, Nicole. In a few hours, you will be gone."

"But I can't make a commitment to you. Not when—"

Something she hadn't seen before erupted from Charles. "Not when you love this American deceiver. This no-good—"

She put her fingers to his lips. "No. You're right. I will likely never marry David." She patted his chest, wondered at her loss of words. "But don't say things in jealousy that are not true. You are one of my dearest friends. Don't say anything that might change that."

He turned, shuffled through the door, and closed it behind him. She sank to her knees and rested her head on the bed. Tears came with force; she pulled the duvet to her face and allowed the dam to be breached. She wouldn't marry David. It was a dream she'd used to escape the darkness. She cried a wordless prayer, a groan that carried more than words ever could, and slid to the floor. David would be her sacrifice, as her father had been. And Gerhardt.

* * *

Nicole glanced at the clock. Eleven twenty. She opened the door, her clothes tied in the bundle she held close to her breast. The two men looked on in silence, their faces drawn. Pascal still sat in the corner.

"I'm ready." It was a lie. She might never be ready for what lay ahead. Not now.

Charles moved toward her and stopped. "You must eat something. You haven't eaten all day." He lifted a plate of squab and potatoes. "Please, let me warm this for you."

"Thank you, Charles. It's fine." He had prepared her food, probably all they'd brought home. She touched his beard, struggled to hold her heart in check, couldn't abide revealing herself to him, now. "Have you discussed your plans for escape?"

Gaston turned from her. "Pascal has promised to have word to us within a week. We will stay in my flat. That will give us a few extra seconds to escape should the Gestapo come."

She choked down a bite of squab. "I pray I will see you both soon."

Gaston looked up, his face as white as ash. "There is something I must say." He swallowed. "I have failed you both."

She stared, wondering how he could ever fail anyone.

He looked away. "I was contacted two weeks ago. The Americans were captured. Somehow, the lieutenant arranged with MI6 to have you removed from the country. He sent a friend to tell you to be ready and instructed you to leave on your own should the organization fail to come for you. I cannot disclose to you the friend. It would be dangerous for him."

She pulled her hand across her face, felt the wetness in her palm, and fought for breath.

Gaston turned to Charles. "I'm sorry. I thought if she knew, she might leave alone. That would have been more dangerous. There seemed to be no need to put you through this, and London's plans so often change. I thought they might find another way."

Charles' mouth gaped wide.

Gaston returned his stare. "I would have taken her myself. I would not have left her in danger. Two weeks, he said. So, I waited two weeks. Then a day—now three. I would have taken her tomorrow. I wanted to give them every opportunity." He dropped his head.

Nicole reached for Gaston's arm. "Your decision was the right one. You failed no one." She fought for breath. "And David is well?"

Gaston stared at the table. "He sent his love and asked that you remember John, chapter fourteen, verse two. And that you remember your name. I assume you know what that means."

Tears came, though she fought them. "Yes." David was alive. He'd gotten word to MI6, had put himself in danger to protect her. Charles was wrong. He was a good man.

Chapter IX

His collar and cuffs were frayed, but the captain appeared freshly starched. "You realize, of course, that your orders were to say nothing."

The accusation incited a firestorm in David's gut. "So, you'd have preferred I let Schneider ferret out the people who saved our lives, sir?"

"Officially, Lieutenant, that wasn't your call to make. You chose to play cat and mouse with this Kraut." Hanson sneered. "How'd you convince him you could execute his lover?"

Heat crawled up his neck. "I never told him she would be executed, Captain, only that Partisans were watching her." He worked to steady his breath. "My warning was in response to his threat. He knows if he goes after Nicole or the others, he's putting Élodie in danger." He waited. "You said it was officially not my call, sir. What about unofficially?"

Hanson scanned the short row of library windows, reached the end, and looked back. His expression had softened. "We just might be able to help you, Dremmer."

He released his breath, was in desperate need of an ally. "Help me how, sir?"

The captain squinted. "When you see this Leutnant Schneider again, you'll need more information on Élodie. We have sources."

Likely goons, but how could the captain be sure he wasn't being played?

Hanson glared. "It's possible we could locate this woman of Schneider's, but you'll have to leave that to us. Our contacts will remain *our* contacts. Is that understood?"

He nodded. "I have no interest in who feeds you information, sir." It was a lie. "I just want to protect those who protected me." He let the discomfort settle. "So, you're convinced I'll see Schneider again, sir?"

49

"Lieutenant, if you've been straight with me, Schneider isn't going to leave you stewing on how you've been taken for a ride, not when he thinks your friends can reach his girl."

He released his breath. The captain had reached the same conclusion as he.

Hanson stretched his neck, freeing it from the constraints of his stiff collar. "My guess is he's using this as a smokescreen, buying time to hide this Jewish girl he's involved with. In the meantime, we'll try to find out where she is."

Doubts rippled the surface of stilling waters. He just couldn't quench the fear that the man was in over his head. "Is it really possible that you could find her, sir?"

The captain shrugged. "I'd say probable. I'm releasing you to continue your transient inspection. Couple of days you'll be back. You'll billet with the bucks and non-coms. I'll have you assigned to the same barracks as Stanislavsky. If he's watching you, we'll be watching him. Meanwhile, I'll check out your story." Hanson's face turned hard. "His story will be checked, too, Dremmer. Don't contact me, and keep what you've told me to yourself."

"I understand, sir, but you do realize you're making me a pariah by separating me from the other officers."

Hanson stared.

He ratcheted his courage. "And how do I know you can do what you say, sir?"

The captain leaned toward him. "Let me read you in on something, Dremmer. I'm your closest friend, and I'm not sure I like you. If you decide to take a piss, you'd best be standing downwind. Last thing you want is for my shoes to get wet. Capiche?" The starched shirt lifted in quick heaves. "I'm thinking you need to get involved on the cleanup crew. And I mean actively."

* * *

Nordlager. Two days of uninterrupted queues punctuated by what were supposed to be medical exams. They weren't exhaustive. He had no doubt the Krauts took note that he was breathing, had four limbs, multiple digits, and at least two orifices. Beyond that, they couldn't have learned much.

He writhed on an excelsior gunny sack fresh from delousing and replayed scenarios that never turned out the way he wanted. Despite the threat he posed to Hanson's shoes, the man appeared to believe his story. Still, he was powerless, and his doubts about the captain's abilities needled him. Nicole's fate hanged, he cringed at the word, on the success of those who might not be proficient in this spy business. Or maybe they were more proficient than he. How could he know? The precariousness of the game made even his prayers seem bleak.

He rolled to his side. Twigs pressed into his knitting ribs, and he closed his eyes and tried to ignore the gnawing in his gut. After his experience in the well, he knew that God existed, and that he was known and heard. That certainty brought a peace that transcended capture and interrogation. But the fear had returned, wormed its way into his soul, and crowded out the light. Now he needed assurance that the God who had restored his leg would keep Nicole safe.

Sound drew him like a mother's touch. He raised his head, stared down the narrow passageway to a group of kriegies gathered in the corner, praying behind their bunks. He edged between the rows and listened. Words flowed, petitions for peace, for family, words rich with King James English. For all that, they brought no more peace than his own. He stood to slip away as the others began to sing, then stopped, revisiting the wooden steps. A holy thrill lifted on a cottonwood breeze. He squatted and took it in.

The hymns resonated like a dream of home or poultices drawing poison from a wound. He couldn't remember hearing them, but he repeated a chorus *sotto voce*. *"And from Your throne shall ever flow, a Love so pure that I may know Your sheltering hand wherever I go."* From somewhere deep, a secret place, a spasm of grief filled his throat and took flight in hushed sobs. Tears flowed down his cheeks, and his body strained with release. He cried for Nicole, for his mother, for Jesse, for Delores and her child, for his failures to meet the needs of those he loved, and for the needs of those he'd failed to love. He cried for his crew, for Dougan, for Ream, for Lioni, for Ito, for Gerhardt. And for the black.

The colt returned on a vapor, his head held high. The days of fear and distrust played before him, days of Dancer resisting his hand. The black was full of power and beauty, raw and unrestrained. When he submitted, something changed. At first it frightened him. He thought he'd taken something Dancer should never have been asked to give.

He leaned against a bunk and felt rough wood press into his

shoulder. When Dancer responded to the urging of the bridle, to hand and leg and voice, something had come alive in him. The colt became who he was born to be. He'd been fashioned for the life he was given. Dancer's will hadn't been destroyed but committed to a purpose. Each time he was saddled, Dancer chose again, and with each release, he became more a creature of destiny—less the indentured and more the friend.

Had the colt not yielded, he would have been free to follow his desires, but he would never have been whole, would have forfeited completion. David caught his breath and embraced the light. He hadn't taken from the colt but given him purpose, love, identity. He breathed the quieting hymns, let the peace settle in, and prayed to be given what Dancer had received.

* * *

David stood, the dark wind whipping past his face, night cutting sharp against the approach of day, twisting streaks of frozen mist between the barracks. It whirled ash from tepid barrels, howled against floodlights, its icy fur pinned against razor wire, driving specks of darkness, blue-black and brilliant against a liquid sky. With morning pitted at its flank, it bayed like a coyote in a trap.

The men in his barracks huddled in their bunks, gathering what warmth they could, bidding themselves to sleep. But morning wouldn't be held. He refused to fight it any longer, left the groans of men too cold to find escape, and wandered to the latrine. He brought his hands to his mouth, tendered what warmth he could to his stinging fingers, and cherished the sovereignty of being alone. He released a silent supplication for Nicole, her safety, her peace, and for himself, to feel the warmth of her voice and see the brilliance in her eyes once more. Then alone in the yard, he breathed in the scent of her, touched a phantom dream, a fleeting softness as she knelt before her bed, her worn gown drawn against her cheek, whispering his name in prayer.

He moved into the darkness of the shadowed stoop. "Thank you," he whispered, and slipped through the door.

* * *

Swanson leaned on his mop. "So, tell me about London, Lieutenant. Those English girls as easy as they say?"

David set his teeth. His second day on cleanup, and the second day of questions about England, the Air Corps, and Ridgewell. He looked from the tub of water warming on the stove, pulled out a pot and began to scrub. "I was only in London once, Corporal. I didn't meet any girls other than to say hello. Most avoided us like the plague, and I didn't blame them."

"Did you like the country? I mean, what did it look like?"

"East Anglia was beautiful. Black and rolling. Rich and wet. The hills were covered—" The door opened, let in a gust of winter. He turned to Stanislavsky, Captain Hanson beside him.

The captain glanced his way. "Dremmer, isn't it?"

He nodded. "Yes sir."

"Lieutenant Dremmer, this is Corporal Stanislavsky. He'll be billeting here."

His chest tightened. "We've met, sir."

"Good. You can read him in on things. Get him settled in."

Hanson didn't wait for a response but slipped through the door into the cold.

David stared a threat at Stanislavsky.

The corporal grinned. "Looks like we're gonna be bunkies, aye, sir?"

"Apparently, we'll be in the same barracks, Corporal." He pointed to the opposite side. "That top bunk's empty. Stow your gear beneath the bottom one. Leave the walkway clear."

"D'you make your appointment the other day, sir?" Stanislavsky smacked his gum.

Swanson edged close, seemed intrigued.

David turned from the tub, dried his hands on a strip of undershirt, and met Stanislavsky straight on. "Corporal, I know your game. You'd best watch your step."

"Yes sir, Lieutenant. Ridden lots of buses. I know how to do that."

He spoke just above a whisper. "Krauts pay you off in chewing gum, Corporal?"

The dark stubble above Stanislavsky's lip strained upward. "That's insulting, sir."

"I intended it for to be. Tell Schneider I said to hire a smarter boy next time."

Stanislavsky's smile flickered. "No idea what you're talking about, sir."

"You know exactly what I'm talking about. There's not near

enough Hollywood in you to pull this off. Enjoy your chewing gum." He burned his anger into Stanislavsky's eyes. "It's apt to be the last payoff you get."

Stanislavsky's face flashed an alarm that was as quickly covered with a grin. There was a movement to his right as Swanson sidled within hearing range.

He turned and smiled. "I recently learned that Corporal Stanislavsky has a close friend I happen to have met. I passed on my regards since you're so interested." He looked back at Stanislavsky. "But I believe we've reached an understanding, haven't we, Corporal?"

Stanislavsky bunched his shoulders and shrugged.

"Do we have an agreement, Corporal?"

Stanislavsky heaved his rucksack over his shoulder. "Whatever you say, sir."

He sank his hands into tepid water and retrieved the potato pot. At this moment, Élodie could be in hiding freeing Schneider to pursue Nicole. She should be out of Belgium, if Henri did as he'd promised, but her life was dependent on so many, including the captain who was either the boon he'd prayed for or the biggest ruse yet.

***

David huddled with the other kriegies in the barracks, crusts of sawdust-laden bread in their hands. They'd returned from morning appell where they'd stood in a cold wind for an hour while the goons worked on their addition and subtraction.

The fire burned low, and their collective breath hovered over the cooking area in the center. At that, it was the warmest spot, though only a double handful of coal remained in the bin. The door behind them slammed against a frigid blast, and he turned to see an unfamiliar face, a private, his thick, red hair pushing an ill-fitting cap off his forehead.

The boy moved toward them rubbing his arms. "Everybody here on the approved list?"

A deathly quiet took the room. A gangly private named Mathews turned toward him, a question on his face. The red-headed boy hesitated, looked around, and took a slip of paper from beneath the wrist band of his right glove. He cleared his throat and held the paper closer to the bare bulb. "All the news that's fit to scribble fast, boys. This in yesterday from the BBC. The Aussies have repulsed Jap attacks in the Ramu Valley and are maintaining their positions.

"Lieutenant General Mark W. Clark, Commanding General of the Allied Fifth Army in Italy, received the Distinguished Service Cross from none other than President Roosevelt while he visited troops in Sicily.

"Thomas Wright 'Fats' Waller died yesterday of pneumonia while in his bunk on *The Santa Fe Super Chief* as it pulled into Kansas City's Union Station. He was returning to New York after a two-week engagement in Los Angeles."

Fats Waller. Dead. David heaved in the unsteady light, felt the world tilt slightly, and remembered the silk fingers racing across the keyboard in utter brilliance.

The private took a breath and looked toward the door. "New York Giant rookie Bill Paschal has put the finishing touches on a closely contested race for individual championships in the National Football League by making off with the ground-gaining title with a one-yard margin. He claimed the distinction by running ninety-two yards against Washington."

The boy went on, something about a murder trial in New York, but David had lost the ability to follow. Fats Waller was gone, his genius never to be offered again. The private wished them a Merry Christmas. "Only nine days, boys. That'll be a feast, won't it?"

David took his watered-down coffee and crust of bread, pushed through the door into the crystal brilliance, and headed to the library. A slight pain niggled at his neck and shoulders when he lay on his palliasse at night. He needed exercise, had wanted to go to the sports field, but he was hungry. Red Cross parcels were due soon. Good chance he could trade his cigarettes for a tin of potted meat, some condensed milk, too, maybe. He'd exercise then.

He pushed the door of the library. *Fats Waller*. The man had left a world hungry for purity, his touch on the ivory as close to perfection as anything he'd heard. It was an injustice, but justice would come. Deep inside, the promise grew despite a world that reveled in its loss.

* * *

Sleeping nine hours a night had become a habit. Some of the older men, those who'd been behind wire for months or years, rose only to eat and make appell or carry out assigned duties. But today was Sunday. David wrapped his fingers around the bread he'd saved, found the tin of potted meat deep in his pocket, and left to find a seat at chapel. He hustled to the library, sat in the center section, and opened his Bible as someone moved into the seat beside him.

"This seat taken?"

"Help yourself." He turned, started to rise.

Captain Hanson motioned him down, picked up his pocket New Testament and put his head down. "Don't look this way. Your shadow attended mass this morning. I'm assuming he won't be at Protestant services." He paused. "I have news."

"Is there a problem, sir?" His stomach tightened.

"Seems Stanislavsky was handled by the same interrogator as you."

He let the vindication settle in.

"You're checking out all right. Thing is, so is he. What I want to know is, why didn't you tell me about him being held with you after your capture?"

"I never saw him before my first morning here, sir, unless…"

"Unless what?"

"Like I said, Captain, I was held in the cellar of a warehouse. After we got there, they separated Bear and me, Sergeant Billington, the tail gunner from my crew."

"Your friend." Hanson's words were scarcely audible.

"Yes sir. They locked me in the bathroom, but I saw Bear and a few others in the cellar. I assumed they were part of another crew. Stanislavsky could have been there." He fell silent, searching his memory. His head came up without bidding.

"What?" Hanson's voice was taut.

"If Stanislavsky is infantry, what was he doing in the middle of Belgium, sir?"

"Says he was in a commando unit sent inland from Messina reconnoitering spots for landing strips. They were shot up. He was captured and taken to Belgium for interrogation."

"Taken to Belgium from Sicily, sir?"

"Stranger things have happened. If that's where they're gathering information on commando raids, then it's possible. Is there anything else you want to remember before I have to find it out on my own?"

"I had no idea Stanislavsky was in that cellar, or if he was, sir. But why would Schneider have been interrogating infantry?"

"You said there was some battle going on over jurisdiction. Maybe your man in blue wasn't a virgin. Could have had a habit of taking the Wehrmacht's dates home."

He bit his thumb. "Or maybe the Luftwaffe has a special interest in where the Allies plan to put landing strips. Which would suggest Stanislavsky spilled the beans."

Hanson's voice was scarcely audible. "That's possible. Our sources say Schneider attended the University of Munich. Before he left, he was seen in the company of a fräulein by the name of Élodie Devillier. Both were well-liked. He went into special training mid-term. Not clear if he requested it, but he said he'd broken it off with Devillier. Thing is, she disappeared at the same time. Some thought she followed him to Düsseldorf in some secret elopement, but most believed she went home to Belgium with a broken heart."

"Interesting." He wished he had a way to check out Hanson's information.

"Here's the pitch. Munich is thirty miles away. Maybe they have unfinished business here. He could have requested this stalag. We've got friends in the woods, and most are associated with the university. We also have work detachments that walk through the woods, capiche? If those two are back, we'll know."

So, that was it. Their contacts were from the university.

The captain's head pivoted. "As long as you're on your knees, pray for patience."

He smiled. "How about I pray for quick answers, sir? I don't want to put any excessive wear on what little patience I have left."

"They're your knees, I suppose."

"Captain Hanson?"

"Yes, son."

He stifled a laugh. "Thanks for your help, sir."

"Let me read you in on something, Dremmer. Your gratitude isn't needed. I intend to use your 'understanding' with Schneider. And when you see him, you're going to convince him that you're both in the right place. For the duration. You capice?"

He felt the stiffness in his neck begin to ease. "And how do I do that, sir?"

"Dazzle me, Lieutenant. Impress me with your ingenuity. That's an order."

He turned to catch the captain's grin before it faded. He was in.

Chapter X

Nicole darted between shadows, the obsidian street rising beneath her. She stopped, gazed into a scrap of moonlight, and caught the muted flicker of Pascal's jacket as he wended through rundown houses with roofs that mawed the darkness with jagged teeth.

Pascal disappeared into an alley. She quickened her pace and pushed into thicker gloom only to lose him again. Her breath caught. She was alone, without David or Charles or Gaston. The street had taken all the fire left in her trembling legs. Before her, a vaguely familiar park emerged, now covered in thickets. Moonlight splashed on leather, and her lungs released their grip on the cold. She fought to refill them, crept after Pascal into the cover of shrubs, and trailed him down a narrow path. He emerged on a brick street glazed and slick with lorry tread, then ran beside a stone wall and disappeared around the corner. Her chest tightened, and she firmed her grip on her pack, ran past the corner, and spotted him ducking beneath yellow light oozing from a window, the house hinting at a life locked away and secret.

Pascal approached a gate. She waited for a creak, but the hinges were silent. He crept to the rear and tapped on a window hidden beneath the cover of a holly, the leaves bent and curled. A limb snapped, and he jerked, scurried toward a shadowed doorway, and motioned for her to follow. The door opened, and she slipped behind Pascal, traced unsure lines in the velvet dark and retrieved a form bent and shuffling toward the corner of the room. A switch snapped, and the man hovered over a solitary orb of light.

Pascal put his hand on her shoulder. "Elisabeth, this is Clement." Her new code name, offered without warning. It would be known only to Pascal and Clement. And MI6. If she were captured, this new contact would know nothing of Nicole or Electra, and Charles and Gaston would know nothing of Elisabeth. "He will guide you through the next leg of your journey."

The man straightened and leaned back. The faint light from his shaded lamp penciled an edge to his grizzled face, added a sunken chin, and a sharp nose. He was likely in his sixties, stooped and thin, with patches of white erupting from his railway cap.

"Thank you for your help." She extended her hand, felt his leer before he spoke.

The eyes glinted, his smile a testament of hunger. "More than welcome, *ma chérie*." His French was gruff, accented with something she didn't recognize.

Pascal stepped between them, offering shelter. "You'll be leaving soon?"

Clement raised his chin and looked around the boy's shoulder. "Perhaps an hour. No sooner." The words were filled with gravel.

Pascal nodded. "Best observe your routine. Your lights should go on and off when they always do, and you must exit the house in darkness."

Clement shot him a fiery glance. "I know all this. I can handle her."

The boy seemed hesitant, caught her eyes, and scanned the room. "Clement will place you on a railway car bound for Brussels where the car will be switched to another train. You will remain in it a day and a half, perhaps two days. In Lyon, you will be met by another railway worker. He will give you directions for the next leg."

She would require food and water for two days. Clement's responsibility, surely.

The man looked away and nodded at Pascal. "It is time I help her change."

A prickly cold moved up her spine.

Pascal wavered. "We will contact you shortly to make sure you are safe."

The promise was for Clement. There would be no further contact. "Thank you, Pascal. I look forward to hearing from you."

He embraced her and dropped something into her coat pocket. She slid her hand across the broad edge of a blade enfolded between smooth handles. "I'll see you soon, love."

She forced a smile. "Until then."

The door closed. Clement took her hand and switched off the lamp. "Come with me."

Her stomach squeezed; she tugged her hand free and followed the bent figure past a dining table into a short hallway. Doors stood at each end, a dimly lit bathroom between, the light she had seen from the street. Clement entered a bedroom on the right and turned on a lamp.

She stopped. The bed butted against two walls. A single window with drawn curtains appeared above the headboard. The only space was a narrow walkway before a mirrored door. A tiny dresser and chair were jammed into the opposite corner.

"You're normally awake at this hour? We shouldn't arouse suspicion." She examined him more closely. He wore overalls, smelled of coal oil, had a deep scowl carved in his face.

He turned, his eyes moving up and down. "I think I have something that will fit you." He placed his hands around her waist and pulled her through the door.

Her lungs emptied in a gust, and she pushed back.

"Just settling on your size, *chérie*." His breath reeked of tobacco and wine.

Information was vital, a way to control him. "How long have you worked with us?"

He stiffened. "I am a dedicated socialist, a member of the Partisans Armés, and I am accustomed to this kind of work."

She shivered, was familiar with their betrayal of political enemies. "I wasn't questioning your expertise, but this is difficult work for strangers."

Something else was hidden in his look. Suspicion? He stepped into a closet, lifted pants from a hanger, a shirt, a scarf, then reached to retrieve a cap. He turned back, looking eager.

A chill prickled the back of her neck. "Where should I go to put them on?"

"Here." Tobacco stains narrowed his teeth as he grinned.

She swallowed and lifted her chin. "Then, of course, you will be so kind as to step outside, monsieur?" She flattened herself against the wall and made room for him to pass.

He released a slow breath, offered a sly smile, and brushed against her, his hand lingering on her hip as he maneuvered past. It required a key. Air froze in her lungs. She fingered the knife, tucked it into the new pants, slid the chair against the door, and dropped the clothes onto the dingy bedspread. She removed her coat and sweater and turned from the door. Her fingers trembled against buttons as the trousers fell to the floor. The faintest rustle whispered in the hall.

* * *

Clement leaned against the wall, peering through the hidden fissure in the frame. The girl was stunning, her skin soft and warm in the amber light. He released his breath. Something frightened her, and she turned her head to the door and reached for her sweater. Her breasts were plump and firm, not large but ample for so slight a thing. Flawless. She turned back, and he drank in the silky flow of her back and buttocks beneath her panties, followed her long, sculpted legs as she turned to the bed and held the sweater to her breasts.

When he was young, women sometimes looked back when he held their gaze. One thing would lead to another, of course. Still, he'd never seen a woman like this.

He stood, leaned away from the door, and filled his lungs. He had hoped to meet someone when he offered to help these people but never dreamed such a woman would be delivered to his door. Until now, there had been only coded messages, reports on trains, the relaying of car numbers. This made it worthwhile.

There had to be a way to have her. He would use caution, of course. She seemed well connected. He bent toward the door, his need growing, watching her wiggle as she stepped into the old trousers, an electric chill coursing his spine at the porcelain perfection of her hips and legs. She pulled the trousers across her thighs, the light sparkling over goose-pimpled flesh. Her hands vanished around the faint depression above her loins as she worked with the buttons, then drew the belt around her narrow waist.

He stepped away and worked to quiet his lungs. "Are you ready, *ma chérie?*"

"No! Don't come in!"

He suppressed a laugh. *It's too late, duckie.*

"All right." Her voice was weak with fear. He stepped toward the door, wanted her to hear him down the hall, opened it to see her standing in his clothes, filling them deliciously.

He scowled and shook his head. "No. You look like a girl. A beautiful girl, certainly, but a girl." He held her icy gaze. "Perhaps we could try larger clothes." He placed his fingers in the loops and tugged. "These were from my youth. It is a shame, of course, but if you tied a towel around your breasts..." He slid his fingers over the waistband and pulled. "I will help."

Her breath left her, and she pushed. "Monsieur Clement, with your experience, I'm certain you know what happens to those who betray others in this work. There are so many dying these days, people seem not to notice when accidents occur."

It was precisely the thing he hated about beautiful women. They always tried to make him appear the fool. "Who is betraying you? Wear what you like. It is your life."

She shook her head. "I'll try larger clothes. Do you have soot for my face?"

He nodded, reflecting on the ways of young women, offering kindness only when they wanted something. He would resist her beauty. "I have furnace ash."

"That will do, thank you. You may close the door while I change clothes."

He felt the shame she intended, but she would regret it. He was no woman's fool.

* * *

Nicole stared into the dark and shivered. Overhead lamps knifed the coal smoke. The tracks, polished by constant grinding, emerged in elaborate curves and angles from the shadows and budded into stems of flowering steel. The roundhouse, a mass of blackened brick, dissolved into darkness. Clement appeared in the closer of two doorways, a lamp in one hand and papers in the other. She stiffened, watched his approach, his steps graceless and slow.

"Hold these." His words were filled with chill. "I'll go back and get another lamp."

She searched his face. "Do you think that's necessary?"

He shrugged. "Do you wish to be in the dark for days?"

She retreated around the corner and fingered the knife. This man frightened her.

Clement emerged with a lamp and stomped across the rows of steel as she debated whether to follow. A voice echoed, shouting orders. Clement lit the lantern and looked her way, seemed irritated that she wasn't behind him. She bounded across tracks and cinders to reach him, and he handed her a lantern, tore a corner from one of the papers, and began scribbling. "Here. This car will go to Lyon. I don't know how long it will be delayed in Brussels. It could be days." He pointed to a string of cars. "Pascal knew nothing."

"Clement." She spoke softly, prayed, hoped God didn't begrudge her asking his help in a deception. "On my next visit, we could perhaps have dinner, become better acquainted."

He blinked, his face slack. "Yes? Soon, do you think?"

"A week. Maybe two. I won't forget what you've done for me." She choked on the words, knew no other way to remove the threat of betrayal.

He remained quiet for a moment, then raised his chin. "I think you mistake me for a fool. You don't plan to see me on your next trip at all."

She stood rigid, couldn't force herself close. "Of course, I will see you. I will need your expertise again. I didn't mean to be hurtful. This work makes one tense, and I don't know you."

He reached to touch her face, and she jerked away, caught herself and leaned in.

He smirked, pointed toward the siding. "Your car is that way. It will have the number I copied for you on the side." He turned and lumbered toward the center of the yard.

* * *

The door was rolled half open, the choking scent of kennels venting into frost. Nicole slid the lantern onto the floor and jumped up, felt her way between pallets loaded with machine parts, and lit the lamp. Sulfur burned her nose as light licked the walls. Wooden crates were stacked in the center with cages in the front. She edged beside crates and climbed atop the first row of kennels, balancing on a pipe frame. A Pomeranian yapped, and she dropped to the narrow walkway, cooing in her best German.

The dog quieted, and she raised her lantern. Keys bristled from heavy wire doors. She removed one from a small cage and placed it in a large one. It popped open, and she quenched the light. A growing lack of ease urged her back to the door. Across the yard, two men stood beneath a light pole, one in uniform, the other shifting from foot to foot. Her breath froze as Clement turned to point in her direction.

She set her lantern down, glanced across the rows of tracks, saw no hiding place within reach, and ran to the highest crate to spring up to the pipe frame. Beneath her a German Shepherd sniffed warily. The next cage was empty, but she had no way to shush the Shepherd if he panicked. She crawled to the end of the row and shoved the key into a lock. It refused to turn.

Gravel cracked beneath boots, words drifting harshly above them. She reached for a middle cage, inserted the key, and the door opened. Scarcely balanced, she threw her clothes inside, held to the pipe frame, and placed the toe of her boot within the mesh in the next row. Rollers on the heavy door squealed, and she stretched to lower herself into the cage. The wire beneath her toe bent, and her boot broke free, slamming her against a wire door, the pipe frame gouging the center of her back. Tears flooded her eyes as she dragged herself inside. Yellow light engorged the dark, and she prayed without thought in a plea too desperate for words.

The sliding door crashed against the stop. "There's ample light now, yes?" German, the diction precise. The speaker went silent for a moment. "Is this also your lantern?"

"No, Herr Feldwebel." A buttery sphere pushed against the gray. "I have only this one." Clement's German was atrocious, even worse than his French.

Nicole wrapped her fingers around the paper he'd given her and stuffed it in her pocket. If she were arrested, he would go, too.

"A railroad lantern. It is one of your compatriots, yes?" The voice was loud. "Looking for a place to sleep, no doubt." Dogs growled. "He appears to have gone back to work without it."

"No! I am certain someone is here. This is the car! This person, a saboteur I am thinking, is hiding in the back. I would wager this!"

Boots hit the floor and scuffed closer, the feldwebel grunting as the Pomeranian began its yap. Something flashed, slamming into a cage. Howls drowned the voices for painful seconds, then dwindled.

"*Um Gottes Willen, Monsieur Vermeulen!* If a saboteur were here, he would have provoked an uproar as you have. Lock the door! Your ghost will be here when the car returns!"

"We'd best look with earnestness, Herr Feldwebel. This car will be departing soon!"

The German laughed. "I need coffee. We'll search for ghosts on a warmer night."

Nicole stifled her breath as all went silent.

"Elisabeth, I made a mistake. This car is going to Berlin. I'll leave the door open just—" The little dog's yap buried Clement's proffer. "You haven't much time."

His boots struck gravel, and she was taken with a thought. He hadn't put her in this car by mistake, and he couldn't afford to have his betrayal brought to light. If he'd planned to betray her before he picked the car, why had he reported her to the Gestapo? He would have had his revenge. It seemed more likely that he'd sought vengeance after putting her on the correct car.

But if she were wrong... Tears warmed her cheeks, and she reached to open the cage. The key was gone! She pressed her cheek against the wire, looked down, and saw a metallic shimmer on the floor. She heaved foul air and moved her head, frantic in the constricted gray to find a closer key. None of the surrounding cages had one.

She pushed against the panic, hadn't noticed whether the dogs had food and water. If they didn't, someone would care for them. Should the caretaker appear before they were out of Belgium, chances were good that he would help. But how long could she stay in this position? Her back throbbed, and her knees ached. Tears began a scalding flow as cars jerked, rolled, then jerked again. She pushed against the top of the cage and stared into a shaft of light coming from the narrowed doorway. A sudden crash pushed her into the wire, and she withered onto the mesh, blood dripping from her nose. The car pulled away, brakes releasing and tugging in quick jolts. The train was made up.

The door rolled wider, and a blue opalescence lit the wall. They were moving beneath the lights near the center of the yard.

"Elisabeth! This is your last chance! Come out, or you will go to Germany!" Clement was frantic. He had no time to search, would be trapped himself.

She brought her fist to her mouth, fought the urge to call for him to save her.

"Please, chérie! All is forgiven. I'll get you to Lyon on another train!"

Clement wasn't concerned with her safety. He would never have called the Gestapo if he were. She began to relax, his desperation a growing solace. He knew she would report him if she had the chance. He was thinking only of the accident she had promised.

Clattering rails suppressed the crunch of his boots before the door rolled shut, the latch clanging. The lid of her coffin could have knelled less dread. Wire pressed against her back, and she lowered her chin. The gold necklace her father had given her slipped from her shirt and dangled below her gaze. She reached to push it back but stopped, taken with an idea.

She lifted it from her neck, clasped the cross to the spring ring, wrapped the chain around her finger, and slid it through the wire, urging it into a lazy swing and easing it toward the shimmer. In seconds it stopped. She rotated her finger, drew the chain to her hand again, then pried the base of the cross around the cage frame. It bent inward, conforming to the pipe until it formed a hook. She held onto the ring, lowered the cross to the wooden planks, and resumed the swing. In seconds, it struck metal. She tugged, but the hook swung free. She tried again, then again. The hook couldn't be maneuvered beneath the bow of the key.

She leaned her head against the wire door, reminded herself that she wasn't alone, and allowed the truth to settle her. Her heart slowed, and her hands steadied as she swayed to the measure of her prayers. The train gained speed, and the wheels grew rhythmic. She opened her eyes, lowered the hook again, allowing the tracks to move the cross from side to side, and thumbed it downward. In minutes it drifted over the key and halted. She allowed the chain a few millimeters, and it flattened. She offered a few more, and it pirouetted, the open end settling. She waited, rehearsed her prayer, and swayed to relieve the pain in her back. The car bounced on rough track, and the hook dropped lower. She held her breath and tugged. The chain had taken on heft, and she lifted, a shimmer rising from darkness. Her eyes clouded, her heart freer as she drew her prize upward and grasped it with both hands. She breathed, slid the key into the lock, and twisted. It clicked, and the door eased open.

* * *

David's footsteps echoed in the murky calm. He pulled his jacket close and watched his breath waste into the corner. The Krauts allowed them nowhere near enough coal to heat a library with mostly bare shelves, but there was an upside. The place offered privacy. He settled into a chair, rested his feet on another, and opened a copy of *The Grapes of Wrath* he'd found in a Red Cross box and claimed as his own. Reading dulled his hunger, sometimes even for Nicole.

He flipped through the pages to find his place. The Joads had passed the country he knew well—Elk City and Sayre and Texola. They'd escaped the red dirt of Oklahoma, wormed their way across the sandy knolls along the Texas/Oklahoma line, past the shinnery he knew for its toxicity in the spring and its beauty in the fall. Further west, red cedar clawed for life on the sand hills beyond Shamrock. In truth, they weren't hills but swells, dry creeks between them, trails of sand lined with cottonwoods that spanned a county or more. He'd ridden a few—Shinnery Creek, Sandy Bottom, and Long Dry—had examined the flats generous enough to offer a few bushels of wheat or sorghum, even cotton for the adventurous. He stared into the dark corner, saw the Panhandle as it lay in its winter meagerness, the sage and grass flowing beneath an open sky.

He caught movement outside the window and lowered his book. Stanislavsky was staring in, a cigarette dangling from his lips. It seemed not to have occurred to the corporal that windows worked in two directions. The narrow eyes dulled, and Stanislavsky moved closer to the door.

David shook his head, returned to the book, and thought of the copy he had at home, a prized possession if Delores hadn't burned it. For all of Steinbeck's sermonizing over the rape of the land, the book made him miss his life before the war, especially his days with Dancer. He read a few paragraphs and snorted. The capitalists heading the vast destruction were, in fact, his neighbors who worked long hours to eke a shallow living from their parcels of earth, land as precious to them as family. He turned as Stanislavsky lit another cigarette and bunched his hands around his mouth before another window. David put the book down, tiptoed to the door, and opened it to behold a blank stare.

"Looking for something, Corporal?"

The dark orbs cut away. "Just a place to smoke."

He stepped out, exaggerated his scan of the barracks, the groups of kriegies, the latrine. "I can see how it might be hard finding a suitable place."

The corporal looked inside and acted as if what he was looking for wasn't standing in front of him. "This spot's as good as any, wouldn't you say, Lieutenant?"

The man was a pitiful hawkshaw. "Can I interest you in a cup o' joe? Likely some left."

Stanislavsky slithered through the door. "No sir. Just gonna take a peek at them books, see if they have one I might like."

He shook his head. "I doubt it, Corporal. They don't have crayons, either."

* * *

David dried a bowl. Mess had been assigned as punishment, but he looked forward to the order it imposed on his days, and the stilling of his worries.

"Any leftovers, Lieutenant?"

He lifted a pan, looked over his shoulder and caught a fresh-starched uniform. Hanson had made a joke. That was one for the newspapers. "None we haven't duly liberated, sir."

Swanson slid across the barracks, began sweeping a corner he'd already swept. It wasn't the same reaction he'd had when he and Stanislavsky butted heads. So, Swanson was likely working with Hanson, knew the secret handshake, and was the proud owner of a decoder ring.

Hanson poured the watery coffee into his cup. "Dremmer, I'm here to suggest you volunteer for work detail."

He studied the captain's face. "Yes sir. When?"

"Tomorrow morning." The captain glanced at Swanson and continued. "Here's the drill. Krauts are making up a crew for the rail yard in Munich. I want you on it." He lowered his voice. "At eleven hundred hours, you'll ask the goon in charge if you can relieve yourself. They have two rubble piles they're using for latrines. If you aren't approached by an old German with a handkerchief in his shirt pocket, you'll repeat the request at fifteen-hundred hours. Capiche?"

It was a bit too cloak and dagger for his taste. "I understand. What do I tell him?"

"Not a thing. He'll tell you. He's been on the lookout for your friends. He'll refer to Schneider as the rooster and Devillier as the hen."

David dried his hands on a worn undershirt and turned to meet Hanson's glare. "Got it, Captain. And how will he know I'm his contact?"

Hanson slipped the empty cup into the warm water. "Don't worry; he'll know."

Chapter XI

Nicole lay cradled in the slow rocking of her prayers as the wheels rang out an iron requiem. She ran her fingers through her hair, stringy from sweat and cinders. It had always been an embarrassment, but David said he loved it. Her heart reached out for him, but his place was with his wife and child, whoever the father of the child might be. She buried her head in her hands, returned him to the altar she'd built in her heart, and wondered what it was that so drew her to what she couldn't have.

Light swelled to white around the door, and she stretched the stiffness from her back, stepped to the cages, peered into the stainless steel canisters, narrow at the top and clamped to the sides of the cages so the dogs could lap whenever they chose. At some point, she might require them to share. But not yet.

She moved around the car to drain the tension. How far had she traveled? Perhaps not far. They weren't moving fast. Brussels could be hours away, and there was no assurance that when she reached it, help would be waiting. She hauled her pack behind the crates and lay down. Hiding was clearly more caution than was needed. No one would open the door of a moving rail car. Élodie had teased her about her constant fretting. So how had she come to be involved in all this?

It was the unfairness. Others seemed able ignore it, even when hurt by it. But it was the shared sense of outrage that first drew her to Élodie, an outrage so like David's. She understood it. With so much cruelty, how could anyone not be offended by the Almighty? The answer came in knowing him, of course, knowing his heart, and in trusting him for intervention. Or consolation. But how could one who didn't know him not feel indignant?

The day was an unvarying string of thoughts marked only by slowing grades and wishes to have David's arms about her, to see the end of war, and to know with certainty that her friends were safe. And to taste clean water.

The rhythm endured. Paling light seeped through vents and door. When the light around the door faded to gray, she wondered, in a fleeting scrap of dream, how inviting death might be. Gerhardt knew, of course. She rode the grinding howl, yearning to ask him until he stood before her smiling, wearing his blue suit with a hint of chalk above the pockets, his delight at seeing her flowing in thoughts that suffered no loss to the meagerness of sound or syllable. She smiled, had missed him. But why, he shrugged. There is no end to life and so no loss. I am as close as thought, as near as the present to the past. As close—it is not presumption, really—as God himself. The future is but a thought away, your life a moment's attention from eternity. And he would always be near with a delicate white dusting on his vest and a joy she had always known would be home. He wagged his head in blissful dissatisfaction at what he could not help her understand.

And your family? The thought came without alarm.

His smile grew. Oh yes, they're with me. And so much more. *Him.*

The brakes set with familiar tugs as each car found the limits of its couplers. Nicole woke to a sadness that the dream had ended, thirsty but rested with no idea how long she'd slept. Time was such a strange contrivance, after all, and the dream so like Gerhardt, she wanted to believe she'd seen him. Was that heretical? Perhaps, though, for the moment, it brought peace.

The train slowed, brakes singing in resistance. The car remained still for minutes, then rolled back. It stopped, then pulled ahead. Cars were being sided and trains made up. Brussels! She stretched, eyeing the dogs' deep canisters. The water was less repulsive, now. Still, she would watch the light beyond the door, wait for it to shift from pink to gray, then disappear.

Voices came, indecipherable, then a sound she knew. Her car was uncoupled. Murmurs rose from darkness, and yellow spattered the walls as lanterns passed. Time ceased and left her with nothing to mark day from night, place from place, or thought from dream. David had talked of his missions. Long hours of boredom punctuated by longer minutes of terror. She understood.

The dogs had accepted her. Even the Pomeranian let her pass without objection. She found a large cage far from the door and slid so she could lie half in and half out with her bundle of clothes beneath her head. If someone unlocked the door, she could retract her legs and hide before they were inside. It wasn't as safe as she would have liked, but it was better than before, and a key hung with the scourged cross around her neck.

Voices bellowed. Iron resonated on iron before another car

slammed hers. The heavy clasp resounded, the car rolled forward, and the slack tugged in pulses as the procession tightened. It stopped again, and blue seeped from the door. The central yard. Requests were offered in French, demands booming in German. Her stomach tightened, and her friends began to sniff and growl. The latch squealed, and she drew back, snapping the wire door behind her.

"All right, my beauties. At your service with beer and bacon." The words flowed with the open-endedness of an evening in Paris. She prayed as dogs growled, unsure that the man's French assured anything good. Something thudded to the floor and slid over wooden planks before he groaned and pulled himself into the car.

"Everything all right in there?" Another voice, the French heavy with Boche. She tensed.

"But of course." The man was defiant. "Just feeding these Aryan mongrels, the prized chattel of the Reich, and acting every bit Hun at the moment."

"What's that, you old fool?"

"Just commenting on the fine bloodlines of these beasts, your deity."

"I shall go for tea." The German was away before his words had dissipated.

"Fine, indeed. Off to your tea and schnaps, you foul smell in fine wool. And have yourself a nap. Lots of shiny track to lay your head on."

She closed her eyes, felt the man's presence, and heard cages open.

He filled the coned canisters, scooped pellets into trays, and mumbled. A Shepherd growled. "You, you bag of bones, are a tribute to your race and higher bred than your Führer or his mother." The man gasped. "And you, mademoiselle! You are a strange breed. Would you frighten an old man who comes only to feed you? Bite my leg, then, and be done with it!"

Her breath was gone.

"Ah, again I forget! I could not remember poetry as a child, so why should I be asked to learn it now? So much unfairness, this war. Don't you agree?" He paused for a moment. "No, I suppose not. Now, what was it? Ah, yes. 'It's spring, and the plane leaves wither.'"

Nicole released the heavy grip of her lungs. "Are you also a reader of Goethe?"

"Too high-minded for me, these Boche poets. How does one make poetry from such grumblings?" The old man quieted. "You have no

71

opinions regarding poetry, Elisabeth?"

"You are my *confrère*?"

"Why else would I translate pig grunts into so noble a tongue?"

"Thank God! Do you have water, please?"

"All you want, mademoiselle, that is, unless you wish to bathe or water flowers. You've not yet started a garden, have you?" He handed her a canister like those hung on the cages. "Don't worry. The owner of this one is not Boche." He chuckled. "Drink. It is clean." He laid a package on the floor. "I have bread and cheese, at least enough for two days."

She stopped drinking to breathe. "And do you have instructions?"

"Ah, yes. You have good fortune, despite your bad fortune. You are to stay on this car. A mistake will be made in the paperwork. It is the war, you see." He raised his hands. "You will be routed through Tourcoing, Roubaix, and Lille before going on to Paris. Ah, Paris! What a fortunate girl!" His voice shrilled. "In Paris, you shall be met by a worker such as myself, though perhaps not so handsome, who will escort you on another leg of your journey."

"Tourcoing? Lille? Am I not in Brussels?"

"You are in Ghent."

"But I was supposed to go to Brussels."

He shrugged. "There was a mistake. I was told to meet you only hours ago."

"It was no mistake. Clement tried to turn me in to the Gestapo when I rejected him."

"Ah, Clement, the dedicated socialist! Perhaps he has a weakness for elegantly dressed women and could not help himself." The old man's eyes were specked with brilliance. "Still, it might be best for you to change before you reach Paris."

"You are being serious?"

"Does this offend your sense of fashion? You will be on holiday with your escort, so you should be appropriately dressed. Perhaps you will spend Christmas there. Such memories!" The old man shook his head. "You will leave your railway clothes in the corner."

Nicole breathed deeply. "Thank you, monsieur."

"I am Marcel, and you should know that Clement is being dealt with. He panicked when asked about your departure and told several stories. All were quite fanciful, of course."

She interrupted. "And Pascal knows of this?"

"Yes, he knows." Marcel twisted his neck. "The interesting thing is that in all of Clement's stories, our dedicated socialist mentioned nothing of the Gestapo. His future is not so bright, I think." His hands rose. "It is best that you remain hidden until the train is underway." He handed her an empty canister. "For your personal concerns. Dispose of it through the cracks in the floor. And more water to wash your face, especially beneath your nose so you are not mistaken for Herr Hitler."

He put his hand on her head and pushed her inside, began a rant about mongrels no Frenchman would own, then scuttled away. "Enjoy your tea, you rosy-cheeked *caboche*?"

"Shush, you old goat. I'll report you and have you deported."

"Deported? I've already been deported. Will you now send me to Stalingrad? *Mon Dieu!* Tell me you aren't thinking of Berlin!"

The feldwebel mumbled and walked away.

The old man turned from the door and whispered. *"Au revoir, mademoiselle."*

"Go with God, Marcel."

"I am staying, and I am sure God would prefer going with you. And who could blame him?" The voice grew shrill as a locomotive roared past. *"Joyeux Noël, mademoiselle."*

The door slid closed and latched, the sound peaceful this time. She pulled the bread and cheese close and felt the bundle of clothes in the bottom of the package.

* * *

David wedged his fingers between the sideboards of the cattle car and squinted into the frigid blue. Beech and chestnut trees stirred in winter starkness, pines shadowing them as the first light drifted from the mountains. Wind burned his eyes, but he refused to look away.

Men huddled in the center of the car, spurning the frigid gusts. He couldn't look at them, was reminded of his helplessness. How could he protect Nicole? Schneider had met his bluff with absence, and he had no way to counter it. He turned his head and stared through the narrow slits. Distant columns of smoke boiled in slanted light. The train rocked toward a tired stop where ash covered the grass and leaves like rime. His gaze drifted across kriegies and caught Swanson's icy glare. He returned it, then glanced toward the train yard.

Less than a hundred yards away, a boy sat in soot and rock, his legs bare in the morning chill. The child poured earth from a jar into small piles, imposing an insubstantial order on his dreary world. David felt the D-bar swelling in his blouse and fingered a crust of bread in his pocket. It was one child. With all the bombing, there had to be thousands. Still...

The train ground to a stop, and the door rolled back. A wasteland of rubble and twisted steel lay beyond. Concrete piers stood akimbo, propped by broken ties. Workers moved through the frigid dream, gray as the ash that covered them.

"Aussteigen!"

He moved behind the others and dropped to the gravel, then found a place in line. His group faced a squat German, the uniform obscured by the heads of other prisoners.

"You veel difide to two." An unteroffizier. He could just make out the epaulettes as the heavy-jowled youngster turned in front, spouting his unique version of English. The boy waved to his left. "Dees half to nord. Dees half to sout."

He blinked against the acid breeze as Swanson moved beside him. "Don't mind if we work together, do you, sir?"

He looked ahead. "I suppose not. You been on this detail before, Corporal?"

"Yes sir. We usually work in pairs."

"Good. Clue me in on anything I might need to know."

"Oh, I will, sir." Swanson smirked and scanned the yard. "Who'da thought we could do all this?"

He stared at the misshapen rail. "We didn't. The Tommies did."

The corporal's head jerked. "Oh, yeah? And how do you know that, sir?"

"I'm Air Corps, Corporal. I'm familiar with most of the places we've bombed. Four months ago, we were hitting strategic targets. Factories. Munitions." The corporal's mistrust was a bur under his blanket. "You were sent to watch me, Swanson. I want to know who sent you."

Swanson looked away. "My superior, sir."

"That could be almost anybody. On either side."

The boy's neck reddened.

"*Roust!*" The unteroffizier pointed to a section of destroyed track.

Two goons flanked them as teams of mules pulled ties from a pile of rubble. A German in railroad garb pointed down a bombed siding and drew a line in the air.

Swanson turned and pointed to a stack of ties. "You wanted me to clue you in on what to do, sir. We'll be carrying these."

It was time he regained control. He nodded, tapped a solid one he thought the corporal would have difficulty lifting. "We'll take this one."

Swanson strained his end of the tie to his shoulder and staggered toward a section that appeared to have received a direct hit. Kriegies shoveled into the crater, had almost reached the level mark. Two civilians offered instructions in broken English.

David slid the tie, carving a groove in the loose rock, and motioned for Swanson to push it back. The corporal bent, and he saw the child tottering along the track, his head down, heeding the placement of his bare feet.

He looked at Swanson. "Hold up, Corporal." He stepped across the roadbed and pulled the D-bar from his pocket.

"Halt!" A goon's voice riveted him in place.

He turned, showed the unteroffizier the chocolate and pointed to the child. "Only wanted to give him something to eat."

The German spewed a clouded breath and nodded.

David extended his hand. "Wish I had more."

Dark hollows widened, and icy fingers burned his palm before jerking away. He pulled a sock scarf from his neck, offered it, and felt the chilled fingers again before turning back.

Swanson stood at the pile, making no effort to conceal his revulsion. "That was quite a show, sir."

"Not a show, Corporal. People died here."

"Not enough, sir. Still too many walking around with bedpans on their heads."

The choler rose. "The kid's folks were likely killed if he lives close."

Swanson stood his ground. "You a squarehead lover, sir?"

He cinched his tongue. "That boy isn't my enemy, Corporal. Neither are these civilians. Just the lie they believed. I can't hate a man for being lied to."

"I can, Lieutenant. I can hate 'em real good."

He squelched the urge to put the boy on his knees. "If you want to know where my loyalties lie, Corporal, just ask me."

"Not good enough, sir. I don't know if you're a stooge, but I'm not taking no chances."

He choked his rage. "What time is it?"

Swanson glanced at his watch. "Ten-hundred-fifty hours, sir."

He kicked another tie, heaved his end to his shoulder, and led Swanson to the crater, offering no quarter to the corporal's slight frame. He waited, dropped his end, and strode to the unteroffizier. "Got to relieve myself."

The German pointed to a rubble pile, broken concrete dozed near the center and left in a 'U.' David ambled around the nearest corner, found an old man, his pants down, squatting against a pier. His coat was open, and a handkerchief bulged from his left shirt pocket. David nodded, and the old man looked away. He buttoned his pants and started back.

"De hen has flown de coop." The words lifted on a sudden breeze.

"What?"

"Not to look dees vay! I say, de hen has flown de coop! Has roost on Munich. Wodenstrasse 27."

A cap bobbed above rubble, and David hit full stride before Swanson reached the corner.

The German shook his fist and hollered something full of gravel.

He reached the edge of dozed concrete. "Appears the old man doesn't like GIs, Corporal. Want me to stay and hold your hand?"

"That'd be swell, sir." Swanson nodded toward the squatting man. "Maybe you could help me understand why you can't hate this poor, misguided, old Kraut."

He dipped his chin. "Doesn't appear to like sharing the facilities with the enemy, does he?"

"The enemy? That would be you or me, sir?"

"He thinks it's me, and I believe he's right." Things were looking up. Élodie Devillier was in Munich, and the rooster was sure to follow. *Wodenstrasse 27.* He repeated it to his step and let it gouge a rut in his brain.

* * *

The curtain rose on a living room constructed mostly from Red Cross boxes. A seductively posed GI with mop tresses splayed across his bare shoulders winked at the audience. His skirt was pulled high, revealing remarkably hairy legs. David laughed, lifted by the illusion, and watched as "Peggy" read letters from "Johnny."

He sat next to an aisle seat, hardly recognized the library, and was taken by the strangeness of having been directed to his seat by a sergeant. The lights went down, and someone settled next to him, the faint wisp of potatoes settling in.

"At the intermission, you'll go to the latrine. Manage to be detained. I'll meet you after the crowd clears out." The captain's whisper was barely audible.

"Yes sir." He stared dumbly at the sack curtains. The lights went on, and he was alone.

* * *

The wind was sharp-edged, the latrine little warmer than the yard. David sat at the end of a row of lidded toilets, hating being in the place longer than was necessary. A remaining kriegie scurried to the door and headed out. He brought his hands to his face to escape the stench. The door opened, and Hanson appeared beneath the yellow glow of a bare bulb.

The captain looked around. "So, what'd you learn, Dremmer?"

"That the hen has flown the coup, sir. Élodie Devillier is in Munich. Wodenstrasse 27."

Hanson allowed a smile. "That's it?"

"That's it, sir."

"Good. You said Schneider was present when this physics guy, Stein, was shot, right?"

"Yes sir."

"And Stein was close to Schneider at the university?"

He nodded, pulled his hands down. "Nicole said Stein treated him like a son."

Hanson stood above a toilet several lids away. "You indicated that there were stories concerning an affair between the professor and your Nicole?"

His Nicole. "Yes sir. Stein's peers were trying to remove him as department head."

Hanson squinted. "But you believe Schneider also had designs on Nicole. Is that right?"

"Yes sir." His gut contracted at what the captain might be thinking.

Hanson turned and locked onto his gaze. "My question is, after realizing that it was Stein who was killed, could Schneider have

77

thrown Nicole's name out as a lure, hoping you'd bite? Could it be he only wanted to know if she was working with the professor?"

It slammed him in the gut. Hanson reaching that conclusion confirmed his greatest fear. If Schneider had a vendetta, his admission had made her even more vulnerable. "He absolutely could have, sir."

Hanson looked away. "Here's the drill. If we're going to keep your girl alive, we'll have to contact this Élodie. One of our young Germans can do that. Élodie will let Schneider know she's gotten word from you, and he'll know she's in every bit as much danger as Nicole."

He nodded, felt the earth tremble beneath him. "Yes sir."

The captain appeared to soften. "You all right, Lieutenant?"

"No sir. You realize I betrayed Nicole, don't you, sir?"

"No, I don't, son. You did all you could with what you had. Schneider just had more information. If you hadn't created the story about Élodie being watched, your Nicole might not even be alive."

The earth spun out of control. "But she's still alive, don't you think, sir?"

"I do. Schneider might be pursuing an investigation, but he wouldn't act without knowing how connected you are, not when his girl might pay the price. And we're working with our operatives to find out if Nicole is out of the country."

"Thank you, sir."

"One more thing." Hanson raised his chin. "I want you to take an active role on the committee. Thing is, you're being watched, and we don't want Stanislavsky to know you're with us. Steer clear of me, and don't bring me up in conversation. In the meantime, we'll find out what the corporal's up to and if he might be working with someone else. Capiche?"

"His contact is the rooster, sir, and Schneider will meet with Stanislavsky himself. I know this guy." He turned. "So, what made you change your mind about me, sir?"

Hanson buttoned his trousers. "Not all of us have, but you've passed our tests so far. You relayed the old man's report just like he gave it to us. No additions or deletions."

He nodded. It was no surprise he was being tested. "Swanson still holding out, sir?"

The captain grinned. "He's softening. How'd you know?"

"He's not keeping it a secret that he doesn't trust me."

"He'll come around. I'll speak with him about wearing his feelings on his sleeve."

"Captain, how is it that a corporal is allowed to investigate an officer?"

"Intelligence doesn't work like normal military, Dremmer. And you're barely an officer."

He looked, caught Hanson's grin.

"In the meantime, work on a scheme for our German friends to contact Élodie. We need your input."

Chapter XII

Her breasts pressed against him, warm and full. The muscles in her back quivered beneath his fingers as he slid them to her waist. David felt the coolness of the dress she'd worn to the cellar that evening. His favorite. He breathed deep, drew in the scent of her, allowed his lips to course her neck, her cheek, her mouth, waiting and eager. He raised his hands to her shoulders, her hair flowing between his fingers, rippling like water over smooth stones. He crushed the dark silk of it within his grip and was shaken by the echo of her heart.

He turned on the palliasse and wished for light. The reverie brought an ache so exquisite that it couldn't be stilled. A shadow crossed the room, the first kriegie up stealing to the stove. A faint glow whispered against the window and carried the scent of an open coffee tin. He slid his boots from beneath the blanket, wrapped it around his shoulders, and suspended himself on his arms in a muted sweep to the floor. Two kriegies slid from their bunks across the aisle, quiet, letting their sleeping brothers find what peace they could.

David stepped lightly, took a double handful of coal from the bin, and eased it onto the smoldering ashes as Private Mathews held the door. He piled it onto hot embers and stirred until a piece ignited, pulled the blanket tight, and stared at the coffee pot on the stove plate.

A gray mustering of clouds swirled outside the window. Whatever was coming couldn't be stopped. There were no options. *He* had to be the one to appear at Élodie's door. The old German could be easily recognized. So could the students. Schneider would have them ferreted out and hanged. He was the only one who could make contact and hope to live.

He leaned against the wall, his thoughts weaving an obscure pattern. Hanson had never mentioned an escape from the stalag. It seemed unlikely there'd been one. Even if he could break away at the train yard, the streets of Munich would be fraught with threats.

He looked up, caught Swanson's stare, and nodded toward the door. A few waking kriegies passed as he edged toward the stoop.

Swanson eased in beside him.

"I need to talk to the boss."

Swanson jerked, looked his way. "Who?"

"Hanson. I need to see him."

"Why you asking me?"

"Don't play games with me, Corporal. This is urgent."

"Yes sir."

He covered his grin. Swanson had caved like an empty can.

* * *

"You're right." Hanson leaned against the wall of the latrine. "There are limits to what we can expect of these kids. Most of them are injured or unfit for military service, but this is war, and people die. That's what they signed up for."

David couldn't fail to make his case. Not this time. "I'm the only one Schneider is afraid of. If I slip into their house and tell her who I am, it'll convince him that I'm connected. Someone could cover for me at the rail yard. How long would it take?"

"That's out of the question. You don't even speak German." The captain stuck his head out of the door. "This place stinks. Give me five minutes before you leave."

David stepped to the opposite side, closed his eyes, and saw the woman wilt within the spray of blood. *No more lambs to the slaughter, Lord.* He opened the door and looked out, as much for air as caution. Someone was standing on his barracks stoop, and it looked like Stanislavsky. Light was failing. Still, he'd give the corporal time to tire of the wait.

Two kriegies, one bent over, exited a barracks beyond his. He watched as they passed Stanislavsky who seemed to take no notice. They drew close to the latrine, and he slipped back, lifted a lid, and assumed the position.

"Second time in a month," the bent one said. "Those rotten potatoes they give us."

The second laughed. "We could go on a hunger strike. That'd teach 'em."

David shivered on the throne, waiting them out. "You, too? I'm afraid to leave."

Private Good Cheer flashed a grin. "Your momma would cry if she knew the thing you missed most about home was toilet paper."

He rose, cinched his belt, and moved to the entryway. The red blush of a cigarette glowed from his stoop. The kriegies stepped behind him. "Believe I'll walk along with you so long as you stay on the machine gun side."

Private Dysentery nodded and Good Cheer laughed. "Sorry, sir. I didn't see the gold bar."

"You're fine, soldier."

They passed his barracks, and he moved to the corner of the next. He bid Dysentery a quick recovery, and circled back, then entered the side door and took a seat beside a never-ending poker game. He looked around, found Swanson, and nodded for him to watch the door.

The game was slow, and he grew bored. Stanislavsky stepped in as the windows went from gray to black. The corporal looked surprised and turned. He caught Swanson's glance.

The boy nodded. Stanislavsky's reaction had been duly noted.

* * *

The Civil War was winding down. Lee had begun to have misgivings about the outcome, and the atrocities on both sides were making the celebrated general doubt that the righteous cause of states' rights was sufficient to justify the butchery. The door to the library opened, and David looked up to see Swanson walking between the rows, checking for patrons.

"Mind if I sit here, sir?"

He stared at his book. "Guess that'd be all right since it's so crowded."

"Look, Lieutenant, I understand you're sore, but I was being careful."

"That right? So, are you convinced I'm not a Nazi, Corporal?"

Swanson nodded. "Captain Hanson told me about the old man in the train yard."

"You didn't know?"

The boy looked away. "Hanson received the information, then set up a meeting to see what you'd do."

"So, I passed muster?"

"Yes sir. You passed the information like you got it—didn't do nothin' with it on your own. That's what he was looking for."

"Glad you were both pleased. So, what brings you to my office?"

"The plan, sir. It's in the works." Swanson delivered the message in low tones.

82

"Tell me about it."

"Here's the drill. We want—"

"Wait. This 'here's the drill' business. Will I have to talk like that if I join the club?"

The corporal raised his hands. "Sorry, sir. Can't help picking it up after a while."

"There's another thing."

Swanson raised an eyebrow.

"Where do you stand? I don't know whether to watch my back or pat yours."

Swanson's neck reddened. "Guess you'll have to wait and see, sir. Like I did."

"I don't have the time. I need to know something now." He leaned in.

The corporal tensed. "What's that, sir?"

"I want to know how Hanson gets his clothes cleaned and pressed in a place like this."

The corporal chuckled. "He couldn't do it without your help, sir."

He squinted.

"You know them bad potatoes you put in water with the peels?"

"Yeah."

"Well, he mashes 'em, strains the water, and soaks his shirts in it at night. Then he irons them with a shellacked brick he leaves on the stove in the officer's barracks."

He shook his head. "The man's a fanatic."

"But it made you think he had connections, didn't it, sir?"

"It crossed my mind."

"Respect ain't easy to come by in this place, sir."

He brought his hands together, wondered if the attention were a good thing. "I guess so."

Swanson sobered. "We've contacted them students that—"

"The White Rose. I'm familiar with them."

"They're laying low right now. No sabotage or nothin', but they can do this."

"So, they're going to make contact with Schneider's girl?"

"Yes sir. You still want in on it?"

He took a breath. "I'm in, Corporal."

Swanson grinned. "Thing is, they can't just show up at her house. They stay alive by not being known. If this Élodie calls the leutnant on them, they're done."

83

The boy was clearly parroting Hanson who'd stolen his speech. "I'm aware of that. So, how can they help?"

The corporal eased. "How about you write this Schneider a letter and have them deliver it? Play him. I mean, you know where he's hidden his girlfriend. That's got to impress him."

He straightened. "Not bad. We could have them deliver flowers and enclose a note. A neighborly gesture."

"Now you're thinking like a spook, sir. The neighbors wouldn't think nothin' about it. We have these White Rose people tail her, deliver the flowers when she's not home."

He surveyed the room. "And how do I get the note to them?"

"We find the old man at the rail yard, sir. He's my contact, so I'll ask him."

"Hanson will have to sign off on this."

Swanson smiled. "You really are thinking like a spook, sir. Don't trust nobody."

Tension in his neck eased. "I learned it from the best, Corporal."

"Glad you feel that way, sir, since I'm gonna be your primary contact. Be more later."

He winked. "Read me in on it, Corporal."

The boy chuckled. "It's not likely Stanislavsky suspects me of being on the committee. You and me have a reason to talk, being on cleanup and all. You and Hanson don't."

"I still want the plan approved. Personally."

"Understood, sir."

Swanson offered a salute, returned the book to its place, and slipped out the door.

David pushed his book aside, folded the fly page on a British history, and ripped it neatly from the book. He pulled a pencil from the drawer and put it to paper.

To a lovely couple:

Welcome to the neighborhood. It's not Krems, but it's home. Looking forward to renewing our friendship and discussing old times.

In the sincere hope of continued good health for all concerned,

2nd Lt. David Dremmer

Chapter XIII

David pulled his coat to his ears, the wind clawing at his hands. Wheels hammered against steel, the uneven track slamming the car from side to side while cinders stung his face. Swanson lay beside him, nudging him insensibly, the boy curling into himself for warmth.

He closed his eyes, imagined the comfort of a shower, a luxury he could no longer tolerate. Shower heads, left in a constant drip so they wouldn't freeze, were draped in icicles that had to be cleared by the first in line. And the Germans were cutting coal allotments, already insufficient to warm the barracks. They had scarcely enough to cook their rotting potatoes. Work detail, at least, offered warmth. For a while. But when he stopped lifting and dragging to catch his breath, malice wormed its way into his bones.

The train drew to a stop, the stilling air draining his will to stand. He wished for a bowl of meat and a warm place to sleep. But in five days, they would eat well. Or so he'd been told.

"*Aussteigen!*" The squat unteroffizier began his harangue.

He winced at the words. Swanson lay at his feet, a contorted fetus, and he reached down to pull at the boy's coat. "Rise and shine, Corporal. We don't want to get old Arndt in a tizzy."

He shuffled to the door, half carrying the boy. Two kriegies, their faces hidden by rags stuffed around their collars, jumped to the ground. He readied himself for the drop, felt the spite of gravel as it reached his spine, then combed the yard with his squint.

For three days he'd watched the old German moving about, making eye contact, then looking away. The man was afraid of something—probably suspected he was being watched. He sucked in the cold and shivered. Schneider's girl had to have the note before Christmas when the leutnant was apt to be home. He had five days.

"You veel difide to two." The unteroffizier's stubby arm sliced through the center of the huddled kriegies, and Swanson moved beside him, ready to be paired for work. He fingered the crust of bread he'd saved to eat with the broth they'd be given at noon. A few more hours.

The old man walked in front, stumbled, righted himself, and offered David a glance.

Snowflakes whirled in misdirection as the wind picked up ash and buried it in his eyes. He grumbled under the weight of a tie, Swanson breathing hard behind him. He shifted the timber forward, took more of the load, raised his head, and was caught by the old man's glare, the German's chin moving faintly toward the latrine.

A kriegie moved a broken board across gravel and smoothed the bed for them to place the tie. David motioned for Swanson to release his end, then centered the tie over the narrow wedge carved from gravel and dropped it in place. He rose, gave Swanson a glance, and turned to the guard. "I've got to use the latrine."

The unteroffizier followed his finger, nodded, and spat something harsh.

"Yeah, you betcha." He walked past the edge of the rubble, passed the old man, and dropped the message, then squatted to stare at the south entrance. The German looked north.

"I need to see the White Rose. *Verstehen Sie* White Rose?"

"Vat you vant?"

He shuddered at the intonation, more Teutonic, but still like von Felder's. "I want flowers delivered. Enclose the paper. Make sure no one is home. Leave them where they will be seen."

"Wodenstrasse 27?"

"That's right."

"Iss important?" The old man's voice lifted, the admonition clear. He stood his ground. "Very important."

"You not to contact no more. Iss dangerous."

He shivered. The old man was risking everything. "I understand. Who's my contact?"

"Young boy, your group, iss vorker. About so tall as you. Iss only boy Deutsch."

He took a breath. If Hanson learned what he was about to ask... "There's something else. I need a map showing the route from here to the house on Wodenstrasse. Can you do it?"

The German stood and began buttoning his pants. "Iss not good. Vy you Vant?" The paper scraped into the man's coat pocket.

"Lives are at stake." He held his breath.

"Yes okay. Boy vill have for you. But he must..." The old man made a scribbling motion with his hand. "He pencil vile he eat."

* * *

David sat opposite the Germans, staring at the boy. A flash of recognition, a nod. He looked away, scanning the yard. The boy looked down, drawing with a stick in the dirt, then scraped the image with his boot. The old man slumped beside the boy glancing to either side.

David's soup had cooled. Wehrmacht troops spoke in silent puffs as he looked on. He dipped his crust of bread, then chewed as the boy strode to the latrine.

Cold seeped through his jacket. He mopped the last bit of soup and popped the morsel in his mouth. The boy appeared at the edge of the rubble as goons crushed their cigarettes.

"*Roust!*" The unteroffizier sneered, seemed to enjoy the sound of his voice.

Kriegies rose and shuffled into line. German laborers followed, talking among themselves. He reached the ties, began tugging at loose ones. Swanson eased beside him.

"Take a breather, Corporal. Grab a shovel. Let someone else do this for a while."

"I'm okay, Lieutenant, just—"

He turned, stopped Swanson's words with a glare. "No, Corporal, you're not. You're ready to collapse. Now, grab a shovel. That's an order."

Swanson dipped his chin. "Yes sir. Let me know when I'm feeling better, will you, sir?" The corporal shuffled toward a group setting ties.

The German slipped quickly into place beside him. David looked around, saw no one close. "You speak English?" The words were only breath.

"Yes." The German turned his head. Just a kid.

"Can you pick up that end of the tie?"

"I believe, yes." The boy blinked, blond hair falling over his brow, his English distinct.

He leaned forward, spoke in a whisper. "What's your name?"

A question mark formed on the boy's brow. "Bertram."

"You have something for me, Bertram?"

"In my pocket, yes."

"Good. You'll try to pick up that end. It will be too heavy. Drop what you have beneath it and let it back down. You got that?"

"Yes." The boy bent forward, slipped his hands beneath the tie, raised the heavy end, and let it drop. He looked up and shrugged.

David motioned him over. He stepped to the larger end and lifted, gathering the paper in a wad beneath his fingers. When the timber reached his boot tops, he nodded for Bertram to lift.

The boy scanned the yard. "The flowers—such a delivery cannot be made today. Tomorrow, perhaps."

The familiar knot formed in his gut. "Tomorrow morning, then. Lives depend on it."

"Just as our lives depend upon not being recognized." He nodded. "Tomorrow morning."

* * *

David drained the last of his morning coffee, drew his hands around the cooling tin, and edged his way to the stove. His hands had improved in the two days he'd been away from the yard, but the coffee hadn't. It looked like the dishwater he threw out after cleanup. The kriegies were saving the best provisions for Christmas and had doubled the percentage of thrice-brewed grounds. He stepped through the door and shrugged his jacket to his ears.

Stalag officers were grouped in the center of the compound, the commandant standing with another officer. He drew his breath, selected a place in the third row, and glanced at the figure standing beside the oberstleutnant. His heart slammed into his throat. Schneider returned his glare, the glint of a razor in his eyes. A chill ran down his spine. He forced a smile and dipped his chin. The note had produced quick results. He only hoped he would survive them.

Chapter XIV

Nicole paced the floor, the planks splintered from pallet skids. She blinked into a sliver of light, placed one hand on the wall, and bent at the waist, stretching her back and legs. The line of pain spread from her hip to her bottom rib. But it was only a bruise. She would heal.

She picked up an apple the old man had left and polished it on the sleeve of her shirt. It had been months since she'd tasted fruit. She bit deep and let her tongue linger over the texture. Did David have enough to eat? And Charles and Gaston? She fought the guilt that arose—and the impulse to return the apple to the bag. She leaned against the door and tried to imagine the hills and trees gliding past. Travel had been a pleasure before the war, before those certain that the world, once recreated in their image, would make men gods. But monotony was a luxury not to be squandered on indignation. God knew what was happening, and MI6 knew where she was. She pushed the core through a hole in the floor. Of course, some thought God and MI6 to be one and the same. Especially MI6.

She eased into a squat, rose and descended until her legs were taut and her muscles warm. The beginning of the war had marked the end of her youth. She was ages older now, though that life was only three years in the past. The University, Munich, Dr. Stein.

A psalm her mother taught her swept over the green hills of her soul. As a child, she'd lost herself in its poetry and cadence. Now it constrained her with its power.

> *Mon âme est parmi des lions;*
> *Je suis couché au milieu de gens qui vomissent la flamme,*
> *Au milieu d'hommes*
> *Qui ont pour dents la lance et les flèches,*
> *Et dont la langue est un glaive tranchant.*
> *Elève-toi sur les cieux, ô Dieu!*
> *Que ta gloire soit sur toute la terre!*

It flowed in beauty, perfectly suited to her mother's lilting French. Her heart spilled over at the memory of her *maman's* breath against her cheek. In this darkness, a clarity remained, resplendent with truth, and she recited the psalm as David might read it.

> My soul is among lions;
> I lie even among them that are set on fire,
> Even the sons of men,
> Whose teeth are spears and arrows,
> And their tongue a sharp sword.
> Be exalted, O God, above the heavens;
> Let thy glory be above all the earth.

The train labored into gray, the light diminishing around the door. She spread the railway clothes on the floor, hummed while sponge-bathing from the first metal urn she'd hung on the outside of an empty cage. The clothes the old Frenchman had provided smelled faintly of lavender, and she lay on them, when she finished, and pillowed her head on her arm.

* * *

Something awakened her. She shoved the clothes across the bottom of the cage and drew herself into a crouch. Brakes were set, couplers slapping behind her. She rubbed her temples. How long had it been since Marcel bid her adieu and closed the door? She lifted the second urn and poured water into the cup the old man had left.

The train ground to a halt, the cacophony of a rail yard blending into a steady hum. French rose in crescendos that drifted across crashing steel and lifted her heart. If this were Paris… She drew her legs to her chest and rested her head on her knees.

The latch bolt scraped against its casting, and she gasped as the door allowed a slow, gray haze to flood the car. The first four notes of Beethoven's Fifth Symphony floated in. The signal had not been used in months, the auditory "V" that was well known to the Gestapo.

"Elisabeth." The word rose over the barking Pomeranian. "'It's spring, and the plane leaves wither.' Come quickly!"

She threw the railway clothes with what remained of her bread and cheese into the corner and stepped toward the door. A murky figure stood silhouetted in gray and extending a hand.

"And are you also a reader of Goethe?" She forced the words from her throat.

"*Pressez, nous allons*." He reverted to French, but had asked in English, as she had responded. The same mistake! Her feet hit gravel, and she stepped back.

"Who sent you?" Her words were sharp.

"I am here to escort you to the Pyrenees where you will cross into Spain."

She edged away, stood out of reach. "Why did you speak to me in English?"

"I was told that you were proficient in it. German as well."

Her spine tingled. Why had that been discussed? Such information wasn't given to operatives. She spun around, bolted up the track, his heavy steps pounding behind her. Hands clamped her shoulders, and his weight pushed her forward. Her legs crumpled, and she slammed into gravel. She huffed as he covered her with his weight.

"Don't say a word! The Gestapo could be anywhere. What's wrong with you?"

The words hissed in her ear. "Who are you?" His answer meant nothing. Had he been Gestapo, he would call for help, not shush her. Unless he hoped to infiltrate MI6.

"I am Émile. Follow at least twenty meters behind until we are among passengers. I will find you. You will take my arm, and we will leave together."

There was nothing she could do. Not now. "All right."

"No more madness?"

She winced at the soreness in her back and said nothing.

He dashed toward the lights and slid into a shadow behind a siding of cars. She ran stiffly and dropped beside him. He pointed toward a building, a train with mostly flatcars between, then sprinted across several sets of tracks to hide behind boxcars. She forged into the gloom, found him, and lay down. He pointed again, this time toward a crowd milling about the platform. "We will wait until another train arrives and leave with arriving passengers."

"Why did you speak to me in English?"

His head jerked. "I'll explain later."

"Tell me now, or I'll go no farther."

"All right!" He rolled over, held to the car, his pale skin shining in flickering light. Sweat glistened above his thin mustache. "We've discussed your qualifications for a mission. Being proficient in English is imperative. I had to know if you could respond without thinking."

"Thank you for your consideration, but I'm not seeking employment. And the Gestapo uses the same tactic. Were you trained by them or are you that ignorant of how agents conduct themselves in the field?"

He turned to watch a train rasp to a stop, stood, straightened his jacket, and marched to the dark corner of the building. Passengers crowded the platform, and he melded into a queue. She scurried through the passengers and merged with those stirring beneath the light. He waved and stepped close to offer his arm. She hesitated, considered twisting it behind him, then draped her hand around the crook of his elbow and strode toward streetlamps waning in the early light.

Chapter XV

David closed the library door, his cheeks spiked with glacial tears. His coffee had cooled, but his fingers still smothered the cup. He'd saved a crust of bread, had hoped to eat it after appell, but he waited, now, for the knot in his gut to ease. He'd won, had forced Schneider to make an appearance, but the leutnant would attempt to turn the tables. He couldn't allow the man's next move to catch him by surprise.

He pulled Bertram's map from a volume of British history to compare with the map of Munich he'd found in a *National Geographic*. Both were without details, but if he could find something, anything Bertram left unnamed on his drawing to put the Wodenstrasse address in perspective, it might prove helpful.

He pulled the book on the Civil War from the shelf, the dust jacket taped from top to bottom by a single strip. It would easily conceal Bertram's drawing if Swanson came in. He left it open before him as if he were reading.

Bertram had labeled only a few streets: Josef-Ritz-Weg, Schwanhildenweg, Hansjakobstrasse, and Sturmiusweg all wound a circuitous route before Wodenstrasse. Not a bad job considering the amount of time the boy had.

The door opened behind him and slammed against the cold. He slid the paper into the dust jacket, rolled the pages to his bookmark, and prayed his little scheme wouldn't be discovered before it was ready for Hanson's approval.

"You don't rise to greet me at this happy time of year, Lieutenant? I would think it most Christian of you since you still hold to such things."

His breath left him. He closed the book and turned. "Glad you finally made it, Herr Leutnant. Welcome to Krems."

The German's hands spread expansively. "Plans are difficult to carry out sometimes. The exigencies of war. I'm sure you can appreciate this." He pointed to his shoulder. "And you failed to notice. It is now oberleutnant."

His fear morphed into a slow indignation. "Congratulations, Herr Oberleutnant. Do Luftwaffe promotions require you to place your lover's head on a butcher block?"

Schneider jutted his chin, the grin melting. "I was aware that you might be concerned. However, you know that I am not reckless."

"Actually, Herr Oberleutnant, I'd begun to wonder about your concerns and whether you really loved this Jewess of yours."

A scalding blush rose above the German's collar. "I will not tolerate having her threatened, Lieutenant. Nor will you demean her in this way."

He stood, his heart crashing against his ribs. "I wasn't threatening her, but our agreement was to keep both Nicole and Élodie safe. When you tell me one thing and do another, I can only assume you've abandoned your pledge."

"It could not be helped. I entered a different service, and my orders were changed. The *stammlager* system is distinctive. Such things happen unexpectedly."

"It wasn't so unexpected that you weren't able to send spies to keep me under surveillance. That sort of thing would appear to take planning."

The color drained from Schneider's face. "I do not know what you are talking about."

"You know precisely what I'm talking about. These prisons are dangerous places. People die here. If Stanislavsky is of any value to you, you'd best remove him."

Schneider waited as if expecting more. "I'm sure whatever happens to—Stansilavsky, is it?—I'm sure it is of no concern to me. Or to Oberst Berger." The smile returned. "I woke reminiscing about the stellar conversations we once had. I am here to invite you to dine with me tomorrow evening. In my office. I hope your social calendar isn't full."

He'd have to clear it with Hanson. "Herr Leutnant, if you're trying to compromise my contacts, you'd best reconsider. My connections are essential to Élodie's safety."

Heinrich raised his hands. "It's oberleutnant, Lieutenant, and I will keep it official. I'll send guards for you. It will appear to be an interrogation. Does that ease your concerns?"

It likely *would* be an interrogation. "Should I bring a date?"

The oberleutnant stepped to the table. "I doubt you would be interested in bringing anyone other than the subject of our agreement." Schneider lifted the book from the table. "Ah, the American Civil War. The history of a country with no past. That should be amusing."

The map. Air left his lungs. It would be impossible to explain the address scribbled at the top. "I— That's preferable to a country with no future, wouldn't you say?"

Schneider raised the book to his face and began to read. "This is interesting. The author states that both Lee and Grant questioned the righteousness of their cause before war's end." The book lowered, the oberleutnant's finger wedged between pages. The edge of the map peeked from the cover. "Do you also doubt your cause, David?"

"Not at all."

The oberleutnant's brow tapered. "Are you all right, Lieutenant?"

If the paper slipped… "I'm concerned, Herr Oberleutnant."

Schneider smiled.

He'd be giving away all he'd gained, but he had no option. "You were relieved when I mentioned Stanislavsky. I take it you wanted him discovered. Why is that?"

Schneider raised the book in a gesture of innocence. "I have no idea what you're talking about." He tabled the book and removed his finger, the corner of the map pointing at David. "Until tomorrow evening, Lieutenant. Eighteen hundred hours."

* * *

David shivered in the latrine but kept his breath shallow. "The oberleutnant was relieved when I told him about Stanislavsky, and I don't know why, sir."

"But you'd mentioned spies. Plural. Right?" Hanson covered his nose.

"I was just testing the waters, looking for a reaction."

"Then you mentioned only Stanislavsky. There's likely an unknown pawn in this game."

He held his breath, tried to take it in. "Who would that be, sir?"

The captain shrugged. "He knew where to find you, didn't he?"

"Goons likely told him, don't you think?"

Hanson shook his head. "You weren't on the goons' radar before

95

today. We've watched them as we've watched you and Stanislavsky. They weren't interested in either of you."

"So, it would have to be someone who knows I'm in the library after appell or morning workouts. Not exactly an exclusive group. Anyone in my barracks—"

"Schneider just got here. He didn't go to your barracks. He went straight to the library. Here's the drill, Dremmer. The goons found a tunnel a couple of hours ago. Your oberleutnant brought the search party right to the barracks where it was being dug."

It shook him. "Someone had to tell him."

"First morning here, and he knows your routine. And he discovers a diversion tunnel."

"Diversion tunnel?"

"Something to throw the Krauts off. We never planned to do anything with it. Thing is, only a couple of us, besides the boys digging, were aware of it. Contacts are limited. I'm the only one that knows all our plans, and I keep up with who knows what. Capiche?"

He capiched, all right. "So, who knew about the tunnel and my daily routine, sir?"

Hanson looked around the smelly hole. "That would be Corporal Swanson. Only one besides me."

He shook his head. "I don't believe it. Swanson hates the Krauts."

"It's not devotion, Dremmer. They have something on him. An interrogator makes him think he's his buddy, gets him drunk, maybe. They swap stories. Kraut tells him something he did in training. Swanson outdoes him. The German offers to forget it if he confirms some information, and Swanson gives him what he wants. Now the Kraut threatens to let his buddies know he spilled the beans if he doesn't give him more. That's the way the game is played."

"What could Swanson have told him, sir? Does he know I'm no threat to Élodie?"

Hanson grinned. "Swanson thinks you're Superman, dreams you're slipping out at night to arrange meetings between Eisenhower and Goering."

"And how would he have gotten such an elevated opinion of me, sir?"

"Maybe it was what I told him. The cover you started seemed good, so I added a little. Now you're a liaison between the Resistance and MI6."

"But the corporal couldn't have talked with Schneider before this morning. I mean, he was in Tunisia with you guys, right, sir?"

Hanson shifted as if he were pained. "Schneider likely inherited him from someone else."

"Then who turned Swanson?"

Hanson brushed the question away. "That's unknowable. The question now is, what do we do with him? Do we use him, leak him bad information? It won't be easy. The kid's smart."

He drew his hands across his face and thought of the danger the corporal posed to Nicole. "Then how'd he get into this mess?"

"Careful, Lieutenant. What'd the Greeks call it? Being too big for your breeches?"

"Hubris."

"That's the ticket. What happened to Swanson could happen to you, too. That's why you give me all you've got. You're not above getting caught with your pants down, either. Schneider got you to confirm that your girl was in Belgium, didn't he?"

A chill coursed his spine. If Hanson knew... "I've been working on something, sir."

Hanson dropped his hands and straightened. "Let's hear it."

"Schneider's aide in Belgium was Élodie's brother. He mentioned things, things Nicole had already told me. Élodie was with the White Rose. She was anti-Nazi to the core. I'm certain she would help us. I want to meet with her, sir."

"Swanson know anything about this?"

"No sir."

Hanson shook his head. "And you're expecting this girl to cut Schneider's throat after he plucked every feather in her nest?"

"The oberleutnant will be more useful to us alive than dead, sir, and I'm sure she wouldn't do anything to hurt him. Her brother wouldn't, either."

Hanson blew into his hands. "Besides, the oberleutnant's your buddy."

It hit him in the gut. "No sir. He's the enemy."

"Here's the pitch, Dremmer. This kraut is your friend. Don't think I don't see it." Hanson waved it away. "I want to know your plan."

The indictment shook him. "It isn't a plan, sir. Not yet. I just thought Bertram could cover for me at the rail yard. We could exchange clothes. Schneider's house is less than two miles away. I could make it there and back before they gather for the return."

"If things work out with these kids, and Élodie looks promising,

I'll consider it. Until then, work on something constructive like making the most of your dinner appointments." Hanson turned at the door. "There's something you need to understand. I intend to use this friendship with Schneider. Think you could handle that? Turning on your buddy?"

* * *

The gefreiter grunted something indecipherable and motioned David in. Schneider sat behind his desk, an amber bottle beside him. Was this man his friend? His last night in the cellar awaiting execution, he'd wanted nothing more than for Heinrich to come down the stairs.

The oberleutnant stacked paperwork neatly in a folder. "Delighted you could make it, Lieutenant. You don't mind eating in my office?"

He pasted a smile on his face. "It'll do." He soaked in the warmth of the room and looked at the leather sofa. A shower and blanket would make it a perfect evening. Two glasses sat beside the decanter, one with a ring of amber at the bottom. A trick, most likely. It was a safe bet that whatever had been in the glass had been returned to the bottle.

Something narrowed the oberleutnant's forehead. "Would you care for cognac, David?"

"I'm trying to cut back." Hungry as he was, the first swallow would go to his head.

Heinrich spread his hands. "You don't have to worry about being outmaneuvered. This is a social occasion, a respectful tête-à-tête between friends."

"Afraid I don't know much about French heads, Herr Oberleutnant."

"Your marks didn't reflect that. You did quite well in French at university."

The floor sank beneath him. "You've checked up on me. Should I be flattered?"

"Oh, I've done more than check up on you, Lieutenant. You have become my avocation." Schneider's finger rocked like a metronome. "I'm sure it was difficult for you when your father was paralyzed. It ended your academic aspirations, did it not?"

He tucked his fists beneath his arms. "Not really. I graduated a few weeks after that."

"But you had plans to remain at university, not be a *cowboy*." The word oozed disdain.

"I liked being a cowboy, Herr Oberleutnant. I had hopes of producing something more than an inflated opinion of my opinions."

"Cows?" Schneider's lips curled.

"Food, Heinrich. And from the looks of it, that would be far more beneficial to this country than strategies on global hegemony."

The oberleutnant raised his hands. "As you wish. So how might your wife and son be celebrating this Christmas?"

He eased into the chair. "I haven't a clue."

"I understand your mail has been held up. I'll see to it you begin receiving it regularly. I'm afraid you haven't any letters from your wife, however. Does that disappoint you?"

His nails cut into his palms. "I can live with it. I thought you were concerned with the rules of war, Herr Oberleutnant. Isn't it disallowed to withhold mail from a prisoner of war?"

The smile was as starched as Hanson's collar. "That is open to interpretation. The rules state that prison staff aren't to withhold mail. I have just become a prison official."

He locked onto Schneider's blue gaze. "Abwehr oversees interrogations. Wouldn't that qualify you?" It was a guess, but Schneider's turning Abwehr seemed likely.

The German lifted his hand. "And what is the connection?"

Answering with a question again. He'd hit the mark. "Abwehr oversees prisoner-of-war camps, don't they?"

"Abwehr prisons are quite unique, Lieutenant. This is not one of them. Your point?"

"Our organization reaches everywhere. You won't be able to escape our eyes and ears. As you learn about me, I'll make you my hobby, as well."

"I would expect no less, Lieutenant. Though you will learn nothing." He grinned.

"Thank you for removing Stanislavsky. Where did you send him?"

"That, Lieutenant, is above your rank, as you Americans are fond of saying. If you are so curious, have your organization find out for you."

It was a challenge he couldn't accept. "When you remove the remaining spy, Herr Oberleutnant, I want to know where he goes. I have little concern with Stanislavsky. Swanson, on the other hand, is a double victim."

The oberleutnant's brow furrowed. "I had nothing to do with Swanson's handling."

He ignored it. "But you were willing to exploit their abuse, weren't you?"

Heinrich seemed rattled. He sniffed and leaned back. "I abused no one, Lieutenant, nor do I require it to obtain information. I'm afraid you've reached an erroneous conclusion."

He smiled. "Then, what is it you're afraid of, Heinrich?"

Chapter XVI

Jesse rolled onto the porch, turned his chair, and pulled the door behind him. The air, sharp with pine, prickled his unshaved cheeks. It hardly seemed like Christmas, and the bows Naomi had wired around the porch did nothing to change that.

What wheat he could see was sparse, green along the depressions, thin on the slopes, but missing altogether on the knolls. Morgan likely hadn't plowed through the summer, letting the weeds suck what moisture came. In the absence of a wet fall, much hadn't survived. There'd be no payment this spring, either. The bigger portion, of course, would be due in the fall when the calves were sold. That would tell the tale. Whatever happened, Morgan couldn't say he hadn't let him try. He released his breath. If only the boy could be home by then.

He stared beyond the clicking elms, bone bare in their winter nakedness, and caught the lone cedar. He had no word for what it was that haunted him about it, but he turned to the empty pens, remembering Dancer's morning nicker as he charmed the boy from his sleep. He ran his finger along the washstand and saw David stopping on his way in from the field.

He steeled himself in his chair. He'd have Morgan take him to the Summit Place, would ask to see the cows. One way or the other, he'd make sure Dancer was all right.

A door slammed inside the house. Isaac's laughter tumbled like water spilling over rock. He grinned, rolled his chair through the door, and bumped over the sill.

The boy was stirred by anything having to do with cowboys. Just like David. Since Jesse had nothing but time on his hands, and had once been handy with a knife, he found a block of pine, one free of knots with grain that ran straight and true, and carved a horse from it. Several, to be truthful. Finally, one emerged to his liking, and he asked Naomi to wrap it in a bandana and prop it inside the little cowboy hat he'd bought. She feared for the boy to have a bandana, and the horse more than filled the hat, so he consented. Issac would still have two more packages to open on Christmas morning.

Delores shuffled from the bedroom, her camisole open in front, likely hoping Morgan was there. Jesse edged his chair back to give her room.

"Coffee ready?" She yawned and padded past.

"Be done soon, dear." Naomi's voice was smooth as silk. Jesse grinned, wondering how long it would stay that way.

Delores wrapped her arms about her. "I'd forgotten how cold this house was."

"Best put more clothes on, then. Morgan will be here soon." The strain was there. He could hear it, and Naomi's lips were as tight as new leathers in a working barrel.

"He wouldn't mind. He's not like y'all."

Naomi wrung the dishrag over the sink. "I'm sure he wouldn't. That's the point."

Delores tilted her head. "He's—"

"He's a man, and he's still very much alive." Naomi turned, her face flushed.

The words got a hold of Jesse and wouldn't let him loose. He rolled toward his room, wanted not to believe what his mind went to. He stopped and leveled his glare. "I'll have my coffee in my room, Naomi. Holler when it's ready."

Delores stood with her hands on her hips, her eyes narrowing. "He can't hear nothin' in there. You'll have to bust his door down to get him to come out."

"Oh, I've heard plenty behind that door, Delores." He closed it, shut them both out, rolled to the window, and watched the land brighten beneath the bitter light. Naomi had drawn a line with her words, had accused Delores of wanting a man, of setting her sights on Morgan. Well, that was clear enough. But the line she'd drawn was between a live man and a dead one, and David was alive. It was Naomi's boy who wasn't.

* * *

The truck crawled the gravel hill beyond the creek and idled past another patch of wheat that David had broke out four years before. A fine piece of ground, it sloped gentle to the east and north and ended where the creek started. It would hold plenty enough moisture for cow peas once the shinnery gave up its hold. Another couple years, maybe. Breaking it out was David's idea. A good one, too, though Jesse hadn't told him so. Wasn't fitting for him to expect commendations. Might make him proud, and Jesse never could abide a proud man.

Morgan tugged at his hat and turned away. "Reckon there ain't much sense in expecting a wheat crop come June."

He looked ahead. "Not this year."

"I know I said I'd make part of the payment out of that, but maybe I can make it up when I sell the calves."

He grabbed the windshield arms and pulled himself straight. "I won't keep your down money if this doesn't work out. I see how it is. The boy will be back soon. Amount to a couple of lost years is all. No more than that. We've both lived through worse."

Morgan shifted, his picket teeth pinching a match. "You ain't talking about taking this place back, now, are you?"

He looked to the east, saw what wheat pasture there was going to waste. The biggest calves could have been weaned, turned out, the cows allowed to gain some condition. It would make a world of difference helping them breed back. And Morgan could hay along the sandy spots and prevent it from blowing. "It's like I said, if it's too much for you, I'll give you back your earnest money. Don't want you hurt over this. You still have your own place. And the store. You're only forty. It won't hold you back."

Morgan's chin jerked toward the creek. "Don't like you thinking that way, Jesse."

"Just saying you don't stand to lose much." The man expected to be released from another payment and allowed to keep going. He wasn't backing down this time.

Morgan's neck twisted. "A man needs something to build on. You take that away—"

"I'm not taking anything. I'm just showing you it won't amount to much, and it's not working for either of us." He glanced to his left and glimpsed the narrow face. It had to be the proper time. "There were only four mules in the horse pasture. Where are the others?"

Morgan's chin jutted to the side. "Them mules was gettin' on, Jesse. Tractors are the future of this country."

He stared at the mottled face. "You saying you sold them?"

"No, I'm saying I bought a tractor. The Farmall dealer took them in on trade."

He raised himself on his arms. A man unable to defend himself was apt to run into rogues, but this... "They weren't yours to sell! This was a lease to see if it would work. It's not, and now you're selling off my mules to stay afloat. And buying a tractor, of all things!"

"Now, Jesse, there ain't no reason to get foolish. It's no time to be farming with mules when you've got this much land to cover. Only way I can do it is to stay up with the times."

It hit him, the truck pulling up the draw to the Summit Place. "None of my equipment can be pulled with less than four mules. Most take six or eight. You've got no teams to change out. Surely, you didn't sell my implements, too!"

"Jesse, I have ground to cover. I can't do it with mules and old equipment like I bought from you."

"You've bought nothing from me! Our agreement was for you to pay me two thousand in earnest money, and you'd lease the place for five years. If you were able to make it work, the lease and earnest money would go toward the purchase. You understood that!"

"Jesse, a man's got to do what he can to make things work. Sentiment don't play much part in it. If I'd knowed you was attached to them mules—"

"Attached? Those mules are my property! You can no more sell them than I can sell your store!" The knot in his gut pulled him forward. "So help me, if you've... Is the black still on the Summit Place? Did you—"

"Hold on! That crazy black is still runnin' them hills. Can't get within a quarter mile of him. He ought to be cut, Jesse. He's not doing nobody no good the way he is."

Jesse worked his jaw, tried to suck enough air to speak. "You cut that horse, Morgan, and I'll see to it you get the same. You won't be sniffing around anybody else's wife ever again."

Morgan pushed his hat back, rubbing his fresh-shaved face. "Now, Jesse, this is gettin' out o' hand. I thought you and me was friends. I've let that horse run on this place out of the goodness of my heart, as a favor, but he's costing me."

"This is my place Morgan, and as of this fall, your lease is done. I know I won't be paid, but you can wean the calves, keep the heifers, sell them, whatever you want, but the rest comes back to me. Cows, steers, and bulls. You understand? And I'm taking the worth of my mules and implements out of the earnest money." Brakes squealed. Morgan kicked the truck out of gear and pointed his finger between Jesse's eyes. "That horse comes behind me when I feed them cows, takes his share of the feed. That costs me, Jesse."

He leaned forward. "That horse should never have milo, and you know it. It could kill him. You were supposed to feed him oats. Come fall, we'll figure out just what he's cost you, and you'll get it back. I'll have my cows and ranch, and we'll call this deal done."

"I don't think so. Our deal's written out. I'll take it to a lawyer if I have to."

His ears burned. "There's more than one of those in the state, Morgan. My boy is coming home soon. You won't want to see him after what you've pulled, and you won't be able to scheme your way out of what'll happen."

Morgan leaned back, gripped the wheel and started the truck.

Delores stood in the doorway, her hair in curlers mounded at the top of her head. Jesse pulled himself from the truck, clung to the door and grabbed his chair from the back. He heaved it beside him, swung down, and dropped into the seat. Morgan slammed the truck in gear and released the clutch, throwing sand and dry grass at his useless legs. The truck bounced across ruts, the door swinging wide.

Delores held to the porch post, her camisole gaping wide. "Where's he going?"

He pushed the fire down. "Home, most likely."

"But he's supposed to have Christmas dinner with us!" Delores released the door frame and let her camisole close.

"You may as well get dressed. He won't be back."

She spun and marched inside. "Thank you for ruining my Christmas, Jesse. I should have known you'd do something!"

Chapter XVII

A tremor climbed Nicole's neck and pirouetted down her spine, and the slender warmth of Émile's arm did nothing to dispel it. It was the shabbiest of deceits, she and Émile pretending to be husband and wife, a lie swaddled in revulsion.

Paris was obscured in darkness. The only smiles were on the faces of Nazi troops, officers for the most part, some in the company of young women. She glanced at her ring finger, wanted to abhor these Parisian girls, to despise their treachery, but her heart accused her more. This man whose arm she held might be responsible for a dozen or more Dutch or Belgian operatives being thrown to the wolves. He had saved her, but she had yet to learn the price.

He slowed his pace and looked around. "We will speak of sensitive matters only while out of doors beyond the hearing of others. Do you understand?"

"Of course." She pasted a smile on her face for whomever might be watching and waited as the pig's gaze moved over her.

"We cannot assume the hotel is safe."

Warmth surged to her face. "You expect me to share your room, then?"

His eyes flickered. "You needn't worry. You may sleep on the couch."

She hid the chill with bluster. "All right."

His mouth twitched. "The hotel is frequented mostly by Boche. The Reich is obsessed with monitoring their own. One never knows where microphones are hidden."

They strolled beneath a panoply of Nazi flags. Not a crèche remained or a single "Joyeux Noël." Candles burned in a few windows, but it seemed more an act of reverence for their new lord and master. No sacred births were heralded. Instead, evil prevailed, a twisted cross emblazoned in the darkness ushering the witless into an unholy millennium.

She remembered her father reading Herr Hitler's writings in which he declared regret that the Mohammedans failed in their efforts to take the continent. The inherent supremacy of the Aryan race, Hitler scolded, would have assured that Germany, supported by the Mohammedans, would now rule a kingdom free of Jewish control and Christian effeminacy and the compunctions that kept the strong from ascending to their rightful place. In Mohammad, he believed, he'd found a prophet keen on ridding the world of Jews and miscreants.

That apparition now held Europe in its grip, even the City of Lights. A chill eclipsed the morning. The Rue des Ardennes, with Nazi banners draped along its sides, was no brighter for the tarnished beauty of Paris. Émile guided her to a table along the street and drew a chair. The outdoor section of the restaurant was empty though a few heads nodded above the windowsills.

He smiled, an attempt at amiability, she guessed. "Your English is impeccable. You could easily pass for a Brit even to a Brit."

"You're British, then?" She hated playing this game but saw no alternative.

"My father is British; my mother is French."

"How convenient." She forced a smile. "In light of your present work, I mean."

The space above Émile's nose compressed as an old waiter approached their table. "We'd like two cups of coffee and croissants, please." His French was flawless.

He looked back. "I spent a good deal of my youth with my grandparents in Chartres. The most important part, perhaps."

She offered a cool nod. "And what is it you want from me?"

He straightened. "Have I offended you?"

She glared. "I find it difficult to offer deference, considering what you've done. And I'm certain you require deference."

"Perhaps I owe you an apology for our meeting, but—"

"Yes, you do." She studied his face. "And much more than that."

A twitch lifted the corner of his mouth.

She stifled her rage. "You're clearly an officer. Upper echelon MI6, I'm sure."

His ears reddened, and his chin receded.

"Your attitude is like a few others I've met in British intelligence. I'm sure it's difficult to hide. You—" She took a breath. "You care nothing for those who risk their lives to help you."

He looked down his nose. "I had assumed we shared the goal of removing the Jerries from your homeland and stopping their attack on mine."

"As did I, once. But if that were your goal, you wouldn't dispose of assets like yesterday's rubbish." She swallowed bile. "What is this job you wished to see if I were qualified for?" Her words hung in thick silence.

"You've undoubtedly heard of the Thomas/Tómas line?"

She felt her breath return. "Of course, though I believe it no longer exists."

"You're quite correct. However, we propose to establish another like it."

"Only you'd like me to be the lamb you sacrifice this time?"

Fire flickered in his eyes. "We need your help, yes. Guiding fleeing Jews and pilots will be left to others. You'll carry information that you are uniquely qualified to gather."

She raised her eyebrows. "And would I be meeting those requesting this information?"

Émile appeared to be in a pout.

She glanced at an older couple walking arm in arm, sensed their trepidation at being watched, and turned back. "My friends have died because MI6 refused to act on reports that agents or safe houses were under surveillance. You had to know they would be arrested."

"Are you making an accusation?"

She clenched her fists. "Why did you order them to go their deaths?"

"You're to be a courier, not a prosecutor."

The waiter appeared in the doorway, strode to their table, and placed the coffee and croissants in front of them. Émile waved two fingers, dismissing him.

She watched the man retreat and brought her hands to the table. "Will I also be murdered when you're through with me?"

"That's preposterous, Elisabeth."

It wasn't precisely a denial. "You said the Brussels to Madrid route was no longer open. Why is that?"

Émile stiffened. "You know why. The agent operating it was arrested."

"Because you failed to protect him *months* after he told you his operation was compromised."

Émile swirled his coffee. "Perhaps you are not the one for this job after all."

She nodded. "Perhaps not. You might need someone less honest. Or more stupid."

108

He expelled a snuffle and looked toward the street. "Then I wish you well here in France and offer my sincere hope that you survive."

An old man stepped through the front door and marched to the street. She took a swallow of coffee to moisten her parched mouth. "You're saying you won't help me leave safely if I'm not willing to sacrifice myself for your plan?"

"I'm saying I'm not authorized to help Belgian citizens escape. If you're not our agent, I will be unable to protect you."

She shuddered at his audacity. "I see. And if I become your operative, will I be allowed to take my reports to the persons requesting them?"

The snuffle again. "All right, yes."

She waited for a show of conscience but saw none. "I'll require that in writing."

"I couldn't possibly—"

"Then I shan't, either." She held her breath.

"We'll need a safe place to store the document you're requesting."

She drew the stilling air. "You will identify yourself by your proper name." She broke a piece from the roll and stirred her coffee. "I want it tonight. I will keep it on my person at all times. If I am arrested, your identity will be known, as well."

He huffed. "We shall both sign a statement. Then my arrest will also mean yours. We will share the risk."

Her heart pounded. It was all she'd hoped for, really, but... "No. You're far too reckless. There will be one document and one signature, and I shall carry it. The American embassy in London will receive a copy. Perhaps that will dissuade you from disposing of me." She took a breath. "And I must know how to contact MI6 directly."

He stared, the piercing green rattling her resolve. "We're proposing something new. Thomas had no reason to be where he was sent. We will establish two identities, provide you with papers and addresses in two places, and give you a reason to travel first between Aberdeen and Barcelona, and then between Toulouse and Brussels. It will give us a better chance of keeping you alive."

"And continuing your mission." She shook her head. "It makes no sense. Two agents would be simpler. And what of the distance between Barcelona and Toulouse?"

He returned his cup to the saucer with considerable delicacy. "Two agents might be simpler. However, it would necessitate a good deal of communication and a courier between them, a weakness we would prefer to eliminate. As to your other objection, you would be required to make that trek on your own."

Her stomach knotted. "Across the Pyrenees?"

"There is a *passeur d'homme* who will aid you the first few times. But if you could cross without him, you would avoid even more of the exposure our former agents incurred." He leaned forward. "And this is the genius of the plan. We have arranged for your employment with a French firm that sells cloth to a garment maker in Brussels. While under their aegis, you will be Elisabeth Leclerc." He offered a self-satisfied smile. "The Belgian firm has been appropriated by the Germans to produce uniforms, but the proprietor is most eager to help and has a background in intelligence. The Toulouse firm also wishes to help and will cover for your absence while away. They will work in concert. As a quality inspector, you will be required to travel between the two locations."

"And how could my presence be explained in Barcelona? I don't speak Spanish."

He smiled. "That's where your second identity comes in. As a Brit, you couldn't be expected to speak Spanish."

"As a Brit? In Barcelona?"

He brought his hands together, his skin translucent in the morning light. "Sometimes war creates opportunities for entrepreneurs that peacetime does not. In our observations of such enterprises, we have uncovered one that is especially interesting. A Scottish shipping firm is operating under a Portuguese name. They find trade between Aberdeen and Barcelona most profitable, though it's certain they're being paid in Reichsmarks, and the Nazis seem to be turning a blind eye as their ships steam in and out of port."

She placed her coffee on the table. "They're shipping German goods?"

"No, they're shipping American goods to Barcelona where they are picked up by Dutch liners and delivered to the Nazis. This firm, since being apprised of the Crown's displeasure, has been enthusiastic in making amends."

"And who will I be while in the employ of the Brits?"

"Your British name is Elisabeth Clark." His index finger rose, a visual exclamation mark. "You will be found at random times on board their ship evaluating space management and fuel consumption."

She nodded. "An efficiency expert."

He shrugged. "You've a background in mathematics, have you not? And since you can never be expected at either place at any given time, you will be difficult for the Boche to find, should you not want to be found."

It had to have been his plan, one created around her dossier. It would explain why he'd yielded to her demands. A stronger position than she'd hoped for. "I shall require two things. I want contact with someone who's likely in a stalag."

"Your American flyer, yes. Lieutenant Dremmer is in Moosburg actively seeking to learn your whereabouts. As you likely know, his efforts resulted in your retrieval from Belgium. He made some sort of deal with the devil. What it was, our man in Moosburg hasn't said." A twitch pulled at his upper lip. "We'll inform him that you are out of Belgium. Beyond that, we cannot commit resources for you to carry on a long-distance romance."

Her heart stuttered. David had gotten information to Gaston. Perhaps... "Even if he is able to provide you with information?"

"If he has any, I'm certain our man in Moosburg can gather it. And the other thing?"

She let her breath still. "I want my partners in Belgium removed. I want them safe from the whims of unprincipled MI6 officers. Like yourself."

Émile smirked. "That's already in the works, though I don't know how safe they will be anywhere. Charles will likely attempt to find you."

How would he know that? "All right, then, I shall read your statement when it's completed. And I will be the one to place it in the envelope."

Émile put the coffee down. "Do you distrust me that much?"

"Yes, though with the proper motivation, you might learn to be more honorable."

He was silent for a moment. "There is another matter, a more pleasant one." He proffered a crooked smile. "Did you celebrate Réveillon as a child?"

"No, though I had friends who did."

He smiled. "We are to celebrate a Parisian Christmas Eve. Do you find that exciting?"

"In occupied Paris? With Nazis all around? I find that insane."

His head tilted toward his shoulder. "It cannot be helped. I must meet with an asset."

Chapter XVIII

The earth trembled in a howling void as a hole in the heavens spewed gray ash. Its molten core quivered near the edge of thought and surged against the encroachment of night, an obsidian window on a glacial hell. Beyond the window, a crimson rush issued from a woman's head, and fine red mist filtered from David's waking dream.

He opened his eyes to a darkness as void of hope as any lie told by man or demon, moved his legs, but could scarcely feel them for a numbing lethargy drawing itself about him like a shroud. He brought his hands to his shoulders, wrapped the blanket tight, then swung on quivering arms. His boots slapped concrete, rimy and unforgiving, and he shuffled to the stove. The iron was as cold as death, and stinging air heaved from the grate.

He stared at the ceiling and spotted a ring of light around the stove pipe. The flashing and cap had blown off. The damper was open, too, had been left wide at the cost of the night's ration of coal. He closed it, and the blistering draft withered.

Kriegies moaned in strained oblivion. He bent low, gathered bark, cigarette packs, and empty match books collected for kindling, then struck a match. A mound of light huddled in the heat of its own extinction and burst upward, lighting the way for him to scrape coal into the chute. Iron creaked as flames licked blackness. He leaned forward, hoarding what comfort he could.

Wind heaved against the walls, baying in vengeance above the stovepipe. He stood, nudged the damper, gathered the remaining coal, and mounded it with a short stick in the firebox, invoking the flames to thaw his bones. A lone figure moved toward him swathed in a blanket, eyes peering into his. "I 'bout froze, Lieutenant." The corners of the private's words were rounded and dulled by heavy wool.

He bristled at the words. "It could have frozen all of us, Private, not just you." It was an inauspicious beginning for a Christmas morning, though one other might rival it. Delores, the woman who would become his wife, a woman he hardly knew, lay naked beneath his tarp, claiming something not meant for her.

He closed the fire door and stood. Schneider's munificence might have saved him, maybe all of them. He felt the strength of it, the vigor of a full meal. The beef rouladen delivered a potency he'd not known in weeks, and Schneider had offered more. He glanced back. "We've got to get the others up, Mathews. Some of these guys really could freeze. It'll take hours to warm this place."

The private put his blanket around the stove, held it there for seconds, then wrapped it around his shoulders and scraped to the south end of the barracks. "You guys get up. Lieutenant Dremmer let the fire go out."

He swallowed the rising anger, pretending he hadn't heard. He was the only officer in the barracks and was apt to be charged with whatever happened. At least by Mathews. He scraped along the bunks and shook the men awake. "Boots out of bed, boys. Everybody around the fire."

The room ascended to a steady drone, men resisting the stupor of their death dreams. Kriegies ambled toward the center and huddled around the creaking iron, shivering shoulder to shoulder and back to shrunken belly. Heads were down, the men fighting the urge to surrender to the sweeter darkness of an undying sleep.

Swanson lowered his blanket. "Thank you, sir. Guess we'd have slept till we froze."

He put his hand to the corporal's shoulder, felt the weight of the boy's betrayal. Retribution was coming, but it wouldn't be today, and he was grateful. "Move over by the fire, Swanson. Get as close as you can."

The men were bone weary from work detail and weakened by reduced rations. Especially Swanson. Some had traded their D-bars and canned milk for cigarettes. He'd gained from the exchange, though not without some nagging from his conscience. Sleep was the respite they lived for, and all gave themselves to it with abandon. Now even that had broken faith.

The corporal needed to be closer to the stove. "Corporal."

Swanson turned. "Sir?"

"Why don't you make the men some coffee? Use fresh grounds and make it hot. We'll start our Christmas early. I saved two tins of milk for those that want a little. It's in my duffle. My gift to the barracks."

The boy smiled. "Yes sir."

"Mathews!" He looked above the gathered mass for the accusing eyes and spotted him close to the stove, hoarding heat. "Break up that empty bunk in the corner. We don't have enough coal to warm this place. We'll need it for kindling."

The private's mouth widened. "Me, sir?"

"A little exercise will do you good. And as soon as you're warm, form a group of your friends to look for the ring and stove cap."

"I don't have any friends, sir."

He stifled a snort. "Then you'd better make a few."

* * *

Hanson pulled a khaki ribbon away from his mouth. "Heard you had some excitement this morning. Why do you think nobody woke up?" The captain removed his gloves; a shirt torn in strips was wound beneath his cap and hid most of his face.

"Somebody did. It happened to be me, sir." David stood beside his chair, the numbing cold stealing his ability to focus. "Blizzard blew the cap off the stove pipe. The damper was left open. Burned up the night's coal, and the wind blew right in."

"Sure looks like somebody would have woken up before it got that bad. So why you?"

His throat knotted. "Because I ate well last night, Captain. The others didn't."

The corners of Hanson's mouth lifted. "Good thing as it turns out. You had the presence of mind to start a fire." The captain seemed satisfied and tucked his hands beneath his armpits. "Here's the pitch, Dremmer. You were in Schneider's office for a reason. A good one. Enjoying a meal provided by the Krauts wasn't an act of treason; it was part of the war effort." He waited. "And another thing—don't let Mathews' bellyaching get to you. He's a bunk lizard, born believing it's somebody else's responsibility to keep him warm and fed."

He chuckled. "You heard about that?"

"He's still whining about having to find the vent cap in the snow. So, what'd you learn?"

"Schneider has been checking up on me. He knew I took French in college."

Hanson blew on his hands. "Finding your transcripts shouldn't be hard. Especially..."

"Especially what, sir?"

"If I were a Nazi looking for someone in sympathy stateside, a college campus is the first place I'd go. You must have heard talk, found a few professors who liked what they were doing."

"There was one—"

Hanson waved his hand and ended the response. "As long as Schneider doesn't connect your speaking French to the information you overheard. So, what else did he find?"

"That my father was paralyzed a few weeks before I graduated, and that I'd planned on staying at the university."

The captain blew into his hands again. "That it?"

"About me? Yes, but—"

"Your dad's accident— you said he fell off a horse, right?"

He shook his head. "The horse fell on him."

Hanson slipped his hands inside his gloves. "He could've gotten that from a newspaper. The Germans probably have a warehouse full of microfilm. And your plans to stay at the university, who did you talk to about that?"

"Couple of faculty members and a friend. But the man I was telling you about was a biology professor. He was taken with this eugenics business and had joined a group called the Human Betterment Foundation. Said the Nazis were doing something we'd needed for decades. Thing is, there were only a few fellowships being offered for graduate work. He was pushing for one of his students to get—"

"Let me guess. It was awarded to you, instead."

Hanson's impatience worsened in the cold. It was irritating, not being able to finish a sentence. "Yes sir. Of course, I didn't get to use it." He leaned forward rubbing the blood into his legs.

Hanson hopped on his toes. "And what happened to this professor's prodigy?"

He shrugged. "By the time I turned the fellowship down, he'd made other plans. Ended up at some Ivy—"

"This professor's likely our source, not that knowing helps. What was the other thing?"

He hurried. "Schneider is Abwehr now. Luftwaffe uniform, Wehrmacht stalag, but Abwehr command. I'm guessing he feeds them whatever information he gets. Well, most of it."

Hanson shook his head. "That's not good. Gives him access to more resources. We'll work with it, though, just like Stanislavsky."

He paused. "The reason I'm here, in the open, is that Chaplain Daniel is looking for you. I was in your barracks, let somebody suggest you were here, and offered to tell you on my way to get a Bible for morning services."

David straightened, wondering at the request.

"Chaplain says you're to help him with communion during the Protestant service. Wants you to be sure you know what to say at distribution. You know what that is?"

"Yes sir."

Hanson's head tilted. "Why you? You and the devil-beater buddies, now?"

He shrugged. "We've talked some, but—"

"Here's the pitch, Dremmer. Chaplain Daniel has invited the commandant and his staff to attend services. Not likely Berger will be there, but he could send an officer or two. You know how that works. I'll go to the Catholic service since you'll be at the Protestant. Want to keep an eye on Schneider. I'm guessing he grew up Catholic before his party affiliations?"

He shrugged. "I don't—"

Hanson bounced toward the door, pulling his overcoat tight. "They've started cooking. Be some kriegies with full bellies tonight. You need a good meal. Another one."

"Sir?"

"Yeah?" Brightness streamed through the windows and silhouetted Hanson's shiver.

He pitched a Bible from the shelf. "What you came for, sir. Merry Christmas."

Chapter XIX

From the hotel window, Nicole could scarcely detect the evil that had wrapped itself around the city. No banners darkened the sky above, and no propaganda insulted her ears. She couldn't gape into the empty shops or see the blank stares on the faces of those brave enough to stay. Still, the thought of it repulsed her, and she stepped back, stumbled into Émile, and lurched. "Pardon me. I was admiring the drapes."

He caught her glance and shook his head. It was an inappropriate response for a wife who had bumped into her husband.

"Darling, I'm sorry for what I said about your mother." She made her voice as compelling as she could. "I know she is dear to you, but I don't want to end our trip with her. We've had a grand time, and I'm so looking forward to going south. I will make it up to you."

Émile winked. "I suppose, though I don't understand why you're so determined to not see her. It would be only one day."

"Apparently, we can't discuss it. You simply aren't reasonable." She stepped into the bathroom and locked the door, moved her hand over a thick towel, inspected the gilded handles of the tub, and read the labels of the toiletries. She had grown accustomed to the apartment, sharing a bathroom with Charles and Gaston at the end of the hall, the plumbing seldom in order. But this was wonderful.

She twisted the handles and water flowed, growing quickly hot. She slipped her blouse over her shoulders, let her skirt fall to the floor, eased into the water, then lay back to let the kindness cover her. A knock sounded at the door.

"What is it?" She shot upright, grabbing a towel.

"I have a little something for you. A gift."

The man was infuriating. "You always think that will fix everything. Just go away."

"It's in the closet. Please look at it, *chérie*."

She stood, wrapped the towel around her, and reached for the crystal knob. A burgundy evening dress was hanging on the rack and rippled in the feeble draft of the opening door.

"Oh, it's beautiful, *mon chér. Merci!*"

"All is forgiven, then?" The voice sounded truly hopeful.

"We'll discuss it."

***

The dress was as beautiful as anything she'd worn before the war and certainly more expensive. She stared into the mirror, admired the supple undulations across her breasts and thighs, the off-the-shoulder enticement, the skirt that fell to a gentle flare at the hem and split in the back, revealing her long legs beneath the stocking seams. The peep-toes glistened, balancing her diamond earrings. It had been ages since she'd dressed for dinner, but never had she dressed so elegantly. It was a comfort to know she could still look fetching. If only it were for David.

She blinked the thought away and stepped from behind the door. Émile was seated at the table with a pipe in his mouth, dressed and waiting. His pipe lowered, and he gazed longer than seemed necessary.

She sought the proper words. "Do you like it, dear?"

"It's quite lovely." He stared. "That is, you're lovely. Beautiful, actually."

His stare made her uncomfortable. Perhaps her assumptions about him had been wrong.

"I have something else for you." He rose, began rummaging through a shipping crate beside the desk, pulled out a black fur stole and opera gloves. "Do you like them?"

"Ah, Émile! Thank you! You have always been good to me. I know I've been selfish at times." She looked at him, held herself in check, frightened he might think her act was real. "If it means that much to you, we will visit your mother when we go south."

He stared, mystified.

***

The rain-slick bricks beneath them returned the rippling blaze of her dress. Paris in moonlight. Nicole breathed in the place, caught the stirring of Nazi flags, and felt the slender glow drain into twilight. She walked beside Émile, their fingers touching as they swayed. She raised her hand and drew the sequined clutch to her waist.

"It will be a splendid evening, something you could experience only in Paris."

She drew a breath. "Is it necessary? Our being so conspicuous, I mean."

"We should stroll the Champs-Élysées. Paris is so beautiful after a rain. And we are about to celebrate Réveillon!"

The strangeness of it wrenched her heart, the discordance of Christmas Eve in Paris and the multiplied death and starvation across Europe.

He began again. "You shan't forget it. We have reservations in the La Salle Principale."

She stopped, waiting for him to turn. "There is a war on. You are aware of this, yes?"

"Yes!" He faced her, his eyes rimmed with light. "That is all the more reason to celebrate. This night. Here. Now. We've been given this time and have only to seize it!"

"And they have only to seize us! Why do you think we won't be recognized?"

His smile widened. "By whom? Who knows you here? Who knows me?"

"You are an officer in MI6 and clearly upper echelon. Abwehr and SD surely know this. The Germans are, how did you put it, obsessed with the proclivities of their officers? How much more must they obsess over the activities of enemy agents?"

He put a finger to her lips. "I'm a good bit higher than you've imagined, *chérie*, and tonight I am in the most beautiful city in the world with perhaps the most beautiful woman in the world. I shall not fail to receive this evening as a gift!"

She grew desperate and wished to slap his hand away. The man was enjoying this! "You are not too high to hang! And I certainly am not. Please, let's go back."

His smile dissolved. "All right. We will go to the restaurant and celebrate in a corner. I'll tell the waiter we wish to be alone. We'll go straight to the hotel and be back before curfew, but we mustn't miss our reservation. It is a sin no Frenchman can be forgiven of."

She wrapped her arms tightly about her waist. "I thought you were British."

He raised his hands in the expansive light. "I am both. I can deny neither."

"Let's walk near the buildings in the shadows." She turned. "You must inform the *maître d'* that we cannot stay through Réveillon. Make an excuse without drawing attention. Please. We will eat, you will meet your operative, and we will leave, yes?"

He shrugged. "It is inexcusable, but yes, we will eat and return."

* * *

Nicole slipped into the shadows as *the maître d'* was attended to. She shrank, desperate to avoid the scrutiny of the German officers. Réveillon in Paris. The whole thing was something born of a fevered dream. Two hours of roast goose and red cabbage, foie gras and oysters. And, of course, champagne. All while sitting with German officers no more than ten meters away toasting the Führer and the progress of the war.

Émile moved through the door and into the shadows of the street.

"Elisabeth, you are delightful." He spoke in English, the champagne levering his volume beyond any safe level.

She looked at him, saw the glow on his skin. "Please don't allow our roles to confuse you. This is our job, strange as it is."

"Of course." He stiffened.

She walked a step ahead, clinging to the shadows. "At the risk of seeming audacious, I think you are beginning to see me as human."

He chuckled. "Yes, quite."

"Then consider this. The lives that were wasted, the lives your organization continues to throw away, are no less human, no less unique than I. Until a week ago, I was one of them."

He stopped. "I don't set policy, you know."

"But you have a conscience, I hope, and a more-than-ample voice. I am certain it would be heard."

Footsteps approached, and he shifted to French. "There is more to this than you know."

"Then tell me."

He glanced at an old Frenchman waiting for him to pass. "I cannot, of course."

He moved close. "We will leave the day after tomorrow. I will accompany you to Mouchard where you will continue to Toulouse by bus, then transfer to rail as far as Bourg-Madame in the Pyrenees. From there, you will take a cog railway up to Osséja. A *passeur d'homme* will meet you there. It will be a moderate climb but a difficult passage, nonetheless. You must be rested." He looked sad but lifted his chin. "You will take the bed, tonight, and I shall sleep on the couch."

Chapter XX

David entered from the broom closet that had doubled as a sacristy in the previous service, aware that he lacked the chaplain's regal bearing, and skulked with the tray of elements to place on the altar. The music carried the weight of things eternal while the denizens of hell blew hard against the walls, threatening to countermand the Almighty's generosity, and demanding to be heard above the Doxology.

The flow of the Sursum Corda was as certain as the coming of spring and just as slow. He waited, breathing it in. The chaplain made the sign of the cross. *"The Lord be with you."*

"And with you." The response seemed weak against the howling wind.

David drifted, scanning the bowed heads, and mulled the coming words of institution. He tasted the sweetness of the syllables, the promise of release that would be held between his fingers. *Take, eat, this is my body, broken for you...* Christ's body broken, skin ripped wide, sinew rent from bone, muscles abraded, joints in raw contortion, all for the asking to be more fully known, the supplicant made one in this completion of an everlasting offer of forgiveness, the divine passion for justice satisfied, the ransom met with an urgent love.

The words rang convoluted and adorned, more complete somehow in his contemplation. *In the same night in which he was betrayed...* Betrayal was something he knew, of course, though never in such completeness. His heart came to rest on Swanson, on the slip that must have cost him his conscience. He wanted to reach out, to help the corporal, but he couldn't. It was Swanson's move to make.

Chaplain Daniel made the Sign of the Cross and held the wafer between his finger and thumb, then knelt, rose, uncovered the chalice, and lifted it. The words swelled, piercing David's heart as he glanced across the room.

A blur of Luftwaffe blue stirred in the far corner, the frigid darkness taking his breath. Maybe it was the fear of his treachery at being discovered, but he didn't want to face Heinrich—wished beyond words to disavow his lie. He was deceiving the man he would be offering the blood of forgiveness. Betrayal was his duty, a matter of life and death, perhaps even Nicole's, but he might also be playing a part in Schneider's undoing. He was duplicity cloaked in divine flesh and blood. His chest shook at the pounding, his heart accusing him with every blow. Only his resolve held his legs in place. He glanced at the communion tray, saw the storm inside him mimicked by the napkin.

The Chaplain began the preface. *"It is truly meet, right, and salutary that we should at all times and in all places..."*

David fought for breath, tried to force his hands to still, moved his knees to stay the threat of collapse. The words wound down, and the chaplain turned, a wafer in his right hand. The chalice rose, but David looked away, followed the darkness, reached the farthest corner, and caught the edge of Heinrich's glare.

Daniel bowed his head. *"You are indeed holy, almighty and merciful God; you are most holy..."*

David forced his breath to steady and prayed for Schneider to return to his seat. Queues formed along the walls. Two kriegies ushered the men by row, the chaplain reciting words that moments before brought comfort. *"Our Lord Jesus Christ, on the same night in which he was betrayed, took bread, and when he had given thanks—"*

A specter of blue moved along the wall. David drew frozen air, took a tray of wafers, and moved to the communion rail. He watched the chaplain step slowly to the right while Luftwaffe blue glided across the transept and edged toward the kneeling kriegies. His lungs refused to release the air. It wasn't his call to make. The charge his heart was leveling was unjust. It was his duty, and his deceptions could save her life.

He extended the paten beneath the chin of a waiting kriegie and placed the wafer on the man's tongue. *"The Body of Christ."* He moved to the next, drew in the frost, and struggled with the words. The gold-ringed sleeve of Schneider's overcoat rested three feet away. He offered the waiting kriegie a wafer and repeated *"The Body of Christ."*

He sidled to the right, raised his chin, and looked down. The oberleutnant's grin faded, the narrowing lips allowing the slightest wisp to pass. He refused to flinch, uttered a furious prayer, felt the steel of it in his spine, and stood with the refusal of stone.

After several seconds, the perfect teeth glinted. "Are you attempting to humiliate me, Lieutenant?" The voice rose, clearly audible to the men around him.

He stared and waited, then shook his head. "This one's on you, Herr Oberleutnant." He extended a trembling hand. *"The Body of Christ."*

Even the wind grew still.

* * *

"What the hell was that about this morning, Dremmer? You trying to wreck the whole operation?" The arteries in Hanson's neck bulged. "You don't have the right to keep some Kraut from getting communion just because you've got a beef with him."

Hanson wouldn't understand. He spoke in a hush. "My apologies, sir. May we take this outside so the men aren't made aware of my role?"

The captain snorted. "I'll take care of that right now!"

His heart slammed against his lungs. There'd be no way to protect her if the captain kicked him off the committee.

Hanson faced the huddled kriegies. "Men, you are aware of my role in this camp. I interviewed most of you when you came. Let me read you in on something and let me make it clear. We don't need any Lone Rangers fighting this war as they see fit. If you have something to settle with your interrogator, or any other Kraut, take it up with the MOC. You can't make some Kraut leave your chapel and you can't decide what he can or can't do when he's there. We have a lot riding on maintaining a working relationship with the enemy. Am I clear?"

A few kriegies exchanged glances, but no one spoke. Hanson raised his chin. "I asked if I was clear."

A rumble grew, the sibilance of their answer rising above the dying wind.

"That is all. Enjoy what's left of your Christmas." The captain turned, glared at David, and pushed his way through the door.

David stepped back, stunned by Hanson's reprieve, and felt the warmth of a hand on his shoulder. He turned to see Swanson, a glistening in the boy's eyes.

"I understand, sir. Interrogation was nasty for some of us. It's hard to forget what they did. Give the captain a few days is all, sir." The corporal withdrew, straightened, and saluted.

He drew himself erect, returned the salute, and felt the crushing weight of the boy's fate.

Chapter XXI

The streets were strange in their stillness. The overnight rain had been tarnished by darkness, frozen, then left with a fragile white dusting where the walk was covered in shadows. Nicole stepped lightly and turned from Émile, the crack of her boots echoing between vacant shops. She shivered, looked away from the swastikas, and wished for Paris to be as she remembered.

"I am not the enemy, you know." Émile stared through the windows of a crêperie.

She stopped a few meters away, her silence an attempt to conceal the flame that erupted at his words. Only last night he had paraded her before German officers for a feast of roast goose and red cabbage. Now, he acted out some charade, a hungry child on a Christmas morning.

"Information is generally routed through Belgian military headquarters in London. Your reports will go directly to MI6." He turned toward her. "As you requested."

She refused to meet his eyes, observing him in the window instead. "The ones who ignored our memos telling them our agents were being observed? Those who took their lives?"

He offered the pathetic pout she detested. "That is your assumption."

She pivoted, her soles squeaking on the skim of snow. "It is not an assumption. You explained the process to me unless you were again lying."

"There is so much information coming in—"

"And we are so dispensable, are we not?"

Émile's gaze appeared unfocused in the glass. "Plans have changed. You will leave in two hours for Toulouse. Upon arrival, you will take a bus to Saint-Girons. Your *passeur d'homme,* Martin, will meet you there. He speaks little French and no English. A man posing as his father will interpret. Your climb will be more strenuous than the one previously planned."

"We are not going back to the hotel?" Her stomach tightened.

"You learned all this just this morning?"

"It is possible that we are being surveilled. Another operative spotted a photographer."

Fire rose beneath her collar. "At the La Salle Principale? And you exposed the operative you met?"

He turned away, appeared to be hiding his slanted grin. "Perhaps not."

"The result of your absurd risk. And all for roast goose."

"I had to meet the operative."

"You met no one. And what of my letter? I won't leave without it."

Émile's pale skin flushed. "You saw no one because you weren't supposed to. And I have your letter." He patted his jacket. "Luggage is waiting at the station. Once on the train, you should be safe."

He was clearly lying, but she forced herself to breathe and considered the risks of defiance. "We will open the envelope together so that I can be assured the letter has not been altered. We will then reseal it."

Émile released a gust of air.

She stifled her revulsion. "The photographer. Was he in uniform?"

"Wehrmacht. He was taken with your appearance, I'm sure. It is doubtful there were girls like you on the cabbage farm."

"Or he was Abwehr. Or SD. We cannot know with certainty until they place nooses around our necks. I hope your Réveillon was worth it."

He turned, his lips white. "Yes, quite, thank you."

* * *

Nicole stepped under the overhang, her beige coat blending with the paving stones of the Saint-Girons terminal. It had been a miserable two days and nights, and no one was here to meet her. A Wehrmacht hauptmann, the one remaining passenger who boarded the bus with her at Toulouse, stood across from her, his stare an open challenge. Or invitation. She shivered, retreated to a wooden bench, and felt the envelope press against her ribs. She had insisted on it, of course, but if she were arrested, it would mean not only her execution but Émile's. She gazed into the Pyrenees, prayed for the swine to leave, and reminded herself that beyond those peaks, Spain began, and that she would be there soon.

A car, large and sleek, whispered beyond the corner of the three-sided building. She turned her head and watched it bounce across the empty car park. It skidded to a halt and splashed the path where the other passengers had walked. The officer rose, looked at her, then turned. She swallowed her nausea, pulled the strings of her woolen bag, and sent a plea above the highest peak that she might live long enough to see beyond it. A rear door opened, and the hauptmann stepped off the platform, ambled to the car, and was motored away.

She sagged against the bench, then stiffened. A man, disheveled and muttering, appeared on the opposite side of the structure. He was perhaps sixty, the collar of his woolen overcoat raised, his lapel torn. He walked along the white stone path but seemed not to notice her. The car turned toward town and disappeared beyond the curve.

The man stopped and faced her. "Mademoiselle, you are Elisabeth, I assume?"

She caught her breath and lifted her chin. "I am waiting for a friend, monsieur. I am certain he will be here shortly." A stupid thing to say.

He shrugged. "You were expecting Martin, I am sure."

"Your name, monsieur?" The tremor in her voice gave her away, as would her shaking hands had he been close. It was contemptible that her body would so betray her.

"I am Laurent, and my English is rather French, wouldn't you agree?"

He *was* speaking English. Her heart pounded in her ears. "Mine is no better. The product of a British nanny, only."

He stared for a moment, then smiled. "You will learn to be more cautious, I am sure."

"I don't know what you mean, monsieur."

He pulled a cigarette from his pocket. "It is spring, and the plane leaves wither."

She looked above the mountains, shamed by her misstep. "Are you also a reader of Goethe?" She caught her breath. "I will learn better. I have made this mistake before."

"Walk with me. Should we be intercepted, you are my niece on holiday from Toulouse. We will speak French."

"Your niece." The thought pleased her, somehow. "Of course."

* * *

Narrow stone houses clung to the side of the mountain. Laurent ambled beside her. "We are likely being observed."

She almost stumbled. "By whom?"

"It is a small village. I am known, but you are not. It will be noticed—especially since you are attractive, mademoiselle. You must appear to be familiar, as a niece would be."

She slipped her hand around the crook of his arm. "It's wonderful to see you, Uncle."

"Uncle Laurent. Yes, that's it." He shuffled on. "The Boche patrol these mountains. They have vowed to stop escapes into Spain whose government now allows them eight kilometers inside their border. If you are discovered, you will be shot. It is possible Martin will be also. He will travel ahead of you. The moon is full, so you will leave tonight."

"Then how will I know—"

"He will wear a bright scarf. If he takes it off, you will hide. You understand, yes?"

She nodded. "Yes. How long will it take?"

"It is usually a five-day trek. You will make it in four days and nights."

"Traveling only at night?"

"After the second day, you should be able to travel in the light, though it will mean you must move quickly. It is exhausting. Are you a climber?"

"Once…" She found herself unable to endure another lie. "Not in a few years, I'm afraid." She thought of the stairs, the many times she climbed them. When they had food, she used them for exercise, ran up them until she was winded. She could do little else except continue the exercises David devised. But she hadn't. And she had accepted Uncle Laurent's invitation too quickly. "And why was Martin not here to meet me?"

Laurent shook his head. "MI6. Who would ask a Spaniard to meet you at a French train station frequented by Nazis? We are forced to reinterpret our instructions, I'm afraid."

She loosed her grip. "I have seen. Initially they were most helpful in organizing our group, but in the last year we have experienced betrayals."

He nodded. "As have we. We are now confident that some in MI6 cannot be trusted, though we don't know who they are." He caught his breath. "When we reach my house, you should sleep. Martin will come at dusk. You have clothes for climbing?"

"In my bag, yes. And boots."

Three burros ambled in a careless maze, searching for a stem of hay. A small house rose beyond, emerging from a cluster of rocks and alders. Laurent climbed steps carved into the side of the mountain, reached his door, and shoved the heavy wooden panel. He looked inside, stepped back, and motioned her in. "The bedroom is in the back. I shall wake you when it is time."

The kitchen was narrow and the hallway short. She closed the bedroom door, removed her shoes and dress, slipped into her climbing pants, and slid the waxed-papered envelope inside her shirt. She dropped the pocketknife Pascal had given her inside her pants pocket, lay back on the soft mattress, and let the stillness take her.

* * *

Something stirred near the door. Nicole tensed, wrapped her fingers around the knife, and turned. Laurent stood in the doorway, holding a tray.

"Martin is here. You must ready yourself." He seemed tense, slid the tray onto the bedside table, and left the room.

She swung her feet to the floor and pulled her boots on, laced them, swallowed the water and pastry Laurent had left, then slipped out the back into a blue dusk. Mountains rose, jagged peaks in stark relief against a cloudless sky. The picture of simplicity. A young man, tall and lithe, stood in dark clothes, just visible in the waning light. A thin white kerchief tied around his neck shown clear beneath the liquid light of the moon.

Laurent handed her the bag, the corded drawstrings replaced with shoulder straps. "I have placed sausages, cheese, and bread for you inside. Also, wine and water."

She patted his arm and smiled. "Thank you, Uncle. It is quite heavy. Perhaps I should leave the wine."

"As you wish. Martin will show you where to refill the water bottle along the way."

Sleep had taken her far from the little valley, and the darkening peaks seemed more a residue of her dreams than the creation of evening. The boy trotted up a goat path. She followed, her breath coming in even depths, the air beguiling and sweet. Her legs tingled with life. She had almost forgotten what it was like to be in the mountains.

The trail switched back, and Saint-Girons lay silvered in moonlight. White stone houses coiled around the southern end of the valley between the obscurity of pine and alder. Red slate roofs melded into blue, and yellow embers shimmered from the windows. She glimpsed the kerchief as she jogged along a path that meandered up and out of the flat peninsula toward a ragged collection of trees. Beyond them, summits rose clear and brilliant, still as distant as they had appeared from below.

Darkness grew, the moon effulgent above the death of day. A breeze chilled her skin beneath her sweat-damp coat, and she shivered, her pace dwindling from the grade. A snowdrift crossed the goat trail, and she slowed beneath a rock face, the first they had encountered. Above it, trees encircled a grassy plain. Martin motioned for her to come. She pushed ahead until she reached him, knelt beside him, and placed her hands on damp earth to gulp diluted air.

"Drink, rest, stretch, and we climb." Martin's French emerged like lines of a children's poem.

She fell back against the earth, pulled her legs to her chest, straightened, allowed the muscles in her back to ease, and drank a heavy draft of the moonlit night.

Martin stirred beside her. "Now we climb."

* * *

Nicole drew a ragged breath, her fingers pushing into the palms of the leather gloves Laurent had left in her bag. He'd removed the fingertips, explained that she could feel the rock and know she wasn't grasping ice. An hour earlier, she'd caught sight of Martin between moon and stone and admired his deftness. Now she wished for him to stop. She pulled herself atop a rock and searched the blue calm. The boy waited on a narrow plain but turned and jogged toward another face. She followed, her legs quivering, the peaks appearing no closer.

* * *

Time was a measure of exhaustion and pain. She thought only of placing her feet so they wouldn't slip, watched for ice on the edges of the rock, and refused to consider her weariness. She pressed her fingers into jagged cracks, squeezed and pulled, then wedged her toes into the space that had held her hands. One reach, one pull, one push. Her lungs burned, and her arms quivered. She paused, allowed her head to rest against the rock, but only for a moment.

"One hour." The words came from above, and she looked up at a protruding ledge. Martin squatted, a shadow against the thin blue, his hand extended. With his other, he pointed to a plateau beyond. "One hour is light. We eat and sleep, yes?"

She nodded and reached up.

* * *

The sky was gray. Martin dragged her up the final ledge. Grass lay matted along a shelf no more than eighty meters wide. Pines emerged from the cleft beneath the jagged wall.

She swayed, consumed thin air, and fought to remain upright as Martin surveyed the emerging valley. He motioned her toward the granite face, urged her out of sight and tapped his water bottle, then pointed to the trickle emerging from beneath the rock. "Drink, eat, and sleep."

Pain dampened her face. The last hour had seemed a lifetime. She drank, refilled her bottle, and scuttled her pack beneath the largest pine, slid beneath it and found more peace than she'd known in weeks. She tore a piece from the baguette and discovered that Laurent had sliced the saucisson and cheese. She blessed him, offered thanks for the food, pulled the pack behind her back, and eased her stiffening legs beneath the blanket.

The saucisson was rich and tasty. She ate a few slices and surrendered. The wool against her cheek brought a comfort like David's hands, his skin rough from gun cleaner and high altitudes, he'd told her. And from the exercises he did in the cellar, she suspected. So, how could his touch have been so comforting? She'd not known such tenderness since her Papa died. Or such adoration. She shouldn't be thinking of him, but it was a comfort knowing she was loved. She would stop the madness of remembrance when this was over, and she didn't need solace... when she was safe, and David's arms were wrapped tightly around her.

* * *

The storm had stilled. White drifts swooped and dove, lifted gracefully over the sports field and beyond the fence. David eased his chair back, went through the checklist, and reached for the throttles. He released the brakes, thrust across the peaks, lifted over pines, and flew on silent wings to Antwerp, Ghent, wherever she might be. He soared above the empty white, surveying plane trees as they pierced a brightening sky. He held at altitude, wished beyond hope, then put down at Saint Peter's Terminal where kiosks brewed coffee and tea, and coal smoke filtered from tunnels where passengers bustled to trains. There were no Wehrmacht troops, no queues of prisoners, no sick and dying airmen. Young girls walked without fear, and old men strolled without shame. She stood facing him, her smile beyond anything he'd known—

"Something wrong, Lieutenant?"

He stirred, straightened in his chair, nodded at Swanson shifting uncomfortably, snow falling in clumps from his pant legs. "No why?"

"You look sort of lost, sir. Didn't notice when I came in."

"I've had that look since they gave me these bars, Corporal."

"You're a born leader, sir. Most noncoms gotta go through OCS to get that look."

He nodded. "So, where do you think I should lead you?"

Swanson straightened. "Vogt, the friendly feldwebel that speaks good English, was looking for you at the barracks."

"The older one? I've seen you talking. Thought you were buddies."

Swanson fidgeted. "He's a Kraut, sir." More snow slid off the boy's boots. "Vogt said Schneider wants you in his office. The men are worried since you embarrassed him at chapel."

"You think I should expect a reprisal?"

"I guess so, sir." The boy looked away.

"I don't believe Schneider would wait this long to put me in front of a firing squad."

Swanson shrugged. "Unless he's wanting to make you sweat."

He stood, checked his smile. "Thanks for your encouragement. And Corporal?"

"Yes sir?"

"There must be a leak in the roof. Seems to be a puddle forming around your feet. There's a mop in the closet. Think you can clean it up before you leave? I keep my office clean."

* * *

An eruption rattled Nicole's bones and brought her upright. She stared through pine needles at a darkened sky. Martin stood partially hidden by an outcropping of rocks, staring at clouds filling the evening with threat.

She caught his gaze, lightning streaking across the valley. "Are we safe here?"

He pointed beyond the overhang. "Rain." He lifted wavering fingers and drew them down. "Good." He drew his fingers to the south. "No good."

She nodded. If the rain came straight down, they could crawl beneath the overhang. If it blew in from the north, they had no protection. She gathered her blanket around her shoulders. Searing pain coursed her sides and ascended the backs of her arms. She fisted her swollen hands, crawled toward the pool of water, wrapped herself in her blanket, and plunged her hands into the icy trough. The ache grew, and she put them beneath her arms until the throbbing eased.

Martin moved close. "You..." The words appeared irretrievable. He extended his wine.

"Thank you, no. Perhaps tonight when we climb."

He reached for her right hand and placed it between his calloused ones. Her fingertips were raw, the pads near bleeding. "You not to climb." He was silent for a moment, struggling with the French. "Your hands not to trust."

What could she do? Certainly not go back.

Martin rubbed his neck. "Tonight we cross glacier. How do you say? We not to climb."

"That wouldn't require my hands. Yes, I understand."

Her answer brought more questions. Martin struggled for a moment. "More easy to see on glacier maybe." He nodded, proud of his achievement. "And is more cold. One day more."

He removed his heavy coat and turned it inside out, the fleece lining a billowy white. It would be less visible against the ice. He removed his cap, stuffed it in his pocket and extended his hand. "You see hat, you to come. No hat, you not to come."

She nodded and tightened her blanket around her shoulders. It was more ivory than white, but certainly less visible than her clothes. She mimicked tying it around her neck and smiled.

He grinned, nodded. "Yes! Good!"

Chapter XXII

Schneider shuffled forms, grunted at the heel stomp, and waved the old feldwebel out of his office. His chiseled jaw glistened like ice as he pulled a folder from his desk, thumbed a photograph from the bottom, and shoved it toward him.

David stepped from behind the chair, his pulse hammering the unease he was sure the blue-eyed Lothario wanted him to feel. The image was grainy, taken in low light, the film pushed in development. A narrow-faced man with a receding hairline sat opposite a young woman, his smile radiant beneath a chandelier. The woman sat with her back to the camera, her dark hair curled and loose about her shoulders, her head turned slightly— The blood drained from his face, and he stared at the curve of the slender neck, the skin, the lines he had traced with his hand.

"I have been asked to identify these enemy agents." Schneider's voice riveted him. "The man is known. I have but to confirm it. He is an MI6 officer known to be friendly with the Soviets. His name is Émile, though that is perhaps a code name. As you can see, the woman—"

"Where was this taken?" He forced the air from his lungs.

"You are not denying it? I expected you to insist that you didn't know her." Schneider's voice shook, his anger unconcealed.

He met the blue ice with a resolve he didn't feel. "Could we discuss this outside?"

Schneider's chin rose. "There is no need, Lieutenant."

"All the same, Herr Oberleutnant, unless you want to discuss our pact more fully…"

Schneider glanced at the goons huddled in the foyer. He pitched the photograph into a drawer, closed, and locked it. "As you wish, Lieutenant."

* * *

David was winded before they made it to the guard shack, his legs pumping through deep snow beside Schneider who walked easily on packed truck tracks.

"Our agreement, Lieutenant, was that Nicole would be allowed to leave the country, not that she be given free rein to act as an operative for MI6."

"I repeat my question, Herr Oberleutnant. Where was the photograph taken?"

Schneider stopped, a venomous glare locking onto his. "Paris, as you likely know."

He waited, stepped into the tracks, and let Schneider walk behind. "If I had known, I wouldn't have asked."

"Since you've taken the liberty, I will also repeat myself, Lieutenant. Our agreement was to allow her to leave the country, not to afford her the opportunity to work as an enemy agent."

"Is Paris not between Belgium and Spain? Seems to me there were only two places they could take her—Spain or Switzerland. You told me yourself any attempt to cross the Channel would put her in the hands of the Wehrmacht."

Schneider turned onto the road and allowed him to catch up. "If she were merely being taken out of the Reich, why was she dining at La Salle Principale on Christmas Eve?"

He was following again, but he couldn't restrain a smile. She'd been in Paris six days ago and was well on her way. He stopped. "The message I passed on said her removal was imperative, Herr Oberleutnant. They would have no idea what might be jeopardized by her remaining in Belgium. Why wouldn't they have sent a key operative to remove her?"

"It was a party, Lieutenant, and she was accompanying an intelligence officer."

He waited for Schneider to turn. "Not a very exclusive party, apparently. Your photographer was there. Besides, her debriefing was procedural. It likely required a higher up, don't you imagine?"

"My imagination is not so fertile. You cannot produce something more believable?"

He looked back at the gate. "So, are we going for a walk like we did at the interrogation center? I miss those, though not the one with your Walther at my head."

Schneider pivoted and marched back toward his office. "I believe you have had your constitutional for the day. That is what you called them, yes?"

He refused to follow, raising his voice at the German's retreat. "This British agent is in the company of a French woman like those your officers occupy themselves with. That's the conclusion you'll reach, isn't it, Heinrich?"

Schneider stopped. "Are you suggesting that I deny knowing her, Lieutenant? Has it occurred to you that they might already know that we were friends?"

Had Schneider slipped? Or was he planting doubts? "Then you'll be risking your life for Nicole as I've risked mine for Élodie. That was our agreement."

* * *

David paced the library floor and wiped his hands on his pants. He stopped, faced Hanson. "Sir, Schneider's girl was part of the White Rose. Maybe not like these kids, risking their lives every day, but she distributed literature early in the war and protested Professor Stein's mistreatment. She and her brother were stridently anti-Nazi."

The captain had confiscated his chair. "And her brother's now Wehrmacht. He was Schneider's clerk in Belgium, wasn't he? So why couldn't she have changed her stripes, too?"

"She's Jewish. The Krauts took several in her family. How pro-Nazi can she be? And Henri got word to the Partisans and had Nicole extracted. The photos confirm it. He's a proven asset." It pleased him, sounded like what a real spook might say.

"Here's the pitch, Dremmer. It's not just your life at stake. You'd be jeopardizing our operations. And what do you have to gain by contacting this woman?"

He leaned on the library desk. "An ally, sir. One with inside information. She has Schneider's ear and can reach people and do things we can't." *And tell me about Nicole's relationship with Schneider.* The thought shook him.

Hanson stood, his finger in the air. "Do you believe she will convince this Nazi to withhold your girl's identity and turn on the man who's kept her safe for years?"

"She was Nicole's best friend. They shared the cause Nicole is risking her life for. And nobody is asking Élodie to turn on Schneider." He stretched to meet Hanson's glare. "If I'm right, she doesn't know Schneider is pursuing Nicole or her friends who just might have been her friends, too." A frisson ran down his back. "And I have a plan, sir."

"Better be a good one."

It wasn't. Not yet. "Schneider wants to know our lead time, sir. I sense it every time we talk. I need to convince him that we receive good information and receive it fast."

The captain stared. "And how do you plan to show him that, Dremmer?"

"I arrange for his girl to be attacked by a band of hellions, *Jungsturm* maybe, and then rescued by the good guys."

"You have connections with the *Jungsturm*, Lieutenant?"

"Won't be necessary, sir. Here's the pit…" He caught himself. "The attack won't really happen. I'll get Élodie to tell it the way we want it, say she was rescued by Resistance. She can't report it to the Nazis, and I'll ask her to wait to contact Schneider. In the meantime, I'll tell the oberleutnant, assure him she's safe, and say our operatives kept her from being harmed."

Hanson tapped his mouth with a clenched fist. "What do you do if she doesn't go along with it, or if she reports you showing up at her house? Can you do what has to be done if she leans the wrong direction?"

"I feel like I know this woman, sir. She was committed. I can find an angle—"

"You play any angles you want but make it clear that her Luftwaffe lunch ticket is about to be punched. Tell her he's planning on running off with your Nicole, if you want, but convince her not to turn on us. Make it clear that if she doesn't stay on our side, it'll all be over."

He couldn't hold the excitement. Or his concerns at Hanson's suggestions. "So, what do we tell Swanson about the German kid taking my place on the work crew?"

Hanson waved his hand in the air. "Nothing. I'll think of a way to keep him out of the game while you're making your move. You work up a plan. A good one. I want every contingency covered, and I want you giving yourself a couple hours leeway. And—"

He held his breath, waited for the other shoe to drop. "And what, sir?"

"If you don't make it back, we'll have to cover for this Bertram kid."

"I'll make it back, sir."

Hanson squinted. "I said *every* contingency, Dremmer."

He nodded. "Then he'll come back with the crew, sir. He'll keep his head down and answer to my name at roll call. Swanson can be confronted, told to keep his mouth shut. Bertram can go back with the next day's commando group. We'll make the switch then."

"And if you're not there?"

"Then I'll be dead. The kid changes clothes and slips away. He can buy me time, not ensure my success. That's all we can ask."

Hanson shook his head. "And if the Germans find you before we can get him back?" Hanson stroked his neck. "Here's the pitch, Dremmer. If you don't make it back *when* you plan to, we'll deal with Swanson ourselves. Either way, Bertram won't be coming back with us."

His heart stuttered. "What are you saying, sir?"

"You like Swanson, and so do I. But if things go wrong, he'll meet with an accident that'll keep him from ever talking to the Krauts again. You capiche?"

Chapter XXIII

Jesse wheeled himself to the edge of the porch. Silver bells jangled in the wind between red velvet bows, of all things. The getup rasped his nerves. Maybe they'd take them down now that Christmas had passed. He turned away and faced a blistering gust. It wasn't in him to consider why people did what they did or said what they said. He had no need to understand the strangeness of the way they figured things and didn't want to make them less revolting. A man's duty was to do what was right, and there wasn't any doubt about what that was. The cost didn't matter. To contend otherwise was to cover an excuse with a lie. It was why Delores prickled him the way she did.

He stared at the lone cedar and saw David swinging his ax into the stump of its mate. A tear blistered his cheek, and he cursed the wind for what it could do to a man his age. Truth be told, being on the ranch, the place his father started, the place he'd spent his life building, the place David sweated and bled over was worse than being at Naomi's. Seeing the lack of regard, knowing the cattle were as neglected as the land, was like having a child taken from your arms and left in need. It would have been better for him to have died. That way, he could have left believing his sister was who he'd thought her to be.

She and Delores had no business here. Neither of them. Theirs was a world of drapes and ribbons and worries about what was or wasn't fashionable. This place was real, with real troubles and real recompense, but he was helpless to put it back together. Nothing was as it should be, especially him.

The door creaked open behind him. "Jesse, what are you doing out here?" Naomi's voice was shrill against the wind. She'd been hiding something, and he hadn't the endurance to pry it out of her.

"Just enjoying the peace." It wouldn't go unchallenged, and he knew it.

"Peace? It's freezing cold! Come back in before you catch your death."

He watched from the corner of his eye but refused her the satisfaction of turning. She shivered in the doorway as if her display would move him to do as she wanted. "I'll be in directly. If you're cold, best go in yourself."

The door squeaked closed, shutting out some light, but he still felt her moving behind him. "Jesse, if what Delores said is bothering you, I'm sure she and Isaac will be safe here. I'll let her know you're concerned. She won't stay long."

The words enraged him so that he couldn't hold it in. "If we leave, she won't come back at all. She has no intention of it. Why you can't see that is beyond me."

Naomi moved around his chair and pushed between him and the cedar, then settled against the railing, bending to meet his stare. "What are you saying?"

He shook his head. "She's staying here for Morgan. They've been planning this for a while. With her here, it'll make it harder for me to get the place back. At least that's what they think. If this goes to court, they'll claim she was acting as my agent, and she'll say whatever he tells her to, just like she does whatever else he wants."

Naomi's glower drifted past his to what had been in plain sight all along. "Are you saying that Delores and Morgan are lovers?"

"If that's what you want to call it. Appear more like alley cats to me." He let the wind cover his choked words. "I asked you before what it was that made you think she'd make the boy a wife. So what was it?"

Naomi fluttered, her head whipping like a weathervane. "She seemed—they were both lonely and needed someone."

"I don't recall the boy saying he needed anybody." He worked to hold the fire in. "Who was she with before David came along?" The thought had haunted him, the girl's taking pleasure from men the way she did. Even Morgan. It didn't seem likely that David was the first.

"Whyever would you— How would I know that?"

Something more than cold was rattling her. Her eyes were skittering like chickens in a hailstorm. He turned his chair toward her. "You were never one to not say a thing straight out, Naomi. What's keeping you from it now?"

"Jesse, I— You're asking me as if I knew."

He leaned in, pinning her with his stare. "That's plain enough. The puzzle is why you're not telling me."

She turned, her hands covering her face.

He raised his voice into the wind and moved his chair in front of her. "Tell me now, or I'll send you both back, and I'll be the one staying."

He watched as she leaned over him, moving her hands to the knob, grabbing hold as if the wind might sweep her off the porch. He made his voice steady, met the one thing he feared most. "This has something to do with Robert, doesn't it?"

She nodded but didn't turn. "Maybe, Jesse. I'm not sure."

"Isaac is your grandson, not mine. That's the whole of it."

"That's not— I don't know, Jesse." Her shoulders stirred in a heavy tremble.

He wheeled his useless legs before the door and spoke to the twisted face framed within a quarter pane. "If you don't know, you strongly suspect it. That's the truth of it."

Her secret spilled into the yellow effervescence of the window, her tears showing clear enough what she'd been carrying.

He nodded and rolled his chair back, let her escape the truth he'd finally taken in. She had arranged it, made sure David and Delores got together, even enlisted his support in letting the boy know what was expected of him, all to save her the embarrassment of having an illegitimate grandchild.

Chapter XXIV

Nicole huddled on a ledge at the base of an escarpment, the glacier a hundred meters below, and pulled her blanket across her shoulders. Cold had cramped her feet, scaled her thighs, and brought an ache that couldn't be appeased. She shivered and fought back tears.

Martin said it would be the most difficult night, told her they would start early in the evening, take the steepest path they'd taken since losing the rope, and stay within the shadows of the stone face. When it was dark, they would climb to the crest. She rubbed her swollen hands and winced at the burning along her sides. Doubts surfaced like tulips in thawing earth, but if she could hold out, by tomorrow evening they would be in cover, perhaps in the sheepherder's cabin feasting on fresh lamb and sleeping in a warm bed. She had but to keep moving.

She sat up, smoothed the scree beneath her, and stared across the glacier. Nothing stirred. The ancient enmity of sun and ice quickened her pulse. David had spoken of such things, the awe he felt in the hills, the wind in tall grass, or oak leaves shimmering along a creek bed. The memory brought a smile that cracked her lips.

She reached beneath the blanket to loosen her boots, already dreading reattaching the oversized crampons. Martin had added straps to secure them, but that kept blood from reaching her feet. She hated asking him to loosen them, then tighten them again before they went on. And it prolonged the danger. Next time, she would be prepared, would have a heavier coat, warmer climbing pants, and her own crampons. And she would be in better condition, able to climb the rock and stay off the ice.

Next time. She shivered, wanted to recline, but when sleep came, her legs crumpled, and she slid to the ledge and woke. She pulled the blanket over her head and fought the brightness of the afternoon sun.

The second day had been colder than the first, making sleep difficult. Yesterday she'd slept less. And then the loss of the rope.

Martin had taken it from his shoulder and left it in the shadow of the glacier. She'd not seen it, had stepped across it, and tripped. He'd grabbed her, held to the pick but lost the rope. They'd made so little progress since. Now they were near the summit. The wind burned like fire, and the cold knifed through her wet boots and climbing pants. Only her breath was warm.

Rocks popped, and she jerked the blanket from her face. Martin crouched beside her.

"You not to sleep?" He extended his bottle. "You want from the wine, yes?"

She shook her head, tensed. "No, thank you." A shiver ran down her spine.

He looked across the valley, shielding his eyes. "Maybe four hours light."

That was what she would have guessed.

"I don't sleep. You don't sleep. We maybe to climb?" He shrugged. "No one is looking, maybe. We are high. More hard to see. And we remain—" He searched for words.

"In the shadows?" She felt the knot in her stomach relax. "It's safe then?"

He shrugged. "Maybe more safe than stay. More far to go." He pointed toward an area of small crevasses broken and spread in a series of alluvial shards. It took her breath.

* * *

Nicole pushed herself against the wall of ice, the staff Martin had fashioned for her propped against the opposing grade. Her arms burned, her raw fingertips recoiling from the wood. Handholds were useless on ice. Perhaps a hundred meters above, the Spaniard slammed his pick into the azure mass and pulled himself onto an upturned sheet. He slipped into a shadow and looked back. In the last hour, they had climbed less than two hundred meters. She watched as Martin removed his pack and settled back to wait.

He hollered and threw his climbing pick as she reached the bottom of the upshift. The pick wedged a few meters away. She trudged toward it and felt her strength drain into the cold. And it wasn't yet dark.

She found a section with sharp edges, slammed the ax above her head, pierced the ice at the end of her swing and pulled. Her crampons wedged against the opposing ridge. She'd gained less than a meter and was considerably more exhausted.

"My hand, yes please."

She looked up, saw him perched above her, hanging precariously from the top of a shard. She extended the ax, motioned for him to secure himself, but hadn't the breath to speak. He slammed it into the ice and grabbed her wrist with his other hand. She lifted slowly, then shot above the ice, her legs flailing. Both were breathless, he on his back and she on her hands and knees in the shadow of the rock face with ice all around.

"Is not possible. We eat and rest before to climb. Is not so hard, maybe."

"We'll stay in the shadows, won't we?"

He nodded, and she sat up, smiling her gratitude. "This broken ice along the edges—you called it serac? Your French is improving. I didn't know that word."

He returned her smile. "Yes, is trying to return."

"I have saved most of my saucisson and cheese. Would you like some?"

His smile drained. "No! Why you do this? Eat! Always to climb you eat!"

She recoiled and edged away. "It's only— I will be fine, I'm sure."

"You eat! You fall. Freeze maybe!"

"Yes, of course. I'll eat. But do you have enough?"

"You eat!" He pushed his back against the ice and shook his head.

She hadn't considered that her weakness might have come from a lack of food. The cold consumed calories. It had become a habit, always keeping something in reserve. She took a bite of saucisson, chewed slowly, and pulled a piece from the baguette. Then the cheese—all tasty. She ate more, drank water she'd kept close to her breast. After a few minutes, the trembling in her hands eased.

* * *

Glaciers sizzled within a haze, the moon casting sable shards across the gray. Nicole's sides throbbed, and her hands flamed beneath her arms as she sheltered them from a blistering wind. Somewhere beyond them Spain began, a place where Nazis didn't hang people, the Gestapo didn't incite more fear than the heart could bear, and rules from agencies no one had heard of weren't dispensed to punish those whose produce kept the tyrants alive. If she could only keep going.

Martin had lied. It had been a lie born of mercy, and she was grateful, wouldn't have gone on had she known. The climb to the crest had been more grueling than anything she'd imagined. Her body ached, but peace lay before her. Freedom and rest. And she was grateful even for his anger, had needed all the strength she could hold in her shrunken stomach.

The boy moved ahead, his coat turned right side out against the peaks, his kerchief a candle in the wind. Her blanket flapped about her as she crept along the ledge Martin had shimmied across minutes earlier.

The abyss at her back was as dark and unplumbed as hell itself. Still, she scraped her boots along the rock, clasped the fissures on her right and prayed for her fingers to hold. Her blanket tugged at her waist as something bound her foot. Her stomach seized, almost pulling her over, and her thoughts froze. She pushed and her foot slipped, her weight heaving as the darkness swept her legs into the breathless dark.

She grabbed a fissure along the ledge, held with all her strength as her knee cracked into stone, her chin slamming granite. She listened without breath as rocks bounced along the wall, her arms quivering as she lifted her leg toward the ledge. The toe of her boot caught then skated across loose scree. It dropped again, her weight suspended from her folded arms and elbows, quivering in a convulsive urge to let the struggle end. She refused the impulse, drew her strength into a burst, and kicked.

Her heel caught the ledge, and she scooted her toe into the wall, drew herself up, and laced her fingers as far as she could inside the fissure. She heaved herself higher and rested, pulled her other leg onto the shelf, and steadied on trembling knees, battling the compulsion to cling to the small safety she had found, to stay until Martin rescued her. Easing her head around, she looked down. A chill ascended her spine. The ledge was narrow, little wider than the length of her boots. The boy couldn't help. There wasn't room for them both.

She reached higher, pulled herself to her feet, and looked at Martin waiting at the end of the ledge. He stood motionless, his mouth wide, her doom reflected in his stare. Bile rose to her throat, and she ejected what was left of the saucisson and cheese. A chill washed over her face, and her stomach settled.

She raised her foot above the freezing vomit, forcing her boot across the rock. Paralyzing pain rose from her knee. She forced a step, lifted her left foot along the ledge, and pulled her right foot after her. The rubble pile where Martin was perched seemed hours away. She urged herself to the side, one small step and then another. Her knee held and grew less spiteful, and the boy gleamed encouragement in the moonlight as she edged toward him.

* * *

"Your leg is bad?" Martin's voice had been unsteady since her slip.

"Only bruised, I think." Nicole stared across the blue landscape and caught a line of darkness. "How much farther before we reach cover?"

"Not much far. One hour, maybe."

An hour to the tree line, and the descent would become a hike. She breathed in darkness and smiled. "Thank you for all you've done."

He wiped his face on his sleeve. "Is nothing. My father is shot by Nazi."

"Your father? I'm terribly sorry. How long has it been?"

"One year in this month."

"Only a year. He was a guide? Is that why they executed him?"

"Yes."

She smiled, doubted he could read her gratitude in the gloom.

He nodded "You will require of me on next climb, yes?"

It took her breath. "Of course. I will ask for you." She shuddered. "Next time."

* * *

The pine was sparse, the air sweet. Nicole trod above the hollows, her knee stiff as she fought through snow. She slipped between the trees, followed Martin's fleeting shadow, caught a flicker of his kerchief in the growing light. The darkness thinned, and she found herself before a sudden slope, the snow deep against the embankment.

Martin stood, a smile covering his face. He sat at the edge of a snow chute, beckoning her with his head, pushed off and skidded like an otter on his back. She could just make out his form at the base of a ravine, his arms flailing in the waking light, bidding her to come.

She hadn't asked, had been too afraid, but she knew now. They were beyond the reach of Nazis. The sky was streaked with scarlet, the prescience of morning laboring against the gray. She stepped to the edge, sat, removed her pack, and pushed into the growing light, helpless and free, careening past rocks and trees, held on track by the slope itself. Snow blinded her, the wind stinging her skin before she slowed and found herself at the bottom of an arroyo, her arms and legs splayed. Martin laughed, clapped, and reached to pick up her pack. She stood, and he pointed down the valley. A house, nestled near the edge of a stream, was partially hidden in snow, its red roof sparkling in the early light.

Chapter XXV

David swayed, the rhythm of the tracks pushing him into a ruffled oblivion. He forced his eyes wide, his gaze drifting through the bunched kriegies in the cattle car. For two days he'd worked with the young German, carrying ties, leveling trenches, and had spoken less than a hundred words. He was sure Bertram understood what he wanted. The boy just hadn't agreed.

The brakes set, the slow descent into camp almost complete. The car jolted as those behind were slowed in a quick succession of heaves. He pulled himself to his feet and shuffled to the opposite side to peer through cracks between the boards. A late wind pushed gray broth from the west, piled it high, and stood it in a boiling heap. He edged through kriegies, waited for the gefreiter to slide the door back, and felt Swanson move in behind him. What was he going to do with the boy? He couldn't allow—

The squeal of dry bearings shivered his spine, and he readied himself for another rousting. Hanson stood at the edge of the bahnhof, engaged him with his stare, then sauntered in the direction of the sportplatz. David jumped, righted himself and edged toward the corner of the building Hanson had stepped behind. Someone touched his shoulder, and he spun. The old feldwebel stood above him, gaunt and angular, his legs wide beneath a frame designed to carry more weight.

A grin parted thin lips. "Oberleutnant Schneider has requested to meet with you."

"At his office?"

"That is correct." The feldwebel shrugged apologetically.

David stepped away from the troops forming lines to be counted and dipped his head toward the obergefreiter and spoke to the feldwebel "You going to tell him where I'm going?"

Hanson emerged at the corner of the building, caught his eyes, and shuffled away as if inspecting the condition of the kriegies.

The feldwebel grated something official, Schneider's name emerging within the mix. The old sergeant nodded and pointed his rifle in the direction of Heinrich's office.

The snow had all but melted, the ruts channeling runoff into the camp. David avoided the deepest slush, and stepped on snow when he could. He stopped outside the command center and cleaned his boots in an unsoiled drift.

Vogt stood beside the door as if he were a bellman. "Anon, Lieutenant."

Warm air rushed past as he entered, the interior clean and polished, part of a world he'd left behind. Schneider stood off-center facing the bookcase and motioned over his shoulder, his drink tilted straight. The door closed, and he turned. "You appear worn, Lieutenant."

"Thank you, Herr Oberleutnant. You appear relaxed." He stood at ease, hands behind his back.

Heinrich raised his glass. "Would you care for a brandy? It's quite good."

"No thanks. I'm on duty."

"No, Lieutenant, you are not. For you, the war is over. Have you forgotten?"

"We see that differently."

Schneider stepped forward, his hand opening toward a chair. "We see many things differently. Please, have a seat."

He sank into the soft leather and fought the temptation to ease.

Schneider sat, his lithe frame more elastic than he'd seen. "Tell me, David, why would an officer volunteer as a work commando? Captain Hanson tells me the work is grueling, and I know your rations are somewhat limited."

"Somewhat? We've been over this, Heinrich. I've been asked to look out for the men, to make sure they aren't abused." The brandy looked delicious. He turned toward the bookshelf and watched his nemesis from the corner of his eye.

"I don't believe you." Schneider leaned forward. "You are involved in espionage."

He forced himself to breathe. "While carrying ties? You give me too much credit."

Schneider shook his finger. "You are being watched, Lieutenant."

His heart pounded, but he managed a grin. "Then I'll prove to be an excellent diversion."

Heinrich coughed. "You are hiding something. I am certain of this."

It was time to turn the tables. "I am honoring our agreement, Heinrich. Nothing more. Don't make it impossible for me to fulfill my part of the bargain."

"And why should I believe this?"

He tried to appear sincere. "Because you know that nothing is more important to me than the principles of our agreement."

The German spread his hands. "The principal's name being Nicole, of course."

He straightened, concealed the anger that rose at the man's recklessness. "The other principal being Élodie, Herr Oberleutnant."

Schneider spread his hands. "I told you before, it is perfectly safe to speak here. I have taken the liberty of having our dinner brought to my office. I hope you've not made plans."

"Nothing I can't reschedule." He rubbed his sweaty palms across his pants. "Are you trying to bring me under suspicion, Herr Oberleutnant?"

"I am not. Would you care to wash for dinner?"

"A shower would be perfect. Do you have a fresh uniform, by chance?"

"Just your hands and face. You remember where the water closet is, I'm sure."

* * *

"So, what did he give you to eat? I want details."

David caught the captain's grin. "Schnitzel, sir, with asparagus and potatoes."

Hanson's mouth went wide. "Good, was it?"

"Not as good as the beef rouladen on Christmas Eve, sir, but yeah, it was good."

The captain shook his head. "You sure he's not fattening you up for slaughter?"

He grinned. "I'm willing to pursue that line of investigation, sir."

Hanson scraped his chin. "That's it? This Kraut sent for you just to invite you to dinner? Didn't want to discuss literature or politics?"

He took a breath. "He asked about me going on commando detail so much."

The captain glared. "What exactly did he say?"

"He asked if I were involved in some sort of espionage, but he was obviously—"

"Then we're canning your visit to the fräulein. It's out of the question."

Electricity charged his spine. "I'm certain I allayed his suspicions. It's safe, sir."

Hanson marched to the bookshelves, turned, and planted his fists on his hips. "Here's the pitch, Lieutenant. It was *never* safe. The risks now are unacceptable. You'll go on work detail tomorrow, but you'll let Bertram know it's off. And don't work with the boy if you can help it. Any contact will be C and Q, coincidental and quick. If there's a chance anyone can see or hear you, walk away. You capiche?"

"Yes sir." He worked to steady himself. "Sir, when Schneider spoke with me before, he said he'd been checking up on me. I told him I'd be checking up on him, too."

"I remember."

"I believe he invited me to dinner to see if I'd found anything. He wants to know our lead time. It could be days before we found out if he moved his girl, got her out of harm's—"

Hanson's hands went up. "I understand that. But why would this woman help us?"

"We have a hold on her, sir. She has a conscience. They both do."

"Lieutenant, Schneider's not just German, he's a Nazi. He's had to sit on his conscience to get where he is. Don't count on him not being able to do it again. Or her, either."

The captain was listening. Chinks of light shone through the veneer. "I don't doubt she'll have reservations, sir, but if I can convince her that I won't hurt the oberleutnant, I believe she'll work with us. It'll give me a chance to glean information about his past, things to impress him."

"Here's the drill, Lieutenant. These kids can learn enough to impress him. Since she worked with this bunch, they just might know who to ask. And I don't believe you're ready to take her out if she indicates that she'll tell Schneider you showed up on their doorstep."

"You mean *kill* her, sir?" The air froze in his throat. "I couldn't—"

"And Swanson hasn't been dealt with, either. Tell your Kraut buddy with a conscience that you want the corporal removed. That's my condition."

"Sir, if I had to take the girl out, my agreement with Schneider *would* collapse, no matter who he thinks is responsible. And we don't know what might happen to Swanson."

"Lieutenant, I'm not going to let you hamper our operation with worries about the corporal or Schneider's woman. Miss Serat, either. Forget about her. She should be in Spain by now. Whatever happens to any of them beyond this point is not your responsibility."

He worked to steady his legs. "Yes sir."

The captain tapped his mouth, then lifted his head. "Lieutenant, I'm going with you tomorrow. I need to assess the situation for myself."

Chapter XXVI

A frozen cauldron stirred within the gloom mounting in the west. David inched his way to the platform, his hands refusing to warm, already feeling the sting of the approaching storm.

Hanson pulled at his jacket. "Looks like a blizzard. Thought they'd cancel this detail."

He grunted. "Kriegies are cheap, sir. They could freeze the whole crew and have a new one made up by noon." He blew into his hands. "Not too late to change your mind, Captain."

"I understand this is delicate, Lieutenant."

"I know you do, sir. There's no one more qualified. It's just that a captain volunteering for work detail is noteworthy, and the Krauts are aware of your role."

"Lieutenant, I've submitted complaints to Schneider about the men being overworked. If you tell him I wanted to check it out for myself, why would he question it?"

David pulled out a red scarf he'd fashioned from the tattered long johns he'd traded his cigarettes for. "The man has instincts, sir."

Hanson shook his head. "His instincts didn't keep his boy from being discovered, did they?"

"Swanson isn't Schneider's boy, sir. The oberleutnant just inherited him."

The captain's face reddened. "Well, they have something on him, and the corporal is no less dangerous than if he were helping them willingly."

He saw Swanson standing alone. "He's following procedure now, sir."

"Don't trivialize the corporal's treason, Dremmer. He should never have allowed himself to be drafted onto the committee when they had their claws in him."

* * *

David shuffled behind the captain to the door of the cattle car. The morning chill had eased, the clouds lifting, but dust and cinders still barraged the kriegies. He squinted, caught the old German's stare, jumped down and sidled to Hanson's left.

"The man in the gray wool coat, sir. That's our contact."

Hanson looked away, pretending to listen to the strutting obergefreiter. "Looks like he's about to bust a gut. You sure he's up to this?"

David felt the dread of whatever threat filled the old man's stare. "Something's bothering him, sir. No doubt about it." He scanned the yard, tried to find something amiss. The four sidings to the south were complete, and three main lines were open. Trains pulled through the yard every few minutes, the southbound at speed.

The obergefreiter caught his trepidation, grinned, and pointed to the pile of ties.

He nodded and trudged south. In less than twenty yards, the old man edged beside them, his gate awkward. "Explosion iss one hour!" The head didn't turn. "Go to latrine when iss explosion. Bertram iss vait for you, yes?"

His stomach clinched. "What's going on?"

"You go today. To Wodenstrasse." The wizened face blazed at his ignorance.

"Wait, I—"

The captain grabbed his arm. "What the hell have you gotten us into, Lieutenant?"

His heart shook him. "Keep walking, sir. I didn't plan this." He scuffed before the stack.

Hanson squatted in front of a smaller tie, grabbed it, and pulled. It raised a few inches and dropped. "I can't do this by myself, Dremmer!"

He bent and tugged, lifted it to his waist. "You'll have to distract Swanson, sir."

"You're asking me to babysit Bertram and the corporal both, Lieutenant?"

"Someone will have to tell the corporal that he's not to pry into our operation, sir. If he sees Bertram in my clothes, he'll know something's up."

* * *

David slid the tie in place and waited for the captain to push back, grew impatient, and looked up. Hanson's gaze was fixed above him. He turned, saw Swanson staring back.

"They gave me a level, sir. I'm supposed to make sure the ties is flat. Some of the boys was setting them uneven."

Hanson dropped his chin. "Tell him!"

He felt the crushing power of the captain's charge and looked at Swanson. "Corporal, we've been made aware of something that compromises your status. For the time being, you won't be privy to sensitive information. If you see anything, keep it to yourself."

The boy's darting eyes settled on the captain. "I never give them nothin', sir. Not nothin' that could hurt us. You know that, sir. And them sayin' they'd hang the boys in my platoon one at a time. I couldn't let them do that, sir. You know I couldn't."

"Everything should have been disclosed when I recruited you, Corporal!" The veins along Hanson's neck bulged. "We could have avoided this."

Swanson's brow contracted, his Collie face tilting at an odd angle. "But I—" He glanced down. "But we talked, sir— " The boy saw something in Hanson's face and held his tongue.

David slid his hands over his gut. "Check our level, Corporal. Don't draw attention."

The corporal dropped to his knees. "I know everything, all about you going to see Schneider's woman. I won't say nothin'. I never would have."

The captain bent close, his brow drawn tight. "Who told you, Corporal?"

"The old German, sir. He started clearing things through me when we was checking out Lieutenant Dremmer. I just didn't tell him to stop."

"And you were supposed to tell us about today?" David looked at the boy.

"I guess maybe they figured I would." Tears appeared in the boy's eyes. He seemed stunned, had failed the captain. He waited, moved the level, and pointed for the captain to scrape gravel beneath his end. "I just figured you both knew, sir. You can still trust me, sirs, I swear!"

Hanson looked down. "Corporal, this changes everything. I'm requesting that you be shipped out. That's the best I can do."

Swanson rose, his skin gray. "You're gonna let them put me in with the Ivans, sir? Starve me to death?" The boy rose stiffly and staggered toward the next two kriegies.

David's gut tightened. "Isn't there some way we can restrict his access, sir? Keep him in camp? What they threatened— Who could withstand that?"

"He's too good. He found out about your plans, didn't he? And his not informing me that today was the day— that's beyond negligent." The captain's anger seemed to settle. "Get another tie, Lieutenant."

He shivered. "Sir, can't you get him into a medical camp or something?"

"A *medical* camp? He'll be going to a bad boy stalag. Nothing I can do about that. And you're the one with the Kraut buddy. You'll do any requesting that's to be done."

"They won't put him in with the Ivans, then?"

The captain shook his head. "I don't know where he got that."

They reached the stack, and he bent to grab another tie, hoped to save his strength in case the hike to Wodenstrasse turned into a sprint. He raised his head. A train, traveling at speed, thundered beyond their siding.

The old German lurched toward them, Swanson following. "Explosion iss not work!" The words came on a gale between clenched teeth. "Everyone iss wait for you!"

The corporal's head raised. "A diversion, sir." The darkness had lifted from his face. "I can give you that!" He turned to the German. "Is Bertram in place?"

The old man nodded. "Yes, but maybe iss not more time."

A whistle blew at the edge of the yard, a train approaching on the nearer main. Swanson saluted the captain. "What I give them wasn't nothin', sir!" He scrambled toward the track.

An icy bolt shot down David's spine. "Swanson! Stop!"

The corporal sprinted to the track, the train a hundred yards away. The boy stiffened before a cold wind. A whistle blasted, and he stepped onto the rails, spread his arms and looked into the clearing sky. A heavy crack rattled the air, and the boy flew toward them.

David scrambled to his feet, but Hanson grabbed his arm. "Don't waste what he died to give you, Lieutenant! Now *go!*"

Goons ran, kriegies pointing toward the train slicing through the chill. The Wehrmacht formed a perimeter, rifles raised. Swanson lay crushed no more than twenty yards away, blood pooling around his eyes.

David spun. The yard was empty, save a crawler pulling ties from the mound of concrete. He sprinted around the edge of the latrine, found Bertram seated against a rock, hands covering his face. He skidded across gravel and began unbuttoning his jacket.

Bertram raised his head. "There was no bomb. You were not seen?"

"Swanson gave them something else to look at." His fingers shook, refusing the buttons.

Bertram threw his jacket down. "I shall give directions. When I finish, you must repeat."

He nodded, squelching the image of Swanson's porcelain face.

"You will cross Sturmiusweg before reaching Wodenstrasse. Turn left there, go south two houses, and turn right. Follow a path to a small building with a door on the south side between the second and third house. Do you understand?"

"Turn south when I get to Sturmiusweg. Go two houses down. On the west side of the street, there's a small building between the second and third house. Door's on the south side."

"Yes. You will knock on the door and repeat: 'I am one who loved not wisely but too well.' You can remember this?"

"Shakespeare. I'll remember."

The boy nodded. "Othello is your code name. You will be given a key to the house on Wodenstrasse and information on the hen's position. She has been observed all morning. Your route is known. If she leaves the house, they will stop you."

He worked with the boy's jacket, strained to pull it over his shoulders and shoved his cap down. "I've got it. Now, how do I get out of here?"

Bertram pointed toward the chain-wire fence. "There. Do you see where the wire is cut?"

"Looks to be spliced."

"It would seem so. You have only to release three hooks." Bertram pulled the cap low, the scarf hiding his mouth. "If you meet anyone, you will walk with a limp. It will appear you have a reason not to be in uniform. If spoken to, respond only 'Heil Hitler!' You will speak as though you have, perhaps, an injury to the brain. Do you understand?"

"Yes." He forced himself to breathe.

* * *

Ice formed in David's veins, his heart compressed by heavy shards. Swanson had offered his life so he could know if the oberleutnant were set on inflicting vengeance on Nicole. Or having her as his lover. The thought took his breath. He hadn't allowed himself to believe it. Now he couldn't push the thought away.

He didn't know how far he'd walked, but women shambled on the other side of the square, their heads covered and faces down. He'd expected lines of people waiting for bread, not a vacant city. He pushed on, his legs trembling, rehearsing the streets he would cross, and watching for street signs.

A couple emerged from a building, the man in uniform, the woman's hands enfolding the man's right arm. They turned toward him, and his lungs refused to fill. He gawked at the familiar gray of a Wehrmacht tunic, saw the man's head rise, a dark stare fixed on his. The *Wehrmachtsadler* on the pocket came clear, and David's legs grew weak. He fought the compulsion to cross the square, revised his limp, hoped to appear to be covering it. Should he be the first to heil?

"*Heil Hitler!*" The obergefreiter seemed eager to impress the girl.

"*Hei' Hitla!*" With practice, he could have done better. He dropped his head, allowing the couple to pass. The clack of heels stopped behind him. Blood roared in his ears, and the clack resumed. He closed his eyes to offer thanks, and Swanson's crumpled body returned.

He opened them to blue porcelain shimmering on his right. *Josef-Ritz-Weg* cleared within the morning mist. He was halfway there. Stone and brick yielded to wood. Houses rose above water, the ones near the river on piers. The street grew steep, and he slowed his pace, glanced to his right and saw dozens of houses razed, all splinters and broken concrete.

Sturmiusweg. He drew a breath. The sign lay cracked beside the street. He abandoned his limp, rushed across, and trotted west. The first two houses were damaged, windows and doors boarded. Those across the street were leveled. A path appeared leading to a wooden gate on the south of the third house, a small shop beyond.

He knocked on the door and waited. "I am one who loves not wisely but too well."

Something stirred inside, the sound familiar. The door opened, and he stared into the shadows, could just make out the polished push rings of a wheelchair.

"Who are you?" The voice was graveled with smoke.

"Othello. You have something for me?"

"Come inside. Quickly." The chair wheeled back. "You are Army?"

"Air Corps."

"Then you did not take my legs." The head pivoted above a slender frame and offered an unexpected smile. Blond hair scattered flecks of light.

He swallowed and tried to steady his breath. "You were Wehrmacht?"

"Motorized Artillery." The man pointed to his dwindling legs. "A sixty-millimeter mortar fragment to the spine. US, of course."

"I'm sorry." He looked away.

"We did what we had to." The man reached inside a drawer and retrieved a key from a tin. "The hen is perhaps upstairs. She takes breakfast early, then spends much of her day in her bedroom. We believe it is the center one upstairs. She has also a radio. Our people have overheard her listening to the BBC. We assume she is still loyal to the Resistance."

He shifted, hoped for something more. "Did you know her before the war?"

"No, though others did." The German shrugged. "I am told she was active. Many have been forced to do things they do not wish to, Othello."

He nodded. "Your English is excellent."

"My father taught English literature. He required me to learn the language as a child." He thumbed over his shoulder. "You will leave through the garden and proceed three houses south, turn right and cross two streets. Behind the houses on the second street, you will find the rear entrance to the Schneider home. The door is blue, the paint flaking. It is the only such door on that street. You will enter the kitchen. The stairs are on the west side of the dining room. You will leave from the rear and walk north to the street you arrived on. Eyes are everywhere."

He clenched his fist. "And the key?"

The German raised his chin. "You will keep it should you need to return. We made another. Swallow it if it appears you will be captured."

Chapter XXVII

Yellow fur erupted from beneath the wooden stoop and screeched in protest at David's presence. He gasped, steadied himself with the rail, waited, and scanned the house. The door was as the man described it, a wearied blue giving way to weathered wood.

He climbed the steps and kicked off Bertram's tattered boots. The key telegraphed his trepidation to the metal plate, so he held it with both hands, and drove it into the slot. The knob, red with rust in the deep furls, turned without a sound. He pushed, felt the squeal of hinges in his bones, and stepped into pale light, stumbled across a rug mounded above multicolored tile, righted himself, and set his boots in front of the sink.

Garlic and dill needled his nose, a faint garble issuing from beyond the kitchen. He eased through the doorway, spotted the dining room table and front door. A voice crackled through vacuum tubes nasaling something British and bleak. He edged onto the carpet, found a polished banister reflecting what radiance remained in Munich, and pulled himself to the second step. The fourth creaked, and he stopped. A click and the voice went silent. Blood pounded, and he imagined tubes darkening in the chill. He lifted his foot. The squeak seemed louder in the silence. Footsteps scurried. He bolted up the stairs, found the second door, threw it wide, and gawked at a perfectly made bed. He spun and ran to the next room.

A young woman was perched in the windowsill, one leg extending into the cold, her skin whiter against a dingy drape wound around it. Her gown was stretched high, and she struggled to force her head beneath the window frame.

"Stop! Please!" His breath came hard. "I won't hurt you."

She shouted something guttural and pointed at the door.

"I'm a friend of Nicole Serat and Professor Stein. I need your help." He watched her, breathless. "I'm David Dremmer. If you could—"

162

"You left flowers. You are Heinrich's friend."

His spine went electric. Was he? "Yes."

"How did you get here?"

"It was difficult. Please, come back in before you're seen."

She held to the window frame, pulled her leg inside, and flattened against the wall.

Her fright guilted him. "You must be cold. May I get you something? A coat, maybe?"

"What do you want?" Her glower was fevered and dark.

He swallowed. "I'm working with the White Rose. I need information."

"You said you wanted to help Nicole and Professor Stein. Which is it?"

"No, that's not—" He changed tacks. "It's too late to help Professor Stein. Oberleutnant Schneider had him shot. But it's not too late for—"

"You're a liar!" She drew her arms across her breast.

He steadied his voice. "Ask him. Before I was captured, Professor Stein was helping me escape. Heinrich had him shot. I watched the man die."

She looked at the floor, blonde hair falling across her face. "That was Professor Stein?" Her gaze locked on his. "Heinrich phoned me. He was saddened by the shooting. But he did not order him shot. Those were Wehrmacht orders."

He needed more. "Why didn't he stop it? Now he's hunting for Nicole."

"I don't believe you. Heinrich would never—"

"Is there another reason? Does he want her back?"

Her eyes flashed. "She was *never* his! She had no interest in him. She was my best friend; I would never have allowed him to pursue me had she been in love with him."

The words hushed his nightmare. "I'm sorry. I had to know."

She lowered her hands and leaned against the wall. Something near a smile appeared. "You are in love with her?"

"Has Heinrich not told you? Not even about her work with the Resistance?"

"He tells me nothing." A muted ache filled her words. "She worked with the British Embassy in Belgium, so it's no surprise. How do you know her?"

His thumbs found belt loops. "I was injured when our plane was shot down. She nursed me back to health. Herr Oberleutnant captured me and assumed custody from the Wehrmacht."

A smile surfaced, a mystery brought to light. "You caused a great deal of conflict between Heinrich and the Wehrmacht, did you not?"

"With von Felder, yes."

Her smile grew. "Perhaps that is why Heinrich is fond of you. A common enemy, yes? And how is Nicole?"

"She's well, and I hope to keep her that way. Heinrich showed me a picture of her that the Abwehr sent him. He was asked to identify her. I need to be sure he isn't having her followed." He waited. "She was wearing an evening dress in Paris during Réveillon."

"Less than three weeks ago." Élodie seemed pensive. "I would wager she was lovely."

"Very." He leaned against the door frame. "She worried about your safety, wondered why you left without a goodbye."

She looked away. "Heinrich found pamphlets I had hidden, He said the Gestapo was looking for those distributing them. He left the university and accepted a position gathering information from captured airmen. He gave up his career to keep me safe."

It fit with what he knew. "And took you to Dresden?"

"To his grandparents' home, yes. The Gestapo did not know about the house, and he paid taxes in his grandfather's name." She looked up. "His oma raised him, but he was not allowed to attend his opa's funeral." She sneered. "The state had become his father, you see."

He nodded. "Nicole worried that you might have been taken against your will."

She shook her head. "No. Heinrich paid a man loyal to his opa to leave food for me and take care of the house. I have been a well-kept prisoner since."

"And what happened to his parents?"

She squinted. "Why must you know?"

"He's learned things about me. I need him to know I can do the same with him. I'm trying to save Nicole. I know you love him, but his compatriots are searching for her."

Her lips parted. "He speaks of duty, but he no longer believes as he did. I am certain."

"Well, I want Nicole safe, however conflicted he may be. I have no intention of hurting him, but I must know he won't hurt her or her compatriots."

The fire in her eyes burned low. "He wouldn't hurt her. I am sure of this."

He straightened. "But would he protect her more than he did Gerhardt?"

Her eyes grew liquid. "He drinks. Since that night, it has worsened."

"Yes." He bit his tongue. The clock was running out.

She stepped to her closet. "I thought it was the war. I did not know of *Herr Doktor*."

They'd come so far. "We have an agreement. Nicole's safety for yours. I intend you no harm, but he must know that we have resources, that we can learn about him, what he's up to."

She pulled the coat over her shoulders. "You are asking me to betray him."

"I'm asking you to protect Nicole. I won't use anything against Heinrich."

"Only deceive him."

"If necessary, yes, but deception isn't fatal. Being turned over to the Gestapo is." He met her stare, prayed for a way to reach her. She mined his face, but he pushed on. "Being anguished by Doctor Stein's death doesn't mean Heinrich has no loyalties to the Reich."

She stepped quickly to the window and pulled it down. Something had been decided. "You swear you will do nothing to bring him harm?"

"You have my word."

"Follow me." She hurried to the stairs. "Heinrich received papers shortly after he came. The man had come before, but I was afraid to answer the door. When he returned, I overheard them. He was an investigator, and he had a Swiss accent."

He hurried. "So, what was in the box?"

"I saw records from a university in Texas. Heinrich had spoken of you, so I took notice." She moved into the kitchen, saw his boots, and stopped. "How did you get in?"

He stood behind the doorway and pressed on. "It wasn't easy. The papers you saw were what I expected. A professor, a eugenics proponent, was in sympathy with the Nazis. It's likely he supplied them. The thing is, I must convince Heinrich that my sources are equally good."

She moved to the cupboard. "To convince him you can retaliate if Nicole is hurt?"

He hadn't expected her to see it quite so clearly. "Yes."

She offered an icy stare. "So, what do you want to know?"

He took a breath. "Anything that will convince him we can get information on him. How did his parents die? Surely that can't be used against him."

She sighed. "His father died in the Great War. An exploding shell or something. His opa convinced him it was heroic and pressured him to join the Luftwaffe. His academic skills might have enabled him to stay out of the war, but—"

He moved into a deeper shadow. "And his mother?"

Élodie placed sausage on a cutting board. "She crawled into a bottle and never came out. Her death changed everything. He became convinced there was no God, or that such a God was not one he owed allegiance to. He abandoned his ministerial studies to pursue physics."

He stepped closer. "He planned to go to seminary?"

"His opa was also shocked by the inclination. Heinrich believes the old man died happy because he chose the military. Perhaps he did."

She sliced sausage and a piece of bread, then dropped the knife into the sink and pulled a plate from the cupboard. "Eat. Heinrich fears you are too thin."

"You're feeding me?"

"I'm providing you with food only." She handed him the plate.

"We must prove to Heinrich that you are being surveilled but that the Resistance has no intention of hurting you."

She pushed her hands into the pockets of her quilted coat. "Am I being surveilled?"

He swallowed and wiped his hands on Bertram's trousers. "Some of your old compatriots are trying to keep you safe. And confirm your loyalties. None wish you harm." He looked up. "What we have planned will require your cooperation."

She looked suspicious again. "And what have you planned?"

"Heinrich must learn that you've been attacked by *Jungsturm*. You will be saved by Resistance operatives, the ones observing you."

Her hand covered her throat. "When will this happen?"

"It won't, but you'll report that it has. And our reports must be similar, though not identical. I'll tell Heinrich before you are able."

She nodded. "Perhaps it will help to know that it is impossible for me to reach him before evening. He forbids me calling early as he fears Oberst Berger will learn of it."

He chewed the spicy meat. "The White Rose will leave a message in a tin beneath your stoop. Check it morning and evening. You will appear to be feeding your cat."

Élodie smiled. "Then you have met Adelina? Are you now friends?"

He rose from the table and took his plate to the kitchen. "She had to leave. Maybe we'll get better acquainted on another visit."

"Then you will come again?" She spoke from the dining room, an appeal in her voice.

A flush crept up his neck. "I will try."

She moved closer. "I would be willing to help the White Rose so long as they are aware that I will do nothing to betray Heinrich."

"They'll be glad to hear it."

She raised her chin. "Will they make it possible for me to communicate with Nicole?"

His spine tingled. "It wouldn't be possible. It's too dangerous."

She softened. "She was the strong one, but she didn't know it. I need to see her."

"She still is, and I need to see her, too." The words unburdened him. "You were Nicole's friend." He waited for breath, needed to tell someone. "I lost a friend this morning—a smart, frightened boy who'd carried too much for too long. He died so I could come here."

She touched his arm. "So much loss. So many boys. All will be as it should be again."

He drew what solace he could from her certainty, bent to pull Bertram's boots on, and hid the tears for Swanson; for Ito and Ream; for the woman and the boy; for the old man; and all who wouldn't see things as they should be again. At least, not here.

* * *

The breeze scored David's flesh. He lay panting, a fallen tree shielding him from the goons. He rolled to his stomach, raised his head, and waited. Two pairs of kriegies shuffled toward the stack of ties, the guards' heads following.

He slithered over the tree and looped a strip of paper through the woven wire—his signal to Bertram that he'd returned. He scurried back and lay staring into the vastness above, drew from the ceaseless industry of heaven to fill the void, and knew with certainty that all creation suffered here. The emptiness of those who'd gone on would be filled, but what about those left behind? What could quiet the wailing of a heart seeking union here?

His hunger flamed, aroused perhaps by Élodie's compassion. It was so like Nicole's. But he needed something sure, craved a connection that couldn't be taken by miscalculation or weakness, or by a boy's need to prove himself. He'd known that presence in the well, had felt it early in the service on Christmas, for blessed minutes in prayer, or in the cellar with Nicole. He'd seen the reflection of it with Swanson, too, in the melding of their hearts and minds to a purpose. But it had ended, as it always did.

Something pinged against the wire, and he spun to stare above the tree. A dark figure stood at the latrine, motioning for him to come. He looked for kriegies, saw them squatting beneath the trees, drinking their thin soup, the goons smoking by themselves. He scrambled to squat before the fence, released the wire hooks, and sprinted to the latrine, unbuttoning the woolen coat as he ran.

He slid beside the boy. "Where's the captain sitting?"

"Beneath the large tree, beyond the others. He is alone." Bertram's breath was as heavy as his own. "If you must do this again, request someone else. It is too dangerous."

He studied the boy's trembling hands. "What happened?"

Bertram threw the red scarf across the rocks. "They had three counts after collecting the corporal. I answered to your name, but I am certain at least one of the prisoners noticed."

He caught the boy's glare. "Were you with the captain?"

"Yes."

"Then you're safe. No one will question it. Just go home."

Bertram lifted his face. "No one is safe, and I have no home."

He tugged his pants and heard the faintness of Élodie's complaint. *So much loss. So many boys.* He pushed his hands into his pockets. "I'll need the key in your right pocket."

The boy glowered. "You have a new contact. He will approach you within the camp."

"A prisoner?"

Bertram's throat undulated. "You will tell no one. You must promise."

The thought of hiding something from Hanson brought a chill. "All right."

Chapter XXVIII

Swanson's death was more potent than what life remained, the boy's absence a smothered groan clawing at David's throat. He shuffled behind the captain. Glances went unmet and whispers grew silent on icy breaths as they passed. He pulled himself into the cattle car, stared into the corner where his friend last sat, and slouched beside the gray-faced captain who had scrounged a cigarette from some kriegie. He'd not seen Hanson smoke before.

They'd completed their work, carried ties where they were pointed, but hadn't spoken. The only communication had been a nod at his return, the captain's sole statement regarding a mission accomplished at the cost of Swanson's life.

He stared through the cracks at the blood-stained rocks and turned away. Even the obergefreiter was silent. The latch dropped, couplings chattered, and the car jerked forward, the wheels starting a rasp that became a dirge before the wind drowned their desperation.

He leaned toward the captain. "I have information, sir. The girl wants to help."

Smoke shot from Hanson's nostrils. "You sure of that?"

"I'd stake my life on it, sir." He felt the captain's stare and turned.

"And how many other lives are you willing to throw in, Lieutenant?"

The weight was crushing, and his head fell back against the plank. He'd felt the accusation since morning, had insisted on the meeting with Élodie, believing she would be loyal. Why? So he could learn more about Nicole's past? Whether she and Schneider had been lovers? He'd told himself it was more, that any information gained could pay off in spades. Maybe it would, but the speculation had cost Swanson his life.

The captain leaned in. "It was reckless as hell, Lieutenant. The whole thing."

"Sir, I had no idea the Germans had set it up, and certainly not today. And I don't know why Swanson did what he did. Or why he didn't tell us what he'd heard." He shook his head.

Hanson cupped his hands, almost touching David's ear. "I should never have allowed you to involve us with Schneider and this Jew girl. I hope your Nicole is worth it."

The words sliced through the wind. "Sir, you said you intended–"

"Swanson is dead, Lieutenant! Don't even consider not taking responsibility."

He dropped his head and willed the blistering wind to slash his exposed neck, to cut a wound so deep the pain would end. The train slammed against the track, thrashing from side to side on uneven rails the kriegies had built. The captain's arm bumped his and recoiled. He edged away, could see no way out except the route Swanson had taken. Unless he could make himself of some use, offer a payment for Swanson's life.

* * *

The door of the cattle car squealed in retreat, and David dropped to the ground. Somehow, he'd expected the place to be different. Everything else had changed.

He shuffled into line, waited for the obergefreiter to begin his count, and caught the old feldwebel's shadowed gaze locking onto his. Vogt offered a scarcely detectable bobble of the head, then ambled toward the front. He could have imagined it, his addled brain birthing chimeras only he could see. The captain moved in beside him but said nothing.

The obergefreiter scanned the kriegies left to right. "Lieutenant Dremmer, you are required by Oberleutnant Schneider. You veel escort veece Feldwebel Vogt."

Hanson's head tilted toward him. "Go on, Lieutenant. Have a drink with your Kraut buddy. The one with a conscience. Enjoy yourself."

His gut cinched tighter. "He's likely heard about Swanson, sir. What should I tell him?"

"Whatever you want. Tell him the truth. Tell him you had the corporal jump in front of the train as a diversion so you could visit his fräulein."

"Sir, you know—"

"Just go, Lieutenant."

* * *

Vogt stepped away from the obergefreiter and shuffled beside the assembly. The feldwebel turned and waited for him to come close, then jutted his chin toward the camp.

David moved ahead and strode toward the main gate.

"Lieutenant Dremmer, it is no great distance that we must travel. Such alacrity is not required. Oberleutnant Schneider will wait."

Something wasn't right. "Okay."

"I would like to talk. You are a great reader, are you not? Do you enjoy Shakespeare?"

He turned, let the German advance. "I once did."

"Before this," the feldwebel's hand circled, "I taught British literature. Shakespeare was my favorite. Have you, perchance, read Othello?"

His heart stuttered. "It's been quite some time."

Vogt chuckled. "You remind me of Othello, though your complexion is lighter."

How was he supposed to respond? "'I am one who loved not wisely but too well.' One of his best lines, don't you think?"

"It is, indeed. That quality is the reason you received your code name, though I believe you are considerably more capable of discerning the difference between love and possession. Are you a possessive man, Lieutenant?"

He didn't trust this Kraut, and the amiability was unsettling. "What do you want?"

"Your cooperation in saving your life—and the lives of your comrades, of course."

"I'm willing to be saved, but who else do you want to keep alive?"

"You are aware of who we are, Othello, as I am aware of your dilemma. In truth, I am more knowledgeable regarding your quandary than you."

He looked back at the bahnhof, his discomfort growing. "I saw you speaking with Corporal Swanson a few times. I'm sure you know what happened."

"I do. He was my friend, as well. That is, I considered him my friend. I tried to save the corporal, but he was unwilling." Vogt eased into the shadows of the storage building.

David followed, stood beside the strange man, and stared into the failing light as it angled across the sportplatz. "He died because of me. Did you know that, too, Herr Vogt?"

"No, Lieutenant, he died because he was no longer useful to Captain Hanson. The corporal had been warned it might happen. In truth, he feared it."

His heart pounded, but he held his tongue.

"Your captain shares your interest in gathering intelligence, but his real desire is to gain a kingdom. Captain Hanson is Macbeth. Do you understand what I am saying?"

He did, and it frightened him. He'd invested his hopes in the man. "He's 'not without ambition, but without the illness should attend it'?"

The lines in Vogt's face tightened, and he nodded. "Unlike Macbeth, your captain isn't lacking such an illness. He may not have shoved the corporal before the train, but he's not without the ability to urge him onto the track."

He glared at the drooping face. "You can't be serious."

The feldwebel's eyes widened. "Quite serious. I tell you this because you are being molded into the corporal's replacement. Guilt is a powerful motivator, Lieutenant. As is the need of a father's acceptance. Should you need assurance, your plan to visit Mademoiselle Devillier was a good one. There was much to be gained."

He shivered at an unexpected breeze. Had Swanson given Vogt the information?

"I know more about you than either Swanson or the captain, and I believe you to be a good man, one valuable to our cause. Perhaps we might discuss it at some point."

Our cause. The idea of their being compatriots brought a shiver. "So, how am I to contact you?"

"You will not, nor will you mention me to anyone. If it becomes necessary to discuss our mutual interests, you will refer to me only as Prospero. Do you understand?"

"Not nearly enough."

* * *

David slogged between the ruts. *Prospero*. He'd have to reread *The Tempest*, but the day had already brought more than he could bear. Swanson was gone, his body still cooling in the lazarette, and Vogt wanted to be his buddy. Could the man be the wizard working the machinery of some Partisan group? He dragged his boots across a scraper planted by the steps.

"Come in, Lieutenant."

He looked up. "Herr Oberleutnant."

Schneider stood in the door, then turned, marched into his office, and motioned for him to close the door. "Tell me what happened."

He thought of what Feldwebel Vogt had said. "You know what happened, Herr Oberleutnant, and you know why. The corporal was forced to give information to his interrogator or see his squad hanged. He couldn't live with what he'd had to do."

Schneider rocked on his heels. "He lived with it for quite some time."

"Everyone has a breaking point, Herr Oberleutnant."

The perfect jaw rippled as the oberleutnant slid into his chair. He opened his hand to the one across from him. "If you intend to persist in this pointless game, we should at least sit."

He sank into the padded leather. "You aren't going to threaten to hang my friends?"

Schneider leaned forward. "And which should I hang first, David?"

He couldn't bear it today. "I don't have the heart for this, Heinrich."

"I'm sorry. I know you were fond of the corporal. Still, I must know what moved him to do what he did. You were working with him, were you not?"

"No, Captain Hanson and I were partnered today. Swanson was working alone."

Schneider straightened. "Captain Hanson was part of the work party? It must have come as quite a shock, losing another subordinate to suicide."

A frisson shot up his spine. "Another?"

"My records indicate that a sergeant on the intelligence committee hanged himself a five months ago. You are aware that Hanson did not arrive with the others, are you not?"

He gripped the arms of his chair. "Never came up, but then I'm not his confidant."

Schneider leaned back. "Your captain has been here for over a year and has been the head of intelligence the entire time. He was taken

173

prisoner in Italy. Surely, you find that interesting."

The shock was settling in. "Not really. Should I?"

"You said you were concerned with Swanson's welfare. Perhaps his comrades—"

"Maybe I haven't taken the interest I should have in my fellow prisoners. Do you think I've been too focused on you? Should I stop following your activities?"

Schneider spread his hands. "I doubt you are finding any of interest, Lieutenant."

"Oh, I've learned a few things. It had to be rough being raised without a father. Then your mother dying drunk. That was painful, I'm sure. And embarrassing."

The oberleutnant stiffened. "I meant anything of substance."

"And this had to be worse." He leaned into the ice-blue scowl. "Not being able to care for the woman who took you in, loved you when your grandfather—"

"That is enough, Lieutenant!" Schneider rose, his face flushed.

"I would think so, but you still offer these thugs your allegiance—the ones who would put Élodie in a camp. Do you consider that loyalty to a cause or the betrayal of someone you love?"

"That will be all, Lieutenant. I understand this is a difficult time, but you are putting our agreement and, therefore, the lives of others at risk. You will leave. Now."

* * *

David stared at the latrine door. He needed someone he could trust. Like Bear. He covered his face, would give the captain a few more minutes. The man would want to know what he'd learned. At least, he always had. Not that Hanson's failure to show was a disappointment.

So much had happened, and he'd relied on Swanson to show him what was real. Now, the boy was gone, and the captain was being depicted as a murderous manipulator. He'd trusted and lost both. Hanson had helped him learn Nicole's fate, and he'd told him of his deal with Schneider. Had he been taken in? If so, what did Hanson have to gain?

The feldwebel had named the captain Macbeth for his ambition, saying he wanted to be king. Was Hanson's need for power that great?

He was the only one who knew everyone on the committee, a perfect position for a puppet master. But that didn't mean he *was* one. And his methods had uncovered Swanson's secret. Or had they?

He buttoned his fly, his belt sliding inches past the wear mark, and stared into the putrid light. Hanson had also interviewed Swanson on his arrival. The boy's secret likely emerged then. The corporal said they'd talked, had repeated that the captain knew everything. If Hanson did know, it would explain the boy's confusion when he was accused of not disclosing it. And if Vogt were telling the truth, Hanson had used the boy's failure to control him.

* * *

David stared into the darkness of the barracks, the suspirations hinting at the peace of boys asleep. But these were men who'd been tucked in by their mothers a few years back, men like Swanson who carried the weight of their friends' survival, of causes that surpassed their understanding, and of threats that outstripped their capacity to counter. But the causes and the threats were as real as the necessity for these boys to carry them, however unfair it was.

His job was to discern the truth, so he needed to know why Swanson did what he did and what threat Hanson might pose. Feldwebel Vogt seemed to know if the man were telling the truth. But how was he to know? Vogt had apparently named every operative. The few he knew had been given the monikers of Shakespearean characters, and each had some trait his namesake was known for. He was Othello, Hanson was Macbeth, and Vogt called himself Prospero.

He needed to understand Swanson's desperation, and the boy's code name was apt to shed light on that. And he needed to know if Hanson were as dangerous as Vogt made him out to be.

Chapter XXVIX

The Bentley drifted across a whitened field, fresh snow dampening what sound it made. Nicole watched from the rear seat, the driver's head swiveling as they neared the road. The car turned, then surged ahead on scraped gravel.

The major pushed himself against the door, had still not spoken, his nose pointing above the open fields. Nicole's stomach roiled, had been in knots since they'd taken off at Santander. It was her first flight, though it was altogether likely that her digestion had been more disturbed by the major's pomposity. Even in the field after they landed, he'd not introduced himself. Not so much as a nod. Of course, she could have overstepped her bounds sitting across from him. It wasn't improbable that he'd expected her to crawl into the boot with his luggage.

She adjusted the fur on her shoulder and pulled it up to obstruct her view. Her hands rested on heavy wool as she watched through the side glass. Snow had settled on rolling paddocks, a sweeping white blanket over the hills. Trees were rimed with a hoary glaze, the bark beneath edged with charcoal from a slight thaw. If she understood correctly, Oxford was behind them, Woodstock ahead, and Blenheim Palace a short drive beyond that.

The envelope chafed her skin. It seemed unlikely the Jerries would catch up to her in Oxfordshire. Still, the agreement might be important. If her role in this plan resulted in her death, she had a signed statement implicating Émile in all of it.

The car swooped, snow and pebbles skidding from beneath the massive wings. The trees obscuring the view fell away, and the palace appeared. She caught her breath, surveyed what could be seen of the estate, straightened her coat, and slipped her hands into the woolen pockets. The niggle in her stomach rose to her throat, and she pressed her lips, hoping to delay the inevitable. "Major, might it be possible for me to visit a water closet before our meeting?"

His delicate chin swiveled toward her. "We shall enter from the south. The servants' facilities are beyond the hall and dining room, quite on the other end of the palace, I'm afraid."

She surveyed the massive edifice. "I see. Are there no closer facilities?"

His mouth pinched. "None that you will have access to."

She swallowed. "Very well, I shall make do with whatever facilities you use."

The chin rose against the setting sun. "I shall point out the dressing rooms to you."

"And they are closer?"

He sniffed. "Yes."

She breathed easier. "Thank you. You're most kind."

* * *

Nicole rinsed her mouth, dabbed her face with a moistened towel, and stared into the mirror. Her mother had always said every nerve she had ended in her stomach. But she couldn't show weakness. Not to these people. She straightened her hair, pinched color into her cheeks, and opened the door into a cavernous hall. A figure advanced, his cane clattering on marble. Another man moved from behind, narrow with a long stride. She drew in ancient air, glanced at gold panels, a Roman goddess in bas-relief, and strode toward the approaching men.

The first looked like… it was so improbable as to make it… could it be? She forced herself into a vigorous pace, demanded that her lungs draw air, took a dozen more steps, and froze. "Mr. Prime Minister?"

His cigar moved, and he emitted a cloud of smoke. "You say that with some uncertainty. Has there been another election?"

"Yes sir. No, no sir, no election. I simply had not—"

He appeared swollen as he presented what chin he had available. "You are Miss Serat, are you not? Our heroine from across the Pyrenees?"

The breath froze in her throat. She stood for a moment without speaking. "I am, sir. That is, I am Nicole Serat and have come from across the Pyrenees."

"Your journey was most courageous. The Realm is in your debt."

She scrambled for the words she'd prepared. "Sir, in truth, I'm not at all courageous. Quite the contrary, in fact. It's just that I find the wastage of human life unpardonable. That is why I asked to meet with—though I had no idea I was asking to meet with you, sir."

"And quite rightly. I'm not among the cannibals preparing to drop you into their soup. I am here on quite another matter but was informed of your case and have chosen to remain to speak in your defense—if you'll have it, of course."

Her hands shook, and she fought to keep them at her side. "My defense?"

"Quite. I shall be delighted to discuss it further, but just now I intend to visit a water closet. Thompson here will amuse you until I return."

She stared at Thompson's expressionless face, the sharp angles a striking contrast to the cherubic prime minister's. The man loomed above them, his glare following Churchill for a moment, then shooting down the hall. She extended her hand. "I'm Nicole Serat, sir."

"Quite." His hand remained in his coat. "The prime minister shall return shortly."

"Of course." She shifted her weight. "Might I ask, sir, whether I am on trial?"

"I couldn't tell you, miss. As I said, the prime minister shall return shortly."

She coughed. "You did, yes."

* * *

Mr. Churchill grunted as he fell into a chair. "Please have a seat, Miss Serat."

She drew against her cheeks to moisten her tongue. "Sir, I believe they're waiting."

He waved away her objection. "I've informed them that I wish to attend the proceedings. I should be most displeased if they start without me. Let them simmer, Miss Serat." He extracted a puff. "I understand you have an objection regarding orders issued to Partisans."

She refused to allow her discomfort to constrain her. "I do, sir. MI6 continues to order agents to safe houses and other locations weeks after being informed that these places are under Gestapo surveillance. Our operatives are being led to slaughter, and quite without mercy."

The prime minister leaned back. "I have no doubt what you say is true, Miss Serat. The current state of our operations is the result of an attempt to—" He scowled. "The sad fact is, England is fighting more than one war. With what brevity I possess—" He removed his cigar. "Our forces are in unity against the Huns. Some among us, however, are not at all desirous of seeing the Crown or the US decide the fate of occupied Europe."

She shuddered at the implications. "Then whom do they wish to restore order, sir?"

"That's quite the point. They would prefer to see a new order, a government above laws, not unlike that established by the Soviets, become a world system, and they see this war as an opportunity to advance their cause. They are quite taken with the Marxian philosophy which they believe to be the embodiment of beneficence. I assure you it is not. Britain, however, is bleeding and is in want of the information these men are able to collect."

"And Britain would assemble this information at the expense of her allies, sir?"

"It is my sincere hope that there will be no further loss of life. It is probable that what has occurred was allowed by these men in the hopes that the Soviets might be placed in a more strategic position. In short, it would help Mr. Stalin achieve his expansionist ambitions. I pledge to you to insert myself into any discussion of Belgian or Dutch resources, though I cannot promise I will be apprised of them. I am informing you so that you will understand what is at stake once discussions are underway."

She waited, tried to sort it out. "And are our fellow attendees among those who hope to see the Soviet Union control Europe?"

A smile appeared around his cigar. "Or perhaps some union like it. That is, the major and Professor Greeves are, as is your friend, Émile. Cambridge men and all that." He drew on his cigar. "It is possible that others could be in attendance, as well."

A door opened behind them and allowed a familiar melody to drift into the hall. Nicole closed her eyes, felt David's arms encircle her as she slid to the cellar floor. The BBC was playing, and the broadcast was unusually clear. Frank Sinatra sang with the Tommy Dorsey Orchestra, and she'd just learned of the plans to extract David, Bear, and Professor Stein.

I'll never smile again, until I smile at you. The melody swelled into the Great Hall and lured a tear from her eye. And then another. *I'll never love again, I'm so in love with you.* Her throat constricted, and she turned away, praying Mr. Churchill hadn't noticed.

Thompson cleared his throat, and she saw him gawking into the expanse behind her. Nicole turned to observe a woman in uniform moving near then spotting them behind the massive pillar. The young woman drew a breath and renewed her approach, timidly, now.

"Mr. Prime Minister, I wasn't aware— Would you care for tea, sir?"

"Good morning, Alice. Yes, a spot of tea would be lovely, specially prepared, of course. And do try to constrain your generosity. We mustn't crowd the brandy." His head orbited a half turn. "And you, Miss Serat?"

She cleared her throat. "None, thank you, sir." She looked at Mr. Thompson.

"He doesn't imbibe. It's quite unnatural, should you want my opinion." He met her glance and waited for Alice to withdraw. Thompson offered a nod, and Churchill continued. "This is what I shall propose in the meeting. First, the loss of any Belgian or Dutch asset involved, even peripherally, in one of our intelligence operations, shall be reported to me. Second, the head of any sector will be subject to charges should his or her asset be required to offer critical information to the Soviets due to the committee's inaction. I assure you this point will be met with strenuous objections. These men see themselves as quite above any code of conduct decent men impose upon themselves. If need be, I shall pursue this through Parliament." The prime minister's head rose. "Do you have any further suggestions, Miss Serat?"

Her efforts weren't in vain. Tears came irresistibly, and she fought to quell them.

Alice appeared, poured the prime minister's cup half full, then finished with a spirit warmer. "Mr. Prime Minister."

"Thank you, Alice." Mr. Churchill tipped the cup and drew himself up from a slump as Alice scurried away. "A second occasion for tears, Miss Serat. I find that both heavy-handed and effectual. I shall, therefore, concede and offer a further pledge. In the future, should you find yourself in need of assistance, I would be most pleased to offer my services." He cleared his throat. "In truth, I would most earnestly enjoy resisting Mr. Sinatra's suggestions and reinstate your smile."

She looked up, overwhelmed. "I don't know how to—"

"Mr. Thompson will supply you with a number. It will allow you to reach him, and he shall advise me of your request."

She smiled, the relief spreading to her neck and shoulders. "—to thank you, sir."

"Nor I you, Miss Serat. The future of Europe has fallen into the hands of a gallant generation, and I am honored to offer service to such an exemplary representative of its virtue."

"Thank you, sir." She hadn't told him! "Mr. Prime Minister, I have something that might be of use to you—to us, that is—in the meeting. It's attached to my person."

"Your agreement?" A second smile. "That document has brought Émile a good deal of anguish among his comrades. It was his plan, you see, and he was quite unwilling to discard it."

She straightened. "I had feared MI6 would be outraged at my placing their agent in harm's way."

"A few were, of course, but I thought it most clever. You seem to have a gift for taking the upper hand, however slight the opportunity." He pushed himself from the chair. "Were you less winsome, your request to be here might have been considered a demand. Still, I must warn you, there are those who are oblivious to your charms for reasons that might not be entirely political."

Chapter XXX

Darkness had infected David's soul. Hanson had withdrawn, creating a fertile isolation that whispered suspicion into every remembered word. And he didn't know if Vogt were more trustworthy than the captain. It seemed laughable that he wanted to turn to Schneider for answers, the man whose betrayal would assure a loss he could scarcely imagine. He longed for the hush of sleep, but as morning approached, he eased to the floor, hoping not to wake Mathews who'd claimed the lower bunk.

Only one knew the truth, of course, and he wasn't talking, as the saying went. Or was he? He pulled the blanket from his palliasse and draped it over his shoulders. His prayers had yielded light before and brought him face to face with certainty. So why was he afraid to ask for it now? A shiver ran down his spine. It was his unwillingness to pry what he desperately wanted from his own hands and allow Benevolence to choose his course.

But he wanted to live. More than that, he wanted Nicole to live beside him, and yielding would require a tendering of his dream, an offering that might divide heart from heart and soul from soul. Could he endure it? He stood in the dark and prayed for morning.

* * *

The thin obergefreiter wavered in the doorway, staring into shadows, his rifle lowered. David buried a chuckle. The boy was no Gary Cooper. He closed a volume of Shakespeare's plays. "What can I do for you, Obergefreiter?"

"You are Lieutenant Dreamer, yes?"

The guttural trill annoyed him. "Unless you're a bill collector."

The obergefreiter cocked his head.

"I'm Lieutenant Dremmer. What can I do for you?"

"You follow veece me to Oberleutnant Schneider."

* * *

Schneider's pen scratched heatedly across a form. He didn't look up, the refusal a declaration of power, David suspected. The young obergefreiter remained at attention, and he stood beside him trying to appear unruffled.

Schneider grumbled, and the obergefreiter's arm shot up. "*Heil Hitler!*"

"*Ja ja, Heil Hitler.*" He waved the boy away and pointed David to the other chair. "Feldwebel Vogt has asked for your assistance, Lieutenant. The widow of a local Wehrmacht hero needs help delivering a cow. You can do this, yes?"

"I've delivered calves. Cows might be difficult."

The oberleutnant raised his head. "Then you will be asked to deliver *calves*. Of course, you are an officer. You may decline just as you could *any* work detail."

He ignored the jab. "Are these cows political, Herr Oberleutnant?"

"I think not, Lieutenant."

"Then I'd be happy to assist."

Schneider folded his arms. "How does Feldwebel Vogt know of your being a cowboy?"

He shrugged. "I mentioned it when he escorted me from the train."

Schneider chuckled. "So, the two of you have become chums?"

"Not as close as you and me, Herr Oberleutnant. You needn't worry."

"I shan't." Schneider tilted his head. "Our feldwebel was a school master. He taught literature, a diversion you might appreciate."

He smiled, wondering if the oberleutnant were remembering their previous dispute. "Literature isn't *verboten* in the Reich?"

Schneider snorted his disgust. "Perhaps you would prefer waiting outside."

"I'm comfortable here, thanks."

"Nevertheless, you shall wait outside."

* * *

The truck slammed against frozen ruts. David glanced at Vogt seated across from him, his Karabiner balanced on thin legs. Another kriegie sat holding a tarp strut. He nodded, the questions of the last two nights burning in his gut. "How far are we going, Feldwebel?"

The angular face sharpened. "You will be given instructions when we reach our destination, Lieutenant."

He drew his arms close, nodded at the kriegie, and chuckled. They'd left the camp, headed south, turned east, but couldn't have gone far. The ruts yielded to canary grass where it ventured onto the road, making it rough, especially with it frozen. He glanced out the back, saw farmhouses on either side. Brakes squealed, and the truck quivered on its springs. He dropped from the tailgate and eyed the farmyard. Fog obscured the house and barns. Low mountains formed green etchings within the ashen sky, the air laden with pine and grass hay, its beauty pushing back a darkness he'd come to believe was inescapable in this country.

Vogt pointed to a large rock building. "Lieutenant, you will find two cows in the barn. You may assess their condition while I show Private Tremble to his work." The feldwebel walked in the direction of a run-down set of pens, pointing Tremble toward a box of hand tools.

The truck spat fumes, and David shuffled to the barn, marveling at their keeping cattle confined. The moisture and manure should have bred infections. Sunlight and fresh air had proven the better option on the plains, but it was wet here, maybe too wet for the practices he'd learned. He looked across the meadow, saw a dozen or more cows picking at hay scattered along the fence. He pulled the doors back, allowing light to drizzle across empty stalls. Two heifers stood at feed bunks on the far end separated by the width of the massive barn. Both were fat, their muscling more prominent than any range cattle he'd seen.

He stepped to the farther heifer first, her paunch strained and rigid, her udder and vulva swollen. The calf inside her would be heavy, too, increasing the odds of a difficult birth. He removed his jacket, looked for a rope, heard something and turned.

A woman, mid-thirties maybe, approached, her dark hair falling across ample shoulders.

He nodded. "I need soap and a pan of warm water, *bitte*."

She jabbed the air with a pitchfork. Vogt shadowed the door, began hollering and scurried toward them.

"I need soap and water to examine these heifers, Feldwebel. I tried to explain, but—"

"She thought I would bring a doctor." Vogt was frantic. "I told her you were qualified."

The words sparked an ember. "But I'm not qualified, Herr Vogt. I'm no veterinarian, and these are valuable animals."

The feldwebel shook his head. "Please, Lieutenant."

"We need to talk, Herr Vogt. She doesn't speak English, does she?"

Vogt wagged his finger. "We shall talk, Lieutenant, but I must first convince her that it is to her advantage to allow you to help."

A groan ascended in the gray. David looked toward the stall he'd just passed. The heifer was going to her knees. "She's having a contraction! She has a much better chance of calving if she's standing. Help me get her up."

He ran to the heifer and pulled her tail. "We'll need a halter and rope." He looked at the feldwebel and tilted his head toward the woman. "Tell her."

German blistered the chill. The woman bawled, ran to the shadowed corner by the doors, and emerged holding a halter. He nodded. "Come inside the stall, Herr Vogt! This heifer's been in labor for a while." He strained against the tail as the feldwebel crept to her side. "Get her head up. Pull her ears. If she goes down, we may not be able to save her."

Vogt stared, sallower now. "I cannot do this."

Heat spread up his neck. "Then move to her tail and pull as hard as you can."

The woman dragged a wooden box with a halter draped over it.

He turned, saw the heifer's sunken eyes, and yanked her ears. "Tell the woman to hand me the halter."

A wadded mass of rope flew across the rail, and he slipped it over the dry nose. The feldwebel shifted, releasing the heifer's tail, and turned to the box.

"Don't let go! Ask the woman what's in the box."

"I saw syringes and bottles, Lieutenant. I have no idea what they are."

David tightened the halter and threw the lead over a joist, then half-hitched the end around the middle. "Is there a rope?"

Vogt shouted, and the woman raised a thick hemp rope.

"That'll do." He hurried toward the heifer's rump, tied the rope to her tail, threw the end over a supporting beam and pulled. The woman howled.

Vogt shook his head. "She says you are hurting her Adda."

"Tell her I'm trying to save her Adda's life. This heifer is too fat to calve."

The feldwebel hesitated. "Her husband's family is quite prominent, Lieutenant."

"I need hot water and bleach. And baking soda. Tell her!"

Grumbles filled the dank air, and the woman ran toward the door.

He removed his shirt, pushed his long john sleeve over his bicep, and shoved his hand into the distended vulva. Round hips filled the cervix, the calf too large to clear her pelvis. He pushed his arm to the limits of his rolled sleeve and grabbed a hind leg. It jerked away. "This calf is breech, and it's too big to turn. We'll have to do a C-section."

Vogt's jaw went slack. "I do not know what you mean."

"A caesarean. Like Macduff."

The long face went white. "'From his mother's womb untimely ripp'd'?"

"That's it, but I'd trade you for a goon who could quote a veterinary manual."

Vogt's head rose. "You have not done this before?"

"A few times, but I'm no vet." His anger rose. "And I didn't ask for this job, Herr Vogt."

"The cows you offered aid recovered, yes?"

He nodded. "Some did."

The feldwebel held his head. "Her husband's family was instrumental—"

"Tell me later." He slid to the heifer's side and felt along her last rib. "Look in the box for suture. I'll need alcohol, a razor, and shaving soap." He caught his breath. "When the woman comes back, send her for what we don't have. I need a calf chain, a scalpel, surgical needles, and a pair of pliers. And I want her to make a solution of water, bleach, and baking soda. Have her boil the water and put the instruments in the pan, then put a lid on it. And don't let her get behind me with anything sharp."

Vogt stilled. "Her name is Marta, Lieutenant."

He loosened the half hitch. "We'll have to cast this heifer, Feldwebel. We'll put her on her right side. Untie her tail but keep the rope tight. And wait until I'm ready. You got it?"

Vogt shook his head. "I thought you wanted her to stand."

"That was for a normal delivery."

The feldwebel straightened. "You are frightened, are you not?"

"No, I'm angry." He covered his shaking hands, couldn't let the opportunity pass. "You've asked me to trust you but kept me in the dark. So, what was Swanson's code name?"

Vogt jerked. "Why are you asking this now?"

"You left me without a contact when Hanson could easily—"

"It is what is required of you, Lieutenant. You are not in charge."

"You're vulnerable, too, Vogt, just like this heifer. I want to help you both, but I need the truth." He returned to the knot, hoping the eagerness of his fingers would cover the tremble.

"There is another rope in the box, Lieutenant."

He pushed the fire down and climbed over the panel. "I'll get it myself."

The box was a treasure trove. Heavy ropes were coiled in a corner. Two scalpels lay in a sealed canister, and a calving chain glistened at the bottom. Two bottles of alcohol stood on a shelf beside flasks of iodine. More bottles were pushed in the corner, the labels indecipherable.

"I named the corporal 'Hamlet.' He needed to prove himself worthy of his father's esteem. Does that seem familiar to you?" Vogt's voice rang metallic behind him.

He turned. "So, Swanson was susceptible to Hanson's manipulation. Just like me."

The sharp chin jutted. "I believe so, yes."

"And how would you know that?"

The door opened, and Marta pushed a wheelbarrow laden with a twenty-liter gas can, several amber bottles, and small boxes. He caught Vogt's glare. "The can was clean?"

"It was, Lieutenant. She uses it for drinking water."

"I need it sterile."

The feldwebel stood like granite. "She filled it with boiling water."

He glared. "Who is this woman, Feldwebel?"

Vogt's nostrils flared. "She is my sister, Lieutenant."

His sister, the widow of a Wehrmacht hero from a powerful family. It smelled. "Do you share political views, Feldwebel?"

"You will see to what must be done, and we will talk, Lieutenant."

* * *

"Pull her tail away from me. Now, Vogt!" David tightened the loop around the heifer's hind legs and heaved. Adda grunted, her legs drawing together as she slumped to the stall floor freshly sprinkled with diluted bleach. Marta sobbed and pulled gingerly against the halter.

He looked at Vogt. "Tell her to keep the rope tight." He soaped the heifer's side. The feldwebel handed him a razor as he lay his forearm below the hip line and sprinkled alcohol along the flank behind Adda's last rib. He took bold, quick strokes to remove the hair. "Iodine." He let a narrow flow course down the abdomen. "Scalpel. Touch only the tip of the handle."

The blade slipped through hide, pale skin dividing like a zipper, a diagonal score appearing from the hip line down. Adda bawled and threw her head against the rope.

He stared a threat at Marta who sobbed as he stripped fat. He cleared a line of abdominal wall beneath the outer incision. Muscles quivered beneath his hand as he rested his palm in pooling blood and plunged his other into hot entrails, found the calf encased in leathery flesh, and reached deeper. A leg took shape within his grip. "I need light. Open the window."

The hinge screeched, and Marta's squeal charged his skin. Blood was spilling from Adda's belly. He pulled the corner of the opening, allowed the blood to escape, and watched for a surge, saw instead an even ooze emerge halfway up the incision. He pushed, and the flow stopped. It was only a vein. "I need pliers, Feldwebel."

Vogt scrambled, the lid of the pan clanging to the dirt floor.

"You need some help, Lieutenant?"

He turned to a dark figure. "Take off your jacket, Tremble. Roll your sleeves up and wash your hands."

Pliers appeared beside him, and he clasped the vein. He drew a breath, extracted a quarter inch or more from the layered muscles, slipped the pliers deep, and squeezed. The blood slowed but didn't stop. "Hand me the suture."

The instruments appeared, the needle threaded as he'd left it. David tied a knot around the bleeder and cut the suture, recalled Barnhill's deft hands, the certainty of the vet's movements. His hands were reluctant and unskilled as he slid them into darkness, found the stretched uterus and lifted. The calf was long and heavy, pushing the womb toward the incision. He found legs and pulled a taut, pale sack from the opening, the form inside it struggling. "Tremble, when I cut this, you'll see hooves. I'll loop the chain above the ankles, and you'll tighten it. You and Vogt will have to raise the calf. Don't get ahead of me. Let me lift the head."

"Yes sir."

He glanced at Vogt. "You ready, Feldwebel? It'll take both of you."

* * *

The sun shone directly through the window and halted in its descent to rest on a western ridge. The calf lay beside Adda's head as David stitched, trying to emulate the parallel pattern he'd seen Dr. Barnhill perform. He'd used most of the boiled water to clear placenta and was sparing with what remained. He slid the womb inside, the tautness replaced by corrugated folds. The stitches were irregular, not as he'd wanted, but they would hold.

He tied off and moved to the abdominal wall, drew the needle through both layers of fascia, trying to replicate Barnhill's baseball stitches. His were irregular and the work tedious. Adda breathed in shallow gasps. He pulled a final stitch and tied it off.

The hide came together quickly, and he drew the sutures tight, then bathed them in iodine. "You can release her legs and loose the halter."

No one moved. He raised his head, saw Marta sitting with her head in her hands. He turned, found the feldwebel and Tremble sitting, their backs against the wide planks. "That other heifer in labor?"

Tremble raised his head. "Wasn't a few minutes ago, sir."

He stretched his neck. "When is the truck due back?"

Vogt stood. "The truck will not come this evening. Marta telephoned the stammlager and Oberleutnant Schneider ordered us to stay. Marta has agreed to feed us and provide us with blankets. We will remain in the barn tonight."

Chapter XXXI

Nicole shuffled papers and glanced around the cabin. It appeared the shipping firm had gotten a discount on gray paint. She rehearsed briefings and read notes. So much, and all so unfamiliar. She'd never cared for the sea, had no interest in the construction or speed of ships, but she would learn. Perhaps she could even make her time aboard enjoyable.

She spread her arms, touched the wall and desk, and fought the unsettledness that came with oscillating floors and tight quarters. In six days, she would arrive in Barcelona, leave the SS *Stewart*, take a train to the Pyrenees, then a bus to a village near Martin's place. She glanced at her baggage, was grateful she would be warm this crossing. And she had crampons that fit. Uncle Laurent would stow her gear, and once inside France, she would become Elisabeth Leclerc, a cloth and clothing inspector.

She drew what air she could and completed her lunges, then turned to the doorframe to begin her pullups. The door came wide, and a man with dark, pomaded hair stood gawking. She saw his uniform and managed to still a shriek.

"Ye're looking a bit peely-wally, lass. Are ye' weel?"

"Sir?"

"I'm no sir, lass. I'm but a thair' mate."

She swallowed, struggling with the burr, and forced a question through her throat. "I see. Is it your habit to open doors without knocking?" It sounded more harsh than she intended.

"Di' I, lass? I'm truly sorrowful. On a ship wi' only men behin' every door, mos' but wee jimmies, I've forgot ma' courtesies. I'll try ta be more canny."

"I'm sure it wasn't intended to harm. It's just— I might not have been decent." She smiled at his flushed cheeks. "What is your name, Third Mate?"

"Robert Grant, lass. And yours?"

"Elisabeth Clark, and I'm honored to meet you, Third Mate Grant."

The officer grinned. "A nod's as good as a blink ta a blind harse."

She missed the meaning entirely. "I beg your pardon?"

"Titles aren' needful, lass. I've come to tell ye that the *Stewart's* a good feeder. The messman and baker are tope notch. Within the hour ye'll be expected ta dispose of what they've concocted. If ye'll forgive me sayin' so, it appears ye're in need o' nairishmen'."

She smiled. "Thank you for your concern, Robert. I'm looking forward to dinner." It was a lie. The captain had been informed she was MI6, and the meeting was apt to be strained.

* * *

"She's a beaut of a ship to be held in such strict confines, Miss Clark." The captain cut his steak but refused to meet her glances, his burr considerably more subtle than Robert's. "Built to sail between Aberdeen and Brazil, not to cruise along the coast of Spain and Portugal. This war—" He lifted his knife. "It makes your job unnecessary. We must stay with the convoy, a difficult proposition in this weather. Stayin' out of the drink takes priority over efficiency."

"You're fortunate, Captain. The war has been more than an inconvenience to many." She touched the steak to her tongue and bit into the smooth texture. "Still, I'd like to try to earn my keep. Perhaps I can find a few ways to conserve space."

"The convoy's the rub here, Miss Clark. A real strain on a pilot's nerves."

He clearly resented her presence. She smiled. "With the *Stewart's* draft of thirty feet, her shallow depth, and the convoy running under your cruising speed, I could likely save you fuel."

He straightened. "We both know why you're here, Miss Clark. There's no need to make additional demands. The men are tired. It's a strain avoiding mishaps, especially with the Navy all about. Boys with armored boats create as much danger as they're resolvin'."

She put the napkin in her lap. "I simply meant that I would like to help make your ventures profitable. It isn't my intent to restrict your crew. And I'm trained in mathematics." She bit her lip, shouldn't have said it, had been warned about references to her real résumé.

Captain Campbell put his fork down. "I'll speak with our purser.

Perhaps he'll find you a few columns to add up. Keep you occupied. Till then, you'll leave the running of the *Stewart* to those with the expertise to do it."

Was the man unaware that she knew what he'd been up to? "It's quite good, you know."

"Beg your pardon, lass?"

"The steak. It's delicious. It would be a shame to allow yours to grow cold." She held her gaze steady. "Captain, I shall withhold my assistance in the restoration of the profits lost due to our exclusion of your trade with the enemy, but if you hinder me in any way—"

The captain stared. "I hadn't meant to be a hindrance, Miss Clark."

She set her fork on her plate. "That would be best for both of us, I'm sure."

He straightened. "You seem sure of a good many things, though some of what you know is but an assumption."

"If it were an assumption, I wouldn't be here, Captain. The Crown takes aiding the enemy seriously."

* * *

Nicole leaned against the stern rail, pulled her collar tight against her face, and stared into the churning water. The night was as gray as her room and almost as cold. Tiny rain hissed as it hit the stacks, covering the decks with a frigid steam.

"Wha' is this? Are ye no' findin' yere cabin ta' yere likin', lass?"

She turned to the third mate, his hands drawn about his mouth, warming them with his breath. "The cabin is fine, Robert. Thank you for asking."

"But ye're no' here for the scenery, are ye?"

She chuckled. "No, you're right. I'm not."

"So, the captain gart ye radge?"

"He what?"

"He gart ye radge. Made ye angry."

She smiled. "How do you know so much, Robert?"

The third mate grinned. "Di' I no' tell ye I was Sco'ish, lass?"

She laughed, felt oddly at ease. "I discerned a slight burr, so I'm not surprised."

"A slight burr? I think no.' Ma burr's a bit deeper than th' Straits o' Gibraltar." The third mate pivoted toward the forecastle. "Late winter may be bonnie af' th' coast o' Portugal, but I ha' somethin' else ta discuss with ya. Somethin' importan'."

She straightened and gripped the rail. "By all means."

"In future communications within the organization, you'll refer to me as 'Feste.'"

She stepped close, needed to see his eyes. "It's spring, and the plane leaves wither."

The Scot grinned. "Are you also a reader of Goethe?" The words flowed on a Scottish breeze, a mere wisp of highland mist remaining.

She forced a breath. "You're MI6, then?"

"No, I'm with an organization that extends into occupied countries."

She nodded. "I'm familiar with Resistance groups."

"In Belgium, perhaps. But the group I'm affiliated with has made efforts to bring cooperation between multiple organizations and has its roots in Germany."

Was it a trick? "But you're known to MI6?"

"We're frequently directed by them, but no' this time. I have things to discuss, but you must first turn to the rail. It would appear suspicious should we be seen standin' together. I shall observe the port side, and you'll look starboard. If I see anythin', you'll hear my burr. If you see anythin', speak quietly in French."

He took a slow breath. "Your airman is alive and well. He was, however, lured into a partnership with a devious fella'."

She forced herself to breathe. "What can I—"

"He's contacted your friend Élodie in Munich. He's in a stalag there, as is Oberleutnant Schneider who will soon be Hauptmann Schneider if we can nudge him in the right direction."

Feste had too much information to be low level. "And how do you know all this?"

He was silent for a moment. "We have sources within the camp."

"German sources?"

Grant stared into the gray. "Schneider has been offered a bad boy stalag. He'd be directly beneath the commandant. The exact location hasn't been revealed. He's delayed his orders and promotion by insisting he's uncovered a Resistance group operating inside the stalag."

She breathed. "Your organization?"

"Yes."

She steadied her voice. "And what do you want from me?"

"Lieutenant Dremmer will be asked to contact your friend Devillier at least once more. This time, however, the oberleutnant will be present. Your lieutenant must agree. It is imperative."

Something wasn't right. "I will ask once more: What do you want from me?"

The third mate cleared his throat. "Lieutenant Dremmer will do whatever you ask."

A fire torched her breast. "If he declines, there is a reason. I will do nothing to place him in danger." Hope wormed its way into her heart. "But if you were to assure his safety—"

"This is war, lass. Who among us can be assured any measure of safety?"

Chapter XXXII

David stirred within the gloom, the cold stealing beneath his blankets. He eyed the shaded lines of the barn doors, drew the blankets around his shoulders, and felt the strength of Marta's pork and lintels. Vogt confessed that she'd canned them, had said it as if her eating the fruits of her labor were a shameful thing, but stopped short of admitting the food was hidden to protect it from the Wehrmacht. Still, it seemed likely.

David stretched his back. The private hadn't talked much, was likely relieved to be away from camp, but something about the thin-faced Tennessean troubled him. He turned to the slender form beneath the blankets in the opposite corner and crept slowly behind him to Adda's stall. The left rear quarter of the heifer's udder had shrunk, and the teat was drawn. The calf had nursed during the night and now slept at her feet.

The path between the stalls was clear, so he padded to the other heifer, his socked feet silent on the packed earth. She stood, too, clearly in no distress. He moved close and leaned against the wide planks, marveling at her compliance.

A hand squeezed his shoulder, and he spun. Vogt pressed a finger to his lips, his words feathering through the void. "We will talk now, Lieutenant, while the private sleeps. Herr Oberleutnant suggested I bring someone to do repairs. Private Tremble was waiting after appell. I do not know who assigned him to work with us."

He nodded. "So, Tremble could be Schneider's plant."

Vogt stared into the opposite corner. "Or Hanson's. It is also possible he preferred working to remaining in camp. But I have things to discuss."

He'd waited too long. "I want to know a few things first."

The feldwebel scanned the corners. "Briefly, then."

"What you said about Swanson and me, the father thing. How did you know?"

Shadows failed to hide Vogt's smile. "You wrote a letter to your father, did you not?"

Cold fingers gripped his lungs. What kind of connections did this man have? "No one saw it except Feldwebel Devillier, and he sent it out immediately."

"Not before transcribing it."

"Then he was already working with the Partisans when I recruited him?"

Vogt nodded. "He was. We are perhaps more organized than you imagined. No matter. What I must tell you—"

"And how do I know you aren't working with Abwehr? Henri, too?"

"Abwehr is no longer a threat. Their blood has been let with others deemed disloyal to the Führer." The feldwebel paused. "Their successors, the RSHA, is far worse. If Henri were a Nazi, he would not have sent your letter or allowed Miss Serat to be removed from Belgium."

The knife in his gut eased. "Then why did you read my letters?"

"We wanted to know what you were capable of should the need arise."

The Resistance knew where he was, just as they knew where Nicole was. It might be the connection he'd prayed for. "And the need has arisen?"

The feldwebel dipped his chin. "It has, Lieutenant."

"And what's your relationship to Hanson? Do you work with him?"

"No. The captain believes he has allied himself with someone who provides him with information from MI6. In truth, his reports come through me. Captain Hanson is told only the portions of the reports we wish for him to know."

The growing light spurred him on. "But you were Corporal Swanson's contact, and he worked with Hanson."

"Walter worked also with us, yes. It proved to be quite a dilemma for him."

"Walter?" His chest tightened. He'd not so much as learned the boy's name. "What kind of dilemma? Could it have pushed him to do what he did?"

"I have considered it. Walter hated working with us, but he was aware that the captain was manipulative. He still needed Hanson's approval, even after learning the man based his plans to build an intelligence network on your connections. Walter believed he was no longer needed. Can you imagine what this meant to him?"

His stomach soured. "The day Schneider arrived, he discovered a tunnel. Did Swanson leak that information?"

Vogt shook his head. "He did not. I know you are aware of the corporal's feelings regarding my fellow countrymen. And the reason for it."

It wasn't enough. "Then where did Schneider get that information?"

"I know only this. After appell on the morning of his arrival, Herr Oberleutnant met with Allied officers who held positions in the prison. He requested their cooperation and promised better treatment in return. It was normal protocol. Before adjourning, he invited any officers who had questions to remain after the meeting. Captain Hanson was the only officer to do so."

The hair on his arms rose. "Then Hanson had the opportunity, but Swanson didn't." He had more questions, but time was running out. "What was it you wanted to ask me?"

The feldwebel paused. "We are requiring you to again meet with Élodie Devillier."

He drew a hitched breath. "It's too dangerous."

"It will be difficult, but I will help. We will hide it from Captain Hanson. And this time, we will arrange it when Oberleutnant Schneider is home."

A shudder took him. "You're sacrificing me."

Vogt seemed unperturbed. "Not at all. The oberleutnant cannot expose you. Moreover, he is making inquiries into our organization. He poses a threat that must be dealt with."

The chill galvanized him. "You want me to *kill* him?"

The feldwebel smiled. "You find this repugnant? Miss Serat is safe. Her compatriots would be difficult to locate, and he is your enemy."

The earth spun beneath him. "I can't do it."

Vogt smiled. "It would indeed be a wretched fortune to be asked to play Brutus to his Caesar. One can only hope his reaction would be the same as yours." He paused. "In truth, we have no desire to kill Herr Oberleutnant as it would only confirm our presence. We would prefer revising your plan to kidnap Miss Devillier. She will be more convincing if she has, in fact, been captured. Our operatives will be disguised as Volkssturm, an increasingly aggressive group of civilians loyal to the Reich. The incident will prove to Herr Oberleutnant that they are dangerous, and you will inform him that the Resistance has saved her life."

He drew in the chill. "But if he's home, Élodie can tell him."

The feldwebel nodded. "You shall inform him first in his office, then appear later at his home. It is imperative the oberleutnant see clearly that you can leave the camp and that you have the contacts necessary to find him. He must believe your abilities exceed his grasp."

David shook his head. "It's reckless."

Vogt's face was blank. "It is not without risk, but Herr Oberleutnant has been offered a promotion and a transfer to another stalag."

His neck tightened. "And you want me to convince him to take the job?"

"His lover will have been captured, and you will have been part of her rescue. He will understand the Volkssturm knows of Élodie, and you will convince him the attempt is likely to be repeated. We know he has resisted the requests of his superiors by telling them he has uncovered a group operating between the stammlager and Munich."

A shiver climbed David's spine. "And you think Élodie will believe this kidnapping is real, even after I discussed a similar plan with her?"

Vogt smiled. "She was to play a role in your plan and will be surprised by this one. And we are quite convincing as Volkssturm. We know them well."

He stared at Vogt, tried to see past his doubts. "But you won't hurt her."

"She will be safe, Lieutenant. She will experience nothing worse than perhaps a bruise."

He glanced at Tremble wrapped tightly in a blanket. "And what about Hanson?"

"We are aware of the captain's subordinates, including Private Mathews. We will keep them occupied while you inform Herr Oberleutnant of Élodie's rescue."

"Mathews. I should have guessed." David spat into a manure pile.

Vogt glanced at the window. "An escape from the prison would be difficult, so we will take you to Munich."

"And if it's discovered that I'm missing?"

The door opened, allowing a stream of pale light into the barn. The feldwebel slipped into the shadows and walked quickly to Adda's stall.

David watched as Tremble rolled away from the light and pulled the blanket over his head. If the boy were a spy, he certainly wasn't a curious one. Marta edged forward, carrying a tray, and Vogt ambled behind, his words muted in the heavy air. The feldwebel took the tray and shouted into Tremble's corner.

David turned back to his thoughts. However little either of them liked it, he and Schneider were friends, and their agreement was his only shield. If they were separated, it could be disastrous. Especially for Nicole and her compatriots.

Vogt stepped behind him. "Please, Lieutenant. Marta wishes to share her food with you."

He pivoted to see the German turning away. "Herr Vogt, wait. You want me to dispose of your greatest threat. What will you do to get rid of mine?"

Vogt's chin lifted toward the rafters. "Lieutenant, I believe Herr Oberleutnant will take you with him. Captain Hanson will no longer have access to you."

His breath came easier. "And if you're wrong?"

"We shall do whatever is necessary to keep the captain from thwarting our operation."

His stomach knotted. Whatever Hanson was, he didn't want another corpse added to his account. "I'm sorry I was rough on you yesterday. It's just that—"

"You did not know whether to trust me. Be assured, Lieutenant, I am also placing my life in your hands, and my wish to survive is as great as yours."

* * *

The bread and cheese filled David, though the coffee was worse than at camp. How had Nicole managed to make ersatz taste like something other than burned barley? He swirled the grounds, pitched them in the straw, and strolled to Adda's stall to gather instruments.

He opened the trunk, replaced the iodine and alcohol, coiled the ropes, and tucked in the suture container. With bottles arranged, he lifted the metal-joined box, carried it to the supply room, and pushed the door with his boot. Marta's pitchfork leaned in the corner with an ax, a grubbing hoe, and two shovels. He unlatched the shutters on the window, and morning painted the opposite wall in brilliance.

A space the size of the trunk was cleared except for a bundle of sacks, and he pitched them aside. Boxes of canned foods lay in an underground cache, the lid open, and all free of dust. He scanned the labels and caught his breath. Footsteps scraped outside the barn. He threw the sacks in place and reached to close the shutters.

"What are you looking for, Lieutenant?" The feldwebel stood with his arms crossed, his nose pointed directly at him.

"Just putting supplies away. I left the instruments out so they could be cleaned. Not likely we'll need them, but it wouldn't hurt to be prepared. Where does Marta stow the supply box?"

Chapter XXXIII

Cerulean skies brightened the teeth of the Pyrenees. Nicole had crossed in four days, Martin guiding her along a steeper and quicker track. She had slept, stayed warm in her climbing gear, and eaten. Still, the little house beckoned like a dream of home—the warm bed, the duck and pork sausage, the pleasure of Uncle's voice. For all that, the tightness in her stomach seemed not to leave when she was on this side of the mountains. She pushed through the chill, Martin's scarf bobbing before her, his pace nearing a jog. He hadn't said so, but she was sure he was hoping to make it to Uncle Laurent's before full light.

How could Martin begin the trek back this evening? And she had sworn not to use him again. It was unfair even to ask it of him. The skies were expanding, and morning bit her skin. A red promise blushed the peaks as Martin's form grew certain, and his stride quicker still.

She pressed harder, stumbled, and touched the path with extended fingers. An open door silhouetted a man lifting his suspenders, and the warm explosion of a match etched Uncle Laurent's lean face against the failing dark.

* * *

Nicole pushed herself into the heavy chair, her legs trembling as shadows dampened the narrowing walls. She drank the oil-laden air and looked toward the bolted door. There was no other way in except through Uncle's bedroom. Martin sat across from her, the notched planks of the table between them. Laurent stepped into the light, the skillet flickering steam before the shuttered window. "I expected you earlier, but I am grateful you are both here now."

Her stomach moaned at the effluence of sausage, garlic, and beans. She smiled. "As am I, Uncle. I hope you're still grateful after I share my news with you."

His chin wobbled. "We shall discuss directives later. You must now eat." He turned. "Martin, you are too thin. Please take more. There is enough."

The boy pointed to his waist. "With so little, I live. No too much for lift over mountains."

Nicole smiled, delighted at Martin's willingness to attempt what French he possessed.

He turned, laughing. "Elisabeth is more good now, yes? She lift me over mountains."

Laurent nodded and caught her stare. "You were better prepared this time. That is good."

"I had no warning last time, Uncle."

"That is often the case. Remember it."

* * *

She woke, rolled her head, and lurched as Uncle stepped close, a finger to his lips. He offered a pitch of his head, and she rose, her back and legs stiff, the distance narrowing between her dream and the warm kitchen. She had insisted that Martin use the bed this time. He would climb at dusk, and it was only fair. The door opened to a blinding light, and Uncle motioned her into the chill and draped a soft blanket over her shoulders as she stepped outside. The latch clicked behind her, and she longed for the rough wool of his chair.

Uncle spoke first. "I regret disturbing you, but it would be best if you slept tonight before continuing tomorrow. I allowed you three hours only."

She rubbed her eyes. "Yes, of course. Was there something else?"

"I wanted also to hear your directives, though I suspect I know. It would not be good for Martin to carry secrets that would only burden him if he were arrested." He paused. "Are they requiring you to re-establish the Thomas/Tómas line?"

She shook her head. "I've been assigned something else entirely, though I am to arrange safe houses. Are you willing to house escaping prisoners and Jews?"

A smile lifted his cheeks. "That is also why I wished to speak with you. In the past, I found it difficult to care properly for those who were escaping over the mountains."

Her chest tightened. "I'm sorry. You have been more than

gracious. I know it has cost you dearly."

He shook his head. "That is not a concern. I have appealed to a friend who provides mutton and cheese. I am now looking for someone to make clothing for the climb."

She nodded. "That would be most helpful."

"I have been working for a year to dig a room beneath the house that could sleep perhaps three. More as I continue. It is chiseled from rock and earth with an entrance beneath my bed. Within a month, I shall complete another entrance thirty meters above us." He pointed beyond the kitchen. "Should the Boche come, my guests will perhaps be able to escape."

She smiled her approval. "Thank you, Uncle. That is wonderful."

"My friend, the sheep farmer, can perhaps keep five. He will guide small groups as far as the couloir on this side of the peaks, where Martin will meet them. It will reduce the boy's risk and save him a day over and one back. Should a sheepherder be found below the couloir, it might not be questioned so long as he is alone. My burros will also be used to transport the injured."

The day took on a sweetness. If only her other directives were so easily accomplished. "And do you still have contacts in Aquitaine?"

"Yes, and Limoges. They are awaiting notification and will require no more than a few hours to be ready to receive guests."

She warmed at his accomplishments and thought of David and Bear's escape. If only they could have received such care. "Shall I now report this to London?"

Laurent looked toward the road. "No, I will do that. I have also instructions for you. After Paris, you are to continue to Ghent, where your operative there has been selected. He is an older man, a Parisian, placed by the Boche in the train yard."

She nodded, her heart lifting. *Could it be?* "And what is his code name?"

"Marcel."

The warmth of it settled her heart. "I'm certain I will be able to locate him."

Chapter XXXIV

Morning appell dragged on for hours, and the weevil-laden soup was barely edible. The commando parties left, and David returned to his palliasse. He stared into shadowed flames coursing the length of the ceiling, the yellow undulations winding around the ridge beam where panels had been removed. Eyes as red as dusk emerged from the grate and rose in a desultory pack beneath the collar joints. He followed a half-light snaking the corners, licking darkness, and chanting a lie that every man has heeded, and he knew that evil hadn't surrendered. It was the real Phoenix, extinguished for a moment, then rising from the ashes of some long-spent delusion.

He'd spotted Hanson twice in the weeks since he'd been to Marta's place, but the captain pretended not to see him. It was as sure a confirmation as he could ask for that he was being watched. Nothing was allowed to escape the captain's appraisal, so someone else had to be providing information. Mathews, most likely. He waited and prayed, slipped from his excelsior pad, and headed to the sports field. They'd received Red Cross packets, the fourth in five weeks. The packets were meant to last one man a week, but only with additional foodstuffs provided by the Germans. He'd traded Mathews his cigarettes for two tins of meat and hadn't fretted this time about denying the man his food.

The day was fine, the sting of appell dissipating, perhaps a portent of spring. He looked west as shadows shortened, sought anyone staring back, rounded the corner of the storage building, and turned to the gate.

"Lieutenant, come this way. Quickly please."

He angled to the door of the coal warehouse and slipped inside. "About time, Feldwebel."

"'How poor are they that have not patience! What wound did ever heal but by degrees?'"

He slid behind the door and waited for vision. "Othello, right?"

"The correct play, Lieutenant, though it was Iago's line."

"Close enough."

Vogt drew a hand over his face. "Our players are onstage. Élodie is being abducted."

His heart slammed against his ribs. "When will I tell the oberleutnant?"

Vogt lifted his chin. "You will proceed to the bars. I had thought you might come later, so you will exercise at a leisurely pace. At some point, a French corporal will approach you, introduce himself as Mark Antony, and ask you to assist him in—how do you say it?"

"He'll ask me to spot for him?"

"Yes. This is the fourth time you have practiced since parcels resumed, always on the day after their dispersal. It will seem normal for you to rest frequently. Your compatriot will stay as well, though you will not acknowledge one another. Remain at a distance."

He looked toward the door. "Understood."

The feldwebel stroked his chin. "You are being watched, Lieutenant. The captain hasn't any contacts among the French, but we do not wish to bring Monsieur Antony under suspicion."

"Who's watching me?"

"Private Mathews stands smoking between barracks three and four. Today he will be detained while you visit Herr Oberleutnant. You will return to exercise afterward. The private should have no reason to suspect you ever left the sportplatz. Captain Hanson is attempting to discover who is responsible for a spate of thefts among the British. They suspect an American, though it is perhaps a German." The feldwebel chuckled. "The others working with the captain are on work detail."

The feldwebel had likely pilfered more tea. "You're sure he doesn't have another disciple waiting in the wings?"

The feldwebel shrugged. "One remains, but he is indisposed. Private Tremble received a tainted tin of meat, the only one in the entire Red Cross shipment."

David eased. "How unfortunate."

"You understand your instructions. There is no need to linger."

He waited for the dark stare. "Maybe there is. I have an idea about how to get out of the camp when I visit the oberleutnant and Miss Devillier."

The feldwebel smirked. "Do you?"

"You inspect the trucks leaving the officer's mess. I've seen you.

You have a driver who leaves here on your errands. How about I slip into the back of his truck, and you can overlook me during your inspection?"

Vogt shook his head. "Should you be discovered, I would be discovered, as well."

"Won't happen. The guys at the gate are gefreiters. You'll wave it through like always."

The feldwebel's brow contracted. "And how will you escape from a moving truck?"

He stared into the brooding eyes. "I saw tins of chocolate in Marta's barn, cases of powdered milk, more of canned pork, a few of rinderbraten and canned cheese. Cases, Feldwebel. Marta is getting assistance from the officer's mess, and one of those drivers knows the way to her house."

Vogt's face was granite. "What are you suggesting?"

He smiled. "That we use Marta's place as a depot. Your driver will make his stop, and I'll slip out. I'm betting she'd be delighted to take me to Munich."

"Marta can take you nowhere, Lieutenant. However, I frequently accompany the driver to the rail yard. I will transport you to a place near Wodenstrasse. It will lessen your exposure."

The muscles in his neck eased. "And how do I get back?"

"We will collect you at a designated time. There will be an alternate plan should you be delayed. You must be sure that Oberleutnant Schneider does not follow."

"And if I'm not allowed to leave?" He waited. "Or if you're delayed?"

"If I tell you, you will find a reason to object, Lieutenant. And rest assured that my pilfering food from the officer's stores is not an egregious act. It is for families with children."

Gloom slipped inside him, shame for the accusations. "Sounds like risky work."

"It is. That is but one reason I will not allow you to involve Marta in our enterprise. Her imprisonment or death could mean starvation for numerous children."

He nodded. "I understand."

***

David's arms quivered from chin-ups, dumbbell presses, bent-over rows, and bench presses. A Frenchman, the only man exercising, seemed oblivious, a glance meeting his only once. David's legs were weak after only two sets of squats, so he moved to the fence that protected the coal warehouse, reclined against it to absorb the sun, and tried not to rehearse his speech. His words to Heinrich needed to convey exigence, not preparation.

A sudden cool interrupted his reverie, and he opened his eyes. The Frenchman stood above him, his face lost in shadow. "I am Antony. You weel to o-fair aid, yes?"

Antony. He leaned forward. "And I'm Othello. How can I help?"

"To o-fair spot, please."

"Sure." He followed Antony to the bench and waited as the man placed his hands wide. He gripped between them, and the bar rose in a controlled lift. Five repetitions. Antony rose. "Ze deed is done." The words were carried on heavy breaths. "It weel not be reported for two hours."

He nodded. "So, tell me, Mark. How do you feel about your dad?"

The Frenchman leaned his head in puppy fashion. "I do not understand."

He smiled and shrugged. *"C'est une blague."*

***

David stood outside the oberleutnant's door and grew heated under the gefreiter's smirk. He'd likely been deemed audacious for approaching the inner sanctum.

"Ja ja!" Schneider stood at the open door, his cheeks red.

The boy issued an obsequious string of grunts.

Schneider turned and stared. "What is it, Lieutenant?"

"Something you'll want to discuss privately, Herr Oberleutnant."

The German hesitated, maneuvered around his desk, and slumped in his chair. An amber bottle stood uncapped amid stacks of paper. "Would you care for a drink, David?"

His name was offered without preamble. "No, thank you, Heinrich."

"And what is your concern today?"

He caught the lowered gaze. "I have disturbing news. It concerns Élodie."

The oberleutnant's finger rose. "If you are attempting to engage me in a dispute, Lieutenant—" Schneider stared, seemed to read his face, then looked beyond him. "Close the door, please."

He pushed it closed and pivoted. "Élodie was abducted this morning."

Schneider erupted, his chair flying backward. "If your criminals-"

"My *criminals* rescued her, Heinrich. She's fine, though I'm told she's upset. Had they not been surveilling her she might not be alive."

The oberleutnant stood. "She is well? You are certain?"

"She was abducted by a couple of thugs, but my friends subdued them."

Schneider sobered, pulled his chair forward and sat. "Where did this occur?"

"I don't know the spot, but they followed her from the market on the square."

"I have warned her." The oberleutnant shook his head, the flush surrendering to gray.

"We are concerned for her, Heinrich. My friends believe she was targeted."

Schneider's head rose, his eyes burning bright. "Targeted? Why?"

He shrugged. "I can only guess, but maybe her past with the White Rose has been discovered. Or her Jewish blood."

The oberleutnant leaned toward him. "Perhaps it was that foolishness before, but… How would they know of her grandfather?"

David opened his hands and let them collapse. "You both attended the university here. Maybe someone in the Volkssturm knew her."

"Volkssturm? And she is well. You are sure?"

"She's home and uninjured. I don't know about her mental state." He let the implications settle in. "Would it be possible for you to move her? Find a house in Moosburg, maybe?"

Heinrich shook his head. "It must be farther away."

He stood, prepared to leave. "Just so you understand, I intend to honor our agreement, but it might be impossible for me to keep her safe if she's far away."

Heinrich stood, his nod nearing a bow. "Thank you for protecting her, David."

He turned from the stare. Heinrich's gratitude cut deep. "Just don't send her where I can't keep an eye on her. My compatriots believe it will happen again if she stays in Munich."

* * *

David watched the shadowed flames lick the panels still attached after the stovepipe repair. Blue and yellow tongues rose above the missing sections and snaked across the ridge beams. Embers hissed dark prayers, wavering supplications to the god of deception and death.

He stared, captivated, his excelsior mattress offering little comfort. He pled for grace to stand against malice, and, as it was beyond his capacity to believe darkness could win, he prayed with certainty. The grave within his heart burst free, and words emerged without shroud or ash, hurling within the hissing dark to offer an evening sacrifice— adoration to blunt the cheer of evil, and truth to staunch the lies. In the corners, darkness trembled where coals as red as dawn flickered to gray, and light slashed spent delusions. He eased, retired from the battle, and closed his eyes in sleep.

Chapter XXXV

Jesse wheeled himself to the window, tugged at the curtains, and cursed them for their worthlessness. He stared at the lone cedar, felt his throat constrict, and spun from the flow of green. Delores had insisted on having drapes, though it seemed clear that whatever she might need to hide would be on display for any man with an interest in seeing it.

He pivoted toward the clock. It had always kept proper time, and he didn't see a reason to suspect it wasn't now. Ben was late again, the old coot less reliable than rain. Eight forty-five with daylight burning. He pulled at the drape again, saw the red Ford creeping up the hill, old Niedermeyer too persnickety to use the accelerator as a man ought. Likely why he was late. That or he'd stopped to rub another coat of wax on the blasted thing.

He rolled out, pulled the door behind him, and pushed himself across the narrow tracks. The wind picked up sand and spat it in his face. Another dry winter, and March was offering nothing wetter than a blistering gust. And threats of firestorms. He woke each morning to air boiling with grit, rolled onto the porch, and sniffed for smoke even before making coffee.

The Ford pulled into place and parked with the passenger door on the opposite side. The old fool never thought about how hard it was for him to wallow his chair across those tracks. He wheeled through the loose sand around the front bumper as Ben's door came wide.

"Jesse, wait! Lemme put your chair in. You put a scratch on my door post last time."

Thunder! Less than a quarter inch long. Couldn't be seen at all with the door closed. "How old is this car now, Ben?"

"Almost three years. Newest one in these parts, though. A Super Deluxe Ford V8, Jesse. Two hundred twenty-one cubic inches under that hood."

He'd heard it all before. It still meant nothing. "You'd think with all that engine, it could have got you here on time."

"Look at that clock on the glove box, Jesse. I'm ten minutes early, and my clock is right. That's as fine a timepiece as they put in an automobile."

"Early? Ben, you were supposed to be here at eight-thirty."

"That ain't so. I told you I'd be here at nine. I come at eight-thirty last time 'cause you was frettin' about gettin' home in daylight. Told you we had headlights. Then we got home with two hours of light left. I said they wasn't no use in me milking early. Said I'd be here at nine."

It sounded familiar. Could have been the way it was. "Well, at least you're here. Finally."

Niedermeyer shook his head. "You ain't even trying to get along, Jesse."

He covered his grin. "Well, you're right about that. Fact is, I'm tired of getting along. Worn out from it." A wool blanket moved over his chair. "What are you doing, old man?"

Ben slipped behind him. "I'm wrapping your chair so's it don't make a hole in my seats or rub agin' somethin'." The voice was silenced by a gust. "Here's what I'm thinkin', Jesse. I'm thinkin' I know why your sister kicked you outta her house."

He grabbed the top of the door and pulled himself straight. "She didn't kick me out. I sent her back without me. Stayed to make sure Morgan didn't sell off everything I owned." The back door closed, and his friend moved around the car.

"That's a pure shame, Jesse, but I cain't say I'm much surprised. Did I tell you—"

"You told me. More than once. My boy told me, too. And Morgan was a cheat long before he wrote those tickets on you when you were out of town. Never would've thought he'd be so bold as to do that."

Ben slid behind the wheel, pulled the door, and stopped it with his hand so it wouldn't slam. "Word is, he helped hisself to more than your mules, Jesse. Folks is sayin'— Well, they're sayin' that girl come down here without nobody around. Morgan shut down to feed ever' day while she was here. Only some say his truck never left your house."

Jesse shifted, unsure of what to say. "Morgan never was much account at tending cattle." He felt Niedermeyer's stare before the two hundred twenty-one cubic inch V-8 fired up.

"Don't think this is done, Jesse. He'll take you to court over it."

He clenched his fists. "Let him. It's in the contract. If he doesn't make payments, it's still mine. He's not made one yet, and when my boy gets back—"

Niedermeyer shook his head. "That could be a while, Jesse."

Fire stirred in his chest. "This war is coming to an end, Ben. You mark my word."

212

Chapter XXXVI

David sank his ax into the stump of the felled cedar. Chips covered his ankles, his feet sprouting roots that grew deep into the sandy knoll, his limbs straining against a blistering wind. Alone. The image swelled from his sleep and shaded the hollow between waking and dream. He rolled over, slipped from his palliasse, and swung his legs into the dark, his socks settling on the barracks floor. He picked up his boots and flight jacket at the foot of his bunk and stepped through the door. The darkness brought a shiver, and he slipped his feet inside his boots, pushed his arms into chilled sleeves, and set off for the library.

The truth had been settled. Hanson had to be who Vogt said he was. He'd examined every exchange, reviewed the captain's eagerness to pin blame on Swanson, to bring the boy's every action into question, had even suggested his execution. And all without cause.

Then the captain blamed him for Swanson's death, echoing the charge inside. There was a reason for the reversal, and Vogt's explanation was the only one he had. Swanson's heart was unknowable, the truth extinguished by the hiss of steam and hurtling steel. He shivered at the loss buried in his bones and stepped through the library door.

"Good morning, Othello. Are you having difficulty sleeping?"

A current shot up his spine. "What the—"

"Do not start a fire. I know you sometimes burn pine cones, but the light would make us visible." Vogt leaned against a bookshelf. "I assumed you would come this morning. Did you wake Private Mathews as you left?"

The pounding in his chest quieted. "I don't think so. If I did, he'll likely think I went to the latrine." He looked toward the windows. "So, why are you here?"

Vogt leaned in. "Today you will confront Herr Oberleutnant in his home. You will leave in the coach—what is it that you call it?—the bus, after supplies are unloaded at the officer's dining hall. We no longer have the lorry."

He coughed. "Was the truck sent to the Front?"

Vogt shrugged. "That is of no concern. I will be aboard the bus to make sure it gets through the gate. The driver is one of us. We will deposit you less than two kilometers from the oberleutnant's home. Do you remember the square and the street called Josef-Ritz-Weg?"

Every shadow of it seemed an incarnation of his dread. "I remember."

"We will leave you at a warehouse there. From it, you will proceed to Wodenstrasse. You also remember the course, yes?"

The feldwebel's composure was irritating. He looked out the windows at the silent barracks. "I do, yes."

Vogt shifted. "Two hours after leaving you, we will return. In that time, you must persuade Herr Oberleutnant that, though the Volkssturm's plan to remove Élodie was foiled, they shall try again. Convince him that plans are underway, and he must leave soon."

He drew a quick breath. "Getting close, is he? What about Mathews and Tremble? They'll report me missing."

The feldwebel lifted his chin. "They have been assigned commando detail in Moosburg, and Captain Hanson will be meeting with British officers at Herr Oberleutnant's request. He wants the pilfering to stop." Vogt chuckled.

* * *

The bus approached the gate, brakes grinding. David curled behind a rear seat, boxes stacked above him. The rear door swung wide, and his gut tightened. Vogt shouted something harsh, and the door slammed shut.

The driver asked a question, and Vogt responded, the German less officious. The first voice was familiar, could have been the thin gefreiter who escorted him to Heinrich's office. He'd taken the boy's grins as declarations of power. Maybe he was wrong.

The bus rolled past the guards and onto the graveled road.

"Lieutenant?"

He lifted a box. "Yes?"

Vogt sat across from him but faced the front. "I must warn you that, should you be detained, we will wait only one quarter hour, though less if we suspect we are being watched."

He saw something in the face. Concern, maybe. "And if the oberleutnant won't listen?"

Vogt lifted his chin. "Then you must stay. Whatever it takes, convince him to take his new assignment. Should you miss our rendezvous, go to Marta's farm. You can do this?"

His gut clenched. "Not a chance. This is only the second time I've made the trip other than by train, and I'm not seeing any landmarks from the floor. I could go to your son's shop."

The feldwebel's nostrils flared. "Perhaps you consider yourself clever, deducing that he is my son." Vogt swallowed and stared ahead. "Yet you are unable to reason your way back to the prison? You will ask your friend, Herr Oberleutnant, to bring you."

David snorted. "Ask the oberleutnant to smuggle an escaped prisoner into his prison?"

"He cannot risk having you discovered. Your friendship is hindering your perception."

The knot grew icy. "Then fire me, Prospero. I never asked for this job."

"Indeed, you did, Lieutenant. When you chose to write your own script in dealing with your interrogator, you took on more than you can now forswear."

He bit his lip. "I'm wondering what Shakespeare had to say about spiteful Huns."

The feldwebel faced him. "If my references to Shakespeare vex you, Lieutenant, perhaps it is because it reminds you that you have not always acted nobly."

He lowered his head. "That's your reading of it. Shakespeare didn't offer a picture of the evil I've seen. His villains recognized it for what it was, then swore allegiance to it. I'm fighting half-truths and damaged pride. You people always seem to believe you're justified."

"I am fighting that, as well, Lieutenant." The words came through gritted teeth. "I told you the truth, and you rejected it. You are unwilling to commit to what you don't direct." Vogt extended a roll of clothes. "Put these on. Leave yours in this box."

* * *

"'Lives, honor, lands, and all hurry to loss.' So, too, must you, Lieutenant."

David released the latch, slipped into the shadows, and watched the bus idle toward the street. He ducked behind a pile of bricks and scanned the square. Women walked in twos and threes, their packages small. The lines he'd expected on his last trek meandered now before lightly loaded vendors' carts.

He pushed ahead, halved the distance to the three women who plodded at an excruciatingly slow pace. His clothes smelled of mildew and death, had likely been taken off a corpse, the one commodity this country produced in abundance. He shuffled, watching for a chance to get around the women. One turned, but the remaining duo sauntered on. He glanced right, saw the sign where it had lain weeks earlier, reached the corner, and turned left. The house with the shop behind it appeared on his right, and he wondered if Vogt's boy would absolve him of his guilt this time. The key to Schneider's house was wedged in the shelf he'd hollowed in his boot heel, but he needed a place to retrieve it and considered imposing on the man. But Vogt was right. His fellow soldier had sacrificed enough for his Aryan messiah's lunacy.

He slipped to the side of the shop, pulled off his boot, and removed the key. He left the boot untied and slipped the knot of the other to loosen as he walked. The street was free of traffic, the window curtains pulled. He crossed quickly, his mouth like cotton, sucked against his teeth to moisten his tongue, and scurried behind another row of houses before catching the blue of Élodie's door.

He shucked his boots, held them in his left hand, and vised the key in his right. The wooden steps gave beneath him but made no sound. Voices. More than two? He put his ear to the glass, heard Schneider's baritone chafing French consonants, and twisted the key. His breath came in ragged spurts, his ears pounding. He turned the knob and pushed, slid the key in his pocket and rushed to the dining room, hoping to find the oberleutnant before he could react. Cold steel slapped his cheek, and he spun to Schneider's Walther pressing into his forehead.

"It's good to see you, too, Heinrich."

"Why are you here, Lieutenant?"

The barrel gouged his skull. "I'm hoping to save Élodie's life. Yours, too, though I'm reconsidering that part."

The oberleutnant released the pressure. "What are you saying?"

"One of my associates heard plans of another attempt to kill her. I had no way to let you know since you were apparently on vacation."

Schneider raised his chin and stared. "Your associate? How did you get here?"

He shrugged. "I'm not familiar with Munich, so I took a taxi."

The oberleutnant's ears brightened. "Lieutenant, I almost shot you!"

He grinned. "And it wasn't your first attempt."

Something moved to Schneider's right. David turned, saw Henri settling beside a satchel, his starched, white collar covering the neck of a fashionable sweater, his slacks pleated and cuffed. "Henri! I almost didn't recognize you without your typewriter!"

Heinrich let the pistol hang. "Clever, Lieutenant."

He nodded. "So how are things in Belgium? Are you here in advance of the invasion?"

Schneider snorted.

"You're among friends, Heinrich. No need to keep up appearances." He turned to Élodie, her skin a chalky white. "And you must be Élodie, the subject of our agreement."

She nodded, her hands clasped. "Thank you for your efforts to keep me safe, Lieutenant."

"Anytime." He turned. "You're a lucky man, Heinrich. She's a catch. Seems you have no choice but to take the promotion, so long as you keep the terms of our agreement."

Schneider stood immobile. "Who informed you that I had been offered a promotion, Lieutenant?"

"The cab driver. They're like barbers. They hear everything."

Schneider lifted his chin. "And how are you going to get back? Shall I call another cab?"

He looked at the clock, had only twenty minutes. "I'm afraid I left my wallet in my suit pants. I was hoping you'd offer me a lift."

Heinrich glanced at Élodie. "I will get my car."

David grinned. "That's it? No time for a chat? I'd like to give you my opinion on what we should do regarding the prison you were offered." Heinrich hurried through the kitchen door, his hand above his head. David turned to Henri. "You're looking well. And how is Celeste?"

Henri lifted his chin. "We are not friends, Lieutenant."

"We're committed to the same cause. That should merit cordiality, at least."

Élodie gave her brother a blistering glare. "I have something for you, David." She pulled a folded paper from her sweater. "Henri brought it to me, but it is rightfully yours."

"Sweet of you, Henri." He stuffed the paper into his pants pocket.

The boy scowled. "I am here to dissuade her from taking part in your madness."

Her eyes flashed. "I must do more than cower before these tyrants."

The kitchen door opened, and Schneider stepped in. "I will return you to the stammlager, Lieutenant. Hurry, please."

"Henri and I are discussing old times, Heinrich. You don't have coffee?"

Schneider looked at Henri. "We will leave with the lieutenant between us. You have a pistol, yes? You will return and stay with Élodie." He turned. "Lieutenant, you will lie on the floor of my car."

He moved beside Henri and crouched as they bustled down the steps, then slipped into the idling sedan. A heavy coat covered him, the door slammed, and conversation began outside the car. In German. All grew silent before the driver's door opened and the car leaned left. "Lieutenant, this adventure of yours was completely irresponsible." Schneider ground the car into gear and released the clutch.

"Élodie is lovely, Heinrich. I'd think you would consider my efforts worthwhile."

"There are things I cannot discuss before Henri or Élodie. Should I choose to leave 7-A, our agreement will be impossible. The new stammlager will be under a different authority. I may have less latitude, and Nicole is now safe."

A flush burned his neck. "I'm aware that Abwehr was dismantled, Heinrich, and I'm grateful you weren't a casualty, but I want in the new stalag. Pull some strings. Do what you have to, but honor our agreement."

The car stopped, idled for a moment, then pulled on. "I cannot. It is to be a prison for incorrigibles—those who are deranged or have a history of violence or escape attempts."

"Then give me a history. Drop me off outside the prison and send someone to arrest me."

"That is not possible." Schneider's voice quivered.

"Oh, it's possible." Perspiration mingled with the stench, and he lifted the coat for fresher air.

Schneider downshifted and pulled to a stop. "Do you believe you can escape again?"

"Of course." He waited, listened.

"Then allow me to arrange your arrest. You will escape only when I tell you. Otherwise, it is likely you will not survive. Do nothing on your own."

He lifted the coat again. "I won't show you my bag of tricks. If we're on your timetable, you'll have to get me out." Sweat rolled across his back. "And I have two requirements."

Heinrich snorted. "You are in no position to make demands, David."

"I want to be held in isolation after I'm recaptured."

There was a pause. "You are afraid of your associates?"

"I also need to be reunited with Sergeant Billington. Unless you lied to me, he's in Krems. It's a Luft stalag. That should make it easier."

Chapter XXXVII

Spring smothered the bleakness in a swelling warmth as David struggled from the woolen clothes, wiped sweat from his chest, and slipped into his ragged uniform.

Schneider moved from under the shadow of the eves and glanced at the guard tower. "You left your clothes behind my office. You must have been sure I would bring you back."

He smiled at Vogt's cleverness. "It was a calculated risk, but you owed me."

"You are attempting to keep Élodie safe, and I am grateful."

He buttoned his pants, bent to slip his boots on, and retrieved the paper from the pocket of the trousers. "I'm doing more than attempting, Heinrich."

The oberleutnant frowned and looked at his feet. "I hope to fulfill my obligations, as well, David, but you must understand that there are things I cannot do."

"You can find a way to get me into the new stalag. Bear, too."

Heinrich pivoted. "Are you certain you wish to be there? It could be quite unpleasant."

"I'm not exactly in the Waldorf, now. If I'm to fulfill my part of the agreement, I need to remain close to Élodie. And I need to know you're doing the same for Nicole."

Schneider nodded and looked toward the gate. "I shall try."

He kicked the heavy clothes into a pile. "You'll take care of these?"

"Place them in the crate you left your uniform in. I will put them in the incinerator."

* * *

David held Nicole's letter to his chest, still shaken by her words. Élodie said it was the reason Henri came, though the boy denied it. But she had the paper folded and ready as if his appearance were expected. He opened it again and began to read.

David,

> I have been asked to persuade you to, once again, visit my good friend, É. I could not request this of you as I do not know the danger it might put you in, nor am I presently certain that the person making this request is reliable. Instead, I have chosen to notify a trusted member of my former group. He will see to it that our friend receives it, and she can give it to you.
>
> Your reading these words means you have chosen to help without my urging. Rest assured you have chosen well since I know this man will have assessed whether those making this request of you are who they claim to be.
>
> I can only plead with you to be careful. Remember your promises to me as I remember your words: "Then you came on whispered steps, gentle as a secret wish."
>
> All my love,
> N. D.

The message had been typed, not written, but the words were hers. He ran his fingers over the paper, felt the coolness of her skin, the course of her body. The final lines offered proof. They were from the poem he'd written that she'd promised to destroy, and the initials suggested his final words when leaving. She'd promised to identify herself as Nicole Dremmer after the war so he could find her. As with the poem, not another soul knew that.

But questions remained. He reread the first paragraph. She referred to É, their mutual friend. So, she had heard of his first meeting with Élodie. Communication existed within the organization. Apparently, a great deal of it.

Vogt knew of that meeting and had demanded that he repeat it, so the feldwebel had likely asked for her help, a little arm-twisting to ensure his cooperation. But a mere operative couldn't have reached her, much less made the request. Vogt was more than he'd claimed. Within the organization, the school master wielded power.

There was something else. Nicole had chosen to use an associate from her former group, someone she knew and trusted. Henri, obviously. And the É had come from a French typewriter. Again,

Henri. But how had she contacted the little man?

It was unlikely he had come from Belgium. If Henri's arrival scarcely preceded his own, as the satchel made it appear, the boy had done so out of uniform. Was he stationed in Germany, then? It would require the coordination of multiple operatives to find him. But he could have come from France. The Nazis required interpreters, and Henri was qualified. If he were high in the organization, he would likely be known by other operatives between London and Paris. That would be feasible, and it would mean Henri was an important contact. More crucially, Nicole was working not only under MI6 but with Partisans. And she loved him enough to want to keep him safe.

The door squealed, and he slipped the letter inside a book before looking up. "You're here in daylight, Herr Vogt?"

Translucent skin sheathed wizened eyes. "What was the oberleutnant's response?"

"He says he wants to help me escape."

Vogt stiffened. "Why would he—"

"The prison they're giving him is a bad boy stalag. Pretty exclusive. Easiest qualification for membership would be to escape and be recaptured. Or be deemed insane."

The feldwebel shook his head. "I do not like this, Lieutenant. Have you considered how much Herr Oberleutnant might gain if you were killed during an arrest?"

He'd taken Heinrich at his word, needed to trust him. "He tried to dissuade me."

"Perhaps Herr Oberleutnant is sincere, but his quick disposal of an escaped prisoner would serve him well, and he is an ambitious man." Vogt paused. "But we shall hear his plan."

He stood to remove his jacket. "Now who's being ambitious?"

The feldwebel shrugged. "I had thought you might be certain by now. The letter was not sufficient proof that we are comrades?"

"I assumed you requested it."

"Would it help to know how Miss Serat received the request?" The German paused. "She was on a freighter. I asked an operative to solicit her help. He reported her to be as suspicious as you, and as concerned for your safety as you are for hers."

He forced himself to breathe. "Where was she going?"

"Spain. I assume she will cross the Pyrenees. It is a well-travelled route, though traffic commonly flows the opposite direction. Where she will go from France, only MI6 knows—and perhaps the

Almighty, should they deem his politics acceptable."

David chuckled. "And why do you think she's going on to France?"

Vogt shrugged. "Who can know the mind of MI6? I do know she works under their aegis. She admitted it to our operative."

He fought the impulse to defend her, but it wouldn't be enough if Vogt were inclined to doubt her. "I have another plan, Feldwebel, should the oberleutnant's prove unworkable."

The German looked out the window. "And what is that?"

"I'll go to Marta's farm. With directions, I could make it there alone. I'm assuming you don't want to appear trigger happy in front of your sister."

Vogt tilted his head. "Trigger happy?"

"Eager to shoot. You don't want Marta to see the dirty side of your job, do you?"

"No more than I would wish to shoot you, Lieutenant."

"I want to believe that, but can I trust you to find me before anyone else does?"

A smile emerged above the sharp chin. "You can, Lieutenant. You always could."

* * *

Nicole slipped into the shadows of the yard office. Everything was covered in coal dust except gleaming arcs of track. She stared at sided cars and smiled, was sure of her instincts regarding Marcel, and had decided to make Ghent her base of operations while in Belgium.

A man crossed before her, pushing a cart filled with canisters. Liquid splashed as he crossed the tracks, and the scent of coal oil weighted the air. She moved to catch him on the second siding, jogging past the front car. He increased his pace but didn't turn. She'd been spotted, drew close to the cars, and angled in. "Monsieur, I do not wish to alarm you, only to ask directions."

He stopped and turned her way. "Who is it, then?"

Her chest expanded. "A friend." She stepped into the light.

"Mademoiselle! You are indeed more beautiful in the light than in the dark. Should you wish to bite my leg, I would submit without a whimper this time."

"Marcel, isn't it? I am Elisabeth."

"Ah yes. I was never good with introductions. I was told I would be contacted, but I didn't know it would be you." He smiled. "Do you come from Paris?"

"I'm coming from… quite some distance."

"As I suspected, you are a princess from a faraway kingdom."

She warmed at his playfulness. "Aren't we apt to be seen here?"

He shrugged. "I would prefer a corner table with an espresso, but, for the moment, we are safe. The feldwebel decided to sleep off his schnapps. Let us hope he forgets to awaken."

She placed her hand on his arm and squeezed. "I'm sorry I had no chance to leave the handkerchief beneath the depot. It is wonderful to see you again."

"And you, Elisabeth. I had worried—" He lifted his hands. "But you are safe, and I am grateful."

"I have things to tell you. Some are not pleasant."

His smile contracted. "Then you have come from Britain. Good news was banished there centuries ago, else someone might have smiled, and that would have seemed improper."

She laughed, thought of the major at Blenheim. "I have learned much about you. You are quite respected among our agents in Paris." She bit her lip. "And I'm afraid I need your help."

His face hardened. "In aiding escaping Jews and airmen? I will do what I can."

"That will be handled by others. We need someone to gather and process information."

His brow contracted. "What do you mean, 'process'?"

"You are an accountant, as I have learned, and we are tracking troops to determine areas of concentration."

His smile returned, his teeth shining in the muted light. "For the invasion, yes?"

She had feared he would be unwilling. "We can only pray."

"I have prayed, Elisabeth, and my prayers are answered! I will help!"

"It will not be easy. You will learn the average number of troops in cars, count the cars, find where those trains are going, then identify the materiel being shipped with them. You will also follow the records others have kept across the Netherlands and Denmark, then share your findings with me. If they should find you—"

"I am old, mademoiselle. I hope to see my grandchildren, of course, but if not, they shall be free to live their lives as they wish, and I shall see them in a better place."

Chapter XXXVIII

David squinted as the image of the thin gefreiter developed between slate drops. The boy's tunic clung to his shoulders, his soaked trousers wrapping frail legs as they stirred the gray.

The boy stepped beneath the library canopy and stomped his boots. "Herr Oberleutnant requests you to heece offeece." The words were chopped by chattering teeth.

David paused and drew the chilled air. "I'll get my jacket."

The boy's gaze swept the room. "Und all else you vish to take, Othello."

He spun. "This is it? How do you know?"

"I do not know. Herr Oberleutnant is leafing for Munich. Vy else should he require you?"

He needed a concession to be sure. "You drove the bus last week. What do I call you?"

The sharp chin rose. "I am Escalus."

He nodded. "The peacemaker prince. Does Prospero know I was summoned?"

"I veel tell him."

His stomach knotted. "He needs to know now."

"I do not know vere he eece now, Lieutenant."

* * *

David sprinted across the yard, jumped an expanding puddle, and climbed the steps. Escalus sloshed behind, moved close, and pushed him roughly into the entryway.

He stood, his heart resonating within clenched fists.

The oberleutnant motioned him in. "Lieutenant."

"Herr Oberleutnant."

"I am informing you officially, Lieutenant Dremmer, that we are aware of your plan to escape. Should you attempt to carry it out, you will be placed in isolation, or, if you succeed in taking others with you, you will be executed."

He drew an unsteady breath. "That is against the rules of the Gen—"

"I believe not, Lieutenant. The presence of prisoners of war among civilians represents a threat. It shall be dealt with accordingly." The performance was convincing. If that's what it was.

"Lieutenant!"

He turned to Vogt half hidden by the open door. "I am charged by Herr Oberleutnant to do whatever is necessary to see that you remain in custody."

His hungry lungs eased. "I have no idea what you're talking about, Feldwebel."

Vogt stiffened. "It is reported by your commanding officer that you have planned an—"

"You are dismissed, Feldwebel!" Schneider's voice boomed.

So, *that* was it. He watched Vogt scurry from the room and turned back. "What's this about, Heinrich?"

Schneider stood red-faced, the vein along his temple distended "You spoke with someone regarding our plan, did you not?"

He shook his head. "Absolutely not."

"You asked for help, perhaps, and now Captain Hanson has learned of it."

"The captain and I haven't spoken since Swanson died. He blames me."

Schneider's brow furrowed. "Why would he blame you? And why would he report an escape attempt by an officer under his command?"

He saw it again, the innocence that made Heinrich vulnerable. "On your first day here, you found an escape tunnel. Hanson was the informant, wasn't he?"

The German stared, his lips pressed white.

David assembled his thoughts. "The captain blamed the leak on Swanson. If he betrayed the corporal and those working on the tunnel, why are you surprised that he would betray me?"

Schneider turned and stared at his books.

"The captain manipulated you, Heinrich. He has no loyalties. So, what did he get from you?" Schneider's right hand was behind his back cradling his left, the knuckles bloodless and white. He pressed on. "Hanson and I worked together. He used my contacts and deceived me. He betrayed Swanson, and the boy couldn't handle it."

Schneider stepped to his desk, pulled a bottle from his drawer, and poured three fingers.

"None for me, thanks."

The oberleutnant downed the liquid and cleared his throat. "Are you ready?"

He straightened. "You mean *now*?"

Heinrich sat. "After evening appell. If the rain persists, it will aid in your escape. I shall make it known that you were warned. It will appear you were attempting to evade detection."

"Just so we're clear, I said nothing to anyone about our plans, Heinrich."

"And I made it clear to Vogt that you are not to be shot. I will make every effort to capture you, but it is the feldwebel's responsibility to search for escaped prisoners."

He nodded. "And where are you planning to take me?"

Schneider leaned forward. "Escaped prisoners return to familiar places. You have but two—the rail yard and the farm where you assisted in the birth of the cows."

Cows. "And which will I choose?"

Heinrich brought his hands together. "The feldwebel will return to the farm before looking elsewhere. Herr Vogt is not aware that I know Frau Beck is his sister."

"And you think he'll be concerned for her safety?"

Schneider spread his hands. "His concern could be lethal, should he find you there."

It unsettled him. Vogt had taken a reprimand to let him know that Hanson had spilled the beans. Now Heinrich was trying to impugn him. Why?

"You will hide in the boot of my car, and I will allow you to exit some distance from the rail yard as I dare not go there prior to being informed of your escape." The oberleutnant straightened. "When I reach my destination, if all appears safe, I'll rap twice on the lid. You will make your escape at a butcher shop. If I do not rap, you will remain in the car."

"And how will I open the lid from the inside? Or find my way to the rail yard?"

Schneider poured another whiskey. "I have attached a wire to the top of the latch. Pull it tight, and the handle will turn. When I return home, I will remove the wire. I have drawn a map, as well." He handed him a paper. "You will commit it to memory, then burn it in the library stove. It should appear that your hope was to board a train bound for the Swiss border, and that will be your explanation should you be caught and questioned. Look for an open car among the centermost sidings. Records show that cars from these sidings are bound for Switzerland."

He caught Schneider's gaze. "This will require sobriety, Heinrich. Can you do it?"

* * *

They stood in the doorway, the rain coming in sheets. David couldn't see the guard towers. It was a safe bet they couldn't see him, either.

Schneider jutted his chin. "We will go now. The guards are less curious in a cold rain."

David climbed into the narrow trunk, sat upright, and pulled his shoulders in as Heinrich closed the lid. He waited. The car clinked into reverse, gears whining. He felt along the lid, found the cable, and pressed to check for tautness. The latch rolled, and splashes of gray appeared around the seams. He grabbed a slender strip of supporting metal and pulled it down. The engine slowed, the brakes growling. Words were barked in some discharge of protocol. The oberleutnant groused as boots splashed near.

The lid was jerked from his grip. His heart slammed into his throat before Schneider released a burst of German. The lid held inches from the weather stripping, then dropped, the latch twisting. The driver's door slammed shut. Tires caught, first gear whined, and they jostled into the slow rumble of water slapping fenders as David dragged a cold hand across his face.

To his thinking, going early was the weakest part of Schneider's plan. Midnight would have been better, when the kriegies were asleep. He could have left the barracks as if he were going to the latrine. And he hadn't been able to bring himself to tell Heinrich that Hanson was having him watched, or that Mathews might get word of his absence to the captain before they reached Munich. What would Hanson do when he learned of his escape? He'd already reported the plan, believing it a lie. Or did he know? If Vogt were working both sides—

The car slowed, Schneider downshifted, and they crossed water.

David retraced the route, most of it the same as his first visit with Élodie. Would he recognize the place in the rain and dark? Heinrich had provided him with pincers to cut the wire around the rail yard. If he could find the breach, it would keep him in familiar territory. But he hadn't thought to create a signal to lead Schneider to him. Now, it was too late.

The car eased to a stop, the rain now reduced to an occasional patter on the lid. They turned right, stopped, then drove for minutes before turning left. Heinrich braked and stopped again. A truck grumbled through an intersection, and they moved on. If he'd discerned the slower turns, they'd traveled south and east toward the rail yards.

It was at least nineteen hundred hours. Maybe later. The car rolled to a stop, the tires touching a curb. Heinrich's door opened and closed. David waited, took a breath. Two taps sounded, and boots receded in the distance. He counted to thirty and pressed the cable. A gray line appeared, and he pushed the lid. Clouds had thinned, breaking to an open sky. But which direction was it? He dropped his boots on concrete and saw only shadows. Windows were dark, but narrow ribbons expanded and contracted on a door to his left. The butcher shop, blackout curtains swaying after Heinrich's entrance.

The street rose toward a hilltop. Above the tall buildings, a mound of light boiled on the horizon, the sunset sallow as bloodless flesh. So that was west. South was to his left. He pushed ahead, stumbled over bricks, an occasional drop of rain stealing down his collar. He prayed for a street sign, saw instead another row of tall buildings, jogged to the corner, and caught the blue shiver of reflected porcelain. *Scheinerstrasse.* He turned left, edged past shops, and followed an undulating walk to the northwest corner of the square.

He saw movement against a shop window and scurried to the shadows. A dog trotted to the middle of the street, black eyes catching what light was left in the sky. He hurried past the place he'd met the Wehrmacht obergefreiter and the girl, reached a row of trees blocking starlight, and remembered them in their starkness. They were budding now, the shoots stealing what brightness leaked into the night.

He slowed, choosing his steps. A light moved in the east, an engine clattered, and he raced toward trees. A branch struck his face, and soft earth rose to meet him. The sound grew, menacing and mechanical, a diesel laboring against the grade. Slit beams shimmered on brick. He rolled into the gloom, limbs scratching his face. The earth shook as a truck strained past, smoke obscuring the gash of light above the bumper. A three-ton Mercedes, likely the one he'd seen on commando detail. He was on the road he'd traveled then, the fence a quarter mile away, the breach maybe a hundred yards north.

He scrambled to the road, saw a flicker. A locomotive panted forward, stopped, and backed. The flicker swelled into a narrow beam. A railway lantern. He turned left, was lost for seconds, then stumbled onto the path he'd taken before. He crouched, heaved ahead. A branch shoved him into wire as the grizzled edge of downed trees took shape.

The toppled chestnut he'd used for cover shone before him, bark flaking, the white trunk slick with rain. He climbed over it, stepped toward the fence, and traced the woven wire with his hand. A sharp edge cut his palm, and he sucked blood, spat, and searched for the breach with his other hand. The splice took shape beneath his fingers, and he tugged at the links, pulled the wire apart, and drove his shoulder through. The open latrine lay ahead, fetid air rising within the fog, concrete shielding him from the light beyond.

Gravel ground beneath his boots. He stopped beside the rubble, saw jointed pencil lines laid out in pairs. New sidings were flung in a dulling series of twos, the main lines glowing feebly. He was farther south than he'd been and was startled at the countless iterations of muted steel. How would Heinrich find him?

He crossed a dozen or more sidings, all burdened with cars, and turned back to see the first one fade to gray. Lightning flashed in the north, the storm still over the stalag, brightening another array of tracks. He was near the center. A row of empty cars secreted a stench that soured his stomach. He held his breath and walked past them, the sidings curving in unity to the west. The remaining tracks changed slightly, arching to the south. On his right, the doors of a boxcar were rolled back, a narrow line of gray piercing the center. He turned, dropped the pincers before the first car, crept back to the open door, and pulled himself up. His muddy boots slid across wooden planks, and he lay in the door staring at the rows of cars. Lightning flashed again, baring the death of the storm.

Darkness came like a flood, and he recited psalms. Minutes drained into hours before a light swooped in a tiny arc. A railway lantern, its crescent glow sputtering through a maze of wheels and dangling lines, its bearer on the next siding. He retreated an inch or two, could scarcely see past the door. The light disappeared, then reemerged.

He took in the swing of the arm above the lantern, the pace hurried but irregular. Iron clanked to the south, an engine hissing between chugs. A heavy clank pierced the calm, returned, then shook the floor he lay on. He stared at the approaching lantern, circling in a narrow swing, turned and looked through the opposite door, too narrow to crawl through without opening the doors and alerting whoever was there. He looked back. The lamp moved quickly, the rumble of wheels and brakes silencing the approach.

"Lieutenant!"

Had he heard or dreamed it? He put his head through the door.

"David!"

The Wehrmacht wouldn't use his name. The lamp was bouncing, the bearer in an uneven jog. "Herr Oberleutnant?"

The lantern dropped, remained still, the car he was in leaving it behind. He jumped to the ground, tumbled, and stood. "Herr Oberleutnant?" The lantern neither flickered nor moved. His heart shook him, and he waited for a slide to fill a waiting chamber with a round. The distance halved. A hand came clear within the glow, the sleeve of a great coat blending into rock.

"Herr Oberleutnant?" He ran, saw the luster of epaulettes, hair blacker than midnight. "Heinrich!" He jogged across gravel, approached the leaning lantern. "Are you all right?"

The lantern hissed, and he raised it above his fallen comrade. "Can you hear me?"

Fingers twitched against sooted rock. Then a growl. He bent, placed the light beside them, and rolled the body over. Heinrich's face was pale. Blood dribbled from his right temple, and his lashes fluttered.

"Heinrich, can you hear me?"

"Let me res..." The German's liquored breath held in the damp air.

He lowered the wick to avoid being seen. "Are you hurt?"

"I am... fine."

He reached around Heinrich's chest and pulled him to an unbalanced seat. "How am I supposed to get you out of here?"

Footsteps pounded, and he scrambled to extinguish the lantern.

"He is drunk?" Henri's weedy voice.

He sucked in darkness "That's my diagnosis, though he did hit his head."

"We kept him from liquor before the call. He had another bottle, I suppose."

David rose and moved to Heinrich's side. "I'm guessing this isn't the first time."

Henri positioned himself beneath Schneider's arm. "There is a political prison in Dachau. Élodie said he discovered two friends had been sent there. Several of his former Abwehr associates have now joined them." The boy shivered. "His drinking has worsened since he learned of it."

PART TWO

*Special Stammlager 457
Waldheim, Germany
June 1944*

Chapter XXXIX

The castle ascended above the earth, the warm, gray rock respiring toward eternity in century-long exhalations. David closed his eyes, raised his head to the sun, and listened for the soft gurgle of the Zschospau. He relived his walk across the bridge after the trip here, the dark beauty of the flow perhaps fifty feet below. Now he waited for its steady babble when men weren't screaming for deliverance from an approaching doom only they could see.

The shell-shocked were locked behind oak doors, suffering a torment as inescapable as the prison. He turned, stared at walls he'd not seen over, closed his eyes, and set his thoughts afoot. He smelled horses, fresh from the field, grass-sweet sweat lathering their flanks. Black-hearted riders appeared behind his closed eyelids, faces hidden by armor, pauldrons gleaming in the sun. "My kingdom for a horse, indeed, Herr Richard."

The joke wasn't worthy of a chuckle, though Vogt might have appreciated it. He missed the feldwebel, wished the man could tell him what was going on. He'd learned to trust him, but faith had come late. And he'd ceased protesting Bear's absence. It would be cruel, demanding such privations of his friend, the finest man he knew. He only hoped things were better at Krems.

"Lieutenant?"

He turned toward the stables, shuffled to the lone kriegie sitting within the wide doors, shielding himself from the tortured screams. "What's up, Langley?"

The Brit looked around, his grin lifting. "Big news, is it, suh? Things is hottin' up." The gangly corporal extended a scribbled note. "Come ovuh the BBC an hour ago."

He took the parceled cigarette packet and spun away from the bright door.

Under the command of General Eisenhower, Allied navy forces supported by strong air forces began landing allied armies this morning on the north coast of France.

He drew a breath. "This is it, Corporal!"

Langley's teeth shone from the shadows. "Ger uz a pint, eh, Lieutenan'?"

"It's on me. You name the pub."

"Is orrigh' then, sharin' wi' the men?"

"Hide your radio. Pick a place as far away from it as possible. We don't want to give the Krauts any hints." He scratched his face. "But the goons likely haven't heard. It wouldn't hurt to let them know we heard it first."

"An' the note, suh? You'll chuck i' away?"

He grinned. "After I memorize it, Corporal. I love poetry."

* * *

David looked down the spiral staircase. The lack of food was taking a toll. Schneider had brought him sausages and bread his last month in solitary after the escape, and Vogt brought cheese and lintels from Marta's store. He'd eaten well, had spent his afternoons exercising, but that had been weeks ago.

Now he watched his feet, the uneven widths of the steps an invitation to disaster. At the bottom of the stairs, he shuffled across the corridor to Schneider's office and stood waiting for the goon to acknowledge him.

The unteroffizier glared, then slammed a fist against the door. David straightened. Schneider had mentioned his name when the first trainload of kriegies arrived, suggested they pick an officer as their Man of Confidence he could deal with. The hauptmann had gone so far as to say that David had been a difficult negotiating partner in the past. It was likely Schneider's disgust that determined their choice. The vote was unanimous, or close enough not to bother with a count. The position assured him regular visits, a duty he was determined to turn into an opportunity. Élodie had to have made contact with the Resistance, but he needed assurance.

The ancient door creaked open, and David stepped forward. Schneider leaned against his desk, his new hauptmann insignias folding inward across his chest.

He smiled. "Good morning, Herr Hauptmann."

The face was gray. "Is it? I should think you would be grieving the losses of your infantry and fellow airmen."

He nodded. Clearly Heinrich had guessed they had a receiver. "I grieve the loss of all lives lost to Nazi aggression, Herr Hauptmann."

Schneider waved his hand. "And what grievances have you to offer me today?"

He lifted his chin. "We need provisions, more than moldy hay or muddy soup."

The hauptmann looked away. "We've been over this. Our trains are being strafed. Receiving Red Cross packets is impossible. Perhaps you can appeal to your *armies* for help."

"Oh, they'll be here, Herr Hauptmann, though not in time for dinner."

Heinrich refused to meet his smile.

His heart stirred. "What's happened will be for the best. It was inevitable, after all."

Lightning flashed from Schneider's eyes. "Don't belittle me with your concern, Lieutenant. Or your propaganda. As you have said, we are not friends."

"You sure about that? Friends sometimes tell us the truth when no one else will."

The hauptmann's cheek quivered. "I am dealing with more than you can imagine."

The reproach fell short. "I've believed lies before, Heinrich. You've found a cruelty in your ranks you didn't know existed, but it's not too late to do something about it."

Schneider's throat undulated. "Get out of my office, Lieutenant."

* * *

Someone pounded at his door and brought him nearer the unformed phantoms of his dreams. David sat up. "Who is it?"

"Lieutenant, I need your assistance. Come with me, please."

He moved to the edge of his palliasse. "What time is it, Herr Hauptmann?"

"You insist the war isn't over for you. Consider this your duty."

He drew his frayed bootstrings as tight as he dared. The private cell was a concession offered him as Man of Confidence, but he suspected it had more to do with Schneider's desire for quick access. He followed the hauptmann into the corridor and shuffled toward the staircase. Shadows faltered along the steps, the salt and pepper gneiss shimmering beneath the beam of a flashlight. He grew lightheaded and stopped. The guard behind him shoved, and he tumbled toward Schneider's feet. The hauptmann lifted him by the arm and released a torrent of German.

David steadied himself and trailed the hauptmann through the door to the appellplatz, shuffled to the stables, and stood outside. A cow was silhouetted in the brighter moonlight of the eastern wall, a withered man before her. Schneider spoke softly, patted the man's shoulder, pushed paper bills into his hand, and pointed toward the door that opened onto the footbridge. The man turned and looked at the cow before leaving.

Heinrich pivoted. "I have purchased a cow. She must be slaughtered tonight so that your fellow prisoners might eat tomorrow."

He gaped and tried to take it in. "You paid for her yourself?"

"She could no longer produce milk, and the farmer was unable to feed her."

He surveyed her in the pale light. "I can see that. I don't know how much meat she'll yield, but..." He looked over his left shoulder at the steaming pot in the center of the appellplatz, baled vegetable stems beside it, the ingredients for tomorrow's soup. At that, nothing but Germany's best topsoil would be left in the pot when the men finished.

"The cooks will divide her into quarters, Lieutenant. We have no way to preserve the meat, but the nights are still cool. It will certainly last four days. The prisoners will consume it in that length of time. No less. Is that understood?"

He drew himself up and offered a salute. "Thank you, Herr Hauptmann."

* * *

Nicole pushed against the wall of her berth, stretched her legs, and considered the approaching trek over the Pyrenees. She wanted to be ready this time, but it wasn't her greatest concern. She'd spied someone in Manresa watching her and had seen him before. Then boarding the *Stewart*, she saw him again, this time talking to the captain. Something about him, his penciled mustache and quivering gray eyes, filled her with revulsion. And he caught her glance.

She ached for David. He seemed to have an instinct for this sort of thing, had accomplished so much and made so many connections. But he'd also taken chances. Her prayer broadened as she pleaded for his safety and added the sincere wish—it seemed an improper petition—that she would know the comfort of his arms around her at least once more.

Peace came without certainty in a release of understanding. She imagined him near, caressed his brow, and whispered assurances that he'd done well.

* * *

David sank onto the excelsior pad, the swift commingling of thought and insensibility coming before he'd fully settled in. Could death be so sweet? Nicole stood before him, his eyelids scarcely closed, her smile as warm as sunlight. Her laugh emerged, a ringing of silver bells, and she tilted her head toward her shoulder in that gesture he loved. "You've worked well, my love. Now sleep."

But sleep returned him to the stable, the two Germans demanding that he pull the ropes and haul the carcass to the rafters. He'd then sawed the bones, had stolen scraps of flesh when they turned away, and examined the cow's mouth once he'd lifted her from the floor. Her teeth were worn away, and she would have died the first full week of cold. Her slow unwinding had been reduced to the sudden peace of the gefreiter's pistol. Was it like what he felt now?

Nicole smiled and ran her hand across his brow. "No, love. Our peace will last forever."

He reached to hold her, but his arms had grown too heavy.

"Just sleep." Her words rose on a silent breeze that wished him into insensibility.

* * *

"Lieutenant, do you plan to sleep all day?"

David stirred at the voice. "Herr Hauptmann?"

Schneider laughed. "What heinous act have you committed? You are covered in blood."

"I dressed beef all night." He pushed up from the pad, his hands fevered.

"Did you not explain that you were an officer and were not required to work?"

His feet fell to the floor. "There are those who don't care about the rules of war, Heinrich."

Schneider stiffened. "And at what hour were you allowed to go to bed, Lieutenant?"

"Oh five hundred."

"Two hours ago. When you failed to appear for appell—" The hauptmann took a breath. "I shall be certain to enforce the rules in the future, Lieutenant."

He knuckled his thigh. "You were afraid I was gone? Would you have missed me?"

Schneider laughed. "I have no fear that you will escape, David. That is quite impossible."

He fastened his gaze on the hauptmann. "You really think so?"

"I should not wish to see you shot, Lieutenant." Heinrich stiffened. "Make yourself presentable and come to my office. There is a matter we must attend to."

He retrieved his boots and razor and headed for the stairs; the bloodied RAF blouse he'd taken from 7-A was draped over his shoulder with his thermal undershirt. The stairs were easier, the scraps of meat he'd stolen returning some of the strength he'd lost. He only hoped it would do the same for the others. A plan had begun to fester in his skull, and he needed strength to complete it.

* * *

David stared into the dirty glass of the stable window and ran a hand over his freshly shaved cheek. He left his blood-stained blouse soaking in a wash bucket, slipped on his thermal shirt, and headed for the hauptmann's office. English echoed off stone as the pock-faced unteroffizier slammed his fist against the door.

"Come in, Lieutenant." Schneider's voice echoed. "We have been expecting you."

He gave the goon lifting the iron latch a wide berth and stepped inside. A prisoner stood bent, his back to him. The man turned in an awkward pivot, black hair falling across his face.

"Hey, College Boy! Looks like you're holding up good." The man was dark and gaunt, the belt around his waist pulled tight, leaving folds of cloth around his shrunken belly.

His breath left him. "What have they done to you, Bear?"

Thin arms raised, awaiting an embrace.

He grabbed his friend's shoulders and pulled him close. "Hauptmann Schneider's kept me alive, Bear. We'll take care of you, too."

Schneider opened a desk drawer and produced a plate covered in wax paper. "Perhaps I can offer something to aid in Sergeant Billington's recovery. Élodie sent a celebratory gift—buchteln made with poppy seeds. There are two for each of you."

Another act of generosity. David caught the German's smile.

Heinrich extended a hand. "Élodie remains grateful to you for saving her life, Lieutenant."

He nodded. "And I'm grateful to you for saving Sergeant Billington's."

Chapter XL

Light stole between the walls swelling the gray with hope. David had a confidant worthy of his trust who could see through manipulation and ruse as if it were a window. Bear was an answer to prayer, and Heinrich's open heart had provided the avenue for its delivery.

He stared at his friend who lay panting on his palliasse. "Are you sick, Bear?"

The sergeant lifted his hand. "Don't think so, Dremmer. Hard to tell the difference between sick and hungry anymore."

David reached for the pastries. "Eat one now. Schneider's cheese won't take you far. We'll be getting beef in our soup today."

Bear looked up. "You're kiddin', right?"

He unwrapped a roll and tore waxed paper to hold it. "Schneider bought an old milk cow. His own money. Krauts made me cut her up. The meat won't go far, but it'll beat haybale soup."

Bear twisted his head. "They give you sawdust bread, too?"

He snorted. "Toughest trees I ever tasted."

"Pride of the *Vaterland*, Dremmer. You say Schneider bought the cow?"

He handed Bear a roll. "I saw him slip some bills into the old man's hand."

"Commandant at 17-B figured the way to keep us out of trouble was to starve us." Bear's eyes fixed on the pastry. "Still gettin' Red Cross parcels, here?"

He watched his friend bite into the crust and expose the filling. "Not in a while. The invasion is apt to make things worse, especially after they set up airbases."

Bear chewed slowly. "You ain't eatin,' Dremmer?"

"I stole pieces of meat while I stripped the bones last night. Best I've felt in a while." He watched his friend take another bite. "Why won't these Krauts surrender, Bear? Once we take France, there's only one way this can go."

Muscles rippled across Bear's thin face, the unruly dollop covering his forehead. "It's faith, Dremmer. They can't let themselves believe they'll lose. It'd mean their little messiah wasn't who they thought he was, and ever'thing they believe depends on him."

Bear put so much into his few words. "I need to ask you something. After we were captured, they separated us. Remember?"

The sergeant nodded, pinching at his roll, his tongue in the corner of his mouth.

"Did you get to know any of the men in the cellar with you? One by the name of Stanislavsky, maybe? Small guy, black hair, bushy eyebrows that almost met over his nose."

"Don't remember any of 'em. They separated us before sunrise. Didn't even see 'em in the light." Bear tore off a corner of the roll. "There's something in this."

David slid from his palliasse. "Could be she's sent us more than food." His friend handed him a waxy shell. He licked it free of filling, then picked at the coating with shaky fingers.

Bear chewed and rose on shaky legs. "What's it say?"

It took long seconds to open. "It's a drawing of a building with a ward. This place, maybe, but it's only part of it." He looked at the other rolls.

Bear shook his head. "Can't waste 'em. Gotta fish out whatever she might o' hid."

* * *

David glanced at Bear. They'd feasted on beef and vegetable stem soup. It was still gruel, but it had strength. He fingered a small piece of copper wire Langley had found in the assembly area, likely stripped from an ignition coil. He hooked something inside the second buchteln, held his breath and gave a gentle tug. More wax paper emerged, and he handed the roll to Bear.

"This one's yours, Dremmer. For tomorrow, if you want to wait."

"Eat it tonight. That's an order, Sergeant. I need you healthy."

Bear scowled. "You ain't using me to test these for poison, are you?"

"Tell you later." David licked the wax paper shell and placed the drawing beside the first.

"Don't seem to fit, does it?"

He raised the first square to the upper right and drug the second beneath and to the left. A border appeared on the outer edge of each. "It does now."

Bear scraped a hand over his face. "Architect's drawing, ain't it? Where'd she get it?"

"Schneider's papers, maybe. Could be a cyclograph copy of a detail drawing." He reached for another roll, recovered a third piece with an X located near the bottom, handed Bear the wire, and nudged the paper to the lower right quadrant.

Bear retrieved a fourth, removed the wax paper covering, and nudged it into place.

David moved his finger over the diagram. "Here's the officer's quarters; this is Schneider's office. That's general population. The lazarette is behind these doors. The outside showers aren't on it, so the drawing was made before they were put in."

Bear grunted. "And where are we?"

"Here. Above Schneider's office. These six cells were set aside for allied officers."

"And who's in 'em?"

"Just us. There's a captain and two first lieutenants in the lazarette. All shell-shocked. I'm the only officer in general population."

Bear rubbed the stubble on his chin. "How'd I rate stayin' here?"

"Guess Schneider thought I could nurse you back to health. He couldn't allow you one of your own. He's German, you know. And the sick ward is full. Some bad cases there."

Billington nodded. "I heard 'em. So, what's under that X?"

"A cellar. The men call it 'the dungeon.' I thought it might be where they kept supplies, but the Krauts don't go in or out. It stays locked."

Boots stomped on the stairs. He scrambled to the wall beside Bear's bunk, pulled a nail from loose mortar, and pried a stone free. "Stick the papers in!"

Bear lay the papers flat, the sergeant's stubby fingers moving nimbly while David slipped the stone in place. The latch rattled, and he hurried to his bunk.

The door opened, and a goon pointed his finger. *"Ihr werdet jetzt in Hauptmann Schneiders Büro gesucht!"*

He glanced at Bear. "Apparently, I've been summoned." He strode to the door, stepped past the pock-marked unteroffizier, and took the stairs with a strength he hadn't known in weeks.

The obergefreiter marched from behind and rattled the door with his fist. Schneider's voice echoed from a grave that had once held him. "Come in, Lieutenant."

He shuffled before the heavy desk and stood straight.

Heinrich grumbled, and the goon closed the door. "Lieutenant, we have a problem. Nicole has been observed in Spain and Paris. She is clearly acting as an agent for the British. I can no longer offer her protection. Our agreement was—"

"To shield her as I have shielded Élodie."

The vein in the hauptmann's temple bulged. "On the contrary, Lieutenant. Our agreement was to allow her to be removed from Belgium, not to aid her in her duties as an MI6 agent."

Fire rose in his chest. "Your Reich is done for. It existed solely to aid the criminally insane in subjugating innocents. Your friends from the university, your compatriots in Abwehr, have been tortured and murdered. For the sake of all that's holy, help her stay alive!"

"And what is holy, Lieutenant? What you declare it to be?"

"You know better. Heinrich, we're friends! I've fought the truth of that as much as you, but you're a good man fighting on the wrong side. Now, do what's right before it's too late!"

The hauptmann's face lifted. "Did you enjoy your buchteln, Lieutenant?"

It shook him. "I haven't eaten any."

"But your friend, the sergeant, has. Am I correct?"

"Yes."

"Because you insisted, I am sure. Do you know how scarce food is, David? Do you have any idea how difficult it was to obtain flour or butter? Giving away what we provided does not make you a good man. It makes you a fool!"

Fire stirred in his gut. "If that's true, you're a fool to have bought the cow. But it's not true, and you know it, so you salve your conscience with alcohol every day to endure it."

The hauptmann sneered. "And what have I been guilty of? Doing my duty?"

He dared not back down. "You're guilty of supporting an evil so great that it's covered half the globe with death and terror."

* * *

Nicole settled in her chair, glanced around the room, and wished for the prime minister to walk through the door. The Cambridge men sat on the opposite side of the table.

Émile sniffed. "Elisabeth, we decided to meet in a room provided by the workers of Great Britain in celebration of the prime minister's absence."

The major and Professor Greeves tittered.

She nodded. "No apologies are needed. The room is adequate."

Greeves scowled and cleared his throat. "The information you supplied corroborates information we had previously compiled, so we have decided to use the network you have established, without requesting changes."

Heat rose to her face. "Help me understand this, Professor. Are you saying that you risked my life and theirs only to test my associates' capabilities?"

Greeves raised his chin. "It is essential that we assess our resources."

She steadied her voice. "Were it not too great an imposition to read the reports we've provided, you would know that my associates have proven themselves time and again. That information was gathered at great risk."

"Be that as it may, Miss Serat, established protocols are indispensable."

"You find your protocols indispensable, but your operatives disposable?"

Émile spread his hands in a display of amiability. "If you are unable to contain your hostilities over whatever imagined grievances you have, Elisabeth, then—"

"Imagined? I'm placing my compatriots in the hands of men who care nothing about their survival. If I were not grieved by this, I would be as debauched as—" She bit her lip.

"We have more missions for you, Miss Serat. Would it be a mistake to place them in your hands?" Greeves waited, tapping his pencil against a polished leather pad.

"While it may be of no concern to you, I must report that I was surveilled while in Spain. Furthermore, I am certain the surveillance extended into France, and I saw the same man observing me after we docked. He and Captain Campbell were having a discussion.."

Greeves was staring at the table. Émile whispered to the major.

The major looked up smiling. "Miss Serat, I find your work satisfactory. I am recommending your network for participation in future missions."

She forced a smile. "I'm sure. Placing my associates in danger hasn't proven to be an issue for you in the past, has it, Major?"

The major's ears reddened.

Émile raised his pencil. "Elisabeth, I have informed the committee of our work together in Paris. Your proclivity for overstatement aside, I believe you are capable of the planned tasks."

She drew a breath. "If only I could say the same. I find you completely lacking in judgment. You dressed me provocatively and paraded me before German officers, all under the pretense of meeting an operative. You met no one, and we both know it." She glanced from Émile to Greeves, then back. "By your own admission, the Wehrmacht photographed us. If I should be observed by the RSHA, they have only to search their files to verify my association with MI6. You have made my job vastly more dangerous and jeopardized your own operation."

Greeves drew his arms about him. "Were you more familiar with this sort of work, Miss Serat, you would know that no operation is flawless. The mark of a superior operative is the ability to adapt to what cannot be anticipated. You helped establish the framework for an operation that appears quite promising. What is lacking is your willingness to follow directives, trusting that your superiors are more capable than you of assessing both risk and reward."

Blood pounded in her ears. "So long as the risk is not their own. It is clear to me you have chosen the wrong side, Professor. In the Reich, you would be less burdened by concerns for human life.

"Whether I am allowed to engage in another mission will be your decision, of course. In the meantime, I shall prepare a letter for the prime minister informing him that you were apprised of the risks both to my person and to this operation." She looked at Émile. "I shall also inform him that the dangers have been compounded by a surveillant that you were informed about, and that the RSHA now has photographs that will tie me to MI6. In the event of my demise, this letter will be delivered to him personally."

Greeves' mouth twitched. "Miss Serat, since you appear to be more successful at cultivating relationships among your own than with your superiors, I shall reluctantly approve you for further missions. Make no mistake, however. I find your recalcitrance disgraceful."

She nodded. "And what, precisely, do you plan to do about the operative surveilling me?"

Greeves narrowed his gaze. "I find it unlikely that a man *observing* you represents a threat. Not having dealt with you before, the man likely found you attractive. Surely, you have been *observed* before. Deal with this man as you must have dealt with others."

Chapter XLI

David crossed the appellplatz, Bear at his side. Both he and the sergeant were stronger, now, an allotment of Red Cross parcels returning quickness to their strides. Each packet had been divided between two men, but the nourishment helped. He stopped before the kriegies he'd asked to meet him and returned their salute. Langley seemed eager to acknowledge him. Mackey didn't.

He smiled. "Couple weeks of increased rations helping? You men feel better?"

"Much improve', suh. An' you?" Langley spilled the words in a bunch.

"I'm well, thanks. You've met my old crewmate, Sergeant Billington, haven't you?"

Langley grinned. "Allo again."

Bear smiled, nodded. "Good to see ya', Corporal."

"You were captured together, weren't you, sir?" Mackey's grin lifted at one edge.

"We were, but the Krauts sent us in different directions."

The smile approached a sneer. "So, is Sergeant Billington connected, too, Lieutenant?"

He held the boy's gaze. "He is, Private. As a matter of fact, we're working on something we need your help with. It'd be voluntary, of course."

Langley's head rose. "I'm quids in, suh."

He nodded. "I'd assumed that, Corporal. You'll be our ears. But we also need eyes. And hands." He looked to his right. "I want to know what's behind those doors."

Mackey tilted his head. "The dungeon? It's locked tight as a drum, sir."

"But you're good with locks. You were known for that back home, weren't you?"

The smirk disappeared.

He pushed his advantage. "Are you willing to use your expertise for the war effort?"

The boy twisted his neck. "There's no way of knowing what kind of locks they have on those doors, sir. Might be a few hundred years old, and I don't have any tools."

"I don't think the old locks are working, Private. They have hidden hasps on the doors. Can't see the locks, but they're likely new, too."

Mackey nodded. "They may be reinforcing the old ones."

He shrugged. "Could be, but we can't know without checking."

The boy glanced at the parapet. "No way I can get to those doors without being cut in two by that Mauser up there."

"Can't tell from here, but that overhang is in their line of sight. Only have a few feet in their field of vision. That could be covered by two men." He waited. "And I'll be the one checking the locks."

Mackey brightened. "You can write down what you see, sir."

He nodded. "Thing is, no one can know what we're doing. Whether you choose to help or not, this is on the QT. If you help, you'll be on the intelligence committee. I picked you both for a reason, and I'll give you until appell tomorrow evening to decide."

The boy nodded, and Bear turned to watch the goons.

David motioned for Langley to follow and stepped from beneath the chapel overhang. "Any news coming out of France, Langley?"

"Things is hottin' up, suh. Yer boys 'ave taken Cherbourg, an' London's under rocke' fire. No way ter figh' 'em."

The muscles in his neck tightened. "It's still good news. We have a seaport. Airfields will follow, and your flyboys will find a way to deal with those rockets. Or your ack-acks will."

* * *

David stared into the dimming sky, the clouds an advancing brightness against a deepening blue. Stars blinked fresh brilliance within the pending dark. He rehearsed a psalm, the pleas of a king pining for justice. Those yearnings had warmed him through the winter, assured him that justice would come. Now his assurance had dimmed. He'd never met a righteous man, one who could ask for justice without accusing himself. Unless, of course, his righteousness came another way.

"What's got you lookin' at the stars, Lieutenant?"

"Justice, Bear. What gives us the right to ask for it when we're guilty, too?"

"And what's your biggest fear, Lieutenant?"

"That we'll be old men, and you'll still be goading me with this 'lieutenant' thing."

Bear snickered. "That your answer, Butterbar?"

He crossed his arms over his narrowing torso. "I guess my biggest fear is failing."

"But that's what life is. And the more doing the right thing matters, the more your failing hurts. It's why you need forgiveness, and why it's got to be a gift."

He nodded. "If you're asking for my forgiveness, I'll have to think about it."

Bear leaned against a rock. "Fair enough. I'll hafta think about askin'."

He looked into the settling dark, grateful his righteousness didn't require being right.

Bear looked away. "How did you know about Mackey?"

"Schneider tried to talk me out of coming here. He'd received boxes of files on the prisoners, some from the War Department. When I was in solitary, he'd go through one box and bring me another. They included statements from fellow prisoners. He just wanted me to see what I was getting into. Wanted my impressions, too, I think. We each made notes before exchanging. I remembered Mackey and a few others. Thought they'd be useful."

Bear nodded. "What about Langley?"

"I didn't get through all of them, but I don't remember seeing a file on him. If I did, it didn't stand out, but I've gotten to know him. You trust him?"

"I do. He's my pick of the litter—at least, the part I've met."

David stretched his back. "Mine, too. For what it's worth, Mackey wasn't a thief. His father was a locksmith in Minnesota. Friends told him they were breaking into a Western Union office to send prank telegrams. He was head over heels for one of their sisters. The boy promised to convince her to go out with him if he helped. Mackey picked the front door lock, one on the inner office, another on a telegraph. While he was busy, the others robbed a cash drawer. They all went to prison except Mackey. Prosecutor let him enlist, even after he refused to testify against the others, but they all swore he didn't know about the theft."

Bear was silent for a moment. "So, he's loyal. Where's his attitude come from?"

"I can't say. I picked him before meeting him, then asked Langley to check him out. I've watched him, too. He'll bend over backwards to avoid conflict. That might be helpful."

Bear glanced at the tower. "And who didn't make the cull?"

He shrugged. "The aggressive ones and a few with questionable sanity. And that tow-headed kid, Perkins. Have you met him?"

Bear tilted his head. "Not that I recall."

"Leave it that way."

* * *

Nicole hurried, melded into a group of travelers, and scanned the train station. There was a time when she would have relished the terminal's Gothic design and the particularities of Barcelona's eateries. She wondered, now, if she would ever enjoy such things again.

If only she could lead the slender man with his pencil mustache and quivering eyes to Professor Greeves' parlor or Émile's favorite French restaurant or to wherever the major got his manicures. That would be justice. She saw the sign for her gate and whispered a prayer for protection. And forgiveness. Justice wasn't hers to dispense.

She stood in front of a large man, his hot breath prickling her neck, and bought a ticket to Girona. If the inner circle wouldn't protect her, she would have to protect herself. She slipped the ticket into her purse. The *Stewart's* captain had likely informed the mustached man that she had disembarked. If so, he would be waiting for her at the bus station in Manresa. She opted to abandon the course they had provided and take a train to Girona where she'd board a bus the farmers rode to Vielha. From there, she could hike to Martin's cabin. It would cost her a day, but it just might save her life. And Martin's.

She smiled at her cleverness, caught the stench of her own conceit, and uttered another prayer. She knew where her help came from, and it wasn't her wits. On her next trip, she would take yet another route. If she survived this one.

Chapter XLII

Fire roared in David's gut and provoked him to take the four steps to the narrow window overlooking the appellplatz. He'd been shuffled into bedlam with only one contact, and she was either unable or unwilling to communicate.

"Dremmer, you're going to wear them boots out. Not too many cobblers here, is there?"

"We've got to get into that cellar, Bear."

"Hard to plan around this rain. How many days has it been?"

"We don't just need a bright day. We need keys." David waited, considered before bringing it up. "But I think there might be a way to expedite things."

Bear dragged his hand across his beard and put the worn picture of Babs back in his pocket. "You've took up schemin' again. That's worrisome."

He shrugged. "That's my job. I come up with this stuff, and you make it work." He twisted his neck against a growing knot. "The place where we shower. You ever notice the drain? Four-and-a-half or five-inch pipe. Leads east toward the walk-through gate. I don't know where it comes out, but unless it changes directions, it should be on the north side of the path they brought you in on."

Bear chuckled. "How do you figure on getting through that?"

"If we can find enough string and tie it to a bottle, we can float information in and out."

Bear sat up. "And how do you keep the Krauts from seeing it?"

"We put a hole a few inches from the opening, tie a string from it to a bottle, and let the water carry it through the pipe. The string will be tied so the bottle stops short of the opening."

Bear nodded. "And how will Élodie know to look for it?"

"That's the catch. We have to talk to her so she knows to check it every few days."

Billington rubbed his stubby hands. "We hadn't had a Red Cross packet in two weeks. Maybe she'll send something. We can write on the plate before we send it back, maybe."

He felt the sting of what he'd withheld from Bear. "We can't count on that. Schneider and I had a disagreement about me giving you my share of the buchteln."

The sergeant nodded. "Schneider's your friend, Dremmer, and he's trying to take care of you. You not taking your share was a slap in his face. You see that?"

"I suppose."

"Sometimes the Lord puts ties in peoples' hearts. It ain't treason, and it might be what keeps you alive—or Nicole, or Élodie, or all of us."

He'd grown uncomfortable with the conversation. "So, where could we write a note on her dish that Schneider wouldn't see it?"

"I don't know, but it wasn't no worse than some of your ideas."

* * *

David stood with his back to the dungeon stairway, gaping at the drainage pipe. If the pipe were heavy, it would take a brace and bit to attach the hook, another item in a list of needed tools. If it were rusty, a hammer and nail might do.

He turned to Mackey. "The padlocks and hasps all have A-B-U-S on them. The doors behind us are probably the same. How long would it take you to pick one?"

The boy shook his head. "Can't do it, sir."

He looked up, surprised.

Mackey continued. "Don't get me wrong—about any lock can be picked. For sure, these can, but it'd take hours in a machine shop to make the tools to do it." He paused. "But there might be another way."

The boy had his full attention. "Let's hear it."

"We need a key to just one of them. I can make blanks from that, file one razor-thin and put it in the lock. If the metal is soft, I just might get an impression and make a key from that."

His neck grew warm. "That's good, Mackey. What kind of metal do we need?"

The boy scanned the appellplatz and nodded toward the stable. "See the hinges on those doors? They're apt to be soft, so they might work. I could scratch them with a nail to be sure."

A shiver ascended his spine. "Those hinges would be missed.

We'll find something that wouldn't. In the meantime, I need a scrounger—someone we can trust. You know one?"

Mackey scuffed. "Got a pal that's been trading cigarettes with a goon. He got tubes for the radio. But receivers aren't a risk. If we ask for tools, it'll scare him. Could backfire, sir."

David scratched his chin. "It'll take more than cigarettes. We'll need something on him. Which goon is it?"

Mackey nodded at the sentry on the west end, a thin kid he'd seen talking to prisoners.

"Does he speak English?"

The private shrugged. "Enough that we can make him understand what we need."

He thought of Captain Hanson and winced. "I want something understood. We may blackmail the people we recruit, but once we've got them, we don't turn on them. They need to know they're safer with us than with their own."

"Yes sir."

* * *

David stepped to the window overlooking the appellplatz, his grasp limited by stone and fir. Some knight had likely found that a comfort. If he had, all he held dear had to have been behind these walls with him. David listened for the river, imagined the flow he'd seen in the spring, the steady undulations of water making smooth stones smoother, its silver course too swift to allow moss to grow. Beyond his sight, chestnuts formed canopies over grass shallows where catalpas sheltered lovers from gentle rains.

How could this place have bred such evil, and how could he protect Nicole or the kriegies from the darkness it spawned? He couldn't. Nor could he extinguish the darkness in his own heart, the reliance on deceit and manipulation. He shuffled to his palliasse, lay on the excelsior pad, and released his heart to the One who'd brought justice to a flawed king.

* * *

The obergefreiter's jagged words frayed the morning calm, though David only understood the *eins, zwei, drei*. He glanced right, wondered at the quiet endurance legible on Bear's face, then looked at the Germans in front. A young officer talked with Schneider, his head bobbing. The hauptmann dismissed the prisoners, and the perfect chin rose, his glower fixed on David. A gloved hand motioned for him to approach. The young man at Heinrich's side drew himself straight and stiffened his narrow shoulders. A feldwebel, his second star adding some distinction.

He ambled closer, saw the face, and released his breath.

Schneider spoke first. "Lieutenant, I believe you know Oberfeldwebel Devillier."

He grinned. "Congratulations on your promotion, Oberfeldwebel."

"Lieutenant." Henri nodded and looked away.

"The oberfeldwebel is here on behalf of Commandant Schuster and is required to speak with the Man of Confidence." Heinrich turned to Henri. "My office is available, of course."

The boy spun sharply. "I have been ordered to use the commandant's office, Herr Hauptmann. I will require nothing beyond that except privacy."

David covered his grin.

Schneider nodded. "As you wish."

Henri marched toward the officer's quarters leaving him with Heinrich. He turned. "You should never have taken his typewriter, Herr Hauptmann."

Heinrich's mouth lifted. "He is Oberst Schuster's representative, Lieutenant. You will do as he says." He paused. "As will I, I suppose."

David followed the boy to the wide stairs. He walked quickly, determined not to let the men see him trailing behind like a scolded puppy. Henri approached the door beyond Schneider's office and pulled a key from his pocket. The little man pointed to a chair, pulled the door closed, and stepped behind the commandant's desk. "I bring regards from Prospero."

He waited, held his tongue.

The boy cleared his throat. "Are you still uncertain who your friends are, Othello?"

"At the moment, I'm only uncertain about you. What do I call you, Henri?"

"I would prefer you not speak of me at all. Life within the Reich is not so dear."

"But you know my code name. It's an unfair advantage."

"I am Laertes. Now, it is important that you listen to what I have to say, Lieu—"

"Wait!" His gut clenched. "What was your connection to Hamlet?"

Henri glared. "Corporal Swanson was given his code name due to his inordinate need for his father's approval. I was given mine because I swore to protect my sister. I had no dealings with Hamlet." Henri sniffed. "May I continue?"

David smiled and tipped his head.

The boy straightened. "Times are difficult. The lives of many close to both of us are threatened. Heinrich is foremost among them."

His chest tightened. "Is he aware of that?"

The small hands lifted. "Abwehr has been dismantled. Some in its ranks were part of the Resistance. Among those imprisoned are several of Heinrich's superiors."

"So, he's under suspicion. And he knows it."

The boy leaned over the desk. "The war is not going well, and someone must be blamed. I need your assurance that you will do nothing that might bring charges against him."

"Are you suggesting that I not do what I can to oppose the enemy?"

Henri's face hardened. "You have a history of taking risks, Lieutenant. Anything that would result in your arrest by the RSHA would almost certainly precipitate Heinrich's hanging. It would take little effort to discover that you have been transferred to his previous posts."

He held Henri's stare. "So I've heard. And what exactly is the RSHA?"

The oberfeldwebel grunted. "The Reich Main Security Office. Himmler used the dismantling of Abwehr to expand his authority. No mercy is shown to those deemed disloyal, and no confirmation is required for anyone accused of it."

Acid filled his throat. "So, Nicole is in greater danger than before."

"Probably. If Abwehr had a file on her, it is now with RSHA, and they are brutal."

David's strangled rage broke free. "And you're asking me to do nothing?"

The boy leaned back, fire in his eyes. "I am not asking. I am demanding that you do nothing that could result in your capture and thereby expose Élodie or Heinrich."

He met the boy's stare. "I've already been captured, Henri."

"My sister sent you a drawing that reveals a breach. She acted stupidly. The drawing was given to her by a fellow operative. It should have been sent to me." He released a breath. "I am left to mitigate any disaster that might result from her imprudence."

He nodded. "And you see me as the most likely source of a disaster."

Henri removed his hat and placed it on the table. "I do, yes."

"But you need me to know how to use this breach, should the need arise. That is, if it's to your benefit. That's how this works, isn't it?"

Henri stiffened. "There is an exit in the room marked with an X. It is covered by beams that appear to support the structure above. In fact, they cover the entrance to a narrow passage used, in the past, for cattle and sheep. The room was an abattoir, and the tunnel sloped so that it could be washed and drained. At some point, the opposite entrance was covered and forgotten.

"The man who discovered it was our operative. That was fortunate. He broke through while building a supply road with a dozer. The fissure is seventy meters from the southern wall and was covered with car parts and branches. Should the Führer refuse to surrender before the Allies reach Leipzig, it will be necessary for you to use it to contact your troops. Or the Soviets. It is my hope you will be able to save those of us in the Resistance. And Heinrich, of course."

David gnawed his lip. "That would be quite a feat. If I'm to meet our troops, I'll need a map of the area, and that would include Heinrich's home. I'll also need steel files, and your key to the door behind me. And I'll require some soft metal to make more keys."

Henri's mouth pinched tighter. "You are insisting on meeting with Élodie, then?"

He held the icy glare. "I can't work in the dark, Henri. I must have communication with the outside."

The boy nodded. "Then you will meet her somewhere other than our grandparents' home. Perhaps a message system could be developed that would not require you to meet. In the meantime, I will supply blank keys. They are used throughout the system."

A chill shot up his back. "A message device is already in the works, but I'll need string and a few water-tight bottles to float down the drain below the showers. And I need to know where the line emerges and whether Élodie can reach it unseen."

The boy scribbled on a notepad. "Someone else will do that."

"Then find them!" He stilled his breath. "If Heinrich and his staff aren't aware of this breach, why is the room locked?"

Henri stared into the corner. "The plans for this prison were initially expansive. It would have required a large staff. That room was to have been used to hold officer's provisions, however, the additional supply room was not needed. Neither was the road."

"And why was the prison not filled?"

The boy raised his pen. "It has proved less costly to hang troublesome prisoners than to house them, Lieutenant. Consider that before devising your next plan."

* * *

Nicole stirred in the soft chair, her limbs heavy with sleep. She rolled from beneath a thin blanket and stared at the July moon. Laurent stood framed in his doorway, a cigarette muted against the bright sky. She warmed at the sight of him. He and Martin had done so much. A niggle urged her up, and she stepped quietly to the door. "Are you not able to sleep, Uncle?"

Laurent chuckled. "I have not slept in years, child. Perhaps I shall sleep soon."

"I pray we all will." She paused. "There are things I must discuss with you."

A shimmer of moonlight touched his shoulders. "I assumed as much."

She examined the lines on his brow, the creases left by worry. "Martin will leave soon?"

"In a couple of hours. He asked that I place food for him beside the bed."

She forced her breath to slow. "I hope not to use Martin again. If I were able to avoid it, I would no longer expose you, either."

He turned in the morning chill. "It is not your war only, Elisabeth. Martin and I also wish to bring an end to this madness."

She steeled her spine. "But I am being followed. That is why I met Martin without notice and changed my routes to reach him."

Laurent straightened. "You have seen your pursuer? Where?"

"I've not seen him since Scotland. I am certain that he followed me on earlier trips, and I believe he and Captain Campbell are working together."

Laurent folded his arms. "If you are going to Paris, you should know the Resistance is planning to rout the Nazis. It will be bloody." His eyes narrowed. "You do not have to go, child. You may stay with me."

Her throat constricted at the tremble in his voice. "The uprising is but part of the reason I am going, Uncle. They need help."

"So, you are coordinating the Resistance and the armies? That is dangerous work. Will they again send you further?"

She looked away. "Yes, to Belgium. Pray that the Germans yield to the inevitable."

He released a breath. "This I pray always, Elisabeth, and that you remain safe."

Chapter XLIII

David tasted the sodden stone leaching into the air, his pulse sharp with the first success he'd known in months. An hour earlier, Langley had found the requested tools beside his receiver. Henri had come through. At least in part.

He scanned the appellplatz for goons, then allowed his hand to drift between two files and his ribs. He'd hidden two others behind a rock Bear had freed from the wall in their cell and puttied in with plaster concocted of crumbling mortar and bread. A hammer rested beneath his palliasse, and four blank keys were jammed into a notch carved above his boot heel. The awl and bits were squirreled into a hollowed beam in the stables, but he hadn't received a map.

Mackey's black hair rose above the group, his attention fixed, waiting for a signal to amble close. David squinted at the tower. The Mauser was lost in the morning luster, and he looked toward the stables. Langley glanced back, dipped his chin, and began a sluggish advance toward the showers, his trousers pinned beneath his arm. The corporal squinted and stepped close. "Big news, is it, suh? The bells a' Notre Dame is a-ringin'."

His heart lurched. "We've taken Paris?"

"Very neah, suh. Fourteen divisions o' Jerries is sho' up. Guns 'n tanks abandon' all roun', and Yanks are comin' across the Seine. Was more than I could wholly catch. Canucks has star'ed a push, and ya' got'a give the Frogs some praise. Resistance star'ed strikes wot turned ter riots. Civvies runnin' inside strongholds an' such. Keepin' the Jerries busy, and savin' lives, wunnit?"

The Resistance. That was why she was crossing the Pyrenees again. His gut tightened.

"I'd a though' you'da been more brigh' abou' it, suh."

He smiled. "It's good news, Corporal. It's just that I have friends in the Resistance."

Langley nodded. "I see. No numbers in ye', suh."

"Mackey will be over in a few minutes. We'd best not congregate."

"I'm off, suh."

"Thank you for the news, Corporal. Might be best if the men didn't know just yet. Let's wait a day or two so the goons will have to guess how we learned it. We don't want them digging up your radio." He looked up. "There's something I've been meaning to ask."

The corporal turned back. "Wha's tha', suh?"

"If I were able to get parts, could you build a transmitter? One with a signal the Air Corps or RAF could home in on?"

Langley twisted his head. "Now tha' would take some doin', wunnit? Transponders was drop' a while back. They call' 'em Eurekas. Wasn't rightly rada', but they was useful. Migh' be less trouble to find one in a closet o' yer undercovuh frien's."

He hid a smile. "I'll ask around, Corporal. Can you stop later? I need help with a plan."

Langley grinned and moved away.

Bear shuffled close. "Reached the end of the Red Cross parcels. Talked to Schneider?"

"No, but I will." He glanced across the yard, offered a curbed shake of his head to warn Mackey away. "The Allies are taking Paris. Sounds like the Resistance is playing a big role."

Billington looked down. "And you're thinkin' that's where Nicole was headed?"

"Seems likely." He looked skyward, his gut churning. "You've seen the bandits?"

Bear tilted his head. "Heard 'em, mostly. Sounds like they're landin' somewhere close."

He nodded. "We're under their approach. May be 190s. They're expecting something, and they'll take out a lot of our boys. Do you remember their range?"

Bear drug his hand across his neck. "Under five hundred miles."

"That sounds right. There's a lot of places within half that distance that will likely be hotspots—Cologne, Hamburg, Frankfurt, Munich maybe. Berlin, for sure."

The sergeant stared. "And Dresden's next door."

"Our boys can't hit a base this close. Tommies wouldn't dare try it at night."

Bear scraped his neck. "They're usin' us for cover. If you got a plan, let me in on it."

He smiled, was grateful. "Oh, I will. You'll have to make it work."

* * *

David leaned against the stone. Where was she? He clinched his teeth. It was always the same. Fear came first, the struggle to release it, then the submission to hands that could change it. But would they? So many had died, and most had prayed to live. He'd seen prayers answered, of course, but the ones that hadn't been still troubled him.

"You asleep, sir?"

He opened his eyes. Mackey stood blocking the sun. "I'm awake, Private." He looked around, saw kriegies at the opposite end of the appellplatz.

The boy shifted. "Didn't look like I was needed earlier. Wasn't sure."

"You're watching. That's good." He looked at the tower. "I have a couple of steel files tucked in my pants. Some blank keys in my boot. Few more things you might need."

Mackey's jaw loosened behind drawn lips. "ABUS blanks? Like the others?"

He smiled. "Just like them."

"How did you— That will save a lot of time, sir."

"Around midnight, you'll go to the latrine. Wear your garrison cap. I'll trade clothes and get the imprint of that lock on one of your filed blanks if you can have it ready."

Mackey stubbed a cigarette. "There's that light, sir. Floods the whole appellplatz."

"I'll watch for goons, stand under the overhangs until the man in the tower lights up."

The boy grinned. "So, you want me to wait in the latrine until you come back?"

He dipped his chin. "If you can teach me how to make an impression on a blank."

"Nothing to it, sir. Push it into the lock and rock it. Be gentle. Catch both sides. I'll file the imprint onto a second blank if I can find a place to work."

He stared into the shadows. "You'll use the stables. Langley will be your lookout. He has blocks wedged in the floor for a vice, and I'll leave the files with him. And one more thing."

"Yes sir?"

"The little goon that got the tubes for Langley's radio. You find anything on him?"

Mackey's smile widened. "I sure did. Other night, I hear Gageby say the kid meets a woman at the walk-through. Gives her chocolate and cigarettes. Kid gets a kiss. Promise too, I'm betting. Thing is, he's sixteen, and she's the supply feldwebel's frau. Bet the brass'd frown on that."

"Feldwebel Beck's wife? That's good work, Mackey. Really good."

* * *

The tyrants had withdrawn from the district but left snipers behind. "Martyrs for hell," Nicole whispered, glaring over peeling paint through the wedge between shutters. The next building had a recessed entry out of the marksman's view. She could make it there before he had her in his sights, surely, and could wait for him to find a target up the street and run while he was firing. The opposite sidewalk was covered, and the sniper would be required to lean out of the window to see her there. Exposing himself would be suicide. Boche marksmen professed their keenness to die for the cause, so long as their death could be postponed. This one would be asked to prove it.

A report rattled the window. Red dust flew from the bricks of a building up the street. She spun, pushed from the doorway, sprinted south, slid into the next entryway, and settled to her knees. The window behind her exploded, showering the entrance with glass.

Two quick shots echoed through the brick canyon. She scrambled to her feet, saw dust settling from the building across from the sniper. A ruse, likely meant to draw her out. She crept back and forced herself to wait. Etienne would hold her papers.

"Vive la France!"

She edged along the entrance and peered up the street. Two women were marching into the intersection and had to be warned. She scrambled from the safety of brick and stone and bolted onto the street, passed the midpoint before her leather soles skated from beneath her. Her knee slammed brick just meters short of the sidewalk. Fire shot up her leg. She lowered herself, and a bullet whizzed above her. She hobbled for cover as another slammed the street behind her.

Pain scaled her leg and reached her spine. Sweat gathered on her chin as she dropped onto concrete and surveyed the street. Revelers were scattering. A volley of gunfire shattered their screams, but they reappeared in an instant, gesturing toward the window.

She released her breath. The sniper had been shot. She straightened her leg and waited for the throbbing to ease. The group drew close, and she forced herself to stand. The print shop was a few blocks away, her forged documents prepared and waiting. Perhaps Etienne would allow her to hide until evening. His posters encouraging the able-bodied to take up arms were everywhere.

A young man left the crowd and ran toward her, jabbering about the Boche sniper who almost killed her. The scent of alcohol reached her before his hand. She smiled, her legs gelatinous, her hands wet with sweat.

She straightened. "Why are you celebrating? It isn't over!"

"You've not heard? Our 2nd Armored Division is hours away!" He pointed behind them. "The Boche still hold the north side, but not for long."

That wasn't the plan she'd been ordered to convey. Paris had been deemed too valuable, and Churchill believed the Germans would burn it as they fled. "Are you sure?"

"It is official! General Leclerc has sent troops to assure us."

There would be consequences—enormous ones for Émile and the major. Unless they'd lied to her. "I will join you for a while. Can you help me walk?"

The man moved to her side, his hand sliding around her waist. She hobbled, pretending to drink his wine. When they drew near Etienne's shop, she held back, acting as if she couldn't keep up. French, sharp and throaty, rose from a bullhorn, and the young man was distracted by the speaker. She sidled through strangers and onto a sidewalk. The edge of a building covered her retreat as she entered a street perpendicular to the Rue Lhomond. She waited, stood in shadows, scanned doors and windows, limped past two more buildings, and saw the chipped white letters of Etienne's sign, then shoved herself against the familiar door. The frame shook, and she recoiled at the bells. The Frenchman emerged in his ink-stained apron, his face first betraying then denying his surprise.

"Yes, mademoiselle? How may I help you?"

Was someone else here? She tightened her grip on the knob. "I believe my husband left an order to be printed. It would be under the name Elisabeth Leclerc."

He swept a heavy brush of hair from his forehead. "Please help me identify it. They are sales forms, are they not?"

No looks or gestures. "Yes, that's it." She moved to the counter's end and waited.

He opened the half door, unfolding his other hand toward the back. "I apologize for the untidiness. I have been quite busy."

She looked over her shoulder and offered a smile. "These are chaotic times, monsieur."

"They will be in the office." He pushed the door. "Please, madame, make yourself comfortable while I find your order." He lowered the blinds, urged her toward a chair, and pushed the door quietly. "Forgive my pretense. The front door was breached earlier this week. I fear microphones may have been hidden. This door was unopened." He unlocked a drawer. "You are planning another trip to Antwerp? You must keep this hidden."

"Of course."

He pulled a sack from a drawer, sweat beading on his upper lip. "I fear the Boche are onto me. A man stood across the street yesterday. Perhaps his absence today means I am safe."

She drew herself up, the chill extending to her hands. "I had hoped to be allowed to stay until I leave for the train yard, but we should leave now, Etienne. Both of us."

"Normally, of course—" The bells interrupted him. He glanced over his shoulder and stepped to the door before turning back. "On my left are rows of lead type in trays. Hide there. Should it be the Gestapo, you can make your escape into the alley through the back door."

He turned and scurried to the front. *"J'arrive! J'arrive!"*

She followed, slipped through stacks of lead-laden pans, and strained to hear the voices.

Etienne drew an audible breath. *"Ah oui, monsieur.* How may I help you?"

A low grumble followed, the words indecipherable. She edged close, the pinched corridor doused in light from the window. Etienne stepped behind the counter as a man in a felt hat moved opposite him. She caught a glimpse of the pale skin, black hair, and penciled mustache and lost her breath. He turned as Etienne opened the half door. Quivering gray eyes grew iridescent in the stream of light, and she crept toward the back. The half door squealed above the man's chilled mutter.

"Certainly, you may see my accounts, monsieur. That is always permissible for someone with your credentials. There is no need to make threats."

She edged toward a rectangle rimmed in light. The muted luster of a doorknob appeared on the right. Pain knifed her leg, and she stumbled, caught herself with her hands, grabbed the knob, and pulled. Light sliced through the leaden gray, and she scrambled toward clarity. Pain compressed her stomach. She pushed forward, hobbled down a constricted path, lurched over a wooden crate, and fell. She pushed herself up, slipped behind an extended brick wall, heard the door again, and looked around the jagged line of bricks.

A gunshot shattered the silence, and Etienne fell through the door, his blood coursing onto the stone path, his mouth opening in a silent scream.

Chapter XLIV

Late September, 1944

Light, stained and gritty, boiled within the hallway and left the stairs shadowed. David motioned the goon away. His legs were weak, and another shove might send him tumbling.

The guard growled and raised the butt of his rifle. "*Gehen!*"

"He fears you for good reason, Unteroffizier. Step back!" *Schneider. English.*

David caught the crystal glare near the bottom step and faced the pock-marked unteroffizier before trailing the stairs to the smooth stone floor.

The hauptmann motioned him to the open door of his office. "Élodie was concerned about you, Lieutenant. She has prepared a meal." Fingers that once threatened to collapse his throat now opened toward an electric daybreak that revealed bowls of sauerbraten and spaetzle.

"But the men, Herr Hauptmann." The words came unbidden. "I shouldn't."

"I will allow you to take some back to Sergeant Billington, but, as you can see, there is not enough for all the prisoners to taste. You must eat, David."

He caught the German's smile. "And if I do, what will you ask in return?"

The smile withered. "At the moment, Élodie and I are enjoying rather good fortune. We wish only to share it with you."

The man was childlike in his munificence, his suspicions unjust. "I'm sorry, Heinrich. It smells delicious. So, what was your good fortune?"

Schneider beamed. "It was an attempt at amends, I suppose. Oberst Schuster sent a telegram explaining that his duties in Munich have increased. He is leaving this portion of his area of responsibility in my hands for a few more months."

David stilled, tried to quash his cravings. "And the progress of the

Allies has nothing to do with his decision? He's left you in harm's way, you know."

The hauptmann leaned close, the bloom of alcohol drifting across the desk. "Prepare a plate, Lieutenant. The sergeant can wait an hour. I would enjoy a conversation as we once had."

David skewered a slice of beef, then ladled spaetzle onto his plate. "Take more sauerbraten, Lieutenant. Please."

He speared a slab. "Thank you, Herr Hauptmann. I'm very—"

"You are hungry. That is clear." Heinrich dipped his chin. "Please enjoy your meal."

The aroma provoked a response that would have inspired Pavlov. He cut a piece, chewed slowly, tried to savor the taste, but swallowed and forked another.

"You see, I was right. Élodie is an excellent chef, is she not?"

"It's wonderful." He spoke between bites. "You will marry her, won't you, Heinrich? When this is over?" He dabbed his chin and looked up at the blank face.

Heinrich roused. "Her records would be searched should we have married, David." A pause. "But as to the good fortune. The commandant's generosity included two hogs and four cows. There was another male cow—how do you say it?—a steer? It did not survive the journey. They are in poor condition, I am told, but will be edible if butchered quickly." The hand appeared again. "A fattened steer was included for Élodie and me. That is the correct term, yes?"

"It is." Leather mounded beneath his heel, the blank keys pressing against his conscience. "When will the men eat, Heinrich?"

"Meat will be added to their rations the day after tomorrow. Three days at the latest. Assuming none of the remaining animals die, there should be enough to supplement their rations for two months—three if we are able to find hay and butcher one at a time."

He swallowed. "Possibly through Christmas. I'm certain the commandant wouldn't have offered the prisoners food had you not insisted."

"I called every day." Heinrich pushed his chair back and tugged at a drawer. "Would you care for a drink? I am sorry I have no wine suitable for sauerbraten."

He'd tasted Heinrich's brandy, but only in his dreams. "That's most generous, but no."

"I am hopeful someday we shall share a drink. That would be splendid, would it not?"

He couldn't— "You said Oberst Schuster is in Munich. Is he overseeing 7-A?"

Heinrich raised his snifter, and the contents lessened by half. "He is there on quite another matter."

He chewed slowly now. "Is he perhaps superintending the prison at Dachau?"

Schneider lowered the snifter, then drew it back and swallowed what remained. "How do you know of Dachau?"

He gathered spaetzle on his fork. "I know you have friends there."

"But what do you know of the prison?"

"It's a death camp, isn't it?"

A blue haze settled in a liquid pool. "Many have died there, yes."

He swallowed. "And your friends?"

The color had drained from Schneider's face. "It is probable they, too, have died."

"For what crime?"

"They weren't Jewish, Lieutenant, if that is your assumption." Heinrich looked away. "You have managed to discover a few things, David, but there is much you do not know."

"I'm sure that's true. I don't know how a good man could embrace such evil, or why you renounced your faith for a cause like this."

The pale skin flushed above Heinrich's collar. "My grounds were perfectly sound. They were based on reason, Lieutenant, a convention you are clearly unfamiliar with."

He shook his head. "Reason. You've advanced beyond notions like right and wrong—so far beyond that you can now justify the execution of even those who disagree with you, since no truth could be greater than your perception of it." The man was feeding him, yet he couldn't quell the fire. "And you weren't bothered when *your* messiah rejected laws that should have kept him in check since he was above any truth." He waited, listened to Heinrich breathe, and wondered why the man allowed him to continue. "I believe you see it, now. It's not too late to reclaim your allegiance."

Heinrich turned to meet his stare. "You make it sound simple. Do you think I could so easily betray my country or my friends?"

"It is simple, though I'm not suggesting it would be easy. You know what's right. It's why you spoke to the unteroffizier in English. You wanted me to know he could understand me."

The hauptmann poured another drink. "I had hoped we might have a pleasant chat."

"I look forward to that, Heinrich, when you're no longer committed to a faith that would destroy all that's good." He put his fork down. "So, tell me why your friends were taken."

* * *

"Everything is fluid, Marcel. And frightening." Nicole cowered in the rail car, the old man's hand on her shoulder. She breathed, refocused. "You have done well with your reports."

"Eh, merci."

She held the watery gaze. "Promise me you will survive."

He leaned into the light and smiled. "Mademoiselle, I shall survive—if not here, then in a finer place, yes? And I shall see you again, either here or there."

It wasn't the answer she'd wanted. "Don't tell me this. And don't ever say such things to your wife. It isn't what she needs to hear."

Marcel squinted. "Perhaps she already knows, though I cannot both say this to her and survive, for if I tell her, it will mean I have not survived. Of course, if we are together, it would surpass even Paris. Do you think there might be a corner of paradise where canelé is served?"

"I'm sorry, Marcel. I didn't know."

He stepped into the light of the doorway. "And how could you know?"

She drank in the gloom of the train yard. "I'm sure you're aware that the push through France was a success. General Dempsey smashed everything the Boche erected. It was quicker even than here, and I hope more thorough."

He smiled. "But there is more, yes?"

"I have another reason why you must live. There is something you must do."

"If survival is our mission, why are you going on? This car is bound for Liège. You are moving toward death, not away from it."

She drew deeply. "It would seem so, but I am not supposed to be here. It is my prayer that it will not occur to some that I would go even closer to the front." She waited, wanting him to understand. "I am being followed, Marcel. I saw my pursuer while in Scotland and then in Paris where he killed my contact. I saw him also in Antwerp. He appeared before a firefight near the docks, emerging from a

German position. He always awaits me in a place I have been directed, you see."

She refused to meet Marcel's gaze. "I reported his presence to MI6 prior to receiving my assignment. They had no reason to send me to Antwerp. It was the same in Paris. Coordination already existed between the Resistance and the Brits. Those same fighters continue now to battle with snipers on the approaches to the city without any directives coming through me."

She raised her chin. "You will find a safe place, and you will stay there. Promise me. Conduct no more surveillance. I am asking you to live not only because I cannot be responsible for your loss, but also to report who must answer for it should I be killed."

His pulse vibrated through the folds beneath his chin. "I do not understand. Are you saying MI6 is in league with the Nazis? It cannot be."

She shook her head. "No. A few at the top are closely aligned with the Soviets, at least philosophically. They want their troops held back—the Canadians and the Americans, as well—so the Soviets will control more territory when this is over. They likely suspect I know their plans, and they fear I will divulge what they've done. It would be better for them if I were dead."

The old man's face withered. "The one following you is MI6?"

She shook her head. "He is Gestapo, but the captain of the ship transporting me is informing him where I go and when—at the request of these traitors, I am sure. This captain needs his records tidied when the war is over, and these officials can do that for him."

His tremble deepened. "These men have taken in a traitor solely to aid the communists?" Fire filled his gaze. "If this Gestapo man finds you in Liège, what then?"

She looked away. "Then I shall go to the Americans in Aachen. If they refuse to help, I will go to Munich where a friend also awaits the Allies."

"You would be going into the lion's den, *chérie*."

"It won't be much longer, Marcel. I can hide so long as MI6 is unaware of my location, and the Gestapo will not expect me to have gone to Germany."

Chapter XLV

Clouds brushed the parapet and left the stone adrift in dreams. David sat, leaning against the stables, his eyes closed. The unmuffled thunder of a radial engine shook the morning gray. Another cranked and fired, both held captive beneath the heavy clouds, bound to the earth like tethered birds.

Something stirred, and he looked up. Bear stood before him, a knowing smile perched beneath the dollop of dark hair. "Single engines. The second one's facin' us."

It seemed an omen. "The BBC says the 190s are at the front. Got to be 109s. Keeping them warm, maybe, but they go up a lot, considering the lack of fuel."

Bear nodded. "You heard we're back in Aachen, right?"

The boys trusted Bear. Even Langley shared information with him. It was good having him, and if something happened— "Yeah, sounds like a bloodbath."

Bear lowered his voice. "You still planning on making it into the cellar tonight?"

"I'd like to go farther, but I have a group activity planned, if your social calendar isn't full. I'm guessing some of the men will be taking showers this evening."

Bear shrugged. "I imagine so."

"Maybe you could help me gather two or three around the drain. Only men we trust. Ask Grip if you want. I need them to stand between me and the goons."

Bear's brow narrowed. "Sounds like you're in a hurry."

"This fog might help us. There's no way of knowing how long it will take for our troops to reach us, but we need to contact Élodie, figure out a way to ground those 109s before our boys get close."

His friend nodded. "And what about Schneider?"

His face grew warm. "We can't let him know. Need to save him from himself. There's Vogt and his crew, too. And Henri. Some ninety-day wonder could line up every Kraut in both prisons and have them shot. We can't let that happen."

* * *

Autumn festered within the damp, the sun lengthening shadows in the appellplatz. David glanced up from where he knelt. "Watch for goons, boys."

He tied string to a sheet metal screw, massaged it into a hole in the drainpipe, then covered the exposed head with gravel. Bear tied a hand-length sliver of wood to the opposite end and shoved it down the pipe. The sergeant stepped to a spigot as if he were testing the water temperature. The wood darted out of sight as David released string. If the pipe surfaced near the footbridge, it could be reached by anyone, and he planned to be the one to find it.

"What are you trying to build, sir?"

He looked at Grip, an affable kid Bear had befriended. "Just trying to help the Krauts with their plumbing. The drains likely need cleaning, don't you think?"

The boy looked at Mackey and Langley, caught their grins and shrugged. "Guess so, sir."

David winked at him. "Tell the men they can start their showers, Private. And thank you for your help. You understand what you just saw never happened, right?"

"Yes sir." The boy grinned and ambled toward a group of waiting kriegies.

"Thinking about putting Grip on the committee, sir?"

"I may need a man or two to sway dissenters, Mackey. He's well-liked."

"Only sometimes he's a little slow. Not sure he can follow detailed instructions, sir."

David glanced at Bear, then back at Mackey. "I'll take it under advisement." He waited. "You know I've been getting help from the Partisans. What you may not know is that some of those helping us are Krauts. They've even provided supplies, risked their lives, and I don't want them thrown to the wolves when our troops get here. Are you still willing to help?"

A slender twitch pulled at Mackey's mouth. "Are the Germans Luftwaffe, sir?"

Langley nodded. "We was thinkin't migh' be the hauptmann, suh."

Deception seemed the best choice. Again. "It wouldn't be fair to ask you to keep too many secrets. If the Gestapo were to hijack the prison, it could be unhealthy for you."

* * *

David paced the length of the latrine and held his breath. He squinted, the fog obscuring what light penetrated the dark. He looked at the tower, a dull projection in the gray. Where was Mackey? He needed the key and had no idea how long it might take to reach the drainpipe.

Gravel cracked beneath boots. A tall figure cleared the west then turned to go inside. The bill of a cap appeared in stark relief as the boy stepped beneath the yellow light.

"Mackey!"

The private ran toward him, removing his jacket and cap. "Two goons were talking by the door, sir. Didn't want to give them any reason to follow me."

"Understood. Stay outside so you can breathe. Listen for Krauts. Go in if they get close." He pulled the key from his pocket. "It's ready to go, right?"

"Yes sir. Polished it with sand. Smooth as silk."

"Good. I'll need your Zippo, too."

Mackey extended his lighter. "I would've finished that key days ago if the goons—"

"Langley told me they've been snooping around." He looked up. "If this works, I'll see to it you get a raise."

He hustled across the appellplatz, a faint luster stirring to his left, and stared into obscurity, continuing toward the door Mackey had exited. A coal scuttle helmet emerged within the gray, a cigarette case glinting. Loverboy, returning from the gate. David skated in front, and the boy flinched then grumbled something sharp. He slipped through the door, held it so that it closed with a gritty hush. Nothing moved. He waited, listened. The slap of the boy's boots faded into the murk, and he pushed the door again and turned east.

The stairs were wet, the night a concession to decay. He found the lock, inserted the key, felt it snap, and pushed. A low squawk chilled his spine. He stepped inside, inhaling a wisp of urine and mildew. Sparks rose when he spun the wheel of the lighter, then died in damp air. He spun it again, and a flicker rose, revealing massive posts on the south wall and litter on the floor—empty cans, buckets, strips of canvas, a pile of trim. He retrieved a sliver of wood, wrapped it with a rag, and moved it to the flame.

Brightness swelled, exposed ceiling and floor, and shadowed a shard of black behind the nearer post. He wedged his fingertips into the space and pulled. It didn't budge. He reminded himself to breathe and placed the burning sliver in a can. Light grew, the reflection of the can forming an irresolute beam. He slid both hands into the crevice and tugged. The post grumbled, steel on steel, some ancient device resurrected. He edged into a tunnel, less than five feet high, pushed the lamp aside, and hurried ape-like across mortar and stone.

Light receded, threatening to disappear, the scent of earth urging him on. He stumbled, fell forward, his fingers sinking in dirt. He reached upward, found a broken edge. Sheet metal lay across the fissure. He straightened and pushed. It scarcely moved, and he scrambled to retrieve the dimming lantern.

The wooden wick had burned half down, its red tip flaking ash. He picked up more pieces, dropped them into the bucket, and skulked to the breach. The lighted sphere revealed an old trunk lid laid across shattered stone, roots snaking between. He rose to his feet, his legs bent, and heaved. The metal lifted at an awkward cant, hair roots snapping. He snatched a chunk of wood, shoved it beneath the lid, and a ragged slice of gray reached halfway around the fissure.

His hands slid into a lighter darkness, and he turned, shook the flame from the wick, dropped it among the detritus in the bucket, and heaved against the lid. The maw of gray grew wide, and he shoved the bucket beneath faded paint, rested his arms against the earth, and slipped his head into the night to drink citrus air.

* * *

David emerged from his tomb certain there was light, and that it would find him. He wandered in a haze searching for the castle wall, fending off branches, and swiping blood from a scratch on his face. If he waited for light, he would miss appell, the goons would see the swinging hasp, and his plans for the airfield would end—his life with them.

Minutes ticked away. He fueled his pace, pushed through darkness, stumbled, and stopped to listen. A rumble emerged, and he scrambled toward it, climbing over fallen trees and jogging across grass. His shoulder collided with stone and took his feet from under him. He stretched his arms to break the fall and found only darkness. The edge of a precipice struck him mid-thigh, and he twisted, reached for stone, grabbed a protruding root instead, and wrapped his arms around it. Thunder roared beneath him as his legs slid from their fragile purchase of earth. *The river.* He threw his right hand to the side, found the comforting edge of rock, and kicked toward the jagged overhang. Debris broke loose and splashed below. He fought for breath and pulled. The rock released, his other arm trembling above his upturned face.

He drew himself skyward, scraped the earth with his hand, found a crevice, and pulled an arm over the ledge. His boot toed something solid, and he thrust upward, released the root, and crawled panting onto wet dirt. He filled his lungs, swiped at the prickling pain beneath his blouse and felt a pasty wetness.

If he were injured, he would receive no help where he was. He pushed the fear away and struggled to clear his head. Henri had said the causeway beyond the west gate was the only way in by car. It had been dozed across jagged peaks while the southern side had been left unfinished. He'd chosen to go the wrong way. The castle was perched above the river from the east. That explained the walking bridge. He had no hope of reaching the drain tonight. Not without a map, and not in this fog. Maybe not ever.

He drew in the milkweed prickle of catalpas and swallowed hard. The castle had to be on his right. He rose, stepped gingerly, was scraped by limbs, and stumbled over rock. The assault of branches stopped abruptly, and he dropped to his knees, fearing another precipice. He reached and his fingers touched stone, smooth and flowing. His heart settled, and he stood, extended his hand to the wall, and edged west toward the tunnel, keeping the wall at arm's length, and praying to find the breach.

Branches, dried and brittle, shoved him back. A tree trunk lay across the earth, gray within the black, leaning against the wall. He turned to crawl over it, saw a yellow glimmer in the dark, a brighter glow beneath. It grew without weight or sound, then disappeared. His lantern? The sliver of wood he'd used had burned down, but he'd left the stub with the other scraps. The bucket that held them was propping the lid. Maybe it had reignited.

He scrambled toward the flame that rose into darkness, edged around trees, working his way toward the breach. Branches repulsed him, and he zagged away, returned, and caught the light again. It was brighter now. A limb snapped before his raised arms and revealed the yawning trunk lid. He edged close, slid inside, and grabbed the bucket, hoping to close the lid. The skin on his fingers sizzled, and he jerked, slinging burning wood across dirt and stone. He hurried to grind the slivers into mounded earth, dropped to his knees, and crawled to the comfort of captivity.

Chapter XLVI

Wind scraped across the road. Nicole glanced at open fields, was pelted by needle-sharp drops, and prayed for the strength to keep going. The day was a line from David's poem, without the redemption of a secret wish. Spent flowers bent in waves, empty husks trembling in the small rain, the chill of bone-deep bereavement on either side pressing at her heart. She set her shoulders and slogged on, had made her choice hours ago. There would be no bartering now.

A growl rose behind her, mechanical and deep. She glanced over her shoulder, saw a motorbike lurching as the rear wheel found traction and was thrown from side to side. Gelid air refused to pass her throat. The Boche had been repulsed, driven across the frontier, but it was certain some had been lost in the woods or consigned to martyrdom. It wasn't unlikely that a German boy had been left with a motorbike and a rifle. She studied the dark figure for insignia or uniform, but he was covered in a mud-spattered driver's coat and crash helmet.

She turned back, resumed her trudge, praying that whoever it was might pass. The machine drew beside her, the exhaust blowing vainly into liquid air. A goggled face dipped, the voice mounting against the wind. "Ma'am, you needin' a ride? Miserable day for a walk."

American. "Thank you, no. I've only a bit further to go."

The helmet bent to the side then turned into the drizzle. "Nothin' on this road for miles. It may not be the most comfortable ride, but it's a durn sight better than walking. Hop on. I'll take you where you need to go."

She steadied her voice. "What unit are you with, soldier?"

"My unit ain't here, ma'am, but I'm with the 25th General Hospital. We're settin' up shop in Tongres." He lifted his chin. "You can sit on them panniers. The engine will warm you some."

He seemed well-intentioned, but how was she to extend her leg above those leather boxes? "Thank you, soldier. I'm most grateful."

"It's Sergeant, ma'am. Sergeant Robert Lee."

She smiled. "I would have thought with a name like yours, you'd be a general."

"If the brass was as insightful as you, ma'am, we'd have already won this war." He stood, allowing her to extend her leg over the seat. "Sit straight and let me do the balancing."

She settled in, taking comfort in his chivalry.

"You're a Brit, aren't ya'? Whata' ya doin' here?"

"I'm Belgian, Sergeant Lee, though I did learn English from a British instructor. And we spoke it at home. I was on a train bound for Liège, but—"

"But the tracks was bombed. Them tracks get…" The engine drowned his response.

She leaned toward his ear. "You're quite adept at maneuvering your motorbike."

"Ain't no motorbike, ma'am. This here's a Harley Davidson WLA. Forty-five cubic inches." The last word rose to a squeal as the machine's rear wheel slid left, then straightened as the sergeant reduced the throttle and steered into the slide. "It's a motorcycle, ma'am, not a toy."

She took a breath. "Well, you certainly know how to handle your motorcycle, Sergeant."

* * *

Nicole sat beneath a canopy outside the barracks watching Sergeant Lee rummage through wreckage. He'd finished two sandwiches in a few bites and wiped his mouth on the back of his hand. She ate half of her first one, a concoction of boiled tuna and eggs, rewrapped what remained, and placed it carefully in the pocket of her coat. Now she sipped warm coffee.

Sergeant Lee slammed a door behind her. "Krauts gutted this place. Bunch of pigs. What they didn't tear up, they crapped on." He stopped, met her gaze. "'Scuse my French, ma'am."

"But you spoke no French, Sergeant."

He grinned. "It's an expression, ma'am."

"I see. Perhaps I could assist you. What are you looking for?"

"I'm looking for a hospital, ma'am. Leastwise, I'm looking for a place to put one. It's temporary. These barracks will do, but they'll need work. You looking for a job? I might be able to offer you one if I can get it approved."

"I... if you wouldn't require my assistance for long. It might be necessary for me to leave without notice, Sergeant."

"Call me Robert." He scratched his head. "This is your home, ain't it? Or is it Liège?"

"Belgium is my home, Robert, but not Tongres or Liège. And I am Elisabeth."

He squinted. "You don't have no home, do you, Elisabeth?"

"I have places I might go. It's rather complicated."

"Ma'am, a woman as pretty as you shouldn't be alone nowhere. It ain't safe."

She smiled. "Thank you, Robert, but this is war. No one is safe."

He nodded. "It's my job to turn this into a field hospital. Then I go to Liège to set up the big one. V-1s is hittin' there now. No place for injured troops. Quick as I get orders, I'll get boys workin' on this. First barracks we get spit-shined is yours till we start movin' in equipment."

She couldn't allow him to— "I'm overwhelmed, Robert."

He pointed. "Ain't much, but we might have the latrine working in that one tomorrow."

"Your offer is beyond generous, but—"

"I don't see no reason why you'd refuse. You could sleep out of the rain, likely in a bed. And I wouldn't hurt you for the world, ma'am. Wouldn't let nobody else hurt you, neither."

The fear of revealing too much quenched her breath. Still, she would have to contact the Americans at some point. "May I confide in you, Robert?"

"Sure, you can, ma'am."

"I've been working with the Resistance, and I pose a threat to the enemy. I have thus far been able to evade them, but I cannot afford to allow others to be able to identify me should their agents be looking in this area. I cannot become too familiar. To anyone. Do you understand?"

The heavy cheeks swelled. "Nobody here'll be talking to the Krauts, ma'am."

"How would you know? Not all Nazis wear uniforms. Some pose as Belgians or French or British. The one pursuing me has done precisely that, and he knows I can identify him. The Allies are gaining control, and such men cannot afford to have their treachery exposed."

* * *

David stole into the darkness of the officer's quarters, his freshly rinsed blouse dripping onto the floor. He shivered in the hallway and tapped the door frame.

The door flew open, and Bear stared open-mouthed. "What took you so long?"

He turned. "Caught a movie while I was out. Turned out it was a double feature."

Bear grabbed a pair of cotton socks. "Musta been a thriller. Got blood all over you."

David grinned, relief setting in. "Those socks clean?"

"Think I'd waste a clean pair?" Bear drew them around his abdomen. "Whadya learn?"

"Not so tight." He winced. "I learned not to do this in a fog."

"Then you made it outside?"

"I did, but I made a mistake. This castle sits on the edge of a cliff on the east. To get to the drain, we'll have to circle the entire castle and grounds. We both had to see that when they brought us across the bridge. Do you remember seeing it?"

"All I remember was the bridge was narrow, and it was a long way to the water. Looked cold, too." The sergeant shook his head. "Best hang that blouse. Just a few hours till appell. Take my blanket. You need sleep."

He glanced up, could only see a silhouette, dissolute in the yellow haze. "I went over the cliffs, Bear. Had to pull myself up. If I hadn't tripped, I'd have walked right off of them."

"Dremmer?"

"Yeah?"

"I'm glad you made it. You had me scared."

He lay on the palliasse, pulled the blankets over his exhausted limbs, and waited for the trembling to stop. He'd failed at his mission, but, for the moment, he was safe. He'd been spared, directed, and he knew it. It brought the deepest peace, one he wanted to share with Nicole. He prayed that she might know such care and be ushered into a dream of peace.

* * *

Nicole ran her hand over white sheets and brought the top one to her nose. It seemed a lifetime since she'd slept in a clean bed. She glanced at the latrine. Tomorrow, she would have running water. She'd sponge bathed with the soap and water Robert had left on the heater after apologizing for leaving her without a shower. The sweet boy had no idea what luxury he'd provided. And he'd placed a lock on her side of the door.

She eased between the sheets, pulled blankets to her chin, and felt the heat gather as rain pattered on the roof. She closed her eyes and offered thanks for a warm bed, for Robert's kindness, and asked that David know the wonder of sleeping in comfort and safety.

Chapter XLVII

Robert paced the floor. "This job'll seem easy at first, but that won't last. Week or two, overflow casualties will be pouring in from the front, and some of them won't have histories. Biggest part of the unknowns will be POWs. You'll have to write narratives and keep track of 'em so their families get notified." He paused. "Colonel Watts' office will write the letters for the ones that didn't make it."

Nicole's breath caught. Would David's name be among them? "But I would be working in an office. Everyone will soon recognize me."

"I told the colonel you was... Well, I said you was shell-shocked and couldn't talk to people, but that you knew English and wrote good." He shrugged. "It was all I could think of."

She smiled. "That's actually quite good. And where would I work?"

The sergeant fidgeted. "Right here. Barracks' gonna be partitioned off. Your office will be in your quarters on this end. We'll store medical supplies in the other end. Me and Colonel Watts is the only ones you'll talk to."

"And the patients? How will I acquire information from them?"

"The worst wounded will be going to Liège after triage. I can help with the ones here when I'm not there, and you won't have to worry with them that's shipped to Antwerp. They won't have the chance to do no fraternizing with the locals."

She held Robert's gaze. "It's not just locals. Your troops could mention something." She checked herself, couldn't tell the sergeant his intelligence officers were her greatest threat.

"Don't you know somebody that can help you? Somebody you trust that can talk to the boys and get info and next of kin? We need to know what happened to their squads. Few of these boys could be lone survivors. They can help us piece things together."

Gooseflesh covered her arms. It would be safer for him here than in Ghent. "You receive your supplies from the Port of Antwerp, do you not?"

"Pretty much everything comes through there."

"And those supplies are then shipped by rail through Ghent?"

He shrugged. "A good many will, once we get them tracks finished. Be a day or two."

She took a breath. "Then perhaps there is someone, though I'm not certain his English is adequate, but he certainly understands who the enemy is."

The boy straightened. "You always call them that. Are you talking about somebody besides the Krauts?"

Blood surged in her ears. "What you are asking— If I tell you, it must remain between us. Will you agree to that? I need your promise. My life depends on it."

The boy stilled. "I won't talk to nobody you don't okay first."

She nodded. "All right. As I said, I have worked with the Resistance. Some in the group I receive orders from are loyal to the Soviets and are attempting to delay the Americans and Canadians and Brits so that the Soviets might gain control of a larger portion of the continent. They are leaking my name to nefarious individuals so the Nazis will rid them of their problem."

The sergeant frowned. "They're turning you over to the Gestapo? Round about, I mean."

"Precisely."

He dipped his head. "And what do they know about your friend?"

"Only his code name. It's doubtful they could locate him, unless..."

"Unless what?"

Her spine prickled. "Unless they know to follow someone who contacts him regularly. I know of no one other than myself, but he works with other Resistance groups, as well."

"So, how can I get in touch with him?"

"You cannot. Under no circumstances are you to try. You must swear, Robert."

His face reddened. "All right, I swear. But the Krauts ain't there no more."

"Their minions are. Rest assured, Gestapo agents are in hiding, as are RSHA operatives, and questions from an American would draw attention to my friend."

He stiffened. "At some point, you're gonna have to let the colonel know about all this." He waited. "But I'll let you make that call after you learn to trust him."

* * *

Sunlight invaded the gloom. It broke first in narrow splashes, then widened, routing the darkness that infected David's soul. The skin across his belly burned in vengeance, not unlike the evil that lay in wait. He faced the Nazi unteroffizier who strutted toward Schneider.

The hauptmann straightened, diminishing the familiar figure on his right. He spoke and an unteroffizier released kriegies to form a line for their morning crusts of bread. Schneider watched them scatter, then motioned him over.

David walked deliberately, hiding his anticipation at seeing Henri. When he reached them, he offered a perfunctory salute.

Schneider returned it. "Lieutenant, Oberst Schuster has again sent his representative and is requiring your official declaration of proper treatment." The German paused. "Along with any requests you might have, of course."

"My previous request for unconditional surrender was ignored, Herr Hauptmann. What assurance can you give me that this one won't be also?"

Schneider wagged his head, smiled, and turned to Henri. "I hope your discussions with him are more productive than mine."

Henri raised his chin. "Follow me, Lieutenant."

* * *

David slipped into the chair, the dressings beneath his blouse pulling at the abrasions.

"What happened to your hand, Lieutenant?"

He rolled it in examination. "A tennis injury, Herr Oberfeldwebel."

The boy wasn't amused. "A tennis injury. I trust no one else was hurt in the match."

He smiled. "I was the only one playing, and there were no spectators."

Devillier seemed to grasp the gist. "I certainly hope that is true."

David stared. "Thing is, without another player, the matches don't accomplish much."

Henri looked puzzled.

"I'm waiting for a partner, Henri. I can't serve without one."

The lines on the oberfeldwebel's face tightened. "I see."

He leaned forward. "You failed to provide anyone. I need to contact Élodie."

"At the proper time, Lieutenant. Be patient."

"Now is the proper time. I also need maps, candles, and a few blocks of beeswax."

Henri shifted in his chair. "Beeswax, Lieutenant? You want to make impressions of keys, I assume. I will try to find dental quality, though it is difficult to obtain."

"And how would you know that?"

"Before the war, I studied dentistry in Paris." The boy smirked. "So, what destinations are you considering for your trip, Lieutenant?"

Henri's insolence was irritating. "Your sister's home in Leipzig. If not hers, I'll need a map to another operative and one to the airfield where the 109s are based."

The boy sneered. "Then you have not yet contacted Élodie. I had wondered."

He was confused. "How could I? You've provided me no support."

"Élodie is concerned with your health, Lieutenant. She sent bierocks." The boy opened a drawer and retrieved a covered plate. "Our grandmother's recipe. It is delightful."

His mouth watered, but he looked away. "The drainpipe emerges somewhere outside the walk-through gate. It has a string with a wooden float attached coming out the end. I need a knot tied at the exact spot it emerges from the pipe, so tell whomever you're willing to provide me what to look for. We can at least begin communication."

Henri nodded. "I shall locate it myself." The slender hand unfurled above the dish, the gesture so like Heinrich's. "Feel free to enjoy the bierock."

"I'll wait."

"You aren't hungry, Lieutenant?"

He glared at the close-set eyes. "The Allies are coming, Herr Oberfeldwebel. I'm assuming you still want to be identified as one who aided the Resistance."

A flush rose above the boy's collar. "Very well, Lieutenant. I shall provide you with a map to the airfield, but you mustn't discuss your plans with anyone other than those required to complete your mission. Is that understood?"

"And your grandparents' home—I assume it's somewhere other than Leipzig?"

The oberfeldwebel pursed his lips. "Do you know how far Leipzig is, Lieutenant?"

The boy had called his bluff. "I haven't a clue."

"Over an hour by automobile. How had you planned to get there?"

He ignored it. "Then where does Élodie live, Herr Oberfeldwebel?"

"You may call me by name."

Fire rose in his gut. "Where is she, Laertes? Or have you forgotten you swore allegiance to someone other than your sister?"

Henri sniffed. "I need time to review other candidates, Othello."

He stood, couldn't wait two more months for an answer. "No! Give me someone now, or I'll see to it the Resistance knows of your refusal to offer aid."

Henri rose and met his stare. "You have no contacts, Lieutenant. You just said so."

"But we have a radio. I can reach London."

A sneer spread across Henri's face. "I don't believe you."

"Then don't expect MI6's help when the Allies arrive. You'll be lined up against a wall at Dachau, just like Commandant Schuster."

The boy's lips pressed in a bloodless pinch. "That is not his proper title. If you had learned this from MI6, you would know that."

"If I had a few days, I'd get an update, but I don't have a few days. Neither do you. Where do Schneider and Élodie live, and how do I get there?"

The thin lips trembled. "You will—"

"I'll make every effort to keep her safe. Now, where is she?"

The boy grimaced. "How can you reach her without Heinrich's knowledge? You must go when he is not home."

His neck eased. The house was close. "Heinrich sometimes stays in his office at night. Maybe he's working, or maybe he's drunk. All I know is, he's here."

The silence was malignant. "The house is near Waldheim, perhaps three kilometers south. There is a short span on the road on the west where you might be seen from the tower."

"Can't I walk beside the road?"

The narrow face pinched tighter. "West of the main gate, the road drops off on either side. It will be dangerous in the dark, even if you stay near the center. The message system would be preferable, but Heinrich doesn't allow Élodie near the prison as she might be taken hostage."

He considered it. "Then I need another contact."

The boy began to tremble. "There is none. At least, not a trusted one."

"Someone delivered our supplies, and I won't leave this room until this is resolved."

"I'm afraid he may no longer be approved."

An ember ignited in his gut. "You've intended to leave me in the dark all along."

The boy's chin rose, the crystal stare locking onto his. "If the choice is between Élodie's life or yours, surely you know which I will choose."

He choked his rage. "Remember, your life will be in my hands soon. As will Élodie's."

Henri nodded. "All right, Lieutenant. I will send a map with the supplies."

"No, you'll draw it now. In front of me. Neither of us will leave the room until you do."

* * *

The corporal at the wheel of the jeep had likely been instructed not to speak. Or perhaps Sergeant Lee's description of her mental state frightened him. Rather than asking for the satchel Robert had provided her, he stepped back. Nicole covered her smile.

The bag was Belgian, as was her outfit. Sergeant Lee seemed always to consider her needs, especially when it concerned her safety. She held the frame of the canvas top as the jeep bounced between potholes, the engine whining. The train yards appeared, the car squealed to a stop, and the corporal turned to help her. She lowered her head, moved to the opposite side, and slid out. If the boy thought her unstable, she saw no reason to convince him otherwise.

She picked up her satchel. "Corporal, which car am I to board?"

The boy pointed. "That one, ma'am. The officer's car. They have your berth ready."

"Thank you."

A G.I. stood at the top of the stairs. She glanced up as he stared unflinching into the car. A Negro, handsome, perhaps David's age. He stood with the aplomb of an officer, though he wore only two stripes. "Your berth is two doors down, ma'am. It's on your right."

She nodded and smiled, took long strides, then stopped when she heard him following.

"If you're wondering, ma'am, your food will be brought to your compartment."

She didn't turn. "And where are the facilities, Corporal?"

"They're in your compartment, ma'am. This is a coach. It was shipped in from the States. I'll let you know an hour before we reach Ghent."

She pivoted and met his stare. "That's most considerate. Thank you."

* * *

Nicole reclined on the leather seat, pushed the curtain back and stared across yellowing grass. Orange leaves mounded before hedgerows and trees, and roads ran rivulets into streams. It was unlike Bruges or Ghent, the villages close together. With red-roofed houses on every hill, it seemed somber and crowded. Still, it had the feel of home.

The car crested a hummock. The hills beyond were charred, the houses reduced to piles of rock and charcoal. At the bottom of a sloping hill, where a widening stream meandered into a broad valley, two Panzers lay abandoned in the mud. Unhinged tracks looped above steel sprockets, the turrets blackened by fire. On the hillside, cows lay in hideous repose, their bellies distended, their legs stiff in the morning chill.

She pulled the curtain. The ham and eggs Robert had insisted she eat congealed beneath the bodice of her dress. War was as repugnant as it was inescapable. She swallowed a sob, was tired of pretending to be strong. She needed someone to be strong for her. She needed David.

She pushed the thought away. The matter at hand was finding Marcel. A shiver ran up her spine. She had assured Colonel Watts that she would bring him quickly, though it was probable he no longer looked for her handkerchief. The thumb of the Boche had been lifted, so he might not even work at night. If he were still in Ghent. Should he work during the day, writing a car number in the coal dust at the bottom of the wall might expose him. She would wait and see what opportunities arose.

Chapter XLVIII

The Mauser on the turret glinted in the sun. David took it in, then glanced back at his friend. "Two days without rain, and a full moon last night—we need to move on this."

Bear scraped rocks with a stick. "Schneider was home last night. You can't go until you're sure he won't be there."

"If he's here at twenty-three hundred, I'll slip out. When I find the house, I'll check to see if his car is there."

"And how you gonna get inside?"

He turned away, hid his grin. Bear could always spot the weakness in a plan. "Tap on the windows and wait for Élodie to open one."

"I don't like it, Lieutenant."

He grinned. "I don't like it, either, but I can't send a telegram." He turned back. "So, I came up with another plan. Want to hear it?"

"I'm not sure. Is it better than the first one?"

He offered a stern glare but didn't wait for it to be ignored. "I'm going to Heinrich's office to ask about Christmas for the men. If he offers me a drink, I'll take it."

The heavy brow contracted. "Why?"

"I'll pace myself, stay until he gets drunk and needs to relieve himself."

"And whaddaya want me to do?"

"Watch from the landing. If I don't get kicked out when Heinrich leaves, tap on the door. I'll pass you the keys, and you'll have Mackey waiting outside the vestibule. He'll need to be ready to make impressions in that wax Devillier got us."

"Too iffy, and you didn't say what to do if Schneider gets back before I do."

"I'll open the office door an inch or two while Schneider's in the loo. If the door's closed when you come back, hide the keys."

The brow squeezed tighter. "And how you gonna get them back in his office?"

"After the hauptmann returns, I'll discover I need to relieve myself, too. Just watch for me." He worried his lip. "I'll need something on my stomach before all this. Been over a year since I had alcohol, and I've lost a lot of weight. One drink, and I'll be sloshed."

Bear leaned back. "Just order fried chicken with extra mashed potatoes for supper."

He shook his head, didn't want to battle that thought all night. "Think the men would give me a little of their soup? The beef has been getting scarce, but a little would help."

The stick between Bear's fingers snapped. "What do I tell 'em? Butterbar's goin' drinkin', and he don't want the hauptmann to put him under the table?'"

He tilted his head. "It's for the war effort, Sergeant."

* * *

Moonlight glistened from tracks curving into couplets. *Couplets.* Nicole smiled. David would love the metaphor. She scanned the yard and watched two locomotives cross beyond the depot. Her eyes followed the first as it moved south on the second main, taking note of the sidings beyond filled with boxcars. She slipped through shadows, her woolen pants and peacoat melding into darkness, and looked back. Her white handkerchief lifted in the wake of another engine, then fell. Perhaps her stealth was unwarranted. The Boche no longer controlled the yard, but it was probable that a few of the railroad workers were providing them with information.

Gravel crunched beneath her boots. The cars on the first siding were latched and locked, and she moved to the next. Opened doors gaped in the sides of three. She crept to the first and glanced inside, slipped the paper and pencil from her pocket, and wrote down the number. A train approached on the nearest main, extending as far as she could see, flatcars covered with tarpaulins, the doors on the boxcars closed.

She moved back into the shadows. Hammering wheels rattled her stomach. Lights appeared beyond the last car, and she hid until it passed. Beyond the next two mains, moonlight etched the outline of a man, his head thrust forward. She ghosted in silence, stepping only on ties. The chin lifted, and she could almost see the tiny folds of translucent skin.

"Marcel?"

He turned. "Elisabeth? It is you, yes?"

"It is, *mon ami*."

His teeth shone beneath the climbing moon. "I found your kerchief, Princess! Why are you here? Have you renounced your kingdom?"

She hugged his narrow shoulders. "I've come to take you back and make you an earl. Or was it a dukedom you wanted?"

He chuckled. "I am a humble man, Your Majesty. I wish only to be a knight. Is it too late? The Parliament, remember?"

Warmth grew in her breast. "You're in luck. In my kingdom, there is no legislature. We're governed by whim, and our currency is French pastry."

His smile shone. "And am I to be a dedicated socialist, like Clement?"

She laughed. "I have a job for you. Are you able to leave Ghent?"

"Now? I have been told to switch tracks for trains. Things might become untidy."

"Then I'll wait. How long would it take for them to replace you?"

"I could tell them tomorrow and leave perhaps the day after, if I have an urgent cause."

She put her hand to her throat. "That would be perfect. You will tell them you have gotten word from your family in Paris. You will say you are needed there."

His face brightened. "Of course, yes! I will need to inform another operative from my group, but yes!"

Had he misunderstood? "Then we will board a train for Tongres. You will help me at an American hospital. It shall not be long before you're bound for Paris."

The smile grew slack. "Of course. It won't be long."

* * *

David stared at the door and listened to Schneider's steps moving close. His stomach churned. He'd had five extra spoons of soup, two filled with tomato stems, one with a sliver of beef, and two more with wedges of turnip. He owed the men on the committee.

The door eased open, the hauptmann leaning against the frame. "Good evening, Lieutenant. Please, come in."

"Is my intrusion impeding the prosecution of the war, Herr Hauptmann?"

"Not at all."

"Then I'll return when it will."

The German smiled and lifted his arm toward the desk. Forms were spread across it. Between the heap on the left and a tidier stack on the right, a bottle stood open, a glass beside it.

"Have a seat, Lieutenant. Would you care for a brandy? It is an inappropriate digestif for vegetable soup, perhaps, but I would think you might not object."

He stared at the bottle as if the decision were difficult. "Will you join me?"

Schneider turned. "Of course. You are not going to insist that you are on duty?"

He smiled. "It's not a weighty matter."

Heinrich pulled a snifter from the shelf and placed it beside his own.

"You're working late, Herr Hauptmann." He scanned the desktop but saw no keys.

"I'm afraid the reputation we Germans have for excessive paperwork is accurate." Heinrich paused. "Again, I believe we're adequately acquainted for you to call me by name. Privately, of course."

"Thank you, Heinrich." He reached for the snifter. "I had hoped to discuss the prisoners' Christmas. We're without a chaplain, though a few of the kriegies have offered to fill in."

Schneider chuckled. "Most of whom are deranged, I am sure."

"Were you deranged prior to losing your faith, Heinrich?"

The German shrugged. "That argument could be made, I suppose."

David lifted his snifter, a trickle crossing his tongue. "Those of us without the aptitude to accept genocide would appreciate an opportunity to celebrate a holiday *we* hold dear."

"I suppose you believe you just scored a point, as you Americans say?"

He lifted a hand. "It wasn't an argument, just a request."

"It was both, Lieutenant." Heinrich paused. "There is a priest in Waldheim who might be willing to offer eucharist to Catholic prisoners. The service would be in Latin, of course." He looked up. "Are you ready for another brandy?"

"Not yet, but it's delicious." He put the snifter to his lips, allowed himself a taste, and covered the remainder with his hand. "I don't know how many of the prisoners are Catholic, but the Protestants might feel slighted." He caught Heinrich's glare. "Have you received word on Red Cross parcels? Even a partial allotment would help—make it seem more like Christmas."

Heinrich poured another drink. "So, your desire to celebrate your Savior's birth is not a wholly spiritual one?"

He nodded. "Maybe not, but it's meaningful to most of us."

The hauptmann replaced the bottle. "Red Cross shipments have not reached a prison within two hundred kilometers. If they do, I shall tell you."

"And all the animals have been slaughtered?"

"The cows, yes, but a hog remains. We can, perhaps, find adequate rations to keep it alive until Christmas. Would you prefer we wait?"

Cows. "Will the beef last until then?"

Heinrich turned, swept his hand across the room. "Over two weeks? It will not be difficult to keep it cool, but it would mean reducing the amount we're putting in your soup."

He looked across the desk. "I see. What's available elsewhere?"

The glare grew razor sharp. "All of Germany is hungry, David."

He pushed his luck. "But you have gasoline. You could send troops to find some."

Heinrich licked his lips. "I'm sure you know our petrol is rationed."

"Is that why you stay some nights? To save fuel?"

The German squinted. "It is a consideration."

"Is there another reason? Are you and Élodie—you're getting along, aren't you?"

"That is an impertinent question, Lieutenant."

"I'm asking as a friend. These are turbulent times. The salient has cost a lot of lives while Allied forces build. You're under a great deal of pressure."

Heinrich released a burst of air, poured a drink, then walked around his desk. "I'm afraid I must visit the water closet."

David stood. "Would you prefer I leave? We can continue later."

Heinrich's grin returned. "Are you now concerned with protocol?"

He looked toward the desk. "I didn't think you'd want to leave me with your brandy."

Schneider chuckled and stepped to the door. "By all means, pour yourself another." The door swung behind him, touched the jamb, and clicked shut.

David rested his glass and lifted the stacks of paper at either end of the desk. Nothing. He looked in a tray containing pencils, pens, and an eraser, then pulled the center drawer. Brass shifted beneath his gaze, and he lifted keys from the corner.

The door edged open. "Dremmer?"

"Got 'em, Bear." A hand reached inside, and he rushed to offer the keys. "Move!" He checked the clock, picked up his glass, and spilled a drop, as if he'd refilled it. He examined the desk, looked for anything he'd misplaced. The clock on the bookcase clacked, and he took another sip and prayed for Bear's return. Minutes dribbled by, his prayers exploding into a recitation of fear, repeated with ever more volume. Boots clacked across the vestibule, and he looked at the clock. Eight minutes.

The door moved toward him, and Heinrich filled the doorway, standing a bit off center. "I've given your request some thought." The words emerged soft and misshapen.

He smiled. "And what have you decided?"

Heinrich lifted his chin. "I will delay having the hog slaughtered and will try to find additional vegetable bales to keep your men fed until Christmas."

He nodded. "Thank you, Heinrich."

Schneider dropped into his chair. "I hope it won't appear inhospitable, but I must finish these reports. Do come again when I have time for a real discussion. Like we had before."

His gut contracted, and he swallowed his brandy. "Have a good evening, then."

* * *

David leaned against the wall, the imminence of Heinrich's discovery a rock in his gut. "Mackey made impressions of every key on the ring, right?"

Bear lay on his palliasse, his hands behind his head. "Even the ABUS key. He figured it was for the office, so he'll make it first. Figured you might need it. Thought he could finish it before morning. First time Schneider steps out—"

He shook his head. "If he notices his keys are gone, I don't think he'll leave his office. I had no idea the wax had to be heated. How'd Mackey do it?"

"Put it in the water with the vegetable bale. He used the showers to make it set. Took some time."

"I should have planned better."

Bear shrugged. "Wouldn't matter. There wasn't no way he could've made them impressions in time. Just got to find a way to get them keys back in."

Chapter XLIX

Bless the Lord, oh my soul, while excelsior prickles my spine, and the dark seeps through my bones. Let all that is within me bless your holy name, for none of this is your doing—not the thoughts that turn to darkness, or the darkness that births my shame, or the shame that steals my hope. You heal my diseases and forgive my iniquities, as I curse the severity of my bed and dread the cost of my faithlessness. You crown me with tender mercies, while I fight chimeras of my own creation and pray for sleep. You redeem my life from the pit and satisfy my mouth with good, so that my youth is renewed to spend with a woman whom I might love more than you.

David turned on his palliasse. It was a prayer born of truth. His recitation of the Psalms had brought him to an end of pretense, though not of insomnia. If the evening had taught him anything, it was that Schneider was as capable of missteps as he, and that he was unprepared to exploit them. Now he had no option; he would meet his nemesis before the man left his office.

Something rasped within the hall, erratic and hurried. He scarcely discerned a tap, raised his head, and pushed his blanket to the side as the door flew open. Muted yellow filtered from below and was as quickly quenched by the towering figure stumbling toward him.

"Goons are coming up the stairs, sir!" The words came on a frantic gust.

"Close the door and get under my bed! They see you?"

"I think so." Mackey dived beneath the narrow frame.

David unfolded the blanket and let it drape to the floor. Voices rattled before the door came wide. He shielded his eyes from the flashlight, the faces of the pock-faced unteroffizier and Loverboy clearing within the void. "What's the problem, boys?"

The edge of the beam inflated the unteroffizier's nose and upper lip. A stubby thumb stabbed the beam. "He see someone below."

David swung his feet to the floor. His boots caught wool and pulled a double hand-width of blanket from the wall. His heart stuttered. "I didn't see anyone. Likely clouds moving past."

The unteroffizier pivoted into the hall, his boots clacking on stone. Loverboy froze, stared toward the gap at the edge of the blanket, and seemed unsure of what to do.

David rasped harsh words. "Does Feldwebel Beck know about you and his frau, Gefreiter? I'll keep your secret if—"

The boy spun before hearing the offer and pulled the door behind him.

He glanced at Bear. "What time is it?"

Bear lifted his watch toward the window. "Oh three hundred ten."

"I need to be at his door by oh six hundred—half hour before appell." He turned and looked beneath the bed. "You have the keys, Mackey?"

They appeared on a trembling hand.

"Bear, go to the vestibule and signal me when the goons reach the west side." He looked at Mackey. "I'll wave from the stairs. Stop at the latrine on your way to your billet."

* * *

David paced. "I'll need an excuse to get into the hautpmann's office. Got any ideas?"

Bear lay back on his duffel. "What'd you talk about?"

"Christmas. Schneider promised to butcher the hog a few days before, so the men would have meat. Then he offered to get a priest for the Catholics. I turned him down. The service would be in Latin. Wouldn't be fair to the Protestants."

"There's your answer. Take him up on his offer. Even if the men don't understand what's going on, they'll attend a service. Make it more like Christmas, won't it?"

He scrubbed his head. "Yeah, maybe that'll get me in the door."

"You're welcome. Now get some sleep."

* * *

David listened for stirring, anything, glanced down the hall, and knocked again. If the hauptmann were gone, he would know his keys were missing. Still, he could use the opportunity to hide them. He grabbed the iron latch, pulled down, and urged the door inward.

The leather couch was covered in a mussed blanket. He stepped in, looked to the left, and froze. Heinrich stood before a mirror in trousers and undershirt, his face lathered. "What are you doing here, Lieutenant?"

An icy hand gripped his gut. "Is this a public event, Herr Hauptmann? I thought we were on a first-name basis."

Schneider turned. "I asked a question."

He dropped the grin. "Right. I came to accept your offer of Christmas services. Most of the Protestants will appreciate the opportunity to attend any Christian service, I think."

Schneider scowled. "When I failed to open the door, did you assume I was gone?"

"I assumed you were under the weather. Last night, you were pretty—" He pushed his hands in his pockets and gripped the key ring. "I mean, where else would you be?"

Schneider looked in the mirror, drew the razor across his cheek, and splashed it in the basin. "Are you certain your being here has nothing to do with my keys?"

His lungs refused to free their grip. "You've lost your keys?"

A sneer appeared on the mirrored face. "And now you're here to replace them, yes?"

Schneider's calm chilled him. He'd expected the threat of a firing squad but released the keys in his pocket and raised his hands. "Check me if you want."

"Sit! I shall deal with you momentarily."

He stepped to the couch, folded the blanket neatly on the near end, and sat with his back to Schneider. Where might the keys have fallen had Heinrich dropped them? The desk had eight posts, two on either side of the center drawer. They might have tumbled behind one of those.

"Did you sleep well, David?"

The voice gave him a start. "Like a baby, Heinrich. And you?"

"I woke and needed my keys. I quickly realized then that you had taken them."

He turned to watch the hauptmann shave. "Well, I'd like to help, but since it appears to have increased your suspicions, I think I'll withdraw the offer."

The eyes in the mirror met his. "I have decided to have the lock changed. Your efforts were quite futile."

He tilted his head. "A wise move, given your level of mistrust."

Schneider placed the razor to his neck. "The unteroffizier saw someone on the stairs during the night. Who do you suppose it was?"

"Clouds, most likely. The closer the Allies get, the more shadows they're apt to see."

"Cloud shadows. Precisely what Unteroffizier Krüger said. I find that interesting."

Krüger. "We discussed it when they woke us, so I'm not surprised." He forced a breath. "They almost broke the door down, Heinrich. It's always open to the fine men of the Wehrmacht. They should know that."

The hauptmann turned. "They almost broke your door, yet you slept like a baby?"

"It was a brief interruption. It's been a while since I had brandy. Besides, having a clear conscience helps me sleep. You likely remember how it was."

A tapping came from the door. The hauptmann growled a response, but no one entered.

David stood. "Want me to open it?"

Schneider nodded, and he stepped to the heavy door. Loverboy sidled beside him and maneuvered a tray around the couch, an anxious expression on his face.

"Need help?" He hid the keys beneath two fingers, took the tray, and stared at the boy. The gefreiter jolted, and sugar spoons clattered to the floor. He placed the tray on the desk and leaned forward as if to help, eased the keys onto the rug, and toed them beneath a fold.

The gefreiter looked at Schneider, his lips quivering, and emitted a string of broken assonance. Heinrich snapped, muffled his impatience, and motioned for the boy to clean it up. The gefreiter moistened a napkin and blotted sugar beneath Heinrich's chair. David pushed the keys deeper into the fold with his boot and moved to the couch to wait.

The boy removed a cup, a roll, and slivers of cheese, then began straightening the desk, the keys in his hand.

Schneider turned. "Where did you get those, Gefreiter?" The question came in English, the answer in stammering German. He turned to David in fierce scrutiny.

He lifted his hands. "Whatever he said."

The hauptmann wiped soap from his face. "The gefreiter says he found the keys on the rug. I searched beneath the desk. Why do you suppose I failed to find them?"

"I guess you didn't look closely." He turned. "What do you think, Gefreiter?"

302

* * *

Darkness boiled in the north, the unremitting gray swallowed by a gathering black cloud. David moved to the front of the assembly and steadied his gaze. Temerity would be seen as guilt, so he offered an insolent pose.

Schneider marched from the officer's quarters, his expression unreadable. The familiar cacophony of German, the *eins, zwei, drei* of the unteroffiziers, and the dissonance of feldwebels deepened the cold. Roll call ended, and a report was shouted. Schneider's response was bloodless, a liturgy directed to a god he no longer revered.

"Entlassen!"

The kriegies moved off. David stayed a second longer, refusing to look away. The hauptmann caught his glare and motioned him over.

"Lieutenant."

"Herr Hauptmann."

"Perhaps I owe you an apology. I reacted somewhat hastily. The gefreiter showed me where he found the keys. They would have been impossible to see from where I sat."

He released the air in his lungs. "As I said, Herr Hauptmann, when neither of us holds an allegiance that threatens the other, we can be friends. Until then, I'm afraid it's impossible."

The German smirked. "In point of fact, you said that about our having a drink, and that was accomplished. Perhaps we shall overcome this, as well."

* * *

The wheels of the dining car drummed rhythmically as they dawdled over newly constructed tracks. Nicole stared out the window and pressed a hand to her churning stomach. The only American in the car, a major, read a newspaper two tables away. He might have been able to hear but taking Marcel to her berth would likely arouse more suspicion.

She smiled and opted for English. "We've never had the opportunity before, Marcel. I'd love to know about your family."

Marcel swallowed coffee and opened his hand. "Where do I begin? It was only Margarette and I for a decade. I had my business, and we were in love, but she wanted children. She was past thirty, and I was forty." He shook his head. "I regret resisting." He grew quiet.

"But you had children, yes?"

"Eventually, though not until Margarette was thirty-six and I forty-five. Our daughter, Simone, came to us early in the war. She was our light in a dark time. And then Michel." He touched the corner of his eye.

Her heart squeezed. "Are both in Paris?"

He shook his head. "Michel was taken prisoner at Dunkirk. It has been four years. We received letters at first, but he was sent to the mines. His letters stopped soon after." He breathed deeply. "Everyone knew that prisoners placed in mines died there. I never spoke of it with Margarette, but she knew, of course." He looked away. "Simone is in Paris with her daughters, Madelaine and Marie-Thereze. Her husband is also gone three years, now."

She squeezed his arm. "And how did Margarette die?"

"When Michel was born something went wrong. She saw her children come of age, knew her grandchildren, but there was bleeding. The doctors helped at first, but it always returned. At last, her heart grew weak. After Michel was lost, she no longer wished to live, I suppose."

"I'm sorry, Marcel. Truly. I wish no less for you than I would for my own father."

He smiled, shrugged. "Our lives seldom go as we plan, though sometimes we plan poorly. Had we begun a family sooner, she might still…"

She wrapped her hands around his and squeezed. "You cannot know this."

"I also cannot deny it." He smiled. "For you this war will end. You have your airman, and you are with the Americans. I think it no accident the sergeant happened upon you when he did. And you will be searching prisoners' files." He brought his hands together in triumph.

Her heart contracted. "I cannot hope for David, Marcel. It is not possible."

"Because he is married? There is a question regarding this, is there not?"

Air escaped her lungs. "How do you know this?"

His expression grew warm. "*Ma chérie*, I have been with the Resistance from the beginning. Did you think I would not also ask questions?"

She straightened. "And do you have contacts in Tongres?"

He leaned in. "Will we be near the rail yard?"

"They are less than two kilometers from the hospital."

He nodded. "It is probable that I will find one within a week. More will follow."

She held his gaze. "I have no way of learning anything except through the British, and that is now impossible. Can you find contacts unknown to MI6?"

He smiled. "Do you remember telling me of your plans to go to Germany should the Americans not offer help? I could not allow that without knowing who you were to meet and who would care for you. Perhaps I have already learned what you must know."

She hesitated, shaken. "I need to know where David is. And I have a friend from the university. She worked with the White Rose in Munich, but—"

His head tilted. "Your lieutenant is in a prison near Waldheim, and Mademoiselle Devillier lives with Hauptmann Schneider. He superintends that prison. She and your lieutenant are directed by a group established in Munich. A good one. I have worked also with this group."

Tears came. "And David and my friend are well?"

Chapter L

David noticed the pattern while waiting for appell. The German fighters took off at sunrise heading west to return after oh nine hundred from the north. They left in pairs or formations of three. He'd asked Bear to sketch the insignias as they circled close. One plane had a double chevron, one had a triangle, and at least three had no chevron at all—a minimum of five planes.

He squinted into the window and dried his sweaty palms on his shirt. The transponders Langley described could guide bombers to the target, even at night, and Élodie just might know how to access one. If she did, she might also know how to contact London.

He leaned forward, his breath fogging the window so that it blended with the appellplatz, and released the words that had risen with the sodden dawn.

> *Western wind, when wilt thou blow,*
> *The small rain down can rain?*
> *Christ! That my love were in my arms*
> *And I in my bed again!*

Bear shifted behind him. "What's that?"

"A poem."

"Not a very long one."

He grinned. "But it says more between the lines than a newspaper could in a page."

His friend shrugged. "Guess I don't get it."

"What do you learn about the people written about in a newspaper? What are they thinking? How do they feel?"

The sergeant grinned. "It's usually politicians, and they're either wanting my money or looking for a way to control me."

He laughed. "Or both. But there's more in this. We know where this man is, what he does for a living, what he feels, and what his greatest desire is. And there's the power of intrigue. We're left with questions and clues that add power to what the poet wants us to see."

"Kinda like getting to the airfield? Intrigue. You like that?"

He turned back to the window. "In poetry, sure, but lives are at stake here, Bear. Forward troops could break through in a matter of weeks. Those planes could take out hundreds of them."

"If you had all this set up and our troops or the Tommies or the Ivans didn't make it for months, what would you do?" His friend dipped his chin. "It'll fall into place when it needs to."

It sounded so simple. Maybe it was.

The sergeant leaned back. "Then there's Nicole. The love that ain't in your arms."

He looked away. "Sure, the poem made me think of her."

"Or she made you think of the poem. Let her go, Dremmer. Your answer's comin'. Not knowing what it is don't mean there ain't one, or that it's the one you don't want."

He shrugged. "But it could be."

"Yeah, it could, but you gotta trust that God will work things out for your good. And hers."

* * *

The small rain down had rained until noon. Now cold seeped through stone and into David's bones. Langley had reported that the rest of Germany was covered in ice and snow, but they were shielded by mountains and warmed by west winds. Two weeks until Christmas, and they'd had only two freezes.

He drank the chilled air, could see the map with his eyes closed, had envisioned what the road to the north might look like in moonlight. He'd imagined the intersection beyond the narrow ridge hidden in thick growth, and the supply route west connecting him to the road to Waldheim.

He pushed the blanket away, let his feet fall to the floor, and walked to the window overlooking the appellplatz. "Bear, you awake?"

The sergeant cleared his throat. "I am now."

"I'll check Schneider's office on the way to the latrine. If he's there, I'm leaving. I'll contact Élodie and be back before daylight."

His friend rolled his feet to the floor. "It ain't raining?"

"No, but it's cold. Freezing, looks like, and clear. Be easier to see."

Bear's hand drug across the back of his neck. "You sure you

wanna do this?"

He put his RAF blouse over the two shirts he had left, pulled his pants over tattered long johns, and slid his flight jacket over his shirts. He removed the stone from the wall and extracted the key to the abattoir and Mackey's copies of those on Schneider's key ring. "It's time, Bear."

* * *

David placed his candle in the bucket, pushed the heavy post from the wall, and slipped into the tunnel. With his back against smooth metal, he lifted the trunk lid into the night, a much brighter one than on his previous escape. He shoved the bucket into the gaping maw, a fresh chill prickling his face, and lifted himself onto the crusted earth.

The moon dazzled all beneath, as definitive as the light surrounding Heinrich's door. Grass and leaves were rimed in diamonds, the rock tinseled with brightness. He moved toward the wall, breathed in freedom, and jogged to the supply road. The moon was lodged between two pines at the top of a peak, the road shadowed by trees on the near end but visible along the ridge. He looked back but couldn't see the turret.

The treetops to the north glistened, the castle behind him sharp-edged and certain. The tower appeared above the wall, and he sprinted to a copse of trees to escape the goons' binoculars. The land rose in celebration, the river's thundering hymns scarcely audible. He drew in the shiver of the few remaining leaves, a breeze lifting then returning them to silence.

From the intersection, he plunged west, ran a short way, and slipped beneath sagging branches. A tremor pulsed behind him; he pulled back and spotted the slitted lights of a truck at the intersection. It had left the prison after him. He sank into a bed of decaying needles and pressed his face against the earth. Were they looking for him? The truck rumbled past, and he lifted his head. An Opel Blitz, its bed covered in canvas, the tailgate down, the rear flap lifting in the wind. The troop carrier. He rose to his knees and brushed needles from his cheek and hair.

The engine gave up its whine, and brakes squealed. Tires slammed a pothole, and chains hammered against the metal bed. He blew damp earth from his lips. Why would the truck have chains in the back?

Unless they'd delivered prisoners.

There'd been no new kriegies since spring. Henri said troublesome prisoners were being shot. Had he lied? The salient, what the BBC was calling the Battle of the Bulge, might be forcing them to take more. Schneider would likely come for him to meet new prisoners. He glanced over his shoulder. The trip back, re-entering the tunnel, and placing the post in position might take twenty minutes. His absence would have been discovered before then. Bear was right. Trust was all he had.

* * *

The house faced east and sat near the edge of town. Windows reflected the moon's glow, the walls effulgent. Another house crowded it on the north, and a narrow drive separated it from the one to the south. He stepped from beneath a large tree that shaded him from sight and followed a stone path around the side. An old stable shone in the rear. He slid beneath its eaves and peeked inside. A late model car sat on blocks, wheels lifted from the dirt floor, a Mercedes emblem reflecting light from the windows. Two more stalls were vacant, another worn with car tracks.

He reached into his pocket, retrieved the keys, and jogged to the back door. The second key fit, and he slipped into an entryway that smelled of onions and cleanser. From the kitchen, brightness whispered through drapes from a room on his left. He turned toward bannisters that mirrored the slotted clarity of windows. Shadows slid across the polished wood of a dining table. He reached the stairs, took two steps, repeated it until he stood at the top in a hallway facing east. Two doors appeared on his right and three on his left.

"Élodie, it's David. I need to speak with you." His exhalations came in bursts. "Élodie?"

"Heinrich?" The voice was mostly breath.

"It's David. We need to talk."

"David?"

His lungs filled with relief. "Yes. I'll wait in the kitchen."

* * *

Élodie scuttled about the sink and slid a kettle beneath the faucet, her hands nimble in the muted light. "And you told Henri of your need to contact me?"

David eased into a chair. "It's been a long battle. He doesn't want you involved in this. I wouldn't ask, but there's no one else. I'm sorry."

"You needn't be. I am willing. You should know also that I have contacts my brother knows nothing about. What do you require other than surveillance of the airfield?" The assonance was clear, the shift to English interrupting the flow of her thoughts.

"Do you have a way there? To the airfield?"

"My contacts do."

The niggling in his chest grew stronger. "I need a Eureka transponder. The British dropped them across Europe for the Resistance."

She lit the flame and placed the kettle on the stovetop. "I know of them. They were brought in with the invasion, as well. Resistance workers collected and carried them to Belgium. Some also made it here." She dumped coffee in a beaker. "The Wehrmacht now has beacon locators. They sometimes find them in minutes."

His shoulders eased. Henri was wrong. She wasn't rash at all. "I'm not asking you to use it. I just need the machine."

"Our radio man has worked with these. He repairs those damaged by air drops." She snickered. "He calls them his babies. Perhaps he has one in good repair."

"That'd be great. Maybe he'll be able to coordinate times and dates with the RAF." He struggled for words. "There's something else. Are you sure of your brother's loyalties?"

Élodie pivoted. "Our father was taken to a camp. Our grandparents. Our uncle. Henri made a promise to them and will die rather than see me harmed."

He spread his hands. "Will he allow all of us to die to keep you safe?"

"Would you not allow all of us to die to protect Nicole?"

Swanson's body dimmed his vision. The three Belgians. "I've failed to protect others." His voice cracked. "I can't fail her."

She tiptoed, a doe catching a scent, and pulled him from the chair to wrap her arms around his shoulders. "We cannot be responsible for all that happens. If we are fortunate, we can protect those we love. It is the same for Henri."

He allowed his arms to take in her warmth. "I should go."

"Without coffee? I have cream, also."

* * *

David paced the floor, his legs still quivering from the sprint across the ridge. "She'll get information on the airfield, try to learn where the planes are hangered. And on security."

Bear sat on his palliasse, his elbows on his knees. "She'll use the string and bottle?"

"Yeah. Said she had someone else that could check it occasionally. He's got to be here."

"We'll find him. So, what else is eatin' you?"

"Élodie. I asked her about Henri's loyalties. She said he was protecting her, like I was Nicole, at the expense of others. I've sacrificed lives, Bear. Swanson, the three Belgians."

"Dremmer, that wasn't your—"

"She saw her words struck a chord. She hugged me. The comfort was more than—"

"And now you think you're in love with her, too?"

"No. I just haven't wanted anyone else since I met Nicole. I never thought I would."

Bear leaned back, his arms extending to his palliasse. "And you're afraid what you feel for Nicole ain't what you thought it was, something that would last a lifetime?"

He turned. "It's not that. It's just that I don't want to want anyone else. Ever."

"It ain't just your weakness, Dremmer. Loving a woman means giving up all the others to have her. When you choose her, you choose her over what you might want when you're at your weakest. That's love."

"Like King David and Ornan. You sacrifice what your heart wants most."

Bear smiled. "Somethin' like that, yeah."

"So, you've wanted women besides Babs?"

"For an hour or a day. Those feelings don't last. You choose a woman every day and those feelings leave. Love is something you do, usually with feelings, but sometimes in spite of 'em."

"I still love Nicole, Bear."

"But do you love her enough to let her go?"

Chapter LI

She completed another narrative, slipped it into a file, and placed it on the stack. Private Norbert Bessinger would receive his WD AGO Form 53-55 and be sent home to Omaha. He would be thinner than his family had ever seen him, missing three toes due to frostbite, but he was alive and healthy. A fortunate man.

Nicole stared through the window, ice forming at its edges, saw the blood-soaked pall of evening settle on stone, and reached for another folder. Corporal James Ray Loughlin. Interned at Stalag Luft 6, deceased. Date of death was marked unknown, though it was logged as occuring prior to the move to Stalag Luft 4 and the march to Fallingbostel. Marcel added a note: *Fellow prisoner, PFC Jorge Sandoval, contracted dysentery on the march, fell behind, and was left to die. He stole grain from a farmer's bin and made his way to British lines. During the interview, Sandoval said Loughlin was sullen for weeks before attacking a guard with a rock. The guard beat Loughlin to death with the butt of his rifle. Sandoval described Loughlin's attack as suicide.*

She collected the form, intending to place it on the colonel's desk to be converted into a telegram. At Christmas, no less. If the family inquired about the circumstances of his death, their pain would be compounded. It was too cruel. She lifted the stack of reports waiting to be written and placed it near the bottom where it wouldn't be reached for a few days.

* * *

Leaden skies drained through the window as David waited for Schneider to stop pacing.

Heinrich turned. "You were made aware of the evacuation of Stalag Luft 6, I am sure."

"Last summer? I heard about it. Your boys didn't want to be taken by the Ivans."

The hauptmann continued to stare. "True, though I am sure you would agree that releasing your enemies to pursue your destruction would be unwise."

"Those men were starving and unarmed, Heinrich. And they were defenders, not aggressors. Will you concede that, at least?"

Schneider faced him. "I will concede that this war was started for unsound reasons and that it has accomplished little." The words came in a sharp hiss.

Fire swelled his chest. "'Accomplished *little*?' It was evil, Heinrich! All of it! Taking peoples' lives, destroying their families, stealing all they'd worked for—innocent people who'd done nothing worse than being born in a country you didn't like or with a pedigree you believed inferior. As if your superiority entitled you. And you believed that lie because your pride compelled you to. Now you're refusing to acknowledge what you've done!"

Schneider raised a hand. "Stop! I understand that we were wrong—that I was wrong. Now we must find a way to lessen the consequences. Can we agree to that?"

He shook, couldn't lid the cauldron inside. "And what can we do to resurrect the millions of lives and restore their bloodied dreams, Herr Hauptmann?"

"Nothing. But perhaps we can prevent the death of over two hundred more."

He squelched his rage. "You're right. So, what is it you want?"

"The Soviets are advancing. Prisons near Königsberg are being evacuated, and more will begin after Christmas."

"How far is Königsberg?"

Heinrich waved it away. "A great distance. Still, the Eastern Front is moving closer. At some point, it will be here. I want your assurance that you will help when it reaches us."

"The Brits, the Canadians, and the US are advancing, too. You should pray our boys get here first."

Heinrich appeared to relax. "Perhaps I have. However, I believe it probable that you will have to take us to your troops or bring them to us."

He nodded. "Certainly, I will. And I'll let them know how hard you worked to keep us alive. If it's needed, I'll testify to it."

"I believe you would, should a trial occur." Schneider turned to the window. "However, that appears unlikely. My request is that you see to it that Élodie is treated well. I swear to you she had no part in this. She never approved of any of it."

"I'm sure that's true, so let's figure out a way for you to take care of her."

Heinrich lifted his chin. "It is dangerous to believe you have a solution to every problem or even that you can understand them. That is precisely what took the soul of Germany."

He shivered at the truth in Heinrich's words. "I must ask you something. Did you receive prisoners last night?"

Schneider shifted, a blue gaze locking onto his. "How did you know this?"

"I believe the proper protocol would have been to notify me." He needed to reassume some control despite his gratitude at not having his outing discovered.

Heinrich turned his head. "There were four men and all quite damaged."

Something wasn't right. "What are you saying?"

The perfect chin turned away. "I was ordered to dispose of them."

He leaned forward. "Dispose?"

"I complained that we hadn't adequate food for more prisoners, and I was told that it would then fall upon me to dispose of them. What would you think that meant?"

David rose from his chair. "What did you do, Heinrich?"

The hauptmann turned away. "They are in the lazarette. I directed that they be given some of the remaining sedatives." He waited. "I am doing all I can to procure more. These men also have seen more than they can endure."

He caught his friend's gaze again. "Thank you, Heinrich." He eased. "Thank you."

Schneider's lips were ashen. "May you awaken to a peaceful Christmas morning, David."

He straightened and offered a salute. "And you, Herr Hauptmann."

* * *

Nicole stood at her window. Thin patches of ice clung to grass as darkness gathered beneath eaves and under branches. A gaunt figure drifted between shadows, hands burdened, a narrow face leaning into his walk. Her heart lifted at the sight of his jaunty gait. She turned from the window and stepped to her desk to retrieve the envelope.

A boot tapped brass, and she hurried back to the door. "Marcel, what a pleasant surprise!"

"You are hiding in the dark? Your subjects will think you have abandoned them!"

"A habit only. Please come in."

He lifted an iron pot, a bag hanging from his hand. "It isn't right to be alone on Christmas Eve, so I brought dinner and wine. Not Réveillon, of course, but more festive than C-Rations."

She began to clear her desk. "How wonderful! Please use my chair."

He set the pot on her desk and untied the towel. "I trust you weren't working in the dark."

"No, though I had thought I might start again. It was entirely too quiet." She placed a finger to her chin. "I'm afraid I have only one dish."

He chuckled. "Then you may wash it when I finish and have what is left."

She reached across the desk, pretending to yank his ear. "That is not so gracious, especially when you consider that your earldom is revocable."

"Since I have again been elevated to a position I never wanted, and since the beef bourguignon smells exquisite, I deem it worth the risk." He winked. "Also, I brought two plates."

She smiled. "Knight. I had so quickly forgotten. Forgive me."

"It is nothing. Fortunes change, but hunger remains."

He drew another chair, turned it sideways, and looked at the window. "You have no curtain? Perhaps we should request one for your safety."

She withdrew her fork and dabbed her lips. "No, I would prefer to have none. With the lights off, I can see whomever might be looking in."

"You are afraid of the Americans? Sergeant Lee, perhaps?"

"No, it would take only a word from some officer to alert Intelligence, and they could contact MI6. Professor Greeves would act quickly. I used my code name. A mistake, but I hadn't prepared another before I met Sergeant Lee."

Marcel laid his knife across his plate. "Perhaps your pursuer has lost interest. He is now in enemy territory and must concern himself with remaining alive."

She drizzled sauce. "A comforting thought, but unlikely. The man pursued me to Paris when a Nazi defeat was imminent. It was the same in Antwerp. For him to have followed me was remarkable. No doubt he is connected to the Committee." She took another bite and let it linger on her tongue. "Wherever did you get this? It is delightful!"

"A woman was recommended by the colonel. She prepares meals for his staff, now, and the Americans provided the beef." He winked. "And the woman is French."

"I will ask nothing further." She laughed. "But isn't Christmas especially difficult for you? You miss your daughter, I'm sure."

The twinkle in his eyes turned liquid. "My first daughter?" His snicker was clearly camouflage. "Yes, of course I miss her. I pray she is well."

She couldn't contain it. "I am certain she is, Marcel."

He froze, stared as she extended the envelope. "*Joyeux Noël, mon ami.*"

"From Simone? Really? How did you—"

"I have been communicating with organizations in Paris. Sergeant Lee has also helped."

"But you had only my code name."

"And Margarette's name, and Simone's, and Michel's. I found Michel first. Records were kept of all prisoners, just as we are doing. How many Michels were taken prisoner at Dunkirk with a sister named Simone and nieces named Madelaine and Marie-Thereze?" She trembled. "Your son is alive, Monsieur Durand."

His mouth opened in silence. "It cannot be."

"He was injured, though the injury kept him alive. After a fall, he was sent to Stalag 4 B. As he had difficulty walking, he was spared the great march. But you must read what Simone has written." She motioned with her hand. "Please."

The old man's lips fluttered. "You are certain?"

She steadied her voice. "Read your daughter's letter. I will wait."

* * *

David glanced across the appellplatz. Kriegies milled, laughter spilling at the extra portions of hay bale soup. Pork could be found in almost every bite, and they'd been promised barley soup that evening, something they hadn't seen in months.

Bear turned from the spectacle. "You trust him? You think he's made a turn?"

"Schneider? Yeah, I trust him. He knew he was on the wrong side even at Moosburg. The Allies are coming, likely the Ivans, and he's convinced he won't survive. He still wants to save his staff and as many kriegies as he can. And most of all, Élodie."

"He don't think that'll happen if our boys don't get here first?"

David tilted his head. "He doesn't expect to survive either way. Stalags in the east are marching west. Hitler wants the kriegies who survive to be moved south, his ace in the hole."

Bear scraped his neck. "That's a heck of a bargaining chip."

Chapter LII

Sunlight glistened in silver reluctance across maize stalks bowing from the night's freeze. Drizzle wrapped them in ice and gossamer and now released them to a slightly warmer breeze. Jesse wheeled his chair across the porch and edged the growing brilliance from his sight. Christmas. His boy was in a prison camp somewhere, Morgan still had use of his place, and that girl lived in the back of Morgan's store, calling herself his wife.

His throat squeezed. There was no way those two could have married. So far as he knew, the boy hadn't even been told Delores wanted a divorce, and he wasn't going to be the one to write those words. It seemed likely David wouldn't object, would probably feel relieved of the matter, but who could know what might go through a man's mind in one of those places? He nodded in accord with his conclusion. It seemed best to let the thing lie, to allow the boy to have something to hope for and not take away what might be a brightness to him.

He'd received no payment on the place—a relief, truth be told. It would make a clearer path to getting it back. McFarley's had reimbursed him for his mules and implements and applied the debt to Morgan's account. He smiled. Of course, he'd had to threaten to turn them in for buying stolen property. They'd known those mules were his. Those boys just wanted to sell another tractor and were willing to do whatever was needed to get it done. Fact is, if it weren't for that money, he wouldn't have been able to buy groceries.

Morgan had done nothing on the place, had even let the dividing fences fall so that the cows came almost to the house some evenings. The Summit Place was likely grazed to the ground, and the man hadn't bothered to move them. The country was better there, the grass richer. There would have been no reason for them to try the fences if it weren't grazed out. The mamas he'd seen were poor, their hip bones pushing against their skin like tent poles. The shape they were in, they weren't apt to breed back. One good thing had come of the neglect. Dancer had begun to visit, looking from behind the tack shed as if hoping to catch sight of David. The horse was thin but faring better than the cows he'd seen. And he'd spied slender scars on the black's pasterns, likely the price he'd paid to breach the barbed wire and come home.

Jesse pulled himself up and looked north. He'd left oats in front of the pens, hoping they'd be seen as a gift. Or apology. But they hadn't been touched, and he had no way to carry them beyond the barn. The grain was old and weeviled, but he had plans to buy a few sacks the next time Ben took him to Grimsland, if the old fool would allow him to put them in his Ford.

He heard a rumble and rolled his chair around. Ben's Ford moseyed up the hill, red paint flashing in the early light, the engine lugging against the grade. If the man went faster than a first-gear idle, that Ford just might start squeaking. Or he'd imagine it had. He shook his head, rolled to the steps, and pushed down the pleasure he found at seeing the old coot. The car rolled to a stop, and the door eased open, old Niedermeyer likely hoping to save the hinges.

"What are you doing here, Ben? Didn't you know it was Christmas?"

"Course I knowed it was Christmas. I milked early just 'cause of it. Brought you some cream to eat with our cake. Or you can make us ice cream if you druther."

Jesse leaned back. Had the man lost his wits? "Cake? When have I ever baked a cake? Or made ice cream, for that matter?"

"It's time you learnt, if you ain't too old for that, too. Brought you a cigar so's we could enjoy ourselves after you feed me."

"I don't smoke, and what brought you to the conclusion I was about to feed you?"

"Just seems the proper thing to do, seein' as how I come all this way to check on ya."

He snickered. "You came to check on me, did you?"

Ben stopped in his tracks, a jar of cream dangling from his left arm, lines squiggling in the chill. Something covered with a towel swung beneath his right hand. "Bein' alone ain't something a man takes to right off, Jesse. Last couple years, you had your sister and grandboy. The girl, too, if you consider her company. Before the war, it was David. This year—well, this year you needed checkin' on. That's the truth of it."

He shook his head. "Since you've resolved to impose yourself, you might as well come inside. I'll scramble us some eggs."

"Eggs? I thought you had beef tenderloin on Christmas. Was you lying about that, too?"

He offered the most wretched stare he could produce without having a feeling for it. "I don't lie, Ben. You know that. The beef tenderloin was when I was a kid. Naomi did it the last few years, I'll admit, but where would I have come up with such a thing?"

"Same place I did, I reckon. And you do lie, Jesse, just not to other people. Now, get outa the way so's I can get to the house. Why is it you park yourself right where I'm a walkin'?"

* * *

Jesse looked past the curtains, saw the first blush of evening coloring the pines, and turned toward Niedermeyer. "It was a fine thing you did. Especially fine." He worked the words around but could find no other way to ask it. "Would you say we were friends, Ben?"

Niedermeyer looked through the window. "I don't know what else you'd call it. You'd be a hard man to bear otherwise."

He snorted. "Well, I have something for you. It's not a tenderloin or a cake, but I came across it in a parts store and thought you might be able to put it to some use."

Ben tilted his head. "You wasn't gonna give it to me lessin' I admitted to bein' your friend? And what was you doin' in a parts store? You got nothing to put parts on. Is that where you was the week before last? Made us late gettin' home, is what you did."

The floor squeaked where it always did when he rolled into the kitchen. He'd moved most everything he needed below the counter, but this one thing he'd left with the woman's dishes. He pulled himself to the worktop, rested on an elbow where she'd always drained her pans, and reached for a can of Simoniz. "I told the man how fond you were of that Studebaker. Told him you polished it about every day, and he said you needed this. Said when you use the regular Simoniz, the polish takes off paint. That helps where it's started to fade, but since yours is bright, it just adds wear. What you do is, you use the old Simoniz once a year or so, and you use this the rest of the time. It's just protection. Won't thin your paint."

Ben looked away. "It's a Ford, Jesse, not a Studebaker."

He shrugged. "And another thing. Man at the parts store said he's putting in a body shop in the back. I told him about the scratch inside your doorpost. Said they put out factory paints you don't have to mix. Cans no bigger than a man's finger, just for scratches. Since your car is covered all the time, he said he could touch it up without painting around it. Said he'd buff it out, and you'd never know the scratch was there. Dollar and a half, and it'll be on me. We can go to town and make a day of it."

"It's not but a quarter inch long." Niedermeyer looked back and caught his stare. "You done this two weeks ago? Before I brung you the makings for Christmas?"

He hid his smile. "Nah, Ben. I ran to Grimsland while you were on the toilet. You gave me plenty of time. I borrowed your DeSoto since I knew you wouldn't mind."

Niedermeyer turned away, put the chore of making conversation on him, but since it had been bothering him anyway, he spoke it out. "I've always wondered about your boy, Ben. I might know some of what you went through, now."

Ben looked frail all at once. "He was born with problems, Jesse. Something in his heart. Neither time nor doctors could change it. And God wouldn't." The words stopped for seconds. "Joseph wanted to be a cowboy—like you, I reckon. Difference was, he knew early on he'd never make one. Took you longer."

Jesse glared, his tears staunched by a chuckle.

"It was a better answer than that, old man." Ben held his stare but only for a moment.

He nodded. "And your wife?"

Niedermeyer looked at the floor. "Caught the influenza. Lived a couple weeks, but never come out from under it. My opinion was, she chose to die. Couldn't go on without the boy."

He waited for words. Nothing came. "I'm sorry about the both of them, Ben. Truly."

"Guess I ought to head back. Evenin' milking an' all." He stood silent. "Been a good day, Jesse. I didn't know if either one of us would know how to celebrate, but we laughed some."

"Well, I sure did. You always give me plenty to laugh at." He waited for Ben to move, but the old coot stood as unbothered as rock, so he forced out more words. Not that he didn't mean them. "I'm grateful to you for doing this. It's good having a friend."

Ben stared toward the cedar, his head nodding brokenly. "It is, even if it had to be you."

Chapter LIII

January 1945

Nicole pulled her sweater close, pushed the button through the piped buttonhole, and placed her hands beneath her arms. She'd purchased clothes after receiving her third two-week pay envelope filled with Allied Military Currency and wished she'd gotten the coat, a full-length, wool Chanel that wrapped around to button on the side. It would have been worth the extra pay. The heat in her quarters was turned high, and she still shivered. She looked through the window, saw only ice, but someone was there. She'd awakened two days ago knowing it, and her stomach had been in knots since.

She returned to her forms, reached Corporal Loughlin's, and wrote a narrative omitting Sandoval's description of his death. She offered a short prayer for the family and placed the form in the stack of death notices for the colonel. Perhaps the Loughlins were able to enjoy their Christmas. Still, she shivered at what they would now endure.

Patients were arriving from everywhere, most from the overflow of field hospitals. A few wandered in after being left behind on the march from Königsberg. One story especially touched her. PFC Marvin Randall, an Indiana boy, had been left to die. Suffering severe frostbite and unable to walk, he was discovered by a German farmer who took him home and shared what potato soup he and his wife had left. The following day, they wrapped the boy's feet and helped him reach British lines. The couple was fed, resupplied, and given a ride west of the advancing Soviet troops.

She tidied her stack, reached for the top folder, and shuddered at the door swinging open.

Marcel stood with a pallid face. "Your Gestapo man has arrived."

Her lungs refused to fill. "Where is he?"

"Displaying your picture among railway workers, saying you are his lost daughter. I alerted two agents to watch for him. I gave them only the description you gave me, but they know Gestapo when they see one. We will eliminate him. We could make it appear as if—"

"No!" She pressed against her stomach. "It is perhaps not him. And if it is, another will be sent. Perhaps several. Killing a Gestapo man is an invitation to more murders."

Marcel closed the door. "I told my friends nothing, but many have seen the photograph." He drew his breath. "It is of poor quality, but you were said to be wearing an evening dress."

Choler boiled in her breast. "And an effeminate snip of a man was standing beside me?"

"No, you stand alone beneath a chandelier." Marcel spoke in a whisper.

Her hands shook. "Of course. He wouldn't want to be included in the search. I hoped this wouldn't happen, but it was too soon for hope." She searched for a plan. "We will leave. This Gestapo man may know nothing of you, but your railway friends might say something. You will go to Paris. Sergeant Lee can arrange it. I will go to Waldheim."

"You cannot! Especially now."

She set her face. "I speak adequate German. Sergeant Lee will supply food, and I will dress as a refugee, quite unlike the picture this man is circulating. I will be one of thousands."

The old man slumped. "It is dangerous, Elisabeth." He paused. "And Madame Bouchard, the woman who prepared our dinner, has become close. I do not wish to leave just yet."

She cupped her hands, warming them with her breath. "I see. Perhaps she could go with you. That would lessen your chances of being recognized should you be seen."

He looked stunned. "I didn't— Perhaps she would agree to that. It is possible."

She saw herself trudging endlessly along frozen roads with nothing more than she could carry. "When this is over, Marcel, how will I find you?"

He brightened. "When this is over, yes. The Café de Flore on the Boulevard Saint-Germaine. There is a message board. Only the notes of the famous remain long, but I will post a message regularly using the code name, Gratiano." He grinned and jutted his chin. "No, no more code names. I will post as Gabriel Durand. Should you not find it, I will find yours to me. You promise, yes?"

She fought to loosen her tongue. "I promise to try. I pray that day comes soon, Marcel." She stepped around the desk and wrapped her arms around him. "Go with God, my friend, and may your life be filled with happiness."

"And may yours be filled with love."

* * *

Shadows descended into darkness. Nicole stared through the window and waited for the nightmare to end. Sergeant Lee would return soon. She was glad, now, that she had told him of her plight and agreed to his telling the colonel. Watts would understand the necessity of her leaving and might know a way for her to reach the Rhineland. Only the Colmar Pocket remained in Nazi hands, and the French First Army had sworn to destroy them. It was south of where she hoped to cross German lines, but it would be treacherous.

Marcel, Monsieur Durand, had to be considered. But arranging transportation for an older couple to Paris should not be difficult now. She closed her eyes and prayed he would be out of the Gestapo's reach before she left.

* * *

The fog that dimmed the outline of the tower had lifted. David surveyed the appellplatz, his narrow window offering a view of the battlement and latrine. He heard the deep breath of sleep and glanced at Bear. How could the man remain so calm? And why could he not?

Metal glinted at the edge of sight. A goon sauntered toward the latrine, light from the officer's quarters catching his *Gott Mit Uns* tunic buckle. The Krauts seemed as drawn to shiny objects as raccoons. He stared, waited for the boy to turn, then scuttled across the room.

"The guard just checked the north end, Bear. We need to see what we caught."

Bear rose from the bed in serene restraint and trundled toward the door. "You add some string to that line, we just might have fish for breakfast."

The drain opened at a proper distance from the latrine for a kriegie to have a smoke. David smiled and moved in front. "Get the cigarettes and matches."

"Got 'em. They're in my pocket."

He moved within a dream, a breeze across stone. Shadows formed within the muted light beneath Schneider's door, gliding toward the bookcase. Almost twenty-two hundred and the hauptmann was still working. He slinked toward the outer door and turned back.

"I'm here, Dremmer. Keep movin'."

He sprang to the steps, stopped, and slipped his boots on, then headed to the drainpipe. "Put a cigarette in your mouth, Bear. Hand me one. Keep a match handy in case a goon sees us."

Bear stepped into position and looked west. David scanned the main billet, then went to his knees. A scream secreted from the lazarette, the first he'd heard tonight.

He squatted. "We clear?"

"Nothin' this side of the tower. Can't see no further."

The string grew taut, released, and went taut again. It felt different, somehow, had less resistance. He looped it between his elbow and hand until it was an inch thick, heard the strike, smelled phosphorus, and turned as Bear put the match near his face. "Step on the string!"

The goon moved toward them as another scream leaked through the heavy doors.

Bear leaned back and raised his chin, freeing what smoke circled his face.

David took a drag, suppressed a cough, and stared at the moon as the goon moved at the edge of vision. "Just play along. Don't be too nice."

Krüger stepped close and pointed to his cigarette. "You have more, yes?"

"Last one. His, too. Decided to enjoy them under the stars. Nice clear night, you know?"

Likely more English than the man could absorb. Krüger glanced at the sky, then back. "We must speak, Othello."

His breath left him. "I don't know what you mean."

"I bring greetings from Prospero, my former schoolmaster and your friend."

He felt Bear's gaze. "I still don't know who you're talking about."

The goon raised his chin. "Retrieve your message, and we shall discuss it."

He drew a breath. "What was your school master's name, and what did he teach?"

The goon released a rolling laugh. "Herr Vogt. He taught British literature, but, of course, that meant Shakespeare. For him, there would be no more English writers for centuries." The Kraut looked up. "He asked that I tell you that Adda is well, and that her calf is now weaned."

He caught a sneer. "The more you speak, the better your English gets."

"It would have been suspicious to have been too fluent, don't you think?"

"And why would you want it hidden? Unless you're a spy."

"I am a spy, though not as you are suggesting. I am not a Nazi."

He looked at Bear. "How can we believe that?"

The quiet laugh shook his heavy frame. "It would be to your benefit if you did. And mine. It would also benefit Herr Hauptmann, and, of course, Élodie."

He stared. "Devillier said there were no contacts here. Why didn't he mention you?"

Krüger's chin jerked. "Perhaps he wanted to keep you from his sister. I placed the note in the bottle and know what it says. It's meaning, however, is unclear to me."

Doubt squeezed his gut. "Why'd you push me down the stairs?"

Krüger chuckled. "I did not intend to make you fall, Lieutenant. However, you have since avoided me, and that has kept me safe."

"So, why is this a good time to reveal yourself, Unteroffizier?"

"Élodie was insistent that you receive the message right away."

David pulled the bottle from the drainpipe and noticed it had been cleaned. He removed a slip of paper and held it up. It was still inscrutable.

"Allow me." The unteroffizier raised an American Zippo.

Light flickered, and David drew the lighter to his chest. *My friend has another baby and insists this one is yours.* He folded the paper and smiled. "Would it be possible to leave tonight?"

"These are perilous days, Othello. The Red Army launched an offensive in East Prussia. Stalag Luft Seven in Bankau began a forced march only last night. In a blizzard. If that message regards your forces reaching us first, it would seem wise to do just that."

He handed Krüger his cigarette. "I heard about the Soviet offensive. Sounds like they're evacuating prison camps everywhere."

The German drew deeply. "Your radio is quite the treasure, is it not?"

There seemed to be a threat in his words. "What radio? Are you accusing me of having forbidden devices?"

The stifled laugh returned. "Why would I? I've grown accustomed to overlooking it."

David breathed in darkness and steadied himself. He'd never seen Langley's receiver. How had Krüger? "You'll look out for me, then? Make sure I'm not spotted?"

The German nodded. "You'd best get heavier clothing."

The unteroffizier hadn't identified himself. "And what name did Prospero give you?"

"I am Aragon. In my university days, I was less than successful in pursuing a young woman that I had hoped to win, and—"

"I get it." The man's sudden warmth irritated him. "You'll let me out of the gate?"

Krüger looked at the tower and shook his head. "No, Lieutenant. You'll have to go through the tunnel as before."

The glance upward eased David's tightening gut. Aragon hadn't wanted to be seen. He turned to Bear. "May I use your jacket, Sergeant?"

A quick nod. "So long as you bring it back without no bullet holes in it, Lieutenant."

David zipped the jacket and dug his hands into the pockets. The key to the dungeon emerged between his fingers.

Chapter LIV

The walls of her quarters threatened to crush her. Nicole forced herself to breathe and stared out the window. Robert had promised to bring Colonel Watts hours ago. She'd written the man perhaps a hundred notes, read his directives almost daily, but hadn't met him. It seemed a ghastly risk. If he were like most officers, he would attribute her concerns to some flight of fancy and notify MI6. Still, she held an ace, though she had to play it judiciously.

She returned to the forms, found it difficult to focus, and began again. PFC Benjamin Herzog, a pre-medical student eighteen months ago, had taken shrapnel in his right leg and shoulder while fighting in Verviers. His prognosis was favorable, though he would be taken to England within the week to begin a lengthy convalescence. Had she omitted anything his family in Hartford might need to know? She scanned the narrative. Yes, he was expected—

The door swung wide, and Sergeant Lee moved to the side. A tall, dark-haired figure entered—General MacArthur without a pipe. He slanted toward her, his angular chin lifted high, a leather jacket open to his waist. The colonel took three strides to cross the room. She stood, her heart hammering.

"Miss Leclerc, I presume." His brusqueness made her more anxious.

She nodded, wondered if a curtsy were more suitable. "I'm happy to meet you, sir."

"I understand there's a matter of some exigence that we should discuss. Please sit down." He hesitated. "I find it difficult to sit before a lady."

She stared, saw a slight lift at the corner of his mouth. "Oh, yes sir. Of course."

She withered behind her desk. He drew Marcel's chair close and sat. "Sergeant Lee filled me in on the basics. I've been given to understand you're an MI6 operative. Is that correct?"

"I worked with WIM, sir, but MI6 recruited me to liaise with the Resistance."

The colonel's brow tightened. "I understood that sort of thing was transmitted on BBC broadcasts."

"The issuing of assignments is, sir, but after being aided by MI6 in escaping Belgium, I was directed to reopen a line across the Pyrenees. I now believe that was a test. After my first crossing, my job became verifying agents and assuring MI6 that they were communicating with their operatives. I was also expected to coordinate Resistance and Allied Command should that become necessary." She wiped her hands on her sweater.

"And did it become necessary?"

Electricity coursed her spine. "Unfortunately, no."

The square chin lifted. "Why is that unfortunate?"

"I was sent on a fool's errand, sir. The job had been done."

The colonel nodded. "And you were sent by higher-ups in MI6?"

She shivered. He seemed to know too much. "I was removed from Belgium because I was being investigated by the Luftwaffe. In extricating me, my MI6 handler believed he had found a puppet too intimidated to object."

"And why were the Germans investigating you?"

"My compatriots found two American airmen outside Brugge. Both were injured, so the Resistance asked that I and a German physicist we were hiding take care of them. The Wehrmacht later captured the airmen and killed Professor Stein."

He nodded. "You and the interrogator had been students of this professor, is that right?"

She felt the blood drain from her face. "Yes."

"I'm also aware that you became close to one of the airmen. It was Lieutenant Dremmer that persuaded MI6 to have you removed, was it not?"

Marcel! You sneaky, sweet little man! "Yes, he did, though I don't know how. I do know he's currently connected to a group in Moosburg run by German dissidents."

The colonel leaned back. "Sounds like the lieutenant has been playing with fire. Are you now wanting to run through the flames?"

"Not at all, sir. I simply don't want those risking their lives for us to be abandoned at the eleventh hour. Nor can I stay here."

The colonel steepled his fingers. "You can if you allow us to dispose of the threat."

She caught his glance. At least, he seemed to believe her story. "The Gestapo wants me dead, sir. Should additional agents replace this one, others will die, as well. That's their policy."

The dark face lowered. "There's no one you can contact directly at MI6 and circumvent the Soviet sympathizers?"

She raised her chin and played the ace she'd been holding. "Not at MI6. There is someone at Blenheim Palace, though I must wait until I've made provision for other agents."

Watts straightened, his hands falling to his lap. "Are you suggesting that you're able to contact the prime minister?"

She held his gaze. "Not directly, but yes. It was he who made me aware of the motives of those now pursuing me at MI6. Neither of us realized they would go this far. The thing is, if I make contact now, I might be extracted, and those I'm hoping to save would be left unprotected." She paused. "Including your informant."

The colonel smiled. "If you're concerned about Marcel, you needn't be. I've grown quite fond of the man. He makes me question the sanity of the Germans for invading France."

She slipped her hands deeper beneath the table, wiping them on her dress.

Watts scratched the dark shadow on his face. "I'll see to it that he makes it to Paris. Madame Bouchard, as well, though I won't pretend to like it. I haven't eaten so well since I left my mother's house." The grin faded. "I can get you to Cologne, but it will come with an assignment. Should you make it to the prison, I want you to make every attempt to turn the prisoners in Waldheim over to General Hodges. I'll inform him of who you are.

"The west side of Cologne is under our control, but it could turn into an inferno at any moment. We have informants who cross the Rhine regularly. There is one willing to take you east, perhaps as far as Kassel, though that will put you almost two hundred miles from Waldheim. I can only hope you make it there before the Soviets."

Over three hundred kilometers. She trembled. "That would be most helpful, sir."

* * *

David stood beneath the tree in Élodie's yard. Moonlight trickled into darkness, thick clouds muting all but the sharpest lines. The gloom had kept him near the center of the road, especially where the dozed stone met sheer cliffs outside the prison. He shifted as light caught the edge of the carriage house, then skulked to the corner, ran for the rear entrance, and extracted the keys from his pocket. He slid the one with the deepest bit into the keyhole, his hands shaking. The shaft settled deep. He turned it, and the bolt slid open.

Outside the pantry, he turned left, the faint luminescence of the kitchen window dissolving before him. He crept toward the dining room, his hand tracing cabinet doors. He bumped a chair, stumbling as it scraped across the floor. Something moved above him, inciting the slightest moan of a floor joist. Footfalls drifted, velvet whispers on spice-laden air. Words emerged in German, what sounded like a question, but the voice held no alarm.

His shoulders eased. "Élodie, it's David."

Soft thuds moved onto the staircase. "I had hoped you would come. I did not want your baby discovered."

His shoulders eased. "That message would have gotten any man's attention."

She laughed. "I suppose, yes. Were it intercepted, I did not want the subject known."

"Then you weren't concerned about sharing the information with Krüger?"

"Hermann? Why do you ask?"

"I just hadn't expected him to be on our side. I'm still not sure."

Her arms folded across her breast. "He has been active from the beginning." She edged close. "Heinrich charged Henri with selecting personnel, so his being here isn't an accident."

So, Krüger was allied with Henri. "How did your brother come to know him?"

"Through Herr Vogt. He taught Hermann and believed he could be turned. Herr Vogt also recruited Henri, though my brother came recommended by others."

It was the answer to a question he hadn't thought to ask.

"My chair proved to be an adequate alarm, did it not?" Élodie hurried past. "Please sit. I will make coffee. You are hungry, I am sure. Heinrich says you have little to eat."

He looked away. "I doubt that you have much, either."

"We still have beef. Also, canned cheese from the Wehrmacht. I would like to send some back with you if you and the sergeant can keep it hidden."

His gut roiled. The men were hungry, too. They'd had nothing but hay bale soup since Christmas. Almost six weeks without meat. "We'll use it only when we have a mission."

She nodded. "Tonight, you are on a mission, yes? I have bierocks. You will eat one now, and I will include another. I have also one for the sergeant." She pushed a small canvas bag toward him. "The transponder is heavy, perhaps fifteen kilograms. It will require strength."

He watched her supple form flowing before the window. "Thank you, Élodie."

Her hand lifted. "We are grateful, as well."

"Your radioman, the one who rebuilds transponders. Can he contact London?"

She turned. "I understood you could reach MI6 directly."

A current ran up his spine. Henri had relayed his claims. "I'll need to contact them more than once to set up an airstrike. We'd be discovered, sending so many messages."

"Of course, and your message through our man must be kept short for the same reason."

* * *

David stood at the front of the formation, weaving from exhaustion. He'd slept just over an hour, the death of yesterday's life falling prey to resuscitation, the raveled sleeve of care left unknitted, sore labor's bath ending with a mere dip into unknowing. He wished, in his odd remembrance of Macbeth, to share what he'd learned with Vogt.

The goons were surly, had held the kriegies at attention for over an hour, had forced them to stand in a cold drizzle, their urge to retaliate growing as the Allies advanced. The BBC reported US troops to be entrenched along the Rhine as materiel was being readied for the coming offensive. The Brits controlled the line north of the Americans and southwest of the Soviets, and Monty was set on taking Berlin. David cared not one whit who would be the first to picnic on the Reichstag steps, so long as the Soviets didn't liberate the prison.

"Dremmer, you okay?"

The whisper came from his left. "Just tired, Bear."

"Think about them bierocks we got waitin'. You can get a nap after that."

He smiled, was about to breathe his response when the unteroffizier stepped in front and chilled them with his stare.

"*Einhundertfünfundzwanzig!*"

He'd heard that one often enough. One hundred twenty-five. All were accounted for. If the other formation were correct, they'd be dismissed.

"*Einundachtzig!*"

Bingo! Eighty-one. Counting those in the lazarette shouldn't be hard, even for these boys. Schneider dismissed them, and he turned, spotted Langley heading to the stables and motioned for Bear to follow.

* * *

Night was settling in, but the colonel's car was warm, the driver obliging though silent. He seemed intent on finding check-in points and examining his watch before each stop. Twice he'd returned to the car with an envelope. Written directions, Nicole assumed. His diligence was reassuring, and she dozed, left the car when they stopped for food and petrol, and once more at a building where he checked in. Still, returning to the idling Plymouth was a comfort.

They'd waited on a convoy only once. The others yielded, she assumed, because their vehicle was a staff car. The men on the troop carriers looked exhausted, their heads hanging, few curious enough to peer into the back seat.

She roused from an unfinished dream, had dozed while considering the day, and looked out the window, surprised to see they were in a town. A row of trees mounted, the moon rising above them, highlighting cows in a pasture. A village, then, crumbling buildings on either side, their windows smashed. An instant rage mounted at the intrusion of the war, and she continued the prayer that had drifted within her emerging dream.

"*Je me couche et je m'endorsen paix, Car toi seul, ô Éternel! Tu me donnes la sécurité dans ma demeure.*" The words poured sweet relief on her parched soul, and she repeated them as David might have read them. "I will both lay me down in peace, and sleep: for thou, Lord, only makest me dwell in safety."

"Beg your pardon, Miss?"

"I was thinking aloud, only. I didn't mean to disturb you."

"Not a bother. Is there anything you need? Aren't you hungry?"

Discomfort rose with his solicitude. The boy's kindness seemed unmerited. "I hadn't considered it. I will eat when you wish to, Corporal."

The driver checked his mirror, a flash of something dour on his face. "We have another check-in. There'll likely be chow left. Be another hour from there to Cologne." He hesitated. "I'm told the place you're going isn't safe. I'll be happy to stay until your contact shows."

She smiled. No operative would reveal himself with a staff car there. "Were those your instructions, Corporal?"

The eyes appeared in the mirror again. "Not exactly, but—"

"I will be fine. Thank you for your kindness."

Chapter LV

Light curled in yellow brilliance, licking the stone of the tunnel walls. David scrolled two corned beef cans into a cone to amplify the candlelight and direct it onto the transponder.

Langley stooped to look inside the back panel, pulled a jackknife from his pocket, and removed screws holding it in place. "A myst'ry, innut? Bat'ry's chargeable, but it's o' no benefit ter us. Sweet contrivance though, suh."

David scratched his neck. "Will it work?"

Langley shrugged. "Can' say, suh. It's sure the bat'ry won' 'old up long."

"I can give them our approximate location with landmarks. They should be able to estimate the time they'll be overhead. How long do you think the battery will last once the transmitter is turned on?"

"I've no idea 'ow much charge we mi' 'ave nor 'ow much juice is used, suh."

David sat on his haunches and tried to stretch his neck. "We'll give them our distance from the target. If they miss the drop point, we could be caught in the bombing. We need that battery to last until we can tell them when they're overhead."

"We, suh? Are yer askin' me ter volunteuh?"

"Are you offering, Corporal?"

A toothy grin formed within the beam. "I am, suh. Surely."

"I appreciate your willingness to help, Langley. Always."

"But you've made plans ter work wi' the sergean'?"

"Yes, but we could use your help with the transponder. I'll see if we can gather extra rations a day or two before. It won't be an easy walk. That thing is heavy."

"Ya' can do that, suh? The rations, I mean."

"It's possible."

* * *

The warm comfort of the car had blown away. Nicole stood dizzied, peering into the dusk of bombed-out buildings and broken glass. She saw no one, though Nazi troops ran through the alleys of her fears, hidden from light, scurrying across dust and crumbling brick.

She wanted to pray, but only one came. "I will both lay me down in peace, and sleep; for thou, Lord, only makest me dwell in safety." Phantoms came to oppose it, the scratch of rats' feet, sharp and pressing against her breast. She repeated the words, this time with breath. "I will both lay me down in peace, and sleep; for thou, Lord, only makest me dwell in safety."

"Shush, you ninny!" The words came in German, an inflection she'd heard only on forays away from the university. And there had been no signal.

"It's schpring and se plane leafs visser." The voice was as feral as the English.

"Are you also a reader of Goethe?"

"The devil's spawn and the Führer's half-brother, that one! I'd sooner read the label from a bottle of poison." The whisper was carried on its own wind, the German guttural and harsh.

"Who are you?" She shuddered. "And where are you?"

A muted cackle rose along a dark wall. She detected a line in the obscurity, a cove created by an extended interior wall. She stepped lightly toward it, trying not to stumble.

"You was speaking English, you ninny! You are insane, yes?" A pause. "Good! That will make you easy to work with."

She swallowed, wished to see whom she was speaking with. "English? I didn't realize."

"None of them Wehrmacht snots is around. I would smell 'em. Still, don't do it regular. Them boys will have you strung up before you can heil that tin god o' theirs."

Nicole stopped. "I'll be more careful. Thank you."

"Come. We'll get you into clothes that won't land you in a Gestapo snake pit. They shoot people for looking like traitors, and you're dressed too finely to be much else."

Something moved within the shadows, and a broad-shouldered woman hobbled into a sliver of light, tattered sweaters unraveling beneath her overcoat. "We'll leave in a few hours. Four o'clock and no crying! We'll be at the Rhine by daylight."

A door opened, light splashed across a wide face, and the squat figure stepped into oblivion. She followed, caught the stench of urine and manure. "This is your home?"

"It was before bein' liberated." The cackle again. "Now it is Gustav's, but he shares."

She stopped. "Gustav?"

"My charmer. They would feed him to the Führer, but that one eats only turnips and children." A stubby finger rose into the gray. "Herr Mustache shall eat the meat of his own arms soon." The woman shuffled across the room. Light hissed from a cranny, and the woman appeared bent, her cheeks flaccid and weathered. Two walls extended on either side of a table, defining what had once been a breakfast nook.

Nicole watched from the edge of a tarp that veiled them from the windows.

The woman turned toward the light. "I will provide you with clothes, yes? You would prefer something that will not get you hanged?"

She stifled a laugh. "I would, thank you."

A thick finger rose. "Then you may not be insane, Elisabeth. So much the worse."

Her stomach squeezed. The woman hadn't offered a code name, yet she knew hers.

Bowed legs shuffled into light where stubby arms held dresses and sweaters, a man's long underwear, and a ragged coat. "These will do, yes?"

She stared. "Which ones should I wear?"

The woman offered a toothless grin. "All of them. Gustav shall adorn the one on top so the Wehrmacht will not want you, but not before you sleep. You shall put them on, we shall sleep, and we leave, yes?" She pointed. "Those you wear I shall sell to Wehrmacht boys. For their girlfriends." The grin again. "We make them happy, and they shall let us pass."

Nicole removed her coat. "I don't know your name. What am I to call you? And what do I say if they ask why we are traveling east?"

The finger rose. "First we are traveling north! Also, I am Elfriede, and I have no silly names. I cross the river to sell what I collect in the west. I give some so that we might pass. But not you. If you do as you are told, I shall give them none of you. Now dress, and we shall sleep."

She pulled another sweater over her thickened sleeves. "And where do I sleep?"

Elfriede's finger poked through the hissing light. "There or there or there. Wherever you wish. Only not with Gustav. He will love only me." The woman tottered into darkness.

And where was Gustav? Had the old woman imagined him? She ran her hands over the floor for something to use as a pillow, removed a thick sweater, rolled it beneath her head, then tucked it tightly, whispering her prayer.

* * *

David stood within the gloom of the appellplatz, his boots perched above the drain, his breath hollow and quick.. He had no reason to be in the open. Twenty minutes of loitering had produced nothing but a chill, the dampness piercing even his jacket. "See any goons?"

Bear glanced to his left. "One's checkin' the locks on the lazarette. Don't seem to be payin' us no mind."

"You can't trust them. If we tried to hide, they'd be on us like fleas."

Bear pivoted slowly to stare at the walk-through gate. "One's coming, walking like his boots is untied, and he's trying not to step on the laces. Got to be Krüger."

He chuckled, pictured the unteroffizier's awkward gate, and looked away. Gravel crunched louder.

"Gentlemen, you appear to be waiting for something. Or perhaps someone?"

David turned and nodded. "We're hoping to catch a bus before the Russkies get here."

"I see." Krüger raised his chin. "And so might anyone else who looks this way."

"Seems to us our message system is obsolete. We have you, now. There's no need to write anything down that could then be read by someone who doesn't need to see it."

Krüger twisted his neck. "Which is precisely why you weren't informed about me earlier. You are putting me in a compromising position, Lieutenant."

"Then give us a way to communicate. We can't wait a month for an answer."

"And what is your question?"

He bent his arm toward the east and let it drop. "How far is Waldheim from the airbase over there? And how far are we?"

The chin lifted. "You are considering sabotage?"

"Just updating our Christmas list—making sure the addresses are all current."

A burst of air passed Krüger's lips. "The airfield is roughly three kilometers east of us. It is perhaps four kilometers north and east of Waldheim."

The same as Henri's map. "Thank you. So, how do we contact you?"

A smile appeared. "You have strings, snips of cloth from overworn clothing, perhaps? Something that could easily be explained by snagging a sock or shirt against rough wood?"

He nodded. "We have a fair supply of worn-out clothes."

"Place a scrap near the base of your door when you leave for appell. I will see it while checking billets and will find you as soon as I am able."

He'd expected a delay and felt relieved. "That'll work."

* * *

"Wake up, ninny girl! I have water and a gift for you."

Nicole jolted at the nudge and stared into darkness. She smelled wet stone and urine, stood, inferred Elfriede's round shoulders from the murk, and drank the water in eager gulps. "I was so thirs—" A hand brushed her temple and cheeks, something warm and... Her stomach seized, and cool water pressed against her throat. She dropped to her knees. "What did you do?"

"Ach, ninny! It is from Gustav." Elfriede cackled. "He made it from the fresh grass of the *Vaterland*. And perhaps some oats I have bargained for, yes? It will keep the Fürher's boys away." The old woman straightened. "And your German! Anyone would believe you are German except, perhaps, a German. So instead, you are insane, yes? Now stand! We will apply Gustav's gift to your dress. The Russkies have attacked you and driven you mad, and you have rolled in Gustav's droppings once again. I try always to stop you, but sometimes I fail."

"Please, no. It's made me quite ill."

"So easily you become ill. What have you not seen of this war that this should make you ill? You have not seen dead children? Stand still! You will ride behind me when we cross the river. I am taking you to your parents."

Nicole turned her face to escape the stench. "Do you think we'll go as far as Kassel?"

Hands moved within the gloom. "Farther. Kassel will bring only more trouble."

It seemed impossible. Perhaps Elfriede really was crazy. "Gustav is your horse, is he not? How can he take us so far?"

The unladen left hand emerged from the murk, a broad finger almost touching her nose. "He is not pretentious, my Gustav. He is a mule, and a very pretty one. Additionally, I have ways no one has dreamed of. Not your Pommies and not your Amies. You must do only this. You must fear Russkies! You see them in the shadows. You dream of them at night, and you will answer the Führer's boys with '*Mutti!*' or '*Pa!*' Nothing else, yes?"

Chapter LVI

The cart rattled across bricks, Nicole's arms bouncing against her ribs in cadence with Gustav's gait. The darkness invited ruminations, though Nicole fought to keep them at bay. She was forced to turn her head every few seconds to capture a breath free of the stench, but if it kept the Wehrmacht away, she would endure it. Elfriede swore she knew the kinder guards at the bridge and promised they would be there by daybreak. The air seemed fraught with fiends and brutes, and not a single streetlamp shone to quiet her fears.

Gustav's hooves slipped as they turned between buildings. Elfriede released a squall, and Nicole drew hands over her head, her heart jolting before she recognized the sound as a melody. The howl hadn't been meant for an observer or even for Gustav, who seemed not at all repentant. He continued to clop evenly, seemed accustomed to the song, a discreditable version of "A Bird in a Gilded Cage."

* * *

"Mutti!" Nicole released her pent-up terror in the single word she was allowed.

Elfriede slapped the guard's shoulder. "Do not touch her, foolish boy! She will bite you, and there's no telling what she has had in her mouth!"

The frail soldat removed his hand, then reached for Nicole's coat, apparently hoping to get a look at what was beneath it.

She lunged. *"Mutti!"*

The boy withdrew in disgust. "She's filthy!"

"She will claw your eyes out! The Russkies had a go at her in the east, and she has not stopped running. I am taking her home. Now stay away!"

The boy looked frightened. "All right! Just go, and don't bring her back! We'll not tolerate imbeciles."

The old woman changed her tack. "Not even one with wares? You want nothing for your girlfriends? I have jewelry."

"Just go!"

"Yes, all right." The old woman turned in her seat. "I will take Gerda to her family, and perhaps they will buy my jewels. Next time, I will show you what I have, yes?"

The boy raised his hand in the waning gray. "Why would they want such a miserable creature? Forget who it was that let you pass."

Elfriede cackled. "Already I forget your name, Werner. And what is it you look like? I cannot recall. A bear of a man, yes? It is quite reasonable that Gerda took you for a Russkie."

"Shush, you old cow, before I change my mind and have your cart searched!"

Gustav began an even plod across the bridge, his mood unaltered. Nicole released her fists, determining the mule to be the only sane creature in Cologne.

"You are tiring, Gustav?" Elfriede cooed as if no one heard, though the bridge was filled with foot traffic. "We shall soon stop, my sweet, and you will eat your fill. In a few days, we shall reach—" She turned and looked back. "You will prefer riding, won't you, my sweet?"

* * *

David stared through Schneider's window, the morning lost in drizzle, damp piercing his bones. The blizzards that blew across Europe were diminished to a cold rain in the Zschopau Valley and washed vainly at the citrus stench of death. Where was she? Was she even alive?

"You have heard about Dresden, I am sure."

He turned from the window to look at the hauptmann. "Yes. I'm truly sorry, Heinrich."

Schneider's jaw flickered in the contracting light. "That is all you have to say? But you believe in civility, do you not? The British and the Americans do not murder civilians, do they? For you, there is no sport in war. Is that not what you said?"

"Whatever pushed Allied Command to do it, it wasn't sport."

Heinrich faced him. "For once, I wish to believe you. I need to know that those I am considering surrendering to value the lives of my subordinates. Now, I fear for them."

He had no stomach for a debate. "You know. You're just angry, and I don't blame you."

"Then you agree it was wrong? Bombing an entire city, taking so many lives?" The hauptmann's words clouded the deeper chill of his office.

"No." He struggled. "I don't know. I'm only grateful I didn't have to make the call, no matter how many troops it saved."

Heinrich slumped, his tremble visible against the gray. "And how many of your troops were near Dresden, David? How many were threatened there?"

He waited, wished the conversation over. The BBC's report of the devastation had shaken him, and he didn't want to defend it. "It isn't that simple. Dresden was the least defended city. It could be hit with fewer losses of crews and aircraft. And your commanders had to be stopped. They must understand the consequences of continuing. It's heartrending, but no worse than all the other lives that have been lost—the Jews, the Belgians, the Poles, the French, the British. It must stop, Heinrich, and to stop it, your commanders must release their dreams of—what is it your Führer demands? Power? Worship?"

Schneider was silent, his tunic contracting. "Worship. Perhaps that's it after all."

A current ran up David's spine. Heinrich had conceded more than he'd dreamed.

The perfect chin lifted. "I no longer remember the reason for it, but the war appeared essential once. Now, I see only that my countrymen are dying." He shrugged. "And others, of course. But I have no notion of what was behind the passions I once held."

David released a breath. "Do you feel a century older than before the war? I do."

The German returned a lean smile but said nothing.

"I suspect youth generates its own passions. Like Scotch." He waited. "You remember that conversation, Heinrich?"

"Yes, of course." The hauptmann's shoulders slumped.

"The fervor of youth isn't apt to change when confronted with the truth. It's a fire that feeds on enchantment and rage. The idea that our enemies might be right was anathema to us. We ached to set things right, and reason seemed treacherous."

"You're saying I was wrong?"

He laughed. "Of course, you were. So was I. I treated people badly, especially those closest to me." He met the German's gaze. "I believed foolish things, and I was angry. I had passion and thought it made up for all I lacked—which was understanding, as it turns out."

"So, the defense of my country is something I shall outgrow as I mature?" The hauptmann stood stone-faced. "As you have?"

"Being young made us susceptible to bad ideas. I don't hate you for believing them, but the ones you held, the ones those around you touted as truth, were vile, and you worshiped them as I worshiped mine. The lies I believed haven't set the world on fire, though some still might."

Schneider's form melted from the stone around him. "You came here to discuss something. I doubt you want to wait for me to mature beyond my folly. What is it?"

He took a breath. "I know you're aware of it, but it's my duty to remind you that the men are hungry. A long march would kill them. They need provisions."

The fresh-shaved cheek shimmered in the gray. "I seek provisions daily, Lieutenant. We are getting little from the west and nothing from the east. How would you have me gather provisions in a country being raped by invaders?"

"That's been a problem in the rest of Europe for years." He waited, let the fire die. "For what it's worth, I know you've sacrificed to feed us. Please don't give up."

* * *

Nicole rolled beneath a blanket, grass poking beneath her collar. Elfriede had allowed her to wash the manure from her face, but the smell remained in her clothes. She wanted to pull the sweater over her head, but the stench made it unbearable, and she shuddered at the thought of having to reapply it. How far had they traveled beyond the bridge? It couldn't have been far. And how many weeks would it take to reach Kassel?

The evening had been spent along a tributary where Gustav grazed while they ate lintel soup. She'd scooped snow from the pale grass beneath the slush until Elfriede was convinced her sweet mule was full. Now, they bedded on spots he'd grazed clean. At nightfall, the old woman took out a bag of oats, poured some, and allowed Gustav to munch until he grew drowsy.

Light pierced the sweetness, and Nicole rolled her head toward the stream where the old woman stirred a kettle above a small fire. Elfriede hadn't heated the soup the night before for fear of alerting Allied pilots, but morning would extinguish its light as surely as snow would contain the flames. She smelled coffee and remembered the comfort of the barracks, pushed the blanket away, stepped to the tumbling water, and splashed her face and hands until the chill reached her bones. Elfriede turned at her approach, a box of K-rations open beside her.

The old woman pointed to the coffee. "Drink a little, ninny girl. You may have half the can of cheese and bacon, but leave the sugar and cigarettes. We must have them to trade."

She smiled, hoping to put her benefactor at ease. "It's yours. I won't take what is yours."

"Ninny girl, you have not yet been hungry. When you are, you will eat even Gustav."

She straightened. "I wouldn't! Would you eat Gustav?"

Elfriede shook her head. "I'd sooner eat what is left of Herr Hitler's left arm!"

She nodded. "And so would I."

The old woman glared, suspicion on her brow. Seconds passed. "All right, you may have milk in your coffee." Elfriede pulled a slotted can from beneath her skirts and pointed it toward an empty cup. "Pour some. I shall watch."

She poured a little and handed it back.

"Take more, but not too much."

"If you wish." She poured the thickened milk and looked up at her friend.

"All right, then. You may have one sugar. No more." The old woman nodded her on. "I have lintels and cabbage. In the mornings, if you rise early, we shall also eat from this K-ration. I have more, but they will be needed for our train ride. Today we will eat from this one only."

Train ride. She sipped the American coffee, tasted the warmth of Marcel's visits, and remembered the comfort of the field hospital. "Where will we meet the train?"

"In Düsseldorf. I sell to Wehrmacht boys there. They control the trains."

"Did Colonel Watts give you the K-rations?"

Elfriede cackled. "I tell him what I see, and he arranges for me to have them. We have our agreements, you see? You are to be protected, yes? Pretty girls are always protected."

She stared into the darting eyes. "Not always, Elfriede."

The old woman shrugged. "Yes, yes. Sometimes to be young and pretty is a dangerous thing. But there is usually a weak man willing to die to keep you safe."

"Some aren't weak." She pointed to the K-rations. "Is the Wehrmacht not suspicious?"

"You are thinking of your airman!" Two teeth pearled along Elfriede's gums. "The Wehrmacht believes I trade for them. I tell them Americans want women's underthings." She cackled. "Both sides believe the other abnormal. Why should I not use such silliness?"

Chapter LVII

David scanned the map and noted an open pasture to the north of the airfield. He reached for a scrap of paper he'd salvaged from a pack of Lucky Strikes, had written all the vital information on one side and now condensed the essential points for the telegrapher on the other.

HAVE EUREKA STOP
109s BASED 4 KM NE WALDHEIM 3 KM E PRISON STOP
WILL GUIDE AIRSTRIKE FROM NORTH SIDE STOP
ADVISE DATE AND TIME STOP
OTHELLO

Vogt had contact with the Brits, so they would have a means to identify him. He reread the telegram, hoped his bona fides were adequate. A nudge from the Tommies might also persuade the Army to include Heinrich among the good guys when the prison was liberated. The hauptmann had turned, and he was the only one who couldn't see it.

Still, his own identification could take days, and the 109s were flying too often to not be engaging troops. They had to be grounded. Permanently. He put the message in his pocket, took a burlap string from his fraying palliasse, left it beneath the door, and eased down the steps, glancing toward Heinrich's office. Every man alive had believed a lie, at some point, that compelled him to act contrary to what he knew was right, and if that lie were repeated often enough, it had the power to make him deaf to the truth in his heart. But it wasn't irredeemable. That truth was now eating a hole in Heinrich's convictions.

He trundled across the appellplatz and stood at the edge of the assembly, a position that offered him a good view of the Germans. He had to be sure Aragon wasn't among them, needed the man to find the string and get the message out.

He stared into the growing light, words of supplication forming within his heart. Assurance came, an echo of the certainty within. If peace were ever to be his, he had to release his demands and surrender what he wanted most. He closed his eyes on darkness and prayed for the ability to release the one he cherished above all else.

* * *

Nicole walked beside the cart, jogged when the grade reversed, and shuffled when it worsened. Gustav could have pulled the load with her added weight, but she wanted to assure Elfriede of her devotion to all things precious, especially her charmer.

Something rumbled, and the old woman turned. "Jump in!"

She scrambled onto the cart, felt a sharp tug at her waist, and looked back. The hem of her top dress had caught the hub, and rose print cloth unwound across Elfriede's wares. She pulled, and a button snapped, allowing her to slip free.

The old woman grunted in the chill. "Should they stop us, ninny girl, call for your *mutti*."

"Yes, of course." A lorry wobbled and revealed a line of vehicles. "It's a convoy!"

"They are late for Adolf's funeral, yes?" Elfriede drew her hand to her breast. "It is coming! You will see."

On either side, leafless trees stirred on a chilled breeze where snow melted into a metallic sky. "They are close!" Neither Elfriede nor Gustav made any effort to surrender the center of the road. "Move over!" Nicole hollered just as the lorry behind them bellowed. The column bore down with squealing brakes, and she pulled what remained of the rose print pleats over her head.

The old woman urged Gustav to the side and maneuvered the cart between two trees. Gears clashed, and a lorry rolled past. More followed, pulling artillery, then dozens laden with troops. She leaned her back against Elfriede's rump and lowered the red-rose pattern below her eyes. The lorries picked up speed, boys visible through sideboards, their faces lifeless as they met her glare. Children who should have been excited to be away from home sat with ashen skin, already half dead, headed to the Eastern Front.

Lorries rumbled for at least two kilometers, she supposed, before the Kübelwagens passed, officers in each. The cars in the rear were marked differently and bore a passenger in front. The last one slowed to a stop. A soldier stepped down, his face bulging and lined, a huge medallion swinging from his neck.

His gait mirrored the defeat bought with years of perturbation. "What are you doing?"

"My job, *Herr Orpo*! I keep your weary boys supplied with niceties, and sometimes things to fill their bellies." Elfriede's annoyance glistened on her gums.

The orpo's lips pulled back, his teeth dark and oddly spaced. "Gut-slick, are you? And what have you taken from the brave men of the Wehrmacht today?"

"Not so much as I have given, Your Grandeur. I have goods, so might I show you a trinket for your poor, saintly wife? Or your girlfriend, perhaps? Or have you given up altogether on having a woman?"

Nicole's stomach tightened as his gaze turned toward her.

"What have we here?" He moved close, then stepped back, lust losing the battle with revulsion.

Nicole grabbed pleated cloth and curled into a ball. *"Mutti! Das Russkie, Mutti!"*

Elfriede stepped off the cart. "I am returning her to her mother. Do not get close, or she will bite you! The Russkies have abused her. She was running west. I have nursed her back to health and am taking her home, you see?"

The man's puffed lip lifted. "Poor, dear girl. A good German, too. One can see she comes from Aryan stock. Look at those eyes!" He shook his head. "*Gnädige Frau*, drive your mule from the road when we approach. We wouldn't want the *fraulein* to suffer further."

* * *

The moon splashed silver across the appellplatz and crested in a brilliant sheen along the parapet. David stared through the window, turned, and looked at the floor. The string from his palliasse still lay beneath the door. "It would have been a good plan if Krüger had done his part."

Bear yawned. "What's that?"

He turned to his friend. "He was supposed to contact me."

Bear scraped the back of his neck. "He's been sick the last few days."

"How do you know?"

Bear rolled over to sit on the edge of his palliasse. "Hadn't seen him, so I got Grip to ask. That little goon, Loverboy, said he come down with something."

"I hired you to tell me what I need to know before I had to ask, Bear."

The sergeant offered a slack salute. "Consider it done, Lieutenant."

"I'm going to make another trip to see Élodie. Think you can find out if—"

"Schneider's in his office. Least, he was an hour ago. And I'll check before you leave."

"That's more like it." He drew the stale air. "Full moon and only a few clouds."

"It'll make you easier to spot." Bear rubbed his hands. "And I don't have a good feeling about Krüger. Think he might o' reported your plan?"

He dipped his head. "Or he might be running from the Ivans."

* * *

Brilliance reigned, darkness trembling amid rags of snow that cowered beneath the shadows of pines. David had emerged from the tunnel full of expectation, thrilled at the cleanness of the air away from the latrine and crowded men.

He drank a scent like cherry blossoms and felt the hope of spring, then forced himself to consider what lay ahead. Taking out the 109s would save lives, but if Krüger were a double agent, the mission could be over, and he and Bear with it. He reached the place where the turret came into view, raised Bear's coat as if hoping to fly, and sprinted toward the trees. He grabbed a limb on the first, dived beneath it, and looked back. Something moved along the parapet under the darkness of a passing cloud, but he couldn't decipher if it were man or bird. It seemed doubtful a goon could distinguish him, either.

The BBC had reported that the Krauts failed to dynamite the Ludendorff Bridge. General Hodges had been ready, Langley said, had rushed in, captured it, and crossed the Rhine. He prayed the general reached them before the Ivans.

He and Bear had stretched the can of cheese until the last few tidbits had to have mold scraped from them before being eaten. They'd had nothing but hay bale soup since. Still, he pushed, willing

Élodie's house to come before he reached the end of his strength. It was almost an hour before he stood beneath the tree, moonlight playing on slick bark, branches bristling with shoots so dense they captured the light around them. The carriage house glistened as he sorted the keys in his pocket. He pushed into the shadows, darted to the rear, climbed the steps, and slipped into the entryway, the familiar scent of cleanser and potatoes biting his nose.

From the kitchen he glanced north, a blue shaft divvying the stairs. He gripped a chair and moved through the dining room to the second step, then the fourth. A door in the upper hallway stood half open, light slicing past. "Élodie, it's David. Don't be alarmed."

"I will be down in a moment." The English was clear.

He slipped from the stairs and moved into the kitchen savoring the warmth, eyed the converted carriage house through the window, and pictured the dusty sheen of the Mercedes.

"I'm sorry to keep you waiting."

He detected the lisp, now, faint but familiar. "If I were able to let you know when I'm coming— It's wrong, breaking into your house." He spied the pinched corners of her mouth. "I've written something for the telegrapher. For London. Will you see that he gets it?"

"I will take it in the morning." Her voice flowed soft and warm.

"I'm also concerned about Krüger. What's happened to him?"

Her pallid skin seemed to lose tension. "Heinrich tells me he is ill. A condition of the lungs, I believe. But Klaus, the telegrapher, spotted him at the railway station the morning before last. He said Hermann was dressed in civilian clothes."

The tingle in his gut grew worse. "The Soviets are advancing. You think he deserted?"

She shrugged. "Perhaps. The train he boarded was bound for Kassel. It is the same train that once went through Cologne, then turned back to Belgium. It is possible he was trying to meet with the Americans. Klaus thinks he is hoping to rescue those of us in the Resistance."

He shook his head. "An unteroffizier? He can't get through his own lines, much less ours." He retrieved the message. "If he shows up, don't say anything about this. Not a word. And don't let him carry messages. Tell Klaus, too. Krüger knows I had an interest in the base, but it's best if he thinks I abandoned my plans."

"So, you think he is loyal to the Nazis?"

"I think we should be cautious. He has no need to know."

She tilted her head. "I've put something back for you. You're quite thin."

He released the air in his lungs, had hoped she might have food.

She moved to the entryway and reached into her pantry. "I've held these out of our gifts from Oberst Schuster. Heinrich knows nothing of them."

He lifted it from her arms, felt the heft of it. "What has the man provided now?"

"C-rations taken from prisoners. I will prepare also a slice of bread with a little butter. You will eat it on the way." She faced him in the pale light. "I have news concerning the airfield. The planes are inside, so we have not determined the number. Security is weak, perhaps because the front is still some distance away, but two guards are at the gate, and we assume an observer is in the tower." She paused. "Won't you at least have a coffee with me?"

He smiled. "Coffee sounds nice. And may I have the bread and butter with it?"

* * *

Nicole spent the morning surveying what had once been Düsseldorf, her exhaustion compounded by what she saw. Rubble was scraped to the side, following uncertain recollections of streets. Tarps were attached to the remaining walls, though an occasional block emerged with buildings still standing, boarded but in use. Gustav plodded, seemed to know his way without prompting, advancing them to the train yards, no blacker than the rest of the city.

The mule drew up before a dock, and a feldwebel stepped forward, one hand on his hip, the other raised in an officious pose. He stared at the cart, looking beneath Elfriede's feet. "You want to go east?" His tone was sharp. "I will need six of those Ami rations to put you on a car."

"Two, and a packet of cigarettes." Elfriede waved her hands, her voice rising above squealing hogs. "And I want a boxcar so we shan't freeze or smell pigs all night."

The gangly man grinned, pushing for an advantage. "I saw several boxes beneath your seat, you old swindler."

Elfriede's cheeks reddened. She stepped off the cart and bustled toward him. "I am a swindler? You can eat three days on what I'm offering with nothing added. American boys do it, and they are fat. But you would let two women starve and leave Gustav and me with no way home so you might have more than enough. You are the swindler!"

Nicole listened, tried to grasp why Elfriede did it. The woman seemed to have no fear of Nazi bullets or charges created from freshly minted regulations. She saw men capable of work sitting before the platform, their coats pulled tight. Some had families, surely, that they could no longer look at without shame. The Nazis had promised they would plunder the rich to provide for all, had fulfilled more than was promised and plundered everyone, save those few capable of furthering the Führer's ambitions. Something settled in her heart. Elfriede had little, but she had more than these men withering in their strength. And she was using what she had to wage war.

"All right, you old sow. Four Ami food boxes. You may board that car when it is pulled before the dock." The feldwebel pointed down the track. "You will also clean the floor after your mule. And next time, I shall not do it for less than five boxes."

"Next time, Horst? Next time, should fortune serve you well, you shall be eating from a large pot behind barbed wire begging some Ami soldat for a scrap of rind!"

The feldwebel jerked. "Such talk is forbidden! I'll have you put before a firing squad!"

"If you do, you shall never again know a week with a full stomach!"

Nicole spotted a shipping crate with buckets stacked inside and eased behind it. The containers were clean and had metal tighteners. She'd dreamed of the showers she'd had in Tongres, wished for more than a face washing. She slipped her hand inside—

"You, there!" Horst's voice rattled. "I knew you were up to no good! Your partner is stealing tankers' buckets as you rant. That is a theft from the Reich, and it will get you hanged!"

"Calm yourself, Horst. She's not in her proper mind. She's been abused."

"So you said. By Russkies, unless the story has changed."

Nicole lifted the lid high and tried to crawl into the crate head-first.

Elfriede ran toward her. "Wait, Gerda! We'll stop our dispute! Don't hide, my sweet!"

Horst followed, his grunts echoing between the crates. "She's hiding?"

"Certainly! She's frightened by shouting men, especially those who act like Russkies."

He raised his hands. "I did not know!"

The old woman pulled at Nicole's sleeve, moved to embrace her, but winced at the sight of her face, and patted her back instead. "You are safe. You are safe."

"Mutti!" She put the full volume of her lungs into her cry.

"I'm taking you to your *Mutti*, Gerda." The old woman cooed as if talking to her mule.

Horst raised his hands. "Where is her *mutti*?"

Elfriede hesitated, then offered a compelling smile. "In Chemnitz."

Horst looked around him. "I will place you on another car. There is a siding bound for Chemnitz. It will save you time and your mule many steps."

Nicole drew a breath. Chemnitz was close to Waldheim. She'd seen it on a map.

Elfriede touched her chest. "That would be most helpful, Horst. Thank you." The old woman looked at the buckets. "I have jewels. Your wife would love them, yes? Perhaps we could use one of the buckets for washing?" She pointed her chin over her shoulder.

Nicole turned, caught the feldwebel's stare, and pasted panic on her face.

He looked away. "The tankers' buckets are for shaving, but yes, they should work well. I will, perhaps, look at your jewelry."

354

Chapter LVIII

David listened from the narrow window as Bear's breath rippled like water over smooth stones. The man exuded peace, his gentle knowing as imperturbable as the tide. Even hunger didn't disrupt his calm.

Why couldn't he live that way? He'd known peace in the well, experienced it in prayer, but it escaped his grasp when he needed it most, and he wanted desperately to hold to it as his friend did. He stepped to his palliasse, his movements practiced and quiet. He'd heard nothing since leaving the message with Élodie, and the BBC reported that the Reds had stopped the Nazi offensive in Hungary and were now in Danzig. The end seemed near, but if he failed to lead the RAF to the airfield, more lives would be lost, and the prison might be liberated by the Ivans. That would likely mean death for Schneider and Élodie.

Bear rolled over and groaned. "What's eatin' you, Dremmer?"

"I heard the planes again this morning. They took off around oh five hundred. It's likely they're strafing our boys, Bear." He turned and met his friend's dark stare. "A lot of lives depend on us taking them out. But I promised Heinrich that I would lead our troops in if it comes to that. We don't know what might happen if the Tommies accept my offer to guide that bomb strike. To either of us. If we don't make it back, who will contact our troops? Schneider might have to surrender to the Ivans, and those men out there depend on us for their lives, too."

Bear scratched his grizzled cheek. "Dremmer, we can't know how any of this will work out. You're taking on more than you can carry. I know you feel like you need a plan, and that's a good thing, but the fact is, your prayers are more important now than havin' another back up plan. Or two.

"You're gonna have to learn to trust."

Bear looked at the floor, seemed unwilling to come out with what he was thinking. "So, what would you be doing if you was on the ranch right now?"

It had become a game, their talking about what might be happening at home, the hills covered in snow, or the first shoots of Rescuegrass peeking through the earth. "I'd be enjoying my second cup of coffee with cream and sugar, or maybe saddling Dancer so I could check heifers. They should be calving by now."

Bear's whiskers snapped beneath his fingers. "Make you nervous, delivering calves?"

"Always. I was scared before I got the heifer in a loop, slid a pigging string around those little shanks and saw the head come out. It was best when I could get the mama to the pens, but sometimes I couldn't. That made it dicey."

"So, why'd you do it?"

He shrugged. "Most would have died if I hadn't, and that was my livelihood. Besides, it made me feel like I'd done something decent, watching that calf nurse his mama."

"That's what you're doin' now, ya know. And it'll be worth it when it all works out."

"*If* it works out. And the lives we're dealing with…"

Bear moved his elbows to his knees. "They're sacred, and you wanna save 'em. But you can't take on everything that happens."

He nodded.

Bear snugged his coat. "Think you could teach me to ride a horse? Look at a cow and know if she's about to calve? Know when the grass was grazed enough that I need to push cattle off one pasture and onto another?"

He stepped close, had asked Bear almost two years ago to consider partnering with him—had dreamed of having him there. They could grow the ranch together. "You think you'd want to do that? You know my father sold the place."

"Think I'd like it. And you said Morgan was apt to lose it." Bear rubbed his hands. "And you talked about gettin' a tractor to break out more land. Be easier to pay for equipment if you had two men to keep it going, and we're both handy with machinery."

He couldn't hide his pleasure. "It might be lean for a few years."

Bear nodded. "It might be."

* * *

Gray mist drenched the morning, a promise hidden in the citrus breeze. Nicole moved away from the boxcar to stand behind the cart as Elfriede adjusted Gustav's harness and kissed his nose. The mule answered with a nuzzle to her shoulder.

The old woman turned. "Should you find a man so easily pleased that he shall go to work each day, you shall marry him, yes?"

She smiled. "I'll try to remember to look for one like Gustav, Elfriede."

"Whether you find one so honorable as my Gustav, I do not know, but your American has your heart, yes?"

She looked away. "He does, though our being together is impossible."

The old woman grew quiet. "Nothing is impossible, ninny girl."

Humiliation flushed her face. "David is married, Elfriede. It wasn't really a—" She swallowed the words, refusing to offer the excuse she'd given herself.

The old woman flung her hand in dismissal. "You are sure he is married? I think not."

She stirred. "Were you told something?"

Elfriede pulled her fist to her breast. "Some things I know." She released her hand. "Stay on the cart until we are away from these boys strutting around with guns bigger than their arms." She drew a finger to her gums. "It is best if they do not know you are young and beautiful. They have learned more than children should know, but they have also learned less."

She glanced across the yard. "I've seen only a few."

Elfriede stared ahead. "I have counted nine. We shall likely see more, or perhaps Uncle Joe has come for them in the night to grind for sausage. If we meet them, they must not see your face, even beneath the manure. Howl. Spit. Do what you must. These boys have no conscience. That was why I chose Horst's dock. He is a pig, but he has a daughter."

Her heart pounded beneath the remaining dresses. "How do you know all this? How many times have you been this far east?"

Elfriede nudged Gustav. "I have come to Chemnitz many times, though not since October. Boys littered the yard then, all dressed in uniforms rolled up so their boots could reach the ground. Where have they gone? To the east, I'm sure. So soon dead, these evil boys."

"Not all are evil, surely." Nicole watched as Gustav wandered through the jumbled tracks. Stacks of pallets toppled onto the road;

concrete and wood crowded narrow streets. The mule clopped while Elfriede's hands twisted the reins, strangling something only she could see. No more children appeared swaddled in woolen uniforms before Gustav turned onto a road covered by trees, their branches bristling with fresh growth. After an hour, the cart broke free of shadows, and a field appeared striped by patches of snow, green between. David could have named what grew here. She was tempted to muse about life with him, one free of deceit, but pushed it away. She wouldn't hope for what she couldn't have.

The old woman shifted on her seat. "Gustav will take us through Glösa, so there will be less destruction for us to see. The countryside, at least, is mostly the same. We will sleep tonight in Altmittweida, and tomorrow we will find your friend, yes?

PART III

April 1945

PART III

Chapter LVIX

The news burdened the appellplatz with gloom. There'd been little hint of Roosevelt's decline, but his body had failed. The Tommies seemed to grieve his passing, too. At least, Langley did. David had consoled him and now felt it himself, kneeling before the drain, as a heaviness in his chest. The president wouldn't see the peace he'd worked so hard to secure.

He pulled the string again. A jar emerged covered in muck, and he unscrewed the lid. "Nothing. And no word from Aragon."

Bear swung toward the officer's quarters. "Schneider's gone, so you can't find out nothin' from Élodie tonight. Maybe tomorrow night."

He released a heavy breath, hated every delay. The Ivans were closing in. "Would you turn on a couple of the showers, Bear? I'll float the jar back down the pipe."

The sergeant scratched his heavy beard. "Reminds me. The boys is wantin' to use the showers tomorrow. They're thinkin' they can stand it if they're quick about it."

"They can shower whenever they want, Bear. They know that."

"Well, I'm thinkin' I will, too. Be warm enough by noon, maybe. Just don't want to stand around wet lookin' for something to dry off on."

He laughed. "Are you asking me to hold your bra and panties?"

Bear scraped his neck. "No, but you might hold them rags we got from the lazarette."

He wiped his grin with his sleeve. "I have what's left of a bar of Lifebuoy from the last Red Cross parcel. I use it first, though."

"Good. You can warm it up."

* * *

The Zschopau spanned more than a hundred meters and moved in a ponderous roll. Pine scaled rock above green water. Gustav plodded in indifference to the beauty as the sun climbed above slick-limbed trees prickling with incandescent spears. Nicole strolled beside him, drinking in the sweetness of emerging buds and the honeyed rot of oranges.

"There, do you see?" Elfriede's stout finger shot through a break in the green toward a red-tiled roof rising above trees and rock. A green roof mounted beyond the red. "That's the prison. Your airman is perhaps standing in his window dreaming of you. If only he knew, he would fly to see you, yes?"

She fought for breath. "How can it be—so high?"

"And so near?" The old woman cackled. "It sits upon the highest rock. It is pretty, yes?"

"It is, though it's likely not so lovely beyond the parapet." She filled her lungs. "The countryside is prettier. Nothing here is tainted with National Socialism."

"But it is!" The old woman's voice rose. "The people are forbidden to eat the fruit growing along these roads. Now it rots beneath the branches as they starve."

She nodded. "That's what I smell?"

Elfriede spat. "And perhaps the latrines from the prison."

Nicole grew faint at the thought of starving prisoners, David among them, all held beneath Heinrich's thumb. She'd thought Herr Schneider a man of exacting requirements, occasionally excessive in his expectations, but never heartless. Perhaps the lure of power had taken him, sated his ambitions at the price of conscience. Had he adopted the proper Nazi attitudes? If so, her attempt to save Élodie might be met with brutality.

She dawdled, wishing to not lose sight of the castle. "How long before we reach Élodie's?"

"A few hours only, though we must still find her house, yes?"

* * *

The morning's apprehensions dissipated with the steam of her bath. Nicole watched the evening sun cradled between maple branches beyond the windows and took in the scent of Élodie's dining room. She pictured her home as a girl, her mother's busy hands, her father's laugh, his evening bowl of pipe tobacco turning the room into a sanctuary. Gone forever. Still, she was clean and fed, and Élodie seemed happy, perhaps relieved, for her to be here.

"Would you care for coffee?" The voice came from the kitchen. "It is only ersatz, but it is hot, and I have canned milk if you wish to cover the taste." The words came in English, the habit reappearing just as if they'd never left the university.

She turned to stare into the taut face. "You've been so kind, Élodie, but I must know what Heinrich will do when he finds us here."

"He must choose, Nickie. He knows, but..." She shrugged. "He learned before we left Munich that Professor Neumann was in Dachau. You remember him, yes?"

Nickie. Only Élodie called her that. "He taught at Ludwig-Maximilians, did he not?"

Élodie nodded. "Yes, he taught theology. He and Heinrich met in Munich and became friends. Dr. Neumann tried to persuade him to go to seminary."

It didn't fit. "But Heinrich isn't—"

"He was then and considered a masters of divinity." Élodie drew her arms tighter. "He abandoned his faith at university. His dark night of the soul. That is when he joined the party."

"I thought he joined because they supported his academics."

Élodie squinted. "He was lost and needed something to believe in. He still does. Eugenics became his religion, though he seems now to see the cruelty in it. Perhaps he also sees the horror of choosing who is worthy of life."

Nicole steadied her breath before exhuming what Élodie might prefer to leave buried. "You left the university without a word. Did he force you to go?"

Élodie glanced at the windows. "I could tell no one. Heinrich was called away. He came to me and found White Rose pamphlets. He was certain I would be caught, so he pleaded with me to leave with him. I chose to go but left the literature behind."

Nicole clasped her hands. "I found it in your apartment. Henri disposed of it, of course." She waited. "Does Heinrich know that you've been working with the Resistance?"

The delicate face lifted in a slant of light. "No, though I suppose now—"

"It will come out, yes. Perhaps Elfriede and I should leave."

Élodie turned back. "It is good that you are here. And your friend. We have days, weeks, at most, before the Soviets come. Heinrich is trusting David to contact the Americans, I think."

It shook her, hearing his name. "You've seen him recently?"

"He is my contact, and we sometimes visit."

Her heart swelled. "How? Why?"

Her friend shrugged. "He comes when he needs help."

She fought to still the pounding in her breast. "How can he? Is he well?"

"He is thin, though healthy, I believe. I give him food when I can, he and his friend. It was as a favor to David that Heinrich brought the sergeant here. Heinrich and David are always at odds, but beneath it all, they are friends, I think."

She nodded. "The sergeant Heinrich brought here. Is his name Billington?"

"The Bear, yes." Élodie stared. "You are pale. Has this talk upset you?"

"It's just that I hadn't thought of David escaping prison so easily."

"It wasn't easy. Not at first." Her friend looked up. "He is so in love with you, Nickie."

She felt a tingle course her spine. "It is impossible for us."

Élodie stepped into a trailing light. "Why is it impossible? The war is nearing an end. There is no reason you should not be together."

"Even if we survive, he will return home." She took a breath. "And he is married."

* * *

A cloud floated before the moon and shaded the road. David jogged beneath the shadows, vowing to not let the gloom slip inside him. Citrus air bore the tang of death, but the C-rations gave him a vigor he hadn't felt in weeks. He moved quickly, dampness growing beneath his shirt. There was so much to be done. He reviewed the points Langley had given him, stopped and caught his breath, his hands on his knees. He listened and moved on, rounded the last turn, and sprinted toward the darkness of the big tree. Moonlight glistened from her windows. Élodie's place had become a respite from his male netherworld. More than that, she was a link to Nicole.

He slithered from beneath the tree to the dripping eaves and darted to the back. He'd learned to avoid the second step, the squeal of nails moving through wet boards, and to expect the higher reach of the last. The key slid into place, and he twisted gently to preserve the hush.

The door eased open as laughter glittered the dark. Two voices, both women. He slowed his breath as the smell of potatoes drifted past, a slender vane of garlic and pepper flowing with them before all went still.

He slipped into the kitchen. A voice like tinkling silver pushed a current up his spine. A second voice answered, disquieted. The first picked up, soothing, offering kindness. It sounded so like... He moved into the dining room. A sliver of light slanted across steps as words toppled in an English cadence, and he moved to the stairs.

"He wouldn't have, I'm sure." *Élodie.*

"But he did." He'd taken comfort in that voice, had been healed through its wisdom.

A third, harsh and inscrutable, punctuated an offering with a screech. The stairs overwhelmed him with promise. The risk of entering that room surpassed reason, the voice likely a phantom of his need. Revealing himself could be fatal. Still his heart insisted, and he took the first two stairs, then the rest.

The voices quieted, and he stopped. The door was half open, the light dividing the hall, hiding the part of him still in darkness as he flattened himself against the wall.

"He must decide, I know, but he cannot separate supporting the Resistance from betraying his friends. So many have died." Élodie's voice was husky.

"If Elfriede and I leave, and he won't be forced to choose. Just understand that you haven't much time. Either of you."

He surged through the door, saw her seated on the floor, her mouth wide.

She rose, her hand at her breast. "David!" The word rang with supplication.

She was alive. She was *here.* He rushed across the room, found her waiting arms and drew her tight. She held him for seconds, then seemed to come to herself and freed him. His hands lifted to her face. "I can't believe it! *Mon âme!*"

Her sobs released all but hope.

He fought for breath. "You shouldn't be here. You should be somewhere safe."

"Just hold me." Her words were stifled by a sob.

He spoke in a whisper. "I won't let you go. Not ever."

"She cannot say vissout my help, yes? She comes to give you to General Hodge, boy!" Stubby hands rose. "I forget to put se rocks into my mouse before I shpeak, *ja*?"

Nicole lifted her head. "David, this is my dear friend, Elfriede. She and her companion, Gustav, have kept me out of the hands of the Wehrmacht for the past two weeks."

He reached to shake the woman's hand, felt Nicole's reluctance as her arm slid down his back. "Thank you for keeping her safe."

"Iss Gustav that bring her, *ja*? And se train. And you can sank Uncle Joe for putting Wehrmacht boys in sausage so zey not in Chemnitz. And Colonel Vatts for demanding it."

Nicole's silver edged laugh came over his shoulder. "The word is 'requesting,' Elfriede."

"*Ja ja*, he request it."

A sliver of yellow angled through the window and moved across the room. It brightened, then flashed from the carriage house.

Élodie lurched. "It's Heinrich! I hadn't thought he would come so late."

A chill coursed David's spine. Schneider had been pacing his office floor when he passed. He looked at Élodie. "Let him know I'm here. I'll explain the rest."

She scrambled past and bounded down the stairs.

He turned, saw the unease in Nicole's face. "He'll come through the back. Hide near the front door. Unlock it so you can run, and don't come out until we know how he'll react."

He skulked down, his steps covered by the rasps and scrapes of their debate, then slipped behind the dining room door. He heard his name and stepped into the light, his feet spread wide.

Schneider jolted. "What are you doing here, Lieutenant?"

"Trying to keep Élodie alive, Herr Hauptmann. And you, if you'll allow it."

Heinrich gritted his teeth. "If you are caught, do you think I will be given a medal?"

"You asked for help in surrendering to the Americans. Arrangements must be made."

Schneider reddened. "And you are employing Élodie in this effort?"

"I have no way of reaching our commanders. It requires a liaison, someone known by our intelligence officers."

"Have you forgotten our agreement, Lieutenant? You were to keep Élodie safe."

"Nicole has come with another operative. General Hodges has

been informed of your wish to surrender and of the sacrifices you've made to keep us alive. You'll be treated well."

The perfect brow contracted. "A Gestapo agent is here looking for a spy, David. A woman spy. I've not seen the picture, but I suspect we have viewed it before." Heinrich glared. "I heard this from an officer who assumed I'd been asked. Do you understand the implications?"

His gut tensed. "You weren't shown the picture, so they might suspect you are in league with her? How did the Gestapo know she was here?"

Nicole stepped from the darkness. "Perhaps I can explain. At least some of it."

* * *

David glanced at the clock on the mantle. Oh three hundred. "We've got to get back to the prison, Herr Hauptmann. It will take some time for me to get in."

Heinrich stopped pacing and stood before the table, his hands trembling. "You have put me in an untenable position, Lieutenant. I am without options."

Heat rose beneath his shirt. "Your allegiances did that, Herr Hauptmann. Nicole has risked her life to save you. I'll do the same, but if you don't do what's right, we'll all die."

"And you have drawn Élodie into this. She will die, as well."

Dark eyes shimmered from across the room. "They drew me into nothing, Heinrich. I work with the Resistance, just as I did in Munich. They are here to help us."

Nicole moved to the table. "I believe it unnecessary to defend myself, Heinrich. General Hodges is waiting for word from me. He will take you into custody along with those under your command. We have only to make our way to him. David will provide statements regarding your treatment of prisoners and testify that you helped secure both our extraction and theirs."

Heinrich straightened. "You said this Gestapo agent followed you from Spain and killed your contact in Paris. But your assignment came from MI6, yes?"

She nodded. "That's correct, though I left Antwerp without their knowledge and worked with the Americans in Tongres. The Gestapo tracked me there. That I understand. This I do not. He arrived here before me. No one knew I was coming except Colonel Watts, and I trust him unreservedly." She stared. "Are you responsible for the Gestapo being here, Heinrich?"

Schneider's head lifted. "No, though I suspect someone under my command may be." He stared. "I believe I am also being surveilled."

Bile rose in David's throat. "Krüger?"

The hauptmann laced his fingers and nodded. "No one knows who might be a spy, but prior to Krüger's trips to Cologne, my actions were never questioned. After I received a request from Oberst Schuster to allow Krüger to visit his sick mother, things changed." He lifted his thumbs. "The unteroffizier claims to be the Schusters' family friend."

His chest contracted. "So, he's been working both sides. He knows the operatives and has likely identified everyone in the area associated with the Resistance."

Nicole and Élodie stood whispering. Élodie turned, tears on her face. "I am among them, Heinrich. I trusted Hermann."

Heinrich nodded, seemed to pale. "As you said, we must return, Lieutenant."

Nicole caught David's eyes and motioned him to the dining room. He rose. "I need a moment, Heinrich."

The hauptmann said nothing but rested his head in his hands.

David stood behind the door, waited for Nicole to turn, and brought his hand to her cheek. So much was left to be said. "We must stay alive. We have everything to live for, now."

She placed her hand on his. "Élodie has received instructions. On 16 April, you are to begin sending signals at zero hundred forty-five hours"

He swallowed. "What day is that?"

"Monday. You have two days only. Also, her associates continue to watch the airfield. There are six planes, though perhaps not all are flying." She removed her hand. "I pray we have occasion to share our hearts."

"We have the rest of our lives, Nicole."

She kissed his cheek. "No, David, we haven't."

The weight of her words crushed him. He hadn't given her up; he'd only deceived himself.

Chapter LX

David stood beside the door of the officer's quarters rehearsing Nicole's words, the moment captured within the revolution of a phonograph, bound at each end by a scratch in his universe. He escaped for moments, but when the words returned, the knot in his gut grew tighter. Worse, a Gestapo assassin was searching for her while he was constrained by rock and wood and unable to lift a hand to protect her.

Cotton whispered on stone, and he turned to Bear sidling toward him from the stairs. His friend had listened as he emptied his heart, had offered no censure when he'd told of the yearning loosed at seeing her or the exquisite pain of her touch.

He nodded and glanced out the entry window. "How's morale, Bear? Are the men adjusting to the news?"

The sergeant glanced at the tower. "About FDR? They're more antsy about being liberated by the Ivans. Schneider looked out for 'em. No telling what the Soviets'll do."

"Maybe we can avoid that. I'm working on it."

Bear drew a breath. "Your plan better not include Langley. He took a spill coming down them stairs last night. Ankle's busted. He's in the lazarette."

He spun. "Why didn't you tell me?"

"There wasn't nothin' you could do, and I was hopin' you'd get some sleep." Bear wrenched his face. "Did Nicole play along about turning us over to our troops?"

"She wasn't playing. Made it halfway across Germany to put us in Hodges' hands."

Bear lifted his chin. "She come for you, Dremmer. Don't think she didn't. It's just—"

"What?"

The black dollop fell across the sergeant's face. "A lot's happened to get us here. Then we was captured by the only Nazi who'd been a friend to the people who took us in." Bear leaned against the wall. "You think worryin' made things work out the way they did?"

He drew his collar tight. "You're saying this was part of a plan? What about Swanson and the three that died in Belgium? Why wasn't there a plan for them?"

"I never said there wasn't no evil out there, or that evil don't have a plan, too. Them people was killed by a man who give himself to it. And God did have a plan for Swanson, but he took things into his own hands. Trustin' is everything."

He nodded. "I know."

"Do you? Then trust there's a reason Nicole made it here alive. I ain't sayin' I know what it is, or that it's what you both want it to be, but you need to know it'll work out for good if you trust God."

He'd tried. "You really think she came for me?"

"I do. But she's had time to think about Delores. That couldn'ta been easy."

David nodded. "You're right about that." So much had to be done. "We've got to be ready for the air strike. We'll need to learn all we can from Langley about the Eureka."

"Yeah, well, you can visit him in the lazarette."

He nodded. "I will. So, how many C-rations do we have left?"

"Jist one, but that'll help."

He zipped his coat, careful not to pull at the fraying stitches. "And one I put in our wall safe for Langley. We'll have to trade off carrying the transponder."

They strode toward the stairs, tried to pass Schneider's office unheard, mounted the first step before a door squeaked behind them.

"Lieutenant, may I speak with you?" Heinrich's words rattled across stone.

"Of course."

Heinrich pivoted. "Close the door, please. Would you care for coffee?"

David pushed against the heavy wood. "I would, thank you."

The hauptmann lifted a cup from the serving tray. "I haven't any sugar, but I have canned milk. Would you care for that?"

"All you can spare." He watched the German arrange spoons and cups with precision. "How are you, Heinrich?"

"It is not as bad as you might think." The man's skin was as wan as moonlight. "I've known for some time that I would not survive this war. My death coming sooner rather than later is something of a relief.

And it appears Élodie might now have someone to care for her."

David shuffled to the leather chair. "I told you the truth. Nicole has established bona fides with the Brits and the US. You'll be treated well."

The hauptmann chuckled. "My conviction is not due to the Americans, David. Surely, you don't think I can pass through Wehrmacht lines. I haven't any orders. No German officer will believe that I am not planning to surrender while marching prisoners west."

He eased into the chair. "What if we didn't have to march?"

Heinrich's brow furrowed. "The Soviets are moving closer. If we wait—"

"I'm not suggesting we wait. I'm suggesting we take a train."

Schneider's face went slack. "I am to arrange transportation for prisoners, including patients in the lazarette, and guards? That's almost three hundred men, Lieutenant."

He leaned against the heavy desk. "Elfriede said most of the Wehrmacht had been removed from the rail yard in Chemnitz."

Heinrich shrugged. "The front is being supplied closer to Berlin. They aren't needed here. And I will not be a party to taking their lives, David."

"I'm not asking you to. Elfriede called them 'boys.' Are they boys, Heinrich?"

The German glared, then nodded.

"Then you can get through to them. Show them false papers. Convince them we will be used as a shield to allow the Wehrmacht to withdraw. Tell them they'll face the Soviets alone if we aren't placed on that train."

Schneider traced a coffee ring. "They have radio communications. My orders must be confirmed."

"But if your orders can't be countermanded, say they were from RSHA, and if you were to insist the Allies are listening to radio communications—"

Schneider shook his head. "I can't leave those boys to face the Soviets alone."

He released a breath. "They're alone now. Give them hope, if only for a day or two. It isn't unlikely that our presence here is an obstacle to British or American troops. They might reach those kids first."

"And where would you suggest we go?"

"Nicole's connections are with the First Army. Take us to General

Hodges."

Heinrich shook his head. "That is impossible. The Wehrmacht has heavy defenses between here and there, and I know of only one train going west. Three days ago, your Third Army took Kassel. The 80th is regrouping there, and Wehrmacht defenses have pulled back. It is likely temporary, but that train is operating only a few kilometers northwest of the city. It would be a short march for the prisoners."

A tingle ran up his spine. "And how do you know that train is operating?"

"It carries our supplies, though it could be taken at any time. A shipment was to have reached Chemnitz yesterday, but it was plundered by the Wehrmacht. Part of our shipment was taken, but the second car is reported to be intact. Its contents should be arriving this evening."

"Does the shipment contain food?"

Schneider nodded. "Bully beef and biscuits seized from the Brits. Perhaps the Wehrmacht could not carry it or none of the officers could read English. In any case, it was spared."

He needed Heinrich to see it. "You understand the danger Nicole put herself in by coming here?"

The hauptmann's brow contracted. "It is no greater than the danger she put us in."

"You'd be in this predicament had she not come, but we'd be without connections" He opened his hand toward the appellplatz. "I don't want you leading her or these men into a trap."

Schneider's gaze began to thaw. "Last night, you asked me to trust you. I now ask the same of you. And you should realize I would not willingly place Élodie in danger."

David eased. "You want her to come with us, then?"

"I insist on it."

"You don't have to. I'm in full agreement." He waited. "I can only imagine how you got us a shipment of provisions."

The hauptmann offered a thin smile. "Élodie's uncle left his Mercedes in the garage. It was new then. It now belongs to a supply officer in Leipzig."

"Thank you, Heinrich. I'll tell the men. Now, how do we protect Nicole and Élodie?"

"You will leave shortly to stay with them. I'll come this evening."

"Let me go after appell. I'll stay with them until they leave."

"What can you do, David? You won't be armed."

"Then leave me with a pistol, at least. You know I'll defend Élodie."

Pale eyelids covered the crystal stare. "I cannot."

"We're on the same side now, Heinrich. Surely, you see that."

The eagle rose and fell above the hauptmann's heart. "All right. I will leave within the hour. You may fly over the walls tonight. I'll stay until you arrive." A fold of translucent skin pulsed against the blue-gray collar. "Élodie has her grandfather's revolver. He hid it beneath the house when guns were taken. I am certain she will allow you to use it."

David straightened. "There's something else. When we make it to the American lines, you and Élodie should be married."

Heinrich's head pivoted. "Why?"

"It's common for your officers to have women with them who aren't their wives. Unless you want Élodie treated like a prostitute, you'll at least claim she is your wife."

The hauptmann nodded. "Yes, of course."

* * *

David raised the trunk lid, the sky widening to a starless gray. The rations had arrived early, and he spread the word that Schneider had put himself at risk and paid the price for them to eat. He didn't need some kriegie trashing his defense of the man when they reached the front.

Nicole was half an hour away. He broke into a jog, felt the strength of bully beef and biscuits, sprinted across the narrow road under the pale froth of moonlight, then slid beneath the pine. He turned to the tower and saw the outline of a goon lighting a cigarette. His breath was easy and deep as he slipped onto the road. His boots, worn to the leather tracings he'd placed inside them, lifted in the steady governance of space and time, and he considered Bear's admonition, wondered how much of life proceeded from choice and how much was directed. At times, it seemed as clear as his friend made it out to be. But not tonight.

He'd yielded to Delores' supplication—had no one to blame but himself. Maybe Swanson's concession to Captain Hanson had been the same, but what about the boys whose blood was mixed with this soil? Would their making right choices have changed their end? It was impossible to believe it would have.

The rumble of a Kübelwagen filtered through darkness, a slitted beam flickering against wet bark. He threw himself beneath a tree as the car dropped a gear and candled the road with a single blackout light. He sucked damp air as the driver leaned forward, the dim glow of the panel offering no more than a silhouette. But it was enough.

"Heinrich!" Brakes squealed, and he ran to the passenger door to stick his head beneath the canvas top. "I thought you were going to stay with them until I came."

The hauptmann leaned toward him. "The plan has changed. My men will return to their quarters but will not leave the prison. I shall tell them that we are to surrender to the Americans and advise them that any mistreatment of prisoners will be reported to their captors."

Blood pounded in David's ears; he couldn't abandon the strike. "When will we leave?"

"Tomorrow. Sixteen hundred hours. You and your men will march to Chemnitz. Prisoners in the lazarette will be moved by lorries the following morning so that we might arrive near the same time. It will be a difficult march. Your men should be encouraged to rest."

He fought for breath, knew only that he had to remain in place. "Let me stay behind and make sure the men in the infirmary make it onto the trucks."

"You do not wish to be in the lead?"

He couldn't think of a reason. "It isn't necessary."

The hauptmann stared. "Then I will also remain and follow your truck."

It seemed likely the man was calling his bluff. Heinrich would want to be at the front to get them on the train. "And when will Nicole and Élodie leave?"

"A few hours before light. They will wait a short distance from Chemnitz, then accompany the prisoners to the rail yard."

His gut tightened. "Alone?"

The hauptmann nodded. "Yes. You will leave the pistol with Élodie. Now, get in the rear and lie down. I'll take you there and drive back."

He opened the door and slid across the seat.

Schneider leaned into the wheel. "Since you are remaining at the prison, I must insist on having Sergeant Billington lead your men. They will follow my orders until they are handed over. Is that understood?"

Blood pounded in his ears. *The mission.* "Understood."

* * *

David stared at the house, moonlight shrouding it in silver, and prayed that if the Gestapo assassin were near, the man would be exposed. He glanced at each of the three corners of the house visible from the tree before he scrambled to the shadow of the eaves. Nothing moved, so he shimmied onto the stoop, unlocked the door, and slipped inside. His shin bumped something hard. Metal clanged within the entryway, and a figure moved into the doorway, a gun silhouetted in the light slanting from the kitchen. "It's me. Don't shoot."

Élodie lowered the pistol, her shoulders falling. "I'm sorry, David."

"David?" Nicole's voice rose from the dining room.

"I'm here."

"Thank God." The words came on a ragged breath. "The alarm worked well, yes?"

They laughed, and he looked down. A pan shone, a toppled stool beside it.

She stepped toward him. "I'm happy you're here."

He moved, too, drawn like a planet to its sun.

Her head tilted, compelling him toward her. "Did you sleep today?"

Can I live without her? "Not at all. Did you?" Light fell across her face, not so brilliantly as Dürer might have seen her, but more lovely.

"A little." She grew silent. "You seem… Is everything all right?"

"Fine." He wanted to touch her, to feel the brush of her lips, but turned to Élodie. "Your alarm gave me an idea. I need a hammer, wire, and pliers. Rods, too, if you have them."

Nicole straightened. "Have you spoken with Heinrich?"

"He brought me."

Light glistened from her face. "Then you know he plans to begin the march tomorrow evening, and that we will leave early in the morning?"

"I'll leave with you. We'll pass the prison before light."

She grew solemn. "And the air strike. The three of you will be able to set up the beacon?"

He met her azure stare. "Heinrich said he'll need Bear to stay with the men and convey orders. Langley is injured. I'll guide the air strike, then come on a truck carrying patients."

She drew a quick breath. "You'll be alone?"

He shrugged. "That's the way it worked out."

"But you can't—"

"What will happen if Heinrich meets the Wehrmacht on the way?" The words drifted from behind Nicole.

He caught Élodie's frantic gaze. "I can't help with the Wehrmacht." She paled, and he struggled to soften his words. "But it's very unlikely he'll run into troops."

"Zose efil boys!" Elfriede shuffled from behind.

He looked across Nicole's shoulder. "Are you ready to travel, Elfriede?"

"No, I veel firs sleep."

He nodded, picked up the pan, and moved the stool to the side, then looked from Nicole to Élodie. "Maybe you could help me set trip wires? We'll let Elfriede rest."

Nicole placed her hand on his arm. "And perhaps we will talk, yes?"

His breath hitched.

"We have wire and tools in the carriage house. Heinrich leaves them near the workbench." Élodie's voice had taken on a shiver.

He took Nicole's hand, slipped through the door, waited for his eyes to adjust, and jogged to the carriage house. The reek of manure escaped the space beneath the door. Dampness muted a solitary squeak, and he stepped inside. Windows on the back wall bled dully across a workbench. Above it, tools were hung, and beneath, bins were filled with screws, nuts, and washers, and Gustav grumbled from the shadows.

He listened to Nicole breathe. "I'm looking for wire on a spool or coil." He pulled a hammer from between two nails, small but adequate. Needle nose pliers appeared in bas-relief.

"And I am hoping you will hear my heart." Her voice was halted by a tremor.

He gazed into the blue, the familiar pain entering his chest. "This war is coming to an end. If we survive, our being together is more than possible. But you insist that it isn't."

She touched his face. "You are married, David. You pledged your life."

He felt his heart contract. "I've lived for the day we would be together. I don't know how to live without that hope."

"God will help us both. I will know that you are safe and complete, and you will know the same of me. He will bring us peace, and we will learn to rest in that."

Chapter LXI

David stared through the kitchen window and sipped the coffee Élodie had left on the grate. The Gestapo man, should he come, would likely check the carriage house first, and he vowed to be ready. He rubbed his temples. Nicole had looked for excuses to stay, but she needed sleep, and he'd insisted she get it. Her presence should have brought peace, but being with her was a painful reminder of the approaching goodbye.

The clock chimed midnight. He started, swallowed herb-scented air, and let his heart still. In three hours, the women would rise. He would help them load the cart, then walk with Nicole to the prison road, and that would be it. He glanced at the vegetable stew simmering on the grate. Élodie had insisted on taking it along with bottled water and blankets. At least, they would eat.

He thumbed the revolver, an outdated Zig Zag smelling of oil and solvent. Though the gun had been cleaned, the lead cartridges were crusted and tinged in green. He shoved it beneath his belt, raised his head, and scanned the corners of the carriage house. The assassin had likely abandoned his mission and gone into hiding or absconded west to avoid the Soviets.

He walked to the front door, his socked feet silent on the polished floor, and peered through the window toward the tree. A gentle breeze nudged its branches, the thatch solid now. A shadow stirred—a gasp of wind most likely, lifting a leaf or scrap of paper. Then a quick agitation near the shadow of the eaves where he'd always hidden. His gut clenched, and he crept to the kitchen and bent to pick up his boots. A thud broke the quiet. The tripwire! He rushed to the front door, hurried onto the stone path, took two steps to avoid the bushes, and ran to the corner. A dark figure struggled to rise, appeared shaken, the narrow face elevating toward the kitchen window. The intruder's thin frame unfolded, and he stumbled to the back.

David pulled the pistol from his belt and sprinted. Loose wire caught his feet, and he soared headlong, the pistol flying from his hand. A muted screech echoed behind the house. The second step. He reached for the gun, found instead a slender peg with wire coiled around it. He grabbed it and eased to the back corner. The man stooped before the door, the tottering flame of a cigarette lighter brightening a sphere around the knob.

He slipped the wire through his hand, gripped the dowel in his right, doubled a section past the width of his outstretched arms and wrapped it around his left, then threw the remaining coil across his back. Grass and rock prickled his feet as he circled behind.

The sound arrested him. Steel probes dribbled clicks from the door. David rushed forward, caught the bottom step and vaulted, slipped from the misplaced top step and pounded the one beneath. The assassin turned, his mouth wide.

David lurched, slammed into the reedy frame, spun him around, pushing his knee into the sharp spine. He yanked the wire over the upturned face, drew too quickly and snared the nose and eyes. A scream chilled the night, and fingers clawed his cheek. He wrenched the wire and tugged it down. It grazed the protruding chin, and he yanked it back. Hands moved to grab the wire as he hove against spasms, the man's ribs arching upward. Shoulders pressed into his forearms, and wire cut into his left hand. He tugged the woven metal, held it until his hunger for air weakened his grip. Darkness, warm and glassy, trickled onto the strand, and the weight grew still and heavy. He lost his grip, and the man slumped across the boards.

The door eased open. A shadowed woman, bent and trembling, crumpled to the sill. He struggled to console her before a cry ascended and reached his soul, and he dropped the wooden dowel to place his arm around Nicole, shielding her from the evil sprawled across the steps.

He drew the darkness into his lungs. "He can't hurt you now. It's over."

"I have to see him." She drew a ragged breath. "I must be sure."

He squeezed her shoulder with his unsullied hand and kissed the top of her head.

She spoke through tears. "Someone will be awaiting his report."

He nodded. "The three of you should leave now. You'll be gone before anyone knows." He drew a heavy breath. "I'll drag him to the carriage house, and you can identify him there."

* * *

David walked behind the cart, the darkness so complete he could scarcely discern the end of gravel or the beginning of forest, could no longer see the blue of Nicole's eyes or read the sweet perfection of her face. He brushed her hand, hoping she would take his. Instead, she walked in silence, the steady clop of Gustav's hooves the only symmetry in the endless dark.

"It's a beautiful place, really." The words escaped without intent. He only knew he'd lost her and was desperate to have her back. "I wish we could walk this road in daylight." He waited, hoped she might offer a perhaps-we-shall-someday, but her withdrawal was complete. Maybe it was what lay on the cart, their march a procession, the three of them following behind while Elfriede muttered her affections to Gustav. They'd covered the body with rugs Élodie had added to Elfriede's goods. A copper kettle of eintopf, bouillon cubes and canned vegetables, sat beside the corpse, both cooling in the gloom.

He'd offered to walk them as far as the river, said he'd dump the man and return alone, but Elfriede refused, declaring herself capable of disposing of such waste. They neared the prison road, and he looked back.

"Is someone following?" Nicole's voice carried a chill.

He reached, drew her close. A glint of moonlight conceded the radiance in her eyes. "I'm only being cautious. Everything's fine."

She freed a breath. "Elfriede has no fear, but that isn't so of Élodie. Will they be safe?"

"Were you safe coming here?" The words pushed sharply from his chest. "We found the gun, at least. You'll be safer than when you came." They stopped, and he placed his wrapped hand over her shoulders and squeezed. "I'm sorry you had to see what you did."

She moved into him. "I would not have believed it was him had I not seen."

He thrilled at her cheek against his. "There's nothing to lead anyone to think either you or that man was at Élodie's home. In a couple of days, you'll be eating hot food and drinking coffee—coffee made from beans."

She shivered. "I wish for us to be together as much as you, David, but our wishes won't bring God's peace, and I cannot live without that."

He touched her forehead with his lips. "I didn't know what it was before you." He looked toward the cart, the clatter of trace chains waning. "Don't presume God won't make a way."

She lifted her head. "I'm not going on, David. I'm staying to help on your mission."

He met the azure flame. "You can't! It's too dangerous!"

"If we die, we might still save many lives. That is what this war has been for us. And we will be together."

He nodded, couldn't deny her that. Couldn't deny himself either.

* * *

David lowered the trunk lid onto the stone fissure and sank beside Nicole. "We should have asked for Élodie's flashlight."

Her hair whispered across his face. "It wouldn't help. The darkness is too great."

He patted the tunnel wall. "I'll leave the quilt beside the stew and bring bully beef and biscuits." He searched for words. "You're okay here? I'd move you into the abattoir, but it might be checked before the prisoners leave in the evening. And it's as dark as this, I'm afraid."

"I will be fine." Her words shivered his cheek. "I didn't mean what I said, David. There is no darkness greater than light. You should go. You must discuss things with Bear."

He felt the warmth of her shoulder and ached to hold her. "The assassin had to be dealt with. Heinrich will understand."

"Dealt with." A rustle rippled the dark, and she rested a trembling hand on his chest. "You should leave. We won't be able to remain this close without— You must sleep."

He treasured the warmth of her breath. "About tomorrow night. Tonight, I mean."

"Yes?"

"Do you understand what I'll be asking you to do?"

"Only that I signal you if anyone approaches while you set up the machine."

"We'll need to reach the airfield by midnight. I'll find the distance from the target and turn the unit on at zero hundred forty-five hours. That won't leave the Wehrmacht time to find us. The Rebecca operator should pick up our signal within fifteen miles. He'll signal, read off numbers, and I'll code them into the machine. You'll wait for the plane and guide them on course. But if something happens to me, you—"

"That part I remember. Please don't repeat it."

He had to be sure. "I'm told the machine is easy to use. I'll show you how to code the numbers in should it be necessary."

* * *

David reached to pull Nicole up the steep embankment then set off across the open field. They'd crossed two roads, sprinting over each, the Eureka on his back offering more resistance than he'd expected. It weighed less than what he'd lost but still seemed heavy. Maybe it was his legs, the gelatinous tremble that made him feel weak. More likely, it was the weight of a life without love that seemed to stretch before him into eternity.

"With no roads, how do you know where we are?" Nicole's words came in short puffs.

He looked up. "See that star? The bright one?"

"There are so many."

"The Big Dipper. Do you see that?"

"Yes."

He smiled. It was a conversation like those he'd imagined. "Beneath it, there's a star."

"I see. The bright one." She smiled, too; he could hear it in her voice.

"That's Polaris. The airfield is east of the prison. If we keep that star just over our left shoulders, we'll end up near our target."

"So simple." Her voice warmed him. "And how did Heinrich react to your dealing with the Gestapo man?"

He stepped over a sheep fence, the staves broken and leaning, and offered her his hand. "He didn't say a word. Just stared out the window."

"He had to follow me to his home, somehow. Had I not come—"

"No, it was Krüger. Heinrich's being surveilled, too. It would have been a matter of days or hours before they sent someone for him. And they wouldn't have spared Élodie."

They entered a dense cluster of trees, the darkness so thick he could scarcely breathe. He stared through overgrowth, looked over his shoulder, and found Polaris between two branches.

* * *

Beyond the trees, Nicole stepped into David's moon shadow. He had been crushed by her refusal. She knew but was helpless to change it. She was broken, too. If he knew what a hypocrite she'd been, telling him what God had for them, unable to bear the thought of a life without him. God would make her whole again, but just now, her future seemed darker than the night that covered them.

He moved as if his vigor hadn't been diminished by privation. He was thin, yet he had brought her bully beef and biscuits, had insisted he'd had all he wanted. Perhaps he had.

They stepped out of the trees, and a road appeared. His hand shot through the gray to stop her as he dropped to his knees. She fell beside him. "What is it?"

He rolled forward into a crouch. "A tanker. There! Got to be Luftwaffe."

Her heart slammed against her ribs as something heavy drew near and grumbled past, its lights scarcely lifting the dark, the air sharp with petrol. "Are they looking for us?"

"No. They're delivering airplane fuel." He watched for a minute or more and rose to his knees. "They're turning. Couldn't be more than a quarter mile south. We're close."

He rose, his hand clasping hers, and pulled her to her feet. He seemed excited.

"This is good?"

"Very good. They're leading us to our target. We've got to move."

He grabbed her wrist, propelled her upward and along a diagonal track toward a copse of hornbeams. Her lungs burned, and she prayed for her legs to stay beneath her. A bleached trunk swelled above the earth. He slid behind it and pulled her into him, cushioning her fall.

Her shoulder compressed inside his hand. "Sorry. I don't know what their sentries in the tower might see." He stared above the fallen tree. "Do you see those slits of light?"

"Yes, what are they?" Her heart pounded.

"Door seams in the hangers, I think. The windows are blacked out." He slid down. "Stay with the Eureka. I'll find the hanger with the most planes and step off the distance."

She wanted to remain silent but couldn't assuage her fears. "Just come back, David. I couldn't bear it if—" He crumpled beside her, drew her close, his hand moving around her waist, his breath awakening her cheek before his lips covered hers. She yielded to his tenderness, the strength of his arms drawing her to his heart. He released her suddenly and moved away.

"We have less than an hour. I need to position the transponder and find a place to observe the plane." He rose and ran into the open field.

She was wholly alone.

Chapter LXII

David had touched her, traced the narrow sculpting of her back, had known the soft caress of her skin. She was everything, but she wasn't his, and the sureness of it shook him to his core. He knew it in a way he couldn't doubt, in a moment cut from time and wrapped in certainty. His love hadn't been proof that they would be together, and learning to live without her would be the hardest thing he'd ever done.

He strode through heavy grass, his gut hollow with truth, and watched the slivers of light growing with each step. The conviction had seized him in a moment, taken him with such force that he'd forgotten to count his steps. He vowed to do it on his return, pushed into a jog, and listened above the rush of blood in his ears. A road appeared before the hangers, a woven wire fence beyond. Neither the road nor the fence had been visible from the fallen tree, and the airfield was larger than he'd imagined.

He sprinted to the road, captured his breath, and heard iron consonants assault the night. Orders were parodied in exaggerated tones. Laughter rose from at least two hangers. Mechanics, working into the night. Would any of them know camaraderie tomorrow? He filled his lungs with prayer, asked for these boys to know the end of war and the lies that birthed it.

He understood it now. It was possible to kill without malice.

The bulbous outline of a Mercedes morphed near the edge of the road, almost hidden by the swell. Beside it, a path ascended the short margin to the fence. He shrank, crept around the car, ran his hand across the warm hood, and climbed the bank to a walk-through gate. The lock had been left dangling, probably by a pilot, stopping to check on his plane.

He peered from behind the hanger and glanced across runways. Three other buildings rose from the darkness, all knifing light around closed doors. The tanker idled between them, its driver dragging a hose to the rear, stopping to chat with a mechanic near the hangers on the west. Slitted headlights exposed three raised lids above underground tanks.

David turned and hurried through the gate. If he added steps to his count, maybe the bombs would hit midway between the hangers and destroy more planes. He started his count at the fence, began at forty, and marched into darkness, his strides lengthening toward the tree where she waited.

* * *

Nicole heard footfalls and rolled to her side. A figure emerged from the grass, his stride long and steady. It had to be David, but why was he walking past her, thirty meters or more from the fallen tree she lay behind? "David?" Her voice was mostly breath.

His hand rose, motioning her down. "Four forty-one." The whisper was gone. He reached the trees and jogged back. "You'll line up behind the big chestnut. It's four hundred fifty yards from the airfield. I'll work the Eureka, code in the azimuth, and you'll direct the plane."

Her heart stuttered. "Yes, all right."

"The Eureka won't be triggered until the Rebecca is fifteen miles out. Gives us over three minutes while they make their sweep. The hangers should be in flames before the Krauts home in on us." He returned to the trees, began erecting the antenna, and pointed. "I'll line you up in front of the tree where you can't be seen by the tower. Holler when they're directly overhead."

She swallowed. "You saw no sentries?"

"No, though I couldn't see the front gate. They're clearly not expecting trouble."

A plane flew between them and the prison, a solitary light burning in the tail. Chill bumps rose on her arms. "Is that—"

"That's it." He watched the horizon. "They're starting the sweep. An A-20 likely carrying four five-hundred pounders. If they trail them, they just might take out the whole base."

She steadied her breath and climbed a stump in front of the tree.

"Keep them in line with the field. Make it a straight shot to the hangers on the north." He seemed calm, his airman's voice surfacing as he pulled the earpiece in place.

She watched the light disappear, the plane nosing their way.

"They've locked on!" His voice was potent.

She scanned the horizon, saw nothing, began to count the remaining seconds. *Ten, eleven...* She reached forty, still afraid to blink. The sky flowed in unbroken gray. Had she lost them? If they were off course... *sixty-eight, sixty-nine...* A light appeared, boring a hole in the darkness, veering slightly to her right. "Turn to my left!"

David mumbled into the headset, and the plane edged toward her, then to her left. "Turn half as much to my right."

She heard him droning into the mic. The light centered, grew bright, plummeted toward the earth, then steadied. "Dead on!" She fought the impulse to seek cover.

The roar consumed her, the light blinding. David hollered something to the crewman. She stared into the light until— "Now!" She spun. The engines shook her, and bombs whistled through the air. She snatched a breath before the earth quaked and the sky caught fire.

She ran toward David, the blistering white blinding her. His arms came through the brightness and grasped her. "They hit just east of center. Go to the road we crossed and hide in the ditch. I'll meet you there."

"Where are you going?"

"If the tanker wasn't destroyed, I'll make sure the west hangers go up, too."

"David, no! We can make it to the prison unseen if we go now!"

He drew her close. "Give me fifteen minutes. If I don't come back, go without me. Find Polaris and keep it off your right shoulder. Watch for landmarks. Cross the sheep fence at the opposite angle. The trucks will assemble early on the west side of the prison. Tell the goons you're a friend of Heinrich's." He kissed her, then ran for the inferno. The blaze lowered, buildings on the north silhouetting steel frames that sagged within a brilliant yellow.

* * *

The hanger on the south had collapsed, and the airframes of at least two planes were shadowed by flames. Men darted like mice beneath the brilliance. David reached the road, scanned the inferno reflected in the hood of the Mercedes, and slid into the driver's seat. The hangers on the north were gone, too, but those on the west were scarcely damaged. A truck with a tank and pump sprayed them down, lessening the chances of their catching fire. A door had been rolled back, the propeller of a plane visible beyond, the fuselage of another beside it.

He slid across the seat, flames glistening from dangling keys. He slipped them out and ran to the gate. The tanker was less than a hundred yards away, the tractor facing east. He stole to the edge of the smoldering hanger. The heavy hose bounced as the pump slugged fuel. He sprinted to the truck, jumped when he reached the running boards, and flung himself across the seat. A clipboard tumbled to the floor; forms and a heavy coat mounded above it. He looked over the wheel. A mechanic with an extinguisher ran north. David sat up, glanced in the mirror. A half dozen men struggled with a fire hose. More dragged a refueling trailer away from the flames.

He looked for a gear pattern, revved the engine, and shoved the shifter left and forward, then eased out on the clutch. It grabbed, but the engine stalled.

The brake!

He found the handle, released it, and pressed the clutch and starter pedal. The truck rolled forward, the starter grinding in a slow roll. It cranked into a compression stroke and stopped. An officer appeared in the passenger mirror, his leather coat glistening with firelight. Black boots mirrored flame, cycling toward the truck, the man's side arm silhouetted above a flashing visor.

David pushed the heavy clutch, moved the shifter into neutral, and stepped on the starter. The engine made a reluctant turn, fired, and came to life. He threw the shifter into first and released the clutch. The truck lurched forward. He checked the mirror and jammed the accelerator. A leather coat glistened but slid away as fuel sprayed toward it, the hose dousing concrete. He caught second, nudged the wheel into a slow right turn, urging the truck off the runway. It veered south, bouncing across a second runway as he wrestled the wheel to the left. The pool of gas ignited where he'd stalled, and men ran from his trailing fire. He straightened and slammed the shifter into third. The circle half complete, he steered toward the west hangers. A door had been rolled back, a plane in full view, half the nacelle of a second beside it.

He aimed the truck between them and leaned to find the hand throttle. Glass exploded above him, shards slicing beneath his collar. He looked up and stared through the bullet-riddled windshield. The puddle of fuel was a burning pyre, the brightest of targets.

He set the truck on a collision course, pulled the hand throttle, slid across the seat, and yanked the door handle. It didn't release. He slid back, coiled his right leg, and kicked. The handle broke, disappearing on the dark floor. He lay on the seat, breathed, drew his legs back, and slammed both heels into the side panel. The door flew open as a second volley of bullets pierced the hood and shattered glass. He raised his head, the cab boiling, and thrust himself into darkness, tumbled across the tarmac, and bolted for the gate.

He'd covered half the distance to the fence when the roof of the west hanger lifted, belching fire. A 109 exploded, throwing him to the concrete, his leg searing with pain. He shook, tried to clear his head, stood, and hobbled on. Flames covered his retreat as he slid down the short embankment and toppled to the car. He inserted the key and hit the starter. The engine came to life, and he popped the clutch, scattering gravel as he spun around.

* * *

An engine screamed, and Nicole slid deeper into her muddy grave. She'd waited longer than he'd asked. Too long, perhaps. Could he have survived the explosion? It was as if Cerberus himself had been set free, his howl scorching the night sky. Had it taken David? She prayed that if he were alive, he would hear whatever was approaching and not allow himself to be captured.

The engine slowed, but she saw no lights. If they were searching for him, their lights would expose— Or were they searching for her? Tires threw pebbles across the ditch. Her heart pounded, and she fought to steady her lungs.

"Nicole!" The words were charged. "Are you here?"

"David?"

"Get in!"

She lurched from the ditch, her hand scarcely able to grip the handle. She pulled her leg in as David wheeled around. "You're returning to the airfield?"

"Only way I know to get to the prison." He squeezed her arm. "Can you drive?'

"Only a— No."

"I took shrapnel in my leg. I'm losing blood. I'll try to get us to Élodie's. If I— Can you find the road to Chemnitz from there?"

She pushed against a surge of nausea. "You won't die, David.

You'll be fine."

"Not without help. I'm bleeding bad."

"I don't— I've never—"

"We'll use Élodie's kitchen. You'll cut some sheets for bandages. I'll leave the car in the carriage house."

Chapter LXIII

White chat captured moonlight and ribboned a pathway through the dark. Flames threatened to quench the boundaries of the road, but David held their speed until the Mercedes yielded to the soft earth at the edge. He eased left, balanced along the crest, and sped on. The tanker protruded through the center of the west hangers as they passed, flames boiling around its sagging frame. Dark figures scurried beneath the inferno as a firetruck idled toward the road, stopping to spray the lost buildings as he and Nicole flew by.

He glanced at her, shifted into high, and released the clutch. The movement set his leg aflame this time, the pain mounting. "Watch behind us. If they recognize the car, they'll follow."

She turned and stared. He held his breath.

"Lights are turning onto the road. A truck, I think." Her voice shook.

He sucked darkness. "We can't lead them to Schneider's house. They'd go to the prison and maybe find the kriegies on the road."

"Do we leave the car?"

"Not yet, but if we have to, I want you to run for cover. I'll walk the opposite way." He reached an intersection, downshifted, avoided alerting their pursuers with his brake lamp, and turned west. He accelerated to a grove of trees atop a hill, coasted to a stop, and killed the engine. "We'll see who's following us. Pray they didn't see us turn." He reached for her hand, felt trembling fingers curl inside his.

Nicole turned to the rear window as he watched the mirror. A command car rolled past, following the arc to Waldheim. She released her breath. "You know the way there, yes?"

He shrugged. "I'll know the road when we cross it. Can't be far."

* * *

David turned onto the gravel road, spotted the dark comfort of the tree in Élodie's yard, and slowed to turn into the carriage house. Lights flashed in his mirror from the road they'd just abandoned. He turned back into the street, pushed the shifter into second, and stomped the accelerator. They raced toward Waldheim, his leg on fire.

Nicole grasped the door pull and glanced back. "Where is your contact?"

He hated quelling her hopes. "I have no contact here besides Élodie. I haven't been further than her house. Watch for a street, a–"

"There!" She pointed to a narrow track, an alley of sorts behind a cluster of homes.

He turned and drove for cover, looked for dust in his mirror but saw only darkness. Houses were clumped in a huddle on the right, more approaching on his left. "We need a place to hide the car."

She nodded and peered out her window. He slowed, spotted a squat outbuilding withdrawn beside the house on his left, both structures in disrepair, the fence between them missing boards. He turned behind the fence, brought the car about, and backed to the wooden door. He lifted himself out, limped to the end of the fence, and stared back at the street. The command car rounded the curve, lights blazing, engine screaming.

He hobbled to the garage and slipped inside. Windows on the north effervesced in steel gray, revealing boxes stacked along the wall, a lathe and press beside them. He shuffled across the floor, stumbled over a box of shop manuals, and glanced back. The sliding door tracks were chained to the wooden frame, preventing the door from closing. But it should open. He moved behind it and pushed. A fresh flow trickled down his leg, and he glanced at his foot. Blood had soaked to the cuff and painted his boot. He needed help quickly. He pushed, and bearings squealed as the door moved wide enough to allow the car inside.

He hobbled out and slid beneath the wheel.

"Are we not going to Élodie's house?"

"We're close. We'll hide the car here and walk. If they find it there—"

"Are you able?"

He had no answer, backed into the shop, and turned the wheel to hide more of the shining blue. "I think it's a couple hundred yards. Three maybe."

* * *

David sat on the steps, drew his right boot close, and pried the key from beneath his heel. His head spun, and he grabbed the railing.

Nicole took a quick breath. "David, are you all right?"

"I think so, but we need to work fast." He stood, grabbed the door to keep from falling, and slipped the key in the slot. "You know where Élodie keeps needles and thread?"

"I'll look." She drew a heavy breath. "Drink water. I'll try to find something to eat. You've lost a great deal of blood."

"Water will help. Look for alcohol and towels."

"Yes, of course." She shimmied to the stairs.

He pulled a chair to the counter, grabbed another to rest his foot on, and stared through the window. The Luftwaffe squad was using spotlights. From here, he could see them in time to hide. And he needed the sink. If the Krauts came in the next few hours, his blood trail would implicate Schneider. If they pursued him, they'd find an empty prison.

Nicole stepped quickly from the stairs. "I found a needle and thread. Also, alcohol and towels. What else will you need?"

He dipped his chin. "Light a burner. Find a pointed knife. An ice pick, maybe—something small and sharp. I need a flat-bladed knife, too. And pliers."

She turned. "Pliers?"

"The needle-nosed pair I used on the wire. You'll need to boil them."

Her eyes widened. "Why?"

"The shrapnel's cutting deeper. Blood flow's worse. Gotta take it out." He waited for her to move. "If I pass out, you'll need to finish. Get the tip of the small knife hot and touch any spot that's bleeding. Use the flat-blade knife to protect the muscle around it."

"David, I can't."

"You can." He held the azure gaze. "I need you."

He cut his left pant leg to mid-thigh, spreading towels beneath his leg and over his lap. Nicole placed a pan of boiled water on the table. A broad knife lay at the bottom. A smaller one was perched on the stovetop, the tip glowing in the dark kitchen. He took a breath. "Bring the candle close and hold the mirror so I can see the wound."

She crouched beside his chair.

"There. Hold it steady." He retrieved the broad knife, allowed it to cool a few seconds, lifted the muscle and slipped it inside the parted skin. Pain shot into his hip, and he fought to keep from vomiting. He stilled, allowed his stomach to settle, then slipped the blade deeper. The tip touched something hard, and an instant sweat covered his face.

He switched hands and lifted with the broad side of the blade. "The bleed's above the shrapnel. Hand me the pliers." He extended his right hand. Dark spots appeared before the mirror. His fingers folded around the handles but refused to grip, and he fought to clear his head.

"David?"

He drifted for a moment and drew a heavy breath. "I need water."

The glass touched his lips, and he felt the coolness in his throat.

"Do something, David. The bleeding is worse."

"Yeah." He waited. "Is it surging or seeping?"

"It's not surging, but there's quite a lot." She went silent.

"Can you..." His ears filled with a swelling buzz, and his head spun.

* * *

Nicole watched as David slumped. She fought back a scream as his right hand released the pliers and his left relaxed on the knife. With every heartbeat, he was losing blood.

I need you. Tears crowded onto her cheeks. She brushed them away, placed the pan of boiled water in the sink and poured alcohol over her right hand, then lifted the broad blade to drain the wound. She slid the blunt knife deep, felt an obstruction, and stared into the gaping hole. Metal glistened three or four centimeters from the cleft. She set the pliers, but the nose slipped free. She raised the knife to give the shrapnel more space, clamped the rough metal again and pulled. David moaned, his head rising for a moment. She waited, lifted the fragment, and gripped the handles as the shard eased into candlelight, glittering with black blood. The flow increased, and she inserted the hot point, lifting the muscle to shield it. Above the waning blush, blood boiled, and she waited. The bleeding was lighter but still deadly. She placed the tip of the pointed knife in the burner, waited until the color returned, then slipped it into the flow until it stopped.

* * *

Nicole stared into the darkness beyond the dining room window. David lay on the rug where she had dragged him, his leg wrapped tightly with torn sheets. She had swabbed the wound with alcohol but couldn't stitch it. Perhaps David would. His steady breath brought comfort, each suspiration a reassurance. He had drunk two glasses of water before she removed the shrapnel, but he had to have food to replenish his blood.

I need you. The words returned, and she dabbed her face. She'd cleaned the kitchen and found three eggs Élodie had boiled, then forgotten in their rush to hide the Gestapo man. She looked at David, wondering how they would make it to Chemnitz in time. The clock read ten past four, and the train would leave at eleven. Lorries would begin loading the infirm at seven, and Heinrich said he would send them back for the remainder of those in the lazarette. He might be able to detain them should the last loads arrive late, but he couldn't wait long.

David stirred, and she came to her feet. "You are awake?"

Groans rose in response. She examined his leg, could find no fresh bleeding, and went to find pants that might fit him. He would need something other than the blood-soaked pair he wore now, the left pant leg cut almost to his pocket.

* * *

The room squared slowly, the uncertainty of something half remembered, the lines irregular and soft, a grainy image emerging from developer. David rolled his head, caught the shine of the banister, the outline of a budding maple beyond a window. A door unlatched, a drawer closed with a thud, and feet whispered on stairs. He struggled to rise but hadn't the strength and eased back, a tension around his leg.

"You are awake?" The words were tinged with relief.

He found her eyes and remembered. "What time is it?"

Nicole stared into the kitchen and bent low. "Four thirty-five. You are in pain?"

"Not so much." He drew a breath. "We need to go."

She shook her head. "I removed a piece of shrapnel and cauterized two bleeders, but you have no stitches. I was afraid—"

He nodded. "It's all right. We'll leave it wrapped."

"You've lost too much blood, David. Élodie left three eggs. You must eat."

Moonlight caught her gaze, the blue piercing his heart. "I'll eat one. You eat the others."

She hurried to the kitchen, and he raised himself with his arms. If he made it to the car, he could drive. Once rolling, he'd shift without the clutch, had learned as a kid to match the engine speed with the load and mesh the synchronizers with the shifter. Getting started was the trick.

She brought two small plates, an egg on hers and two on his, a knife and fork across each. "Can you stand?"

"Help me to the stairs, and I'll pull myself up."

She placed the saucers on the table and grabbed his hands. "The chair is heavy. Use it."

"Yeah, good idea."

She lifted his good leg, swiveled him close to the table, and drew the chair to his left arm. "Roll over on your right knee."

He pulled himself up. The sharpness had been replaced with a deep ache. "Eat while I get the car. Wait for me behind the carriage house and bring my egg."

The deep grumble of a straight eight sounded only a moment before a spotlight burst through the front windows, down the hallway, and across the yard. His words emerged on a shallow breath. "The command car!"

Their eyes met, exchanging something final.

Chapter LXIV

Light splashed through the kitchen window. "Get down!" David grabbed Nicole's arm and rolled beneath the cabinet, his leg refusing the insult of a crawl. The Steyr roared in the street and incited a tremble. "Do you know how to use Schneider's phone?"

She lay curled into him. "If the system hasn't changed."

He loosed his arms from around her shoulders. "Try to reach him. Introduce yourself as Élodie for whomever might be listening. Ask him to call off the dogs."

She crawled to the dining room, skulked back, unrolling the phone cord, and extended a red book. "While at university, Élodie kept a list of numbers on the inside cover."

He reached for the counter, grabbed matches, and lit one. Names, most abbreviated, extended down the page. At the top was an "H" followed by 65-30-14.

She dialed the number and tipped the receiver so he could hear. It buzzed for seconds before clicking, then "Hauptmann Schneider."

"Heinrich!" Her voice was breathy, *"Das ist Élodie."*

A chill gathered on the line as the Heinrich withheld a response.

Determined consonants rasped for seconds before Nicole spoke. He replied, and the line went quiet. David leaned in, heard Heinrich's voice, barely audible. He was speaking with someone else, perhaps on his radio.

Orders echoed in the street, and light exploded against the tree before burning southward.

Nicole hung up. "I complained of Soviets in the street. He assured me they were Luftwaffe, then radioed the feldwebel and said the squad was frightening his wife and her guest, Frau Schuster, Herr Oberst's wife."

David pulled himself to the window. "Won't the feldwebel call Schuster?"

"They won't wake so powerful a man or tell him of the attack before capturing those responsible." She faltered. "I am certain Heinrich suspects I directed the attack."

His chest tightened. "If we make it back, I'll let him know who's responsible. Do you think the Luftwaffe knows the Gestapo is investigating him?"

"I can guess only, but I would think not. The Gestapo discloses nothing. It is how they maintain power. Everyone fears their having information. Or inventing it."

The Steyr rumbled down the street, and he drew a heavy breath. "If we are found here, Schneider will be shot, and the kriegies caught before they reach Chemnitz."

Nicole rose slowly and looked through the glass. "I know we must leave, but you must also eat, David. I wish for you not to lose consciousness again."

* * *

Eggs sloshed in David's gullet and threatened to come up more quickly than they'd gone down. He hobbled the two hundred yards to the derelict shop and threw the mop handle crutch into the Mercedes. Nicole stood at the end of the fence watching for the Steyr as he cranked the engine, pulled out, and let a front wheel drop into a track to avoid using the brake. He looked through the open window. "See anything?"

"Nothing." She slid in, her face glistening with moonlight.

"I'll find a street perpendicular to the road to Chemnitz." He glanced at the clock on the dash. Oh five hundred ten. His leg trembled against the clutch as he backed the car toward Élodie's gate. "I need to cover our tracks. The ones I left with the mop handle could be followed in daylight." He ground the transmission into first, revved the engine, and slid his foot from the clutch. They sped down the alley to meet the street on the curve, and he mashed the accelerator, scattering gravel into the dark. Houses pressed in on either side, dulled by a deathly gloom. A major street appeared, dark and coursing north. He threw the car into the turn.

Nicole wrenched a breath. "This will lead to Chemnitz?"

"We should cross that road if this one doesn't end first."

Granite pavers led hellward between slab buildings and closed storefronts. Signs jutted through darkness, sliced a quadrangle from the center of the street, and offered a tapered inlet to the intersection. He braked, downshifted, then sped through, barreling up the next hill.

Nicole looked back. "They're coming!"

He looked into the mirror. Spotlights scalded the intersection, then turned after them.

"Will you know the road when you see it?" Nicole's words surfaced on a pant.

"It's north of town. Watch for something familiar." It wasn't an answer, and he knew it.

A building rose in the street—a town hall, maybe. He hit the brakes, slid into the square, skated right, then left, and left again. On the opposite side, he re-entered the street. Businesses gave way to houses, then to countryside. They crested a hill, placing it between them and the retreating spotlight. He watched the skyline, passed another road, and spied a stand of trees. The shape, the sequence—something was familiar. He hit the brakes and spun around.

"Was that the road?" Nicole's voice trembled.

"I think so." But he wasn't sure.

Tires rumbled onto gravel, trees shadowing the road. Atop the first rise, slender shafts ran diagonally across shaved rock and vibrated through the steering wheel. He remembered their sharpness beneath his worn soles. "This is the road. I'm sure."

She released her breath. "So, have the plans changed? Will we return to the prison?"

"I want you to hide near the turnoff. I'll take the car to the first bridge and run it into the river. The water's fast from snow melt. It should be out of sight before it sinks."

She shook her head. "You can't walk. The bleeding will start again."

He tried to smile. "I had a great surgeon."

They topped a hill. The car lifted on its springs, then squatted hard. He felt for the light switch. Beams blistered beneath shimmering green branches that fluttered on either side. If the squad took this road, he might lead them to the prison—to Langley and the wounded, or to Heinrich pacing his office floor. Better to go on, hide Nicole and allow himself to be captured.

He glanced at the clock. Kriegies had been marching for thirteen hours and were less than two hours from the train yard. If they'd held up. Heinrich had likely provided one of his officers with orders. The hauptmann hoped to meet the marching kriegies before they reached

Chemnitz, and the man left nothing to chance. So, what would Heinrich do if they didn't make it back? The lives of his staff and the prisoners were at stake. Élodie's, as well. He'd proceed as planned. It was all he could do.

"You're right." David turned, catching a shiver of blue. "We'll go on, make it as close to the train yards as we can. Are there any bridges near there?"

She nodded. "There is one quite close. It is also high, as I remember."

He eased his hand over his throbbing leg. "Good. We should catch up to the kriegies before then. We'll dump the car and wait for Heinrich. He'll be in the first truck. Or near it."

"You are sure?"

"He won't trust anyone else to get us on that train." David spotted the turnoff, switched off the lights and glanced in the mirror. The wheels bounced from the chuck hole near the turnoff to the prison. He slowed and let his eyes adjust to the pale light trickling through pines. "It'll take a couple of hours to reach the train yard. We can't travel fast without lights."

She squeezed his arm. "I'm not eager for our time to end, David."

He fought the insurrection of his heart, wanted to rail against the injustice of their parting, but he forced the scream to still.

* * *

Mountains skirted his vision, offered climb after climb with valleys between. David wearied of the unremitting deliberateness of their pace. The blackness of a solitary rock shadowed gravel where it stole light from the gray, and he switched the lights on. They reached a crest, and a cutback drew him away from the words crowding his throat. He checked the mirror, eased into a valley lush with moonlight and winter wheat, and let the Mercedes idle to a stop. Rock gave way to moist loam that bore the imprints of boots from edge to edge. He smiled. "Our boys are up ahead, and there aren't any vehicle tracks covering theirs."

Nicole nodded. "Then they are safe. There are more foothills, but I'm sure we're close."

He moved the shifter forward and released the clutch, his leg quivering with pain. He touched his pantleg but felt no blood. The car skimmed over soft earth, the absence of rock offering a calm, the breeze easing his doubts. He found her hand beside the shifter and entwined what hope remained within their grip.

The river came to lure the road, enticing and withdrawing in a coquettish dance of glistening water and granite-shouldered earth. The car glided beneath the shade of a leafy roof, dimming the edges of trees. He slowed, stared into the gray, was arrested by a boiling shadow that gave way to the unsure forms of lax shoulders and bent necks. He killed the lights.

Nicole squeezed his hand. "There is a guard in the rear, yes?"

He pulled to the side of the road and rolled his window down. A new weakness had crept into his body—and an ache. "Likely several of them." Kriegies shouted in the distance, and he looked at Nicole. "There are things you need to know if something happens."

"We will survive, now, David. Both of us."

"I believe so, but in case I don't, there was a man in Moosburg, a feldwebel."

She stirred. "Was he the evil man you became involved with?"

A current shot up his spine. "Who told you I was involved with someone evil?"

"A contact. A Scot with the code name Feste."

The muscles in his neck eased. "The evil man was American, a captain, the head of intelligence. The feldwebel's name is Vogt. He set up a Resistance group, gave the operatives Shakespearean code names. It's more than likely he recruited your man, Feste. When 7-A is taken, our troops need to know that Vogt is a hero. He can identify those who worked under him. Promise me you'll do all you can to save him."

She placed her hand on his shoulder. "Of course, yes."

He nodded, took in the peace. "How far is the bridge?"

She moved closer, let her head rest on his shoulder. "It's quite near."

He listened to her breathe in the stilling gray, wanted to fill what time he had before— She turned, captured him with her stare. He cupped her face and kissed her. "I know you're right. I don't want what isn't best for you, or what hasn't been given to me."

She pulled away and turned. "I asked that I be allowed to see you, that I would know you were safe and well. I thought it would be enough."

He drew her to him. "I prayed that, too, but it isn't enough. Not by a long shot."

She seemed to ease. "If only you could hold me until I slept, I would choose to never wake." She waited. "I've repeated something every night. Words from a psalm. It is no secret to the One who hears that I've wished we could pray it together."

"And what was your prayer?"

She straightened and touched his face. "I will both lay me down in peace, and sleep: for thou, Lord, only makest me dwell in safety."

He drew her close and kissed the crown of her head. "I'll repeat it every night. For both of us." He moved away, started the car, and edged to the hilltop, a budding pink lifting the eastern sky. He followed the road with his gaze, saw men crossing a bridge, aegis arms of iron covering them.

When the last man cleared the final span, he eased the car to the bridge, backed to the side of the road, and waited for the men to be swallowed in silence. Nicole stepped from the car, holding his crutch, and stood half hidden by trees. He looked at her in wonder. The pain had worsened, the ache spreading to his back and shoulders. A deep chill had risen, and he turned to the turbid green, lighter by half beneath a waking sky. Four saplings blocked the path between the bridge and the pines. With speed, the car would crush them before plowing over the edge. He only had to clear the door.

He grabbed a small branch, eyed the distance between the seat and floorboard, and placed it between the glistening bumper and fender. It gouged paint before it broke, and he shivered, half amused at his own disgust at scratching a car he was about to destroy. He threw the branch across the seat, slid inside, and started the engine. His right foot on the clutch, he pushed the shifter into low, shoved the broad end of the branch against the accelerator, jerked his leg from the clutch, and threw himself to the road. The car surged, veered slightly to the left, scraped the bridge railing, bounced over saplings, and plunged into the gorge.

He lifted himself with a draining effort and offered Nicole his hand. "Let's wait on the other side. It'll give us time to identify the truck and maybe Heinrich."

She moved beneath his arm. "And this day has only begun."

He drew her to him. "But it's the first day in a long time that I'm where I want to be."

Chapter LXV

The Opel mounted the bridge, the engine's report assaulting the river and ricocheting through trees. David crawled forward. "That's the one!"

Nicole slipped behind him. "How do you know?"

His head spun as he pulled himself up. "It's the truck they used to deliver supplies to the lazarette. Prisoners, too. The bumper's bent on the right front."

"And you're sure Heinrich will be in it?

He steadied himself on quivering legs. "If not, he'll be close."

The engine lowered in pitch, and the front springs squatted. Two goons were perched on the seat, staring. Another engine whirred, and he scraped to the side of the road. Schneider's car braked behind the Opel, and David waved the truck by. A goon jumped out, his Mauser leveled. Schneider marched from behind, spat something gruff, and the obergefreiter lowered his gun.

Nicole stepped behind David. "Henrich told the corporal you couldn't keep up. The boy asked why you were wearing civilian trousers, and Heinrich said he loaned them to you."

He faced her. "Did the obergefreiter ask about you?"

"He is rather afraid to, I suspect." She placed her hand on his back. "His staff car is full. Will we be left behind?"

He looked. Three kriegies sat in the car, all officers. The shell-shocked from the lazarette, he guessed. "May we crowd in, Herr Hauptmann?"

The truck pulled away, and Schneider stepped close, his face reddening in the early light. "You betrayed me! I told you I would have nothing to do with the killing of my comrades."

"And you didn't. I carried out the bombing entirely on my own." He swallowed. "It's possible to kill only for survival, Heinrich. How many died?"

"I have had no report on that. I will take you there if you wish to express your concern."

"I'm getting on the train, Heinrich. It's likely the Gestapo has sent someone to murder you, too, so I suggest you do the same."

Schneider trembled with rage. "We will place the officers on the next truck. As MOC, it is appropriate that you will arrive in my car. Perhaps I can prevent further bloodshed."

David shivered, covered in a sudden sweat. "That's precisely why I had to eliminate the planes." He breathed deep, trying to clear his head. The captain sat opposite the driver's seat, and two slack-jawed lieutenants teetered in the rear.

A second truck mounted the bridge, and Schneider opened his passenger door. "Captain, step out, please." The hauptmann nodded. "Help your comrades, Lieutenant. They've been sedated and might have difficulty walking."

* * *

Kriegies sat within the shadows of half-leafed oaks. Schoolboys stood above them fidgeting in sagging uniforms, their Mausers leveled. David dragged himself away from the command car, breathless at having to stand. He looked up, saw a glint in the eyes of a soldat. The boy looked to be no more than thirteen, his trembling finger sliding inside the trigger guard.

Nicole stepped close, and he pushed her behind him. "If anybody sneezes, these kids will unload on us, Heinrich."

The hauptmann nodded, turned to the boy, and spoke in even tones.

"He is explaining that the Wehrmacht lost Kassel a few days ago." Nicole's words washed over David's shoulder. "He is saying the prisoners are to be used in an exchange for their troops being allowed to retreat. Should these soldats not cooperate, he says the exchange will not take place, and these few boys will be left to face the Soviets alone."

Another cold sweat covered his face, and he slipped his hand behind his back, found her warm fingers and squeezed. "Pray they believe him." He scanned the kriegies. A lone figure rose from beneath a tree and faced him. Bear, trying to get his attention. He nodded and motioned him forward.

The boys lowered their Mausers, and Schneider patted the

shoulder of the closest, then glared at David. "The trucks need to return for the remainder of the infirm. You will go with them. It might be necessary for you to liaise on my behalf."

"I can't, Herr Hauptmann. I've been injured. I took some shrapnel and have a fever."

Heinrich's nostrils flared. "You have managed to put everyone in danger with your killing spree, Lieutenant, and now you are unable to fulfill your duties!"

Nicole moved in front. "He needs medical attention, Heinrich. Food and water, as well."

The hauptmann spun. "You ate at my table and slept beneath my roof. You enjoyed my protection while planning your murderous attack." The words emerged in a hiss.

David leaned close and gripped the Luftwaffe tunic, Heinrich's back hiding him from the boys with Mausers. "I set up the attack, Herr Hauptmann. She came here only to ensure a bloodless release of prisoners and personnel. Including you."

Schneider released his breath. "Then you are culpable for the deaths of those men, Lieutenant."

He released the lapel. "That's correct. Those planes were lengthening the war, helping the aggressors to maintain the illusion that they could continue to kill with impunity."

Bear edged beside him. "You're sweatin', Dremmer. What's wrong?"

"Took some shrapnel in my leg, Bear. Would have bled out if Nicole hadn't removed it."

Heinrich moved back, straightened his tunic, and released a flurry of German. The boy in front hurried to the truck. "The soldats will begin loading the infirm onto the train so that the trucks may return to the stammlager. These boys will then accompany us to Kassel. The medics will come with those still in the lazarette."

David nodded. "Thank you, Herr Hauptmann."

Schneider motioned to an obergefreiter and spat a directive, then turned to David. "He will take my car. You and Miss Serat will go with him. You will receive what medical attention they have to offer. I have ordered that water be left in the car for you."

***

David eased into the rear seat, pain spreading to his neck and shoulders.

Nicole placed a hand on his forehead. "You need help."

"The wound's infected. I just hope there are still enough meds to treat me."

She asked the driver something in German and received a sharp retort. The obergefreiter waited for a moment, his lip jutting outward. *"Um unser leben zu retten?"*

David rested his head on the seat. "Wha'd he say?"

She lowered her voice and watched the mirror. "I asked if he spoke English and told him we were here to help. He fears that surrendering is a betrayal of the Führer and deems the saving of his life of no concern. In truth, I wanted to know if he would understand what I must tell you."

He drew a hard breath. "Whatever it is, you'd best say it quick."

***

Sunlight riveted the window with brilliant blasts, dimmed to a halcyon green, and exploded again in vivid white. David dragged a hand over his face.

"We are nearing the turnoff, David. The obergefreiter says there are two medics still at the prison. They will help. Please hold on."

The docs. He struggled to remember their names, was blanketed in a miasma too dense for breath. The wave passed with a chill. "I'm really sick."

"I know, my love."

"You have to make it back." He waited for breath. "Leave me in uniform. If the Ivans come—" He had no breath, wanted to reassure her they would care for him.

"I will not leave you."

"Take my Bible. It's beneath my palliasse."

She caressed his forehead. I will find your Bible, but I will not leave without you."

***

"We keep sodium hypochlorite and boric acid made up. Mix it every morning. I'll debride the wound and follow that with a sulfa packet. That should keep him alive till we reach the hospital."

The words emerged from David's dream. "I'll make it."

Her hand was on his cheek. "Corporal Taylor agrees that your wound is infected, David." Nicole paused. "The guards are loading the lorry but will wait for us."

Light exploded at the back of his skull. "Got water, Doc?"

"All you want, Lieutenant."

* * *

Nicole watched him slip into darkness and felt an odd relief. He was out of pain, and the burdens ahead were beyond his knowing.

"You and the lieutenant took the airbase out?" Doc spoke above the whine of the truck.

She glanced at the thin gefreiter perched before the open flap, grabbed the tarp brace, and leaned in. "Corporal, I appreciate what you're doing for Lieutenant Dremmer, but we are still in the custody of Germans. Much could happen before our rendezvous with General McBride. Please don't ask for information that would compromise us before we reach Kassel."

Taylor edged forward, his voice like gravel. "We all knew the lieutenant was working with the Resistance, ma'am. I mean, we didn't doubt he was all in for the war effort, but I can see he had other interests." The medic scaled her length. "Something closer to his heart, I guess."

She glared and leaned away. "I have covered much of the continent, Corporal, and have been in Germany only three weeks. The lieutenant's efforts have been to save you, not me."

He smiled. "No disrespect intended, ma'am. I don't blame the man one bit." He leered and turned away. "You may as well read to him. Seemed to quiet him."

She pushed for redirection, thought it unwise to obey too quickly. "He called you 'doc.' Were you a medical student before the war?"

"No ma'am, I was studying economics." He shrugged. "They call all us medics 'doc.'"

"But you have seen many injuries. Wounds like Lieutenant Dremmer's, perhaps?"

The corporal tilted his head. "Enough. If you're asking, he'll likely make it. Next seventy-two hours will tell. He's not gangrenous, at least not yet. Likely more fragments down deep, but no bleeding, so they'll probably clean the wound again, give him penicillin if they have it, and leave the shrapnel. It likely won't do as much damage as digging it out."

The words drew a tightness around her breast. "Are you saying it would have been better had I not removed the shrapnel?"

"Not if it was making him bleed. You had to see to that."

She released a breath. "Thank you, Corporal."

Chapter LXVI

Under the canvas firmament, a frigid curse settled in David's bones. Then the voice began.

> *In the beginning, Chaos reigned in unrelenting madness above a desert sea, and God drew the heavens over the earth, hovered across the face of the deep, and dispersed the gloom with a winded Word. And within the Word was Idea, pure and holy and scalding white.*
>
> *And the void was filled with pain as waters gathered above and all beneath clawed for light. So, God divided the waters from dry ground, blessed them both and besought the Earth to offer grass and fruit and herbs. He rooted life in the sea, divided dark from light, and day from night; He saw that it was good and bent low in a violent embrace like wind on the hills, cradling all He'd made.*
>
> *David drew in the exultation, knew with certainty that life would go on, that all he'd known was but a breath, and that his days were without end. Brilliance sorted what was given from what was withheld, the thousands of tomorrows, and the sweetness of the voice that whispered him from one world to the next. The loss was anguish, but only until parting ended.*
>
> *He wasn't of the darkness any longer and hungered for the light. Regret had been swallowed in forgiveness as surely as death had been in victory. And neither Delores nor her child, the woman, the boy, or the old man sinking beneath the window— not even Swanson was his burden. The truth of it brought the sweetest peace, the yielding of his love to One greater and more certain than morning.*
>
> *But with the Voice, he paused...*

* * *

Nicole placed David's Bible on the planks and squinted tears into the bright shafts burning through the cattle car. Something had happened in the transfer to the train, and she knew it. "I thought we'd lost him, Doc." She dabbed her eyes. "How much longer?"

The corporal smirked. "Don't know how far Kassel is, but we're not moving fast. Nazis could be anywhere." He lifted his chin. "Maybe you ought to pray for the rest of us a while."

Bear placed a hand on her shoulder. "Just keep reading. You're reachin' him."

She glanced up, saw Bear glaring at Doc, and picked up David's Bible. "Which book does he most often read? I opened to Genesis, but—"

"You're doin' all right. There's something there he needs."

The words gripped her heart. "I thought he'd died, Bear."

"He can't die no more than you or me. I don't know if he'll be with us, but I know he loves you, and that won't end. And I suspect if he has a choice, he'll stay."

She struggled to hold the tremor from her breath. "I told him we couldn't be together. I took away his reason to stay."

"You were doing what you had to. God will show him what he needs to see."

She picked up the Bible and opened it.

* * *

Words fell like rain on his parched soul. He was both dust and spirit, just as she, both fashioned by Perfection. And she, not molded from his rib but from his heart, had returned so that, at last, she would be bone of his bone and flesh of his flesh.

Would she? Would she? Would she? The rhythm rose from a metallic core, serpentine and hissing, venom dripping along two rails, taking purity from nakedness, crafting lies from fruit, luscious and alluring, and in reprise, pushing toward an enmity that could not die until it hissed its last and recoiled beneath the Grinding Heel, a serpent's squeal of coal-hot iron, its fangs unhinged in the death of death.

* * *

The door screeched open. Nicole stood, let her hand remain on David's, was reassured by the warmth beneath the blanket. She glanced at the descending sun, turned back to the corpsman, and offered a silent plea.

Doc nodded. "I picked out a few boys in decent shape. They've had two days of full rations. They'll make it, trade off carrying the litter and get the lieutenant to the 80th. You know where McBride is, right?"

"I know only that US troops are headquartered on the west side of the city, Corporal." Her words were tremulous. "Perhaps Herr Hauptmann knows."

The corporal raised his face. "The side we're approaching from?"

She nodded, and he grinned.

Bear put a hand on her shoulder. "We'll stay with Dremmer."

Heinrich appeared at the door, his face flushed. He mumbled something to the two gefreiters and looked up. "Sergeant Billington, you will follow me as will Miss Serat. My men will carry the lieutenant. We'll remain at the front of the group. Be sure Lieutenant Dremmer's flight jacket is visible. Yours as well, Sergeant."

Nicole tensed and looked at Bear. He winked. "It'll be fine. They're in better shape than our boys. They'll get him off the mountain quicker."

"And Élodie and Elfriede?"

"They'll likely stay with the guards from their car till they surrender their rifles."

She edged across the rocks, her legs quivering, the litter bearers descending ahead.

General Hodges knew of her mission, but General McBride did not, and the brass would want her story verified. Without a statement from David, she couldn't prove any connection to MI6 or the airstrike. Bear would vouch for her, of course, though he was also unknown to the Resistance. But she still held her ace.

Her boots slipped, and she skidded across a lichen-covered rock slick from rain. She felt a hand grasp her arm, found a foothold, and eased toward an alluvial wash where gefreiters turned to stare. The ground leveled, and she regained her place behind the litter, opened David's Bible, and read.

* * *

Adam called her Eve, the life birthed in his heart, his children's flesh, the sharer of his dreams, and that before his being sent to work the dust, to sate Earth's lust for death, to battle hell to stay alive. He'd been driven from the presence of Perfection, consumed by terror, and thrown against the gates of Sheol. Yet he rose, stood at the edge, and stared at flaming swords unsheathed before the Tree, its fruit unblemished by his labor, its promise sure. He had only to surrender the fight, to release his hold and be free.

* * *

Lines of machines converged at the edge of the trees, lorries and half-tracks, tanks and troop carriers, men covered in grease, cigarettes suspended from their lips like hangers on a clothesline. Nicole stepped onto gravel, saw Heinrich grow rigid to her left. She let the Bible hang at her side and looked above David's tattered jacket.

A lieutenant approached, a string of men with rifles, following on either side of the road. The officer raised his hand and brought the column to a halt. "What the flaming—"

Heinrich's chin jutted. "I am Luftwaffe Hauptmann Heinrich Schneider, Acting Commandant of Special Stammlager 457. I wish to surrender to your commanding officer. We are without supplies. I request medical attention for the prisoners needing it and provisions for all others."

The lieutenant scanned the kriegies still spilling from the woods, some with hands raised in a silent cheer, others with open mouths. "Sonuva—" He turned to the man on his right. "You ever see anything like this, Sergeant?"

"Not in this lifetime, sir."

"Get a message to Major Marsh. Tell him what we've run into, and ask—"

"Beg your pardon, sir. I'm Sergeant—" Bear lowered his voice. "I'm Sergeant Amos Billington, Acting Man of Confidence. Our MOC is Lieutenant Dremmer, here, but he's hurt bad. There's others and some is shell shocked. They need ambulances, sir."

The lieutenant looked at David. "What's the matter with him, Sergeant?"

"He took shrapnel in his leg takin' out a Luftwaffe airbase. Has an infected wound."

The lieutenant scratched his forehead. "The one near Waldheim? He did that by himself?"

"No sir, this woman helped him. She's with MI6. She guided the bomber in."

"No, I—"

The lieutenant spun toward his sergeant. "Radio in a request for ambulances and troop carriers. Get these boys some help. And separate the ones that need to go to the hospital." He looked back. "You need help, Sergeant?"

"No sir, but the men could all use a hot shower and a bed. A little food, maybe."

Nicole shook her head. "If it's possible, I would like to stay with Lieutenant Dremmer."

Bear stepped close. "Until the lieutenant can tell you hisself, we'd like to ask for special care for Hauptmann Schneider, sir. He's done all he could to keep us alive. Put hisself on the line for us. You can ask the other men. We want him treated right, sir."

Chapter LXVII

Nicole drew trembling hands across her pants. After all they'd been through, the major's insinuations seemed especially unjust. She stiffened and looked him in the eye. "Since you're unable to reach General Hodges, I'm certain Colonel Watts at the 25th General Hospital in Liège will vouch for me, Major Marsh. I was in his employ, and he's familiar with my ties to MI6."

The major grinned around a sodden cigar. "Bet there's officers all over the continent that would vouch for you, honey. It'd be hard saying no to a face like yours."

The lieutenant stepped forward. "Sir, reports from prisoners confirm that Miss Serat was instrumental in taking out the airbase. She was the one that contacted the British."

She stiffened. "That's not entirely accurate."

Marsh's jowls shook. "Oh, I'll bet it is. I'll bet you've made a lot of contacts with the British. And the French. And probably the Germans."

It was time to play her ace. "If you are able, I believe a phone call might end your misapprehensions, Major. Can your commanding officer patch a call through to London?"

Marsh leaned over his desk. "This is my post, Missy— closest you can get to General McBride. What's the number?"

She held her breath, hoped the hour wouldn't preclude a response. "Whitehall zero-zero-one-three, Major. Mr. Thompson will arrange a return call. Just mention my name."

Marsh sank back, the sneer draining from his face. "Whitehall? You sure about that?"

"Quite sure."

He straightened. "Then we'll wait till morning. General McBride might want to be brought in on it." He paused. "He appreciates me keeping him apprised of these things."

This man was wasting her time. "I see. Are you at least authorized to arrange transportation for me to the hospital where they took Lieutenant Dremmer?"

The major's jowls reddened, and he turned to a corporal. "Call my driver and have him take her by the mess on the way. Don't want the Brits hearing we mistreated her."

She stood. "Thank you for your kindness, Major."

"I want you here in the morning, Miss Serat. That understood?"

* * *

Nicole sat in the hallway outside David's room, the fried eggs and bacon roiling in her stomach. The staff had been cleaning when the driver delivered her to the cafeteria, but they gathered bacon and eggs and served them, swimming in butter, of course. An American staple, it seemed. But she would grow accustomed to it.

And where had that thought come from? It was odd, her returning there unbidden. She had no need to adapt to American ways. David would soon be placed on a train bound for the coast where he would board some ship to the States. And she would stay.

Soft soles whispered across granite. "Are you with Lieutenant Dremmer, Miss?"

She looked up. "Yes, how is he?"

The doctor stood beneath a knitted cotton cap, his face mask untied at the top. "It's a little early, but it's likely he'll recover quickly. We debrided the wound, found two fragments that might have created problems, more that would have caused additional damage to extract." He paused. "The sergeant said Lieutenant Dremmer had been unconscious for hours. That's not something I would have expected. He's septic, of course, but his temperature and the wound site wouldn't indicate that it's critical. So, what happened?"

The fear of offering too much won out. "There was an explosion."

The surgeon lowered his chin. "The two of you guided an air strike, as I understand. But how was he injured?"

"A hanger containing planes was left intact after the bombing. Lieutenant Dremmer found a fuel lorry and drove toward the hanger. He jumped before smashing into the building." Her breath hitched. "He was hit by shrapnel as he ran away."

"Did he lose much blood?"

"Yes, it seemed a great deal to me. There was a puddle in the seat of the car he commandeered. He lost consciousness while removing metal from his leg."

"There was a larger fragment, then. That explains the wound. You cauterized the area?"

Her heart sank. "Two veins only. Did I do something to cause this?"

"If the bleeding was heavy, you likely saved his life. We didn't understand why the wound was cauterized, or why he was unconscious. I assumed a fragment entered hot, though that wouldn't explain his blood pressure or the size of the wound." He smiled. "The blood loss is likely responsible for his failure to regain consciousness. He's on IVs and penicillin. We'll increase the flow rate and rouse him in the morning if he doesn't come around on his own."

She drank the disinfected air. "Thank you, Doctor."

"You're welcome to stay, of course."

"Might I stay near Lieutenant Dremmer?"

He nodded, smiled. "I'll have a cot set up in his room."

* * *

Her voice had ceased. An ocean of days thimbled into a dreamless dark, and David woke not to brilliance but to the cotton-lint dryness of a November frost. The Eve of his belonging, the seed of promise, had withdrawn the width of an ocean from his numbing hands. He struggled to move, found a blanket, warm and comfortable, and slid his hands beneath it. The absence of her voice overwhelmed him with emptiness, and he retreated into unknowing.

* * *

The dry rustling of muslin scraped the edges of her sleep. Nicole pushed against her fatigue, rose, went to David's bed, and reached for his hands. Both were covered by heavy wool. Had he awakened enough to push them beneath the blanket? She thrilled at the possibility, wanted to shake him awake, but knew he needed rest. Tears reached her cheeks, and she returned to the cot, lay back and thanked the God who knew no darkness for the approaching light. In a few hours, she would see his smile and hear his voice.

* * *

A grip encircled her shoulder and took her from her dream. Nicole drew hard for air, pushed the blanket aside, and blinked.

The overgrown boy who had driven her to the hospital stood above her. "Sorry ma'am, but Major Marsh wants you in his office." He paused. "He wants you now, ma'am."

She waited for her heart to settle. "What time is it, Corporal?"

"Oh six twenty, ma'am. Be light soon. The major likes his people on the job early."

"I don't fit that description, Corporal. I'll require time in the water closet. Where is it?"

"Bathroom is down the hall. I'll wait in the jeep, ma'am."

The stern-faced nurse stared as the corporal passed, then waved her close. "We have packets for the boys—washcloths, toothbrushes, soap. And I have a hairbrush. Would that help?"

Nicole smiled. "It would, thank you."

The woman reached into a cabinet and presented her with a small, towel-wrapped bundle. "Don't let the major frighten you. He interrogates everyone he can, especially those from the front. He's not seen action and seems to want to humble those who have."

Fire rose to her throat. "There are places he could be sent to rectify that."

"I suppose, but it won't happen. He's General McBride's brother-in-law, and the general's wife insists that he be looked after. That's how he ended up here." The nurse released her breath. "At least, that's the scuttlebutt."

Nicole weighed the possibility of falling out of McBride's good graces and smiled. "Will you watch Lieutenant Dremmer until I return?"

"I'd be happy to."

"And please tell him—" She checked the impulse to trust too quickly.

Doherty softened. "If he wakes, I'll tell him you were with him every minute."

"Thank you, nurse."

"It's Lieutenant, Miss Serat, and you're welcome."

* * *

The damp air did little to dry Nicole's frizzing hair, though the brush helped. Brakes squealed outside the white stone building. The Nazi banners had been pulled down, and a sign reading "US Army Northern Area Command" flapped loosely above the shaded entrance.

The corporal turned in his seat. "The major's upset. He wanted you in his office when he got here at oh six hundred, ma'am."

"Is there a reason he didn't tell me that?"

The boy flinched. "Didn't tell me, either, ma'am, but he's fuming. Guess you were supposed to know. Or maybe I was."

"I see." She slid from the little car and walked quickly to the front door.

A slight-framed boy pushed against the heavy door. "The major is waiting for you in his office, Miss Serat."

"Thank you, Corporal." She marched to the door and pushed, annoyed that the clasp in her stomach was likely what the major wanted her to feel.

"I've been waiting, Miss Serat."

"So, I've been told. Had you mentioned the time, I would have been here."

He lifted his upper lip above his cigar. "I said 'morning.'"

She raised her chin. "That's generally believed to occur between midnight and noon, Major. Has the general's office returned your call?"

"We've not placed it yet." He glanced at the clock. "We'll patch it through in a bit."

Bile rose in her throat. It was still too early. She turned, her gaze settling on his coffee mug. The major had everyone jumping with—

"You're wanting coffee, too?"

She forced a smile. "I'll take mine with cream and sugar, please."

Marsh looked at the corporal, his cheeks reddening. "Get her coffee, Mayfield."

* * *

Nicole paced, wondered how many jackboots had scuffed these marble floors, and if Marsh might have been a better fit with the previous tenants. But there would be justice.

That word again. She stared at the major's door. It was almost noon, and the general hadn't called back. Meanwhile, David lay helpless, and she had no idea whether he was conscious or if his condition might have changed.

The major's door crept open, his aide standing with his back to her, nodding into smoke. The corporal spun around. "The major wants you, Miss Serat. Now, please."

She stepped to the door, saw Marsh with a phone to his ear, his cheeks fluttering. He pivoted. "She's here now, Horace—uh, General." More quick nods. "Yes sir." He extended the phone and bent toward her in something resembling a bow.

She took the receiver. "Yes, General?"

"Miss Serat, I understand we are in your debt."

"It really wasn't me, sir."

"You took part in a dangerous mission, and you succeeded. Furthermore, I understand you have a history of taking on difficult assignments. I spoke with your boss."

If the major suggested— "My boss, sir?"

"We called the number you provided. The prime minister had been informed you were deceased. He was quite relieved to learn that wasn't true and has promised to call when he can."

"I'm very much alive, sir, though Lieutenant Dremmer— I had to leave him at the 115th."

"So, I understand. We wish him well. I'll hang up now in order for the line to remain open. Again, our sincere thanks for the lives you saved, Miss Serat."

"Thank you, sir." She handed the receiver to the major, who avoided her glower. "If you'll excuse me, Major, I'd like to freshen up before the PM calls."

The major's cheeks shook. "Make it quick."

* * *

Nicole leaned against the wall, her knees threatening to cede.

The phone rang.

"Major Wallace Marsh, at your service." There was a long silence. The red face grew redder, and the fleshy tremble resumed. "She is here, your excel... uh—" He extended the phone and stepped to the side, chinning toward his chair.

She took the receiver but remained standing. "Mr. Prime Minister?"

"Miss Serat!" Silence followed. "On our last meeting, I witnessed a tearful response to a rather somber melody. Can you tell me where we were and the title of the song?"

"We were in Blenheim Palace, sir, and the song was 'I'll Never Smile Again.'" She glanced across the room, saw Marsh's chin lower.

"I regret the discourtesy of the question, but I am certain you appreciate its necessity."

"I understand completely, sir."

"I am told that your lieutenant has been injured. I trust the prognosis is favorable."

She caught her breath. "He's not regained consciousness, sir, but I'm praying."

"I can divine no soul on earth whose prayers I would so covet as yours. Your surviving is ample persuasion that you and the Almighty are on favorable terms." He paused. "Regrettably, I must ask that you leave your lieutenant yet again. It is a matter of justice. Men who make agreements with those set on the destruction of this cherished island must be dealt with." The grumble quieted. "Your testimony is essential in establishing their complicity with the enemy."

She searched the air and felt a grip in her stomach. "When do you want me there, sir?"

"A plane shall arrive around sixteen hundred hours. I am assuming the major can get you to the airfield."

The earth shook beneath her feet. It couldn't end this way. "Might I ask that you make that request directly, sir? The major has concluded that I'm of less than reputable character."

The line went quiet. "Then I shall inform him otherwise. I am requesting an extraordinary sacrifice of you, but I hope to provide recompense."

She bit her lip. "No recompense is needed, sir. Justice is its own reward."

"I shall eagerly await your arrival, Miss Serat. I cannot express my delight at knowing I'll see you soon and in proper health."

"Thank you, sir. I look forward to seeing you, as well."

She handed the phone to Marsh, caught his rattled stare, and stepped to the door.

* * *

Nicole ran her hand over David's arm, both hoping and fearing he might wake. What would she say if he did? Certainly, not all she wanted. She touched her lips to his.

"Ahem."

She turned to see Doherty in the doorway.

"I wanted you to know that Lieutenant Dremmer was thrashing about earlier and appeared uncomfortable. We medicated him. It's unlikely he'll awaken for a while."

Her eyes turned liquid. "I'm afraid I must leave. It's urgent. Will you tell him—"

"I'll give him your love." The lieutenant closed the door.

Nicole turned back, traced the lines of David's face. "You can live without me, my love, however much you wish not to. And I can live without you, though, at this moment, I would surrender all other hopes not to have to. Perhaps we love each other too much to fulfill what we've been given to do. I'm letting you go only to gain what is essential. For both of us."

Something stirred behind her, and she turned to Major Marsh's driver who shifted from foot to foot. "The plane is waiting, ma'am."

Chapter LXVIII

David pulled himself up in bed and peeked around the half-open door. Green fixtures coned brilliance over the nurses' station, spotting a nicotine-stained ceiling above and Lieutenant Doherty below, her pen lifting the heavy fold under her chin as she sat in a ponderous pose. He lay back, the heaviness of waking without Nicole pressing against his heart.

The door squeaked wider, and Bear blocked his view. "You looked better when you was unconscious, Dremmer."

He lay back and offered a grin. "Where've you been?"

"Trying to keep you out of trouble. Intelligence officer's lookin' to talk to you. Name of Marsh. He wants to know the people connected to the groups you worked with."

He drew a shallow breath. "Germans, too?"

"I 'spect so."

"Good. I thought I'd have to find someone. I told Nicole about Vogt when we were running from the Wehrmacht. She knows most of the others, but I have no idea what she's having to deal with there. Seems unlikely she'll have a chance to pass that on."

Bear twisted his neck. "You might make a list for her in case she don't make it back in time. I don't know 'bout this Marsh."

He winced at the thought of not seeing her again. "And what about Schneider?"

Bear shrugged. "He's in the brig, but the boys is tellin' the officers he helped us escape."

He stared at the floor. "I can't believe she's gone, Bear."

"She'll come back if she can. Told me so. Churchill called her. *Churchill,* Dremmer. Sounds like he's takin' care of the ones that tried to have her killed."

His heart lifted. "At least that part's turning out the way it should."

***

The prime minister cleared his throat. "I have news, Miss Serat. I anticipated your departure for the States and arranged proceedings to spare you any further delay. You will be deposed by your colleagues' barrister and myself. Rest assured, I won't be daunting, and I shall do my best to manage Baldwin's comportment." His cheeks lifted. "Should our efforts prove successful, these men will face prosecution."

The prime minister was supplying her with a happy ending to part of this nightmare, at least, though she wished none of it depended on her. She scanned the columns shimmering in the Great Hall. "I'm afraid my going to America is impossible, sir. There are obstacles." She found her breath. "That is, there are reasons the lieutenant and I cannot be together."

The prime minister's frown further compressed his face. "I promised compensation for taking you from your lieutenant's side, did I not?"

She nodded. "None is necessary, sir."

He softened. "My staff is quite adept at unearthing information. In their search, they discovered that mail bound for the prison in Waldheim was routed through Aachen. As our troops have held that region of hell for months, the American Red Cross had already been granted possession of all mail belonging to American prisoners of war. However, my associates were most persuasive in unburdening these noble souls of all packets addressed to Lieutenant Dremmer." The scarce chin lifted. "I should like to think my plea influenced them. I cannot sanction our opening of this gallant lad's posts. You, however, are under no such constraint." He drew on a cold cigar. "An as-yet-unscheduled flight will deliver his mail in a diplomatic pouch, whereupon you shall be given an envelope sent from a Texas solicitor named Archer. It will have been stamped in Amarillo, Texas, and the solicitor's office informed my own that it will contain a document demanding a marital annulment issued on behalf of Delores Faye Dremmer. Should the lieutenant be willing to sign it, he shall be forever free of any legal obligations to Mrs. Dremmer. His only loss will be the pay he would have received for his period of service which has been disbursed to her. However, I believe I can warrant reimbursement of an amount surpassing his loss since the document was executed over a year ago while he was engaged in protecting the Crown. That is in addition to your own pay, meager as it is." He smiled. "I trust you find this acceptable."

She fought for air, her lungs threatening to explode as she moved toward him, reached around his soft shoulders, and squeezed. He stood without returning her embrace, and she stepped back. "Forgive me, sir. That was inappropriate."

"Was it, indeed? Had I known, I assure you I would not have found it so delightful." He turned to the ancient doors. "Are you ready for Mr. Baldwin, Miss Serat?"

She smothered her bliss. "Thank you for what you've done, sir. David might well have shipped out without me."

"Rubbish! Save those tears for the stenographer. The man has been utterly brutal in capturing my blunders. Perhaps you might reach his heart."

* * *

David rolled his leg, felt the familiar stabbing pain, and recoiled at the figure in the door.

"I need you to be quiet, Dremmer. Don't say a word. I'll try to keep the major in the hall, but if I fail, pretend to be unconscious. You understand?'

"I'll talk to him, Lieutenant. He can't—"

"I'm trying to help you, Dremmer. All you need to do is close your eyes and not move." Doherty turned and let the door drift closed, her service pumps scudding marble.

"I'm here to see Lieutenant Dremmer, Nurse. Which room is he in?" The voice boomed.

"It's Lieutenant, Major."

"I'm told the man is conscious, and I have questions."

David lay still. Why was this man a threat?

"My job is to care for my patients, Major, and he isn't up to an interrogation."

Interrogation?

"I'm not asking for your permission, Nurse. Which room is he in?"

A breathless silence preceded heavy heels pounding beyond his closed door. It swung wide.

"I'm Major Marsh, Lieutenant. I need you to wake up. I have questions."

He reached for the headboard. "Major, I'm really not feeling well, sir."

"I need to know who you've been working for. I'm reasonably sure it's the Gestapo. It will be easier if you admit it. You don't want me to do this the hard way."

Had the man actually— "What? I—we just took out a Luftwaffe airbase. Why on earth would you think I was working for the Krauts?"

"It's Major, Second Lieutenant. You'll address me as 'sir.'"

He steadied his breath. "Why would you accuse me of working with the Krauts, sir?"

The major dammed the stream of light flowing through the half-closed door, his feet wide, and his hands lost beneath a roll of flesh. "Some say you turned a truckload of these Nazis, taught them the Star-Spangled Banner, and made Truman supporters out of them."

"I have no idea what you're talking about, sir. I didn't turn anyone."

The tip of the major's cigar turned scarlet. "This sergeant of yours—Billings, is it? He says you had Krauts eating out of your hand. Now I find out that Miss Serat traveled with an old German and the commandant's wife. That didn't arouse your suspicions?"

He gathered his thoughts. "Both were operatives in the Resistance, sir."

The door opened wide, brightening the bloated face before Bear stepped from behind. "Major Marsh, I think you misunderstood me, sir. I didn't mean—"

"I was making the lieutenant aware of inconsistencies in his story, Sergeant. Didn't you tell me that Lieutenant Dremmer worked with Schneider and some other Krauts?"

"Yes sir, but what I was sayin' was that Lieutenant Dremmer worked with the Resistance and that Schneider took as good o' care of us as he could. He even put hisself under suspicion doin' it. And he spent his own money feedin' us, sir. A few other Germans—"

"That's enough! I don't intend to give you boys a chance to correct your stories."

David pulled at the bedpost. "We aren't the enemy, sir."

Marsh turned. "Looks that way to me, Lieutenant."

He pulled at his throbbing leg. "I confess, sir, that your questions strike me—"

Bear cleared his throat. "Maybe you ought to tell the major about the names you give Nicole so MI6 would protect them." He swallowed. "The Germans, I mean."

David nodded. "The ones who worked with the Resistance? I'm sure she's given those names to Churchill already, Sergeant."

Marsh bit on his cigar. "You've given this information to the Tommies? Why would you do that, Lieutenant? That's an act of disloyalty!"

"On the contrary, sir, the Brits directed the Resistance."

The major's face reddened, the dewlap beneath his chin quivering. "So you know, I can get you shipped home whenever I want. Your little missy would be disappointed, I guess, but there you go."

Chapter LXIX

Doherty pushed David's wheelchair onto the elevator, the squeak of rubber tires echoing down the hall. She pulled the scissor gate, and they clattered skyward, reached the top, and rolled onto an observation deck. Beyond crumbling bricks and collapsing tile, mountain crests bristled with new growth above a wide, lush valley.

David rolled around. "Thanks for this, Lieutenant."

"I hope it makes you feel better, Dremmer. I know it's hard without Miss Serat. She was with you every minute she could be." Her voice faded. "She loves you, you know."

He nodded. "And I love her. More than I can say."

She stepped in front. "It would have been better for you to have been unconscious, but I never say, 'I told you so.' It's not a good policy."

He laughed. "Any idea why Marsh is so intent on taking us down?"

"He's assumed this role of intelligence officer. Missed out on seeing action. He's General McBride's brother-in-law and was given this post, so what can we do?"

"But what does he have to gain by it?"

She shrugged. "The man wants to be a hero. Proving you a war criminal and having you hanged might be his last chance."

"So you know, I'm not ready to be hanged just to add credits to his record."

The elevator door opened, and Bear stepped between long shadows.

She winked. "The sergeant's here. Discuss it with him. I'm going back to the floor."

His friend stepped toward them, stopped, and readied himself to salute.

"Sergeant." Doherty hustled past.

"Lieutenant." Bear grinned and pulled a Bible from his rucksack.

David winced. "You here to preach or take up an offering?"

"Nicole asked me to give it to ya', but if you're feelin' generous…"

His heart shrank at the finality hidden in her request.

Bear looked away. "Dremmer, you ever read about Gideon?"

"It's been a while." A serrated breeze filleted his cheek and whistled through the spokes of his wheelchair. "I assume there's a reason you asked."

"You remind me of him is all."

"I didn't remember the mighty man being that handsome."

"Yeah, well, memory may not be your only problem." Bear glanced over his head. "God asked a lot of him, and all he could think was that he wasn't qualified. 'My clan is the weakest, and I'm the least of 'em.' You remember that?"

He smiled. "Sure, but he got it done. Not by himself, of course. Is that the point?"

"No, my point was it was God's askin' that qualified him. Nothin' else. You were given things to do nobody wanted, and you complained the whole time that you was too weak. But your weakness made you dependent on God, and that made you strong."

He caught the scent of it. "I'm too weak for this, too, Bear."

"But God can give ya grace to do it. I don't know how, but he'll come through.'"

David forced himself to meet Bear's gaze.

The sergeant turned, looked beyond what either of them could see. "There's somethin' I ain't told you. Year and a half before Irene was born, Babs and I lost a baby. Her name was Catherine. She lived eleven weeks."

The words compressed his chest. "Why didn't you tell me?"

"Didn't ever seem like the right time." Bear shrugged. "It's made it harder not being there for Irene." A tremor reached the fresh-shaved chin. "We loved that baby, Dremmer. Losin' her was more than either of us could stand. But you know what I remember most about it?"

He shook his head, watched Bear's breath begin to ease.

"The Lord's tenderness." A tear slid down a flushed cheek. "It's what I pray for you. There's a comfort that can't be had no other way. When your hurt's the worst, it's bigger."

He nodded. "On the train here, something happened. I can't explain it, but I heard Nicole's voice as she read. I breathed the words she read, and they became more than her words. I saw that sorrow had an end. If not for her, I would have gone on." He caught a breath. "I was given absolution for the lives I'd failed to save, all those lost or broken because of me, even before the war. Having that lifted brought such peace. And his presence—" The words wedged in his throat.

Bear leveled his gaze. "When you was in the well, you had peace. How long did it last?"

"A week. Maybe two. I knew God loved me, but I thought he would change things, and when he didn't—"

"I know that fight, Dremmer. When it starts, the peace fades." Bear stared into the waning light. "After all o' this, I feel like I'm losing Catherine again. When I get back home, she won't be there."

His chest ached. "I'm sorry, Bear. I wish I could help." He couldn't meet his friend's eyes. "But I don't want to believe that God takes the ones we love."

"He don't, but the losses are still real. Sometimes we bring 'em on ourselves, or others bring 'em, or they're brought up from the pit o' hell, but mostly they're just a part of livin' in a world that turned wrong at the start. Thing is, when we run after what we've lost more than we do him, we lose sight of his loving us, and that's the biggest loss of all."

* * *

Nicole watched for a moment before moving closer to the prime minister who sat in a plush chair, the spirit warmer beside him. He'd chosen the Green Writing Room for the morning's convocation, possibly for fear of being overheard in the Great Hall. The 1st Duke of Marlboro posed in black on his left while Thompson stood on his right. In yesterday's session, Baldwin had contested her every word, though the PM rebutted each attack. Still, she'd slept very little through the night.

Churchill's head pivoted. "Please join us, Miss Serat. Alice insists on plying me with biscuits." He lifted his cup against the green damask wool coverings. "Diluting my brandy is offensive enough, though as an Englishman, I dare not refuse her tea, but biscuits are too great an imposition, even for one who esteems convention. Please do enjoy them for me."

She caught the twinkle in his eye. "I'm not at all hungry, sir, but I would be delighted to sit with you."

"Well done. I'll not have to look at those drab oligarchs first thing."

She snickered. "You believe the barrister has communist leanings, then?"

"He would prefer 'socialist' as it seems more benign, but with an adequate sprinkling of references to the people's this or that, which are, in fact, things he hopes to embezzle from them. These men fancy being among those few determining the peoples' needs which is considerably less than what they would allocate for themselves." He placed his cup in a saucer. "Our socialist brethren are perhaps the least apt to associate with the workers they so stridently claim to represent. They deem their inferiors disposable and detest the royals whom they find common."

She saw the sadness and wished she could lift the pain as he had lifted her fright during yesterday's depositions. "I'm sure most Britons believe as you do, sir."

He sat without stirring. "After such suffering, I fear too many have grown content with exchanging their liberties for an allowance that will keep them in corned beef and stout. They don't yet realize that once their liberties are gone, their allowances will unavoidably be depleted."

An awkward young man in a tight suit rushed from the hallway, an envelope tortured in his grip. "Beg pardon, sir, but this just arrived by courier. It's from Mr. Baldwin. He rang up asking for assurance that you received it and awaits your reply."

Mr. Churchill pulled a folded slip from the envelope, read it, and released a rush of air. "Thank you, William. I do not wish to respond."

"But he's on the tele, sir."

"By noon he shall, perhaps, have apprehended that I do not wish to defer to his ruse."

William dithered past the corner, his fingers clasping and reclasping the empty packet.

Nicole clenched her hands. "Forgive me, sir, but does this concern my deposition?"

"Quite. Mr. Baldwin has declared himself unwell." Churchill relit his cigar. "Did you, perchance, mention that you entertained hopes of going abroad soon?"

Her heart pounded. She had sensed Baldwin's keenness when she'd said it. "I told him I wished to return to Germany to see someone in hospital before he shipped out."

"Yes, well, Mr. Baldwin no doubt hopes to pressure you into

omitting parts of your testimony to avoid being further detained and is purposely delaying the proceedings."

"I'm sorry, sir. I never intended—"

"You incorrectly assumed you were no longer dealing with the enemy. Unfortunately, you will pay the highest price for your innocence, principally because you still have it." He went silent for seconds. "I shall do my utmost to return you to your lieutenant as soon as possible, but I must insist that you deliver every whit of evidence tucked within your cranium."

"I won't compromise the truth, sir."

He fixed her with his eyes. "I'm certain you won't, Miss Serat."

* * *

Noon had passed without a word. Not from Nicole, and not from Bear. David pushed himself into the hall, risked both Doherty's wrath and the major's accusations. "Lieutenant, are you busy?"

"Of course not, Dremmer. These are recipes I'm reading, not patients' charts."

He looked at the stack of clipboards. "Sorry, Lieutenant. I'll come back later."

"No, you won't! You'll stay in your room, and I'll drop by when I'm able."

He nodded. "All right."

She winked. "Go on, Dremmer, before I decide to forget that I like Miss Serat and run away with you myself."

He spun his chair. "It's Second Lieutenant, Lieutenant, so don't get fresh." He rolled toward his room, caught her grin as he closed his door, and struggled to pull himself onto his bed without contracting his quadriceps. He dragged the sheet over his legs, and felt the ache subside.

Billington stepped through the door, and David's heart lifted. "Glad you're here, Bear. I have something—"

"Wait!" Bear's thick hand rose. "Marsh is after Schneider. Wants him hung. Schneider admitted to being a party member, and Marsh figures that makes him a war criminal."

He pulled himself up. "And where is Heinrich?"

"In the brig they set up on the floor of the Henschel Building. I'm thinkin' Marsh won't do this without makin' a show of it. We got time."

"We can't take that chance, Bear. Can you get the men there?" He threw the sheet back and pulled his leg to the edge of the bed. "I want you there, too. The men trust you." He let himself into the chair, turned it around, pulled his gown lower on his legs, and rolled through the door Bear was holding open.

Doherty stood before him, her finger pointing. "Dremmer, I told you—"

"It's an emergency, Lieutenant. A man's life is at stake."

"Two men's lives are at stake, Dremmer, and one of them is yours!"

"The hauptmann who—"

"I heard. If you get a doctor to order it, I'll administer an enema on the man."

"Can you get me to the offices of the tank factory?"

She shook her head. "Not without your jacket. Let me see how many ambulances we have available. I can't allow you to take the last one."

* * *

David wheeled himself toward the crumbling entrance of the Henschel Building. Rock and concrete had been shoveled to make paths, and he chose the shortest.

"Sir?" The driver hurried toward him. "These signs are saying this entrance isn't safe. There's likely another entrance off the street. Let me push you around."

"Thank you, Corporal." He eased his grip on the wheels. "Do you read German?"

"No sir, but these signs run up this street a few blocks. Path of the bombs, I guess. Most of the buildings on this side are okay in back." The boy breathed hard. "Doherty said to take care of you. She'd skin me alive if you were to die, sir."

"I appreciate your concern, Corporal."

The boy moved around a concrete shard. "This building was used to manufacture small parts and was where the big wigs had their offices. It's used for hearings and high-ranking prisoners now. Your man must be important."

Men in uniform moved in and out of the second door, and officers' cars lined the street. "Everyone's important, Corporal. Except Major Marsh." He pointed. "Try that door."

The boy pushed him across concrete strewn with pebbles, the chair pounding him into exhaustion. He leaned back, lifted the weight from his leg, grew weak, and eased himself down. "Corporal, can you let me rest for a minute?"

"Sure, sir, just let me get you to the door first."

David struggled to hold himself up. They reached the door, and he lifted his chin. "Leave me here, Corporal. That's an order. Someone will come along."

The boy pivoted and hollered back. "You can have somebody give Doherty a call when you need a ride back. I'll give her your best, sir."

He drew a heavy breath. "Along with my remains."

* * *

David pried the door back, wheeled down the hall, and withered. He stopped, tried to read the hand-written numbers, wrapped his jacket around his hospital gown, and wished Doherty had insisted he wear trousers. Two rooms had been set up for conferences with long tables and empty chairs. It seemed likely those with closed doors were in use.

"May I be of assistance, Lieutenant?"

He wheeled around, stared into the black face of a first lieutenant, and noted a sword and pen on his collar. The name tag read Franklin. "I was just released from a stalag near Waldheim, sir. I'm told our acting commandant is here and has been charged with war crimes."

"Are you a patient somewhere, Lieutenant?"

"Yes, but this is urgent. The man has been unfairly charged, and Major Marsh is threatening to execute him."

The dark forehead tightened. "What's this hauptmann's name?"

"Heinrich Schneider, sir. He kept over two hundred of us from starving, and he cooperated with the Resistance in getting us here."

"Can you get signed statements to that effect?"

"A Sergeant Billington is on his way with as many prisoners as he can gather, sir."

"Follow me." Franklin pivoted.

He hesitated. "I can't, sir. I just had surgery. A little low on vinegar—and the rest."

A slight smile lifted the lieutenant's face. "All right, Butterbar. I'll push, but if I'm mistaken for an orderly, I'll see to it you're charged with indecent conduct."

He chuckled, liked the guy already.

Franklin slowed at an open door, then pushed him inside. "Wait here, Dremmer. Junior Leader Blake will entertain you while I get the hauptmann's file."

A dark-haired girl, looking all of fifteen, glanced up and giggled. His face warmed as he pulled his jacket lower on his gown.

* * *

David surveyed Franklin's office. The secretarial pool was nicer. Diplomas hung on either side of his desk, a typewriter perched beside it. Boxes of Court Martial Reports were stacked in the corner and a Judge Advocate's Manual lay open on the desk, but the tiny room hadn't a single file cabinet. "Nice office, sir."

Franklin looked up. "As nice as your stalag, Lieutenant?"

He nodded. "Really close, sir."

"I may not be the most revered man in the group, Lieutenant, but I assure you, I'm capable. More importantly, I'm all you've got. Might be best to overlook my deficiencies."

"I haven't seen any, sir. I just noticed you didn't have any open files."

Franklin's face contracted. "I'm a pariah here. You can guess why, but whether you intended to or not, you've now requested me as defense advocate for a Nazi, a man who sanctioned killing in the name of racial purity. You'd best not push your luck."

"I don't doubt you're qualified, sir, and they put you in a closet. That's wrong. But Hauptmann Schneider put his neck on the block to save the men who chose me to represent them. My job is to see he isn't lynched for it."

Franklin nodded. "I'll do what I can, Dremmer."

* * *

Lieutenant Colonel Tilley looked as if he were growing hams above his eyebrows. "This will be a new avenue of defense, Franklin. Different rules than you're accustomed to. I'm going to turn this over to an advocate more experienced in dealing with nuanced cases."

David rolled his chair between the colonel and the north wall of the Henschel Building. "Permission to speak, sir?"

"Go ahead, Lieutenant."

"I was urged to request Lieutenant Franklin, sir. I was told he's the best advocate here."

Tilley's face reddened. "Are you implying that MI6 keeps track of our personnel?"

His mouth went dry. He hadn't intended— "It's my understanding that MI6 communicates with OSS on issues of concern, sir, and Colonel Donovan supplies whatever information they need."

Tilley glared, his overgrown brow bright against the evening sun. "Very well, Dremmer. It's your pet Nazi." The colonel slapped the folder onto Franklin's open hand. "So you know, Lieutenant, this is a waste of your time."

"I just want justice, sir." Franklin saluted and David followed suit. The door closed behind Tilley, and the lieutenant pivoted, his mouth gaping wide. "Who at MI6 recommended me, Dremmer?"

"I never said MI6 recommended you, but the clerk you left me with thinks very highly of you, sir."

The lieutenant blinked. "And Colonel Donovan?"

He grinned. "MI6 provides him with information all the time, sir. I'm sure it's reciprocal."

Franklin leaned close. "Be advised, Dremmer, the colonel will likely cast the deciding vote on the Preliminary Investigating Official who will preside over your hauptmann's case. You'd best stay on his good side."

The advocate turned to the kriegies assembled in the parking lot. "Gentlemen, Hauptmann Schneider is safe for now. He will remain in custody until a determination is made regarding his case."

A restrained murmur rose.

"However, stenographers will take statements regarding the hauptmann's treatment of prisoners. It's not possible to depose all of you, so it might be best to select the twelve or fifteen most knowledgeable regarding his attempts to improve your conditions. Those of you aware of his dealings with the Resistance should be included. The remainder may sign a letter requesting leniency." Franklin looked at his watch. "I'll need a list of those being deposed by sixteen hundred hours tomorrow."

The men dispersed, most grumbling.

David looked up. "Why is this case a waste of your time, sir?"

Franklin stretched his neck. "The Allies have been planning to prosecute Nazis for months—the worst of them, anyway. They will be tried in international tribunals. If I were assigned a case and won, it would be a big feather in my cap. This won't be one of those cases."

"So, Tilley wants you to let Schneider hang, sir?"

"He just doesn't want to answer to McBride if a Nazi gets a pat on the back. I'll defend your hauptmann to the best of my ability, but I'll need help from the kriegies, and you're their MOC. Get word to them that they're expected to deliver the goods. Are we clear?"

"Yes sir."

Chapter LXX

Nicole ran her hand over the pistachio bed cover and stepped to the marble hearth. The fireplace bore no heat, though she was certain that, should she ask, a servant would light it. Still, the chill rose from her heart, and a warm fireplace wasn't apt to change that. She ran her fingers over a tapestry where lions and harts were drawn in claret tones. The pitiable creatures struggled fiercely against Olympian huntsmen but were clearly doomed. Not unlike herself.

She pushed the thought away, regretted allowing it to surface, had prayed for help and would release the ends to bigger hands. However desperate things might seem, she had to trust that they'd be dealt with.

She tugged the bed cover back, lay down, and pulled a pillow to her face. The prime minister had been negotiating with Ernest Bevin over labor issues and spending his evenings cajoling members of Parliament. He'd told her at breakfast that he'd asked the clerk to delay the barrister until he could resume. But since she was now without assistance, Baldwin was demanding that they restart immediately. If he persisted, it seemed unlikely that justice for a few traitors would deter the PM from prosecuting the war.

All this, and David was apt be ordered home before learning that Delores had filed for an annulment. Would he change his mind if their dream became a possibility? She hadn't been a part of his life before the war, the part he longed for now. And the newspapers predicted that it might take a year for war brides to be processed. Perhaps he would be unwilling to wait.

* * *

"You're weaker than you thought, aren't you, Dremmer?" Doherty stood with a clipboard, her pen supporting the flesh beneath her chin.

David straightened his sheets. "I'm grateful you don't find it good policy to tell your patients that you told them so."

She cackled. "Was it worth it?"

He hadn't heard her laugh. "I suppose, but now we have to keep Marsh from learning what we're up to."

"Which is?"

He rolled his leg. "Lieutenant Franklin, at the JAG office, has agreed to go to bat for Schneider."

Her eyes widened. "The colored advocate? And Tilley allowed him to take the case?"

"The colonel tried to nix it but allowed him to represent us when I requested him. Why?"

"Long story. Franklin is supposed to be a whiz kid, top of his class and all that, but Tilley won't turn him loose. Most think he's pushing the man out because he's colored."

He shook his head. "That fits with what I know of him."

"The colonel's a doozy." She waved her hand. "But go on with what you were saying."

"Bear picked fifteen kriegies from those who offered to make statements. Now he's with the intelligence committee explaining what happened these last few weeks. Schneider could have had us all shot and gotten away, but he chose to get us to safety."

"Decent of him." She shrugged. "That sergeant of yours is quite the asset."

"That he is. We're going into business together when we get home."

"What sort of business?"

"Cattle ranching. It's what I grew up doing. I'm hoping we can take advantage of a rebuilding boom in the next few years."

"Will Miss Serat be able to go right over, or will you have to wait?"

It hit him in the gut. "You didn't know? I assumed…" He drew a sterile breath. "I'm married. At least, officially."

Doherty's smile dissolved. "Does Miss Serat know this?"

"Of course. She—"

Doherty spun. "I can't believe she let you get away with it!"

He leaned forward. "Lieutenant Doherty?"

She stopped, her hand on the doorknob.

He sipped the chilled air. "Maybe you thought I deserved her. I don't. Knowing her has been a gift. I'd marry her in a second, but we can't, and that's my fault."

438

* * *

A throat cleared loudly and drew him from his sleep. David sat up, lost for a moment, then saw Lieutenant Franklin standing in the light of the doorway, a small bundle beneath his arm. "Morning, LT."

"Just barely, Butterbar. Sorry to wake you, but I talked with Hauptmann Schneider, and he denies any involvement with the Resistance. Says he'll face execution before testifying that he has." The advocate glanced toward the nurses' station. "If he persists, it may make his defense impossible."

His weariness was bone deep. "You want me to go with you, sir? Now?"

Franklin stepped close. "We need to get this prepared quickly."

"What time is it, sir?"

"Oh two hundred. Almost. Hope you got to bed early."

It had taken hours to get to sleep after his row with Doherty. "Yes sir." He hooked his left heel with his right foot, swung it from the bed, and descended onto his good leg.

Franklin extended a pair of rolled trousers and a shirt. "Thought you might prefer these."

"Thank you, sir."

"If you need help dressing, Lieutenant, I'll get a nurse."

Doherty was likely off duty, but— "I'm fine, thanks." He leaned against the bed, pulled a trouser leg over his left foot, and slid it up his thigh. "Sir, Schneider just wants to be a good German. Would it be possible for me to question him with a stenographer present?"

Franklin went silent for a moment. "If it's on record and this goes to trial, the prosecution will review it. You don't know the law. You're apt to make mistakes or coach him."

"But I know the man, sir, and I know what questions to ask."

The lieutenant lowered his head. "Then question him. I'll hide. I can't use what he refuses to tell me, but it'll give me a starting place for my questions."

He twisted his neck. "I don't know about hiding and listening, sir. He's expecting to be betrayed. Happens a lot in his circles. And he's smart."

Franklin's head raised. "So am I, Dremmer."

"Guess that makes me the odd man out, sir."

439

* * *

David stared down rows of workstations where lathes and presses had been unbolted from the floor. Bare bulbs lit blackened concrete, the shallow imprint of machinists' boots still embedded in old cutting oil. Cots straddled concrete pedestals, and men in gray lay beneath green Army blankets, arms shielding their eyes. Between stations, banks of steel bars were welded to anchored bolts where explosions of slag were recorded in black. At the end, a green tunic was draped over a prisoner's head, his socked feet protruding from beneath his blanket.

Franklin pointed. "Behold, the man."

David rolled toward the cell, caught a few flickering stares from prisoners, though most eyes were fixed on Franklin. "Herr Hauptmann, we need to speak with you." He gripped the bars. "I guess you've figured out the war isn't over for you, right?"

Heinrich pulled the tunic from his head, his face offering no hint of sleep. "So it would seem. Are you well, Lieutenant?"

"I'm better." He rolled back to allow the MP to open the door.

Heinrich rose, his eyes drifting over his comrades, some still feigning sleep. "This is a strange hour for an interrogation, First Lieutenant."

"We have lots of criminals to deal with, Herr Hauptmann. I've been assigned—" Franklin appeared to catch himself.

David picked up the cue. "Lieutenant Franklin will prosecute your case, Herr Hauptmann." He caught the judge advocate's smirk and wheeled toward the door.

* * *

Franklin turned from a new filing cabinet and looked at Schneider. "I need to go down the hall. Would you care for coffee?"

David wheeled his chair beside the hauptmann's. "Lieutenant Franklin is your advocate, not your prosecutor. We didn't want you to appear to be a collaborator to your friends."

Schneider sat like stone. "They are compatriots, not friends."

"Fair enough."

"You want me to say I colluded with the Resistance. Would I not then be a traitor?"

Franklin stepped in front and leaned against the arms of Heinrich's chair. "If you're still a Nazi, then you *are* a traitor. But if you're asking for a distinction between being a traitor and aiding the Resistance, it's significant. A good German would sacrifice to free his country. A Nazi would work to keep it in chains. Which will you choose, Herr Hauptmann?"

"I am—" The voice shrank. "I hope I am a good man, First Lieutenant."

"I hope you are, too, because Dremmer has asked me to defend you, and I don't want to waste my time if you're using me to help you die a quick death. Is that your plan, Captain?"

Heinrich met the dark stare. "I have little choice. If I claim to have aided the Resistance, my compatriots will have me killed. If I refuse to admit that I allowed your operatives some latitude, Major Marsh will hang me. Which would you choose, First Lieutenant?"

Franklin glanced at David then turned back. "We don't operate by those rules, Herr Hauptmann. We have a code of laws, and we follow it. Major Marsh can bring charges against you, but he can't hang you simply because he wants to, nor can he bring you before a tribunal without evidence." He turned from the steel blue gaze. "I don't have the proper forms, Dremmer. Stay with the captain. I'll put the coffee on while I'm there."

He watched Franklin leave, a pen and tablet in his hand, then positioned his chair so that he could see the door over Schneider's shoulder. "The things you did were precisely what a good man would do, Heinrich. You kept us alive."

Schneider smirked. "I provided food. That was not cooperating with the Resistance."

"When you received the shell-shocked men, what were you told to do with them?"

Schneider sneered. "You know very well—"

"You had almost no supplies. Keeping them alive was a sacrifice."

"And not disposing of them might have prolonged their deaths. It was probable that sparing them from execution might ultimately be more cruel."

"Your intent was to save them." He leaned back. "You disobeyed orders—refused to kill them. Before that, you bought a cow to feed us. You got Bear out of Krems and likely saved his life. You traded Élodie's Mercedes for our rations."

Schneider jutted his chin. "None of those things involved the

Resistance."

"What about the picture of Nicole you were asked to identify?"

"We had an agreement. You know quite well…" Heinrich raised a finger. "There is something you must know. When we met the train near Chemnitz, I accused you of murder. Do you remember this?"

"I thought it was genocide."

Heinrich's face lifted, neared a smile. "Not precisely, but I did mention a killing spree, I believe. I have only today learned this from my fellow prisoners, and I find astonishing."

He nodded for Heinrich to continue.

"Only one man was killed in the attack, and he died after the bombing. An oberleutnant, it seems, decided to pursue the fuel truck you commandeered. The others, all of whom had sought shelter in a ditch after seeing the plane, again fled the area. The oberleutnant alone died pursuing you after he was sprayed with fuel."

"I'm sorry, Heinrich."

"You are sorry?"

"A man died a horrible death. I prayed that wouldn't happen."

"The only one to die was pursuing you, David. Do you not find this astonishing?"

"He was deprived of his life. Who knows what good he might have accomplished after abandoning the lies he'd believed?"

Franklin stepped through the door, offered David a flinty stare, and placed forms on the table. "I chased these down. I'll see if the coffee's ready. You take cream or sugar?"

David nodded. "We take both, sir." Franklin was out the door, his heel strikes fading into darkness. He waited a long while, then opted for a redirection. "Heinrich, I know it created a dilemma when you were asked to identify Nicole's picture. You didn't want to withhold information, but you did what was right, just as I would have protected Élodie from the Gestapo had Nicole not been there."

Anger flashed from his eyes. "It is not the same. The Gestapo was following Nicole. She placed Élodie in danger!"

He worked to quench the ire. "She had connections with General Hodges, Heinrich. She'd arranged a way to get you out. How long before the Gestapo would have sent an assassin for you? Do you think they would have spared Élodie?" A leaf of paper lifted outside the door. "And when you learned that Krüger and Vogt were working with the Resistance—"

"Feldwebel Vogt worked with the Resistance?"

He'd gotten it in Franklin's notes, at least. "He set up a network, had lots of contacts, kept me in touch with London." He waited. "Élodie received directives from him, too."

Heinrich glared. "Why are you telling me this? You would not have told me had—"

He raised his hand. "Just one thing. Who did you fear was most apt to kill you when we made our break for Kassel? The US or the Wehrmacht?"

"You know this also." Schneider turned his head. "Is Lieutenant Franklin listening?"

He looked at the door and waited, half expecting Franklin to step out. Heels clattered down the hall, and he shrugged. "Apparently not."

* * * *

David stared at the dingy walls while Franklin scribbled. When the man paused, he pounced. "Do we have a case, sir?"

"We certainly could have a defense, Dremmer, but Schneider must admit to the things you brought up without being prompted."

"So, do I—"

Franklin's hand went up. "And he must tell us without alluding to whatever agreement you two had. Making deals with the enemy is *verboten*, Dremmer, even if this Kraut's a saint. It's altogether possible the preliminary investigation will end this, and you can go home, but we can't allow things like this to get into your statement. Or the hauptmann's testimony, should this go before a tribunal. If Marsh were to learn of it, the whole thing could blow up in our faces." He leaned back. "I'm also told he's tight with McBride."

"It's apparently a close family, sir."

443

Chapter LXXI

Baldwin seemed genuinely offended, his tirade filling the Grand Cabinet Room with righteous indignation. Nicole sagged beneath his ire, and no one countered on her behalf.

"...furthermore, we cannot allow these men to have their lives and careers suspended simply to accommodate Miss Serat's delusions or the prime minister's political ambitions. I demand these proceedings be allowed to continue!"

She looked at the magistrate, who seemed overcome with boredom, and lifted her hand. "I'm unfamiliar with this process, so without representation, I am unable to respond unless Mr. Baldwin is suggesting that only one side be allowed to pose questions or offer rebuttal."

Baldwin stiffened. "Certainly not. That was for the record. And I will be most happy to provide a barrister."

She saw the hint of a smile beneath Greeves' penciled mustache and knew she'd made a mistake. "Haven't I the right to select my own counsel, sir?"

Baldwin bent toward her, his neck veins bulging. "Miss Serat, I'm certain everyone here knows your choice of counsel. However, Britain can ill afford to suspend its government while you bring charges against those who offered their all to save her."

Heat boiled in her breast. "I believe you're confused regarding which nation these men made sacrifices for, sir."

Baldwin smirked. "Miss Serat, you are neither allowed to bring charges, nor assume the role of prosecutor. I shall have a barrister for you by noon."

He'd tried to use her plea of ignorance against her, and it ignited a fire in her breast. "You haven't one of your allies waiting in the hall, sir?"

The door swung wide, and the prime minister waddled in. "It won't be at all necessary, Mr. Baldwin. Though less skilled in the art of verbal fabrication than yourself, I am perfectly willing to provide Miss Serat with assistance."

She released the breath she'd held all morning.

Baldwin stood. "Are you suggesting that I have given false information, sir?"

Churchill sat without looking up. "I am suggesting nothing, Mr. Baldwin. I was, in fact, awed by the boldness of your intuitions regarding my motives and those of Miss Serat." His head hinged toward her. "Will I suffice as counsel, Miss Serat?"

"You certainly will, sir."

He leaned close and whispered. "You stole my thunder, and quite admirably. I had hoped to introduce motivations at a later time, but your statement regarding their allegiances was most gratifying." He drew a gust of smoke and turned to the magistrate. "We're delighted to allow Mr. Baldwin to proceed, assuming he's had sufficient time to concoct a strategy since requesting a postponement."

A warm comfort rose in her breast.

* * *

David needed sleep, but Schneider's words charged him with adrenaline. The threat Heinrich's fellow prisoners posed was real. Rumors had it that a movement was afoot to rebuild the shattered Reich from an underground network. Heinrich could flee to another country, of course, but few would accept a former Nazi, and some that would were apt to have him shot. On the other hand, if he were known to have helped the Resistance—

He pulled the pillow from beneath his neck, rolled it tight to relieve the pressure in his shoulders, but was unable to relax. The door opened slowly. He waited, praying it wasn't Marsh. Rubber soles squeaked close before Doherty appeared beside his bed, a clipboard in her hand. She seemed timid, her chin receding.

"How are you, Dremmer?"

"Okay, Lieutenant. And you?"

The drifting door sealed off the slant of brilliance. "Mind if I switch on the light?"

"It's your hospital, Lieutenant."

She stood pink-faced in the sudden luster. "I know I come across that way."

"It was a joke. It didn't mean anything."

"Sergeant Billington came earlier. He explained about your marriage, that you never really lived with your wife, and that you learned her baby wasn't yours."

"I don't believe he is, no."

She sucked a quick breath. "And that she was with another man after you married."

He felt a peculiar sympathy for Delores. The charges seemed harsher than she deserved. "It wasn't just her. She needed more than I could give her, and she was scared, brought into a world she didn't know and left to raise a baby alone. I was relieved when she found someone, and I let her know it."

"Still, it's different than I thought. I know you love Miss Serat. I'm just sorry it won't work out for the two of you."

He nodded, tried to smile. "So am I."

Bear slipped from behind, panting. "Marsh found out about Franklin. He knows the men are giving statements, and he says he's puttin' us on a train to France."

"Help me up, Bear. We'll have to find Franklin. He'll need our statements."

"Dremmer—"

"I know, Doherty, but it can't be helped."

"That's not it." Her hands rested on her hips. "I'm the source of your problems."

He looked up. "What do you mean?"

"I told Marsh where you were." Her arms dropped. "I'm sorry. I just thought that a man who would do what I thought you did to Miss Serat didn't deserve my protection, so when he asked, I told him you were with Lieutenant Franklin."

He hid his irritation. Tried, at least. "It would have come out anyway, Lieutenant."

Bear pushed his wheelchair close and extended a hand.

* * *

The chair battered David's leg as they crossed the remains of another ziggurat meant to last a thousand years. He pointed to the side door where the meeting with Tilley took place.

"Dremmer, you got to get some rest. Doc said the infection could come back."

"I'll sleep when they put us on the train."

The wheels whirled quickly down the hall. He spotted the door to Franklin's office and pointed. "It's this one. Looks like he's not here."

"I'm right behind you, Dremmer."

Bear rolled him around, and he saw the fresh-shaved face of the lieutenant, a cup of coffee in his hand. "I was afraid you'd gone to your quarters for a nap, LT."

Franklin slid his key in the door. "I slept a couple of hours and grabbed a shower. What are you doing here?"

Bear spoke first. "Major Marsh is on to us, sir. Says he's gettin' us on a hospital train and sendin' us to France."

The advocate shook his head. "The man won't quit!"

David leaned forward. "Can you get a stenographer, sir? I don't want to be shipped out without leaving a statement."

Franklin set the coffee on his desk and looked down the hall. "I'll find a conference room. I'm leaving the light off. If anyone knocks, don't answer it."

* * *

A slit over the door trained light on Franklin's desk. "Will you find a pencil and paper, Bear?"

His friend scurried in the half light, searching the tiny desktop.

Footsteps pounded in the hall, moved close, and stopped. The door shook beneath a heavy fist. "Franklin, are you in there? I need to speak with you now!"

Marsh. David's chest threatened to explode. Bear crept forward, paper in hand.

"Franklin, I smell your coffee! Now open the door, or I'll kick it in!"

Another voice, muted and indecipherable, emerged from the hall. Marsh's rose above it. "Sergeant, where's that Negro lieutenant?"

"Entry into this area is by permission of JAG only, sir."

An MP.

"I didn't see any guards, and I don't see any signs to that effect!"

"It's generally known, sir. You may petition Lieutenant Colonel Tilley if you wish, but until I receive further instructions, I must insist that you leave, sir."

"I'm ordering you, boy! I need to see that Negro advocate!"

"If you'll follow me, sir."

Seconds grew into minutes while David parceled his breath and listened.

A key scraped in the lock, and the door opened. "Any storm damage in here?"

The light switched on, and he caught Franklin's glittering eyes. "We survived, sir."

The advocate rubbed his hands. "This was our lucky day, boys! You just witnessed the one event that will ensure Tilley's allowing a Nee-gro an even break."

David's neck eased. "You said the colonel won't preside over the PI, right sir?"

"He won't, but he'll likely select the man who does. And now he'll do his best to influence what happens. I was afraid he'd withdraw from the process to keep from crossing McBride, but he won't tolerate having his authority challenged. Every advocate on the wing witnessed Marsh's tirade, and they weren't happy. Tilley's getting a review of the major's performance as we speak." Franklin grinned. "A stenographer is setting up in room 116. I scheduled it for the rest of the day. Anything you want to tell me before we start?"

Bear shook his head.

"A couple of things." David wheeled close. "I was helped by an old feldwebel named Vogt in Moosberg who set up a network of Resistance operatives. He'll be able to identify his agents, but I want to leave some names with you, including Henri Devillier."

Franklin pulled at his throat. "You mentioned the feldwebel when you were grilling Schneider. Why not give the names to MI6? You certainly have a contact there."

"If the stalag is liberated by our troops, sir—"

"All right, I'll get them to an intelligence officer. A real one."

"Sir, there's another man we want protected, a guard at Waldheim. Just a kid. His nickname was Loverboy. Never learned his real name, but the prisoners can identify him. Could I get it all on record?"

The lieutenant grinned. "I'll see to it that Tilley knows about this prior to the PI. Would Marsh have prevented getting this information on record? If so, mention it."

He nodded. "I also want to testify that Schneider's fear of his comrades is justifiable."

Franklin's chin rose. "We'll get it in there, but there's really nothing we can do."

"There may be, LT. If you were able to offer him exile in another country, he might be more forthcoming in his own defense."

The advocate nodded. "I'll make some calls, see what I can do."

* * *

"On your feet, Lieutenant!"

David lurched in his hospital bed, his left quadriceps screaming above Marsh's order. His breath came in a blast. "Ssssir!"

"I'll have a truck waiting for you and Sergeant Billings out front in half an hour. Tomorrow morning, you'll be placed on a train in Cologne. On the twenty-second, you'll board the SS *Argentina* in La Havre bound for New York." Marsh paused and grinned. "I'll arrange for you to resign your commission stateside. Billings will have his papers expedited, too. I want both of you out of this man's army, and I want you out as soon as possible!"

"Yes sir!" His heart rattled in his throat.

Doherty stepped from behind the door, switched on the light, and caught David's stare.

Marsh spun. "Nurse, I want this man out front at zero six hundred hours! Understood?"

"Every patient on this floor understands, Major."

Marsh turned back. "You've been a thorn in my side since you got here, Dremmer. I won't let you destroy my case against this Nazi buddy of yours."

He straightened in the bed. "You're intent on killing an innocent man, sir. If you're successful, a precedent will be set, and the prosecution of real war criminals will be hindered."

Marsh's glower glinted beneath the light. "Dremmer, I'll see to it that your insubordination will be mentioned in your record. At this point, however, you're half an hour away from being out of my hair."

* * *

The Rhineland had greened, except the land being readied for planting. Mules drew lines across gray stubble exposing the blackness hidden beneath. The car sped quietly, the converted Pullman slowing in areas where track had been recently repaired. Wheels rumbled, and

David pictured shivering kriegies waiting for them to pass. He'd awakened at dawn, thinking of Nicole who would likely be in Kassel soon. His chest squeezed with the weight of it.

"You ready for breakfast, Dremmer?"

He glanced up, saw Bear approaching with a tray. "Well, look at you. Aren't you afraid I'll get too fat and lazy to do my share of the work?"

"Been worried about that ever since I signed on for this deal, but I figure if I demand overtime, you'll get motivated."

He grinned. "We're going to be partners, Bear. I count the money, and you do the work. And partners don't get overtime."

Bear lifted a lid. "Real eggs. Bacon, too. No biscuits and gravy, though." The sergeant chinned toward the window. "So, what are they doin' out there?"

He glanced at the window again. "Moldboarding. Turning under last year's crop and getting ready to plant this year's."

His friend grinned. "Seen an old boy with two of them plows chained to a Jeep. The back half was crushed, but he'd hammered it out and chained a plow to the frame."

David scooped eggs. "Wonder where he got his fuel?"

"A still, maybe." Bear placed his fork on the tray and glanced through the window. "Nicole's gonna come back for ya. You know that, don't ya?" The voice had grown pliant.

He nodded, struggling to swallow. "Doherty will let her know what happened."

Chapter LXXII

Nicole glanced into the mountains, heaving with new growth, and squinted to avoid the brick-strewn streets flung chaotically in a maze of debris. The plane banked, fixing what was left of Kassel in her window. She would have had to press her face to the glass to see the end of destruction and the beginning of life. Still, David was here.

She lifted a hand to her face. The four additional days of testimony had left her exhausted. Baldwin had blistered her with questions, most of which were weighted with accusations. He pounced at any opportunity to help his friends escape retribution for murdering hers, while she was portrayed as a traitor. She released the crumpled straps of her leather duffle. The prime minister had countered the man's every attack, though only time would tell if truth would prevail.

The plane swooped low, leveled, and headed for a runway she could no longer see. Would David be willing to wait? No doubt he would sign the annulment papers and escape the trap he'd helped set. But might he choose a new life unburdened by memories of war and death? The plane squatted heavily on the tarmac, and she fought for breath, her hands shaking with the immensity of her message. And his choice. She rose and stepped to the open door.

A young corporal approached as she descended the steps. "Miss Serat?"

The boy's demeanor concerned her. "Yes?"

"Lieutenant Doherty sent me, ma'am. I hope you don't mind riding in an ambulance."

"I'm most grateful, Corporal." The boy dawdled, and she held herself from stepping ahead. "How did the lieutenant learn of my arrival?"

His head bowed. "Some Brit called—a higher-up, I think. He asked about Lieutenant Dremmer's condition and told her you were on the way."

The back of her neck tingled. "And how is Lieutenant Dremmer?"

"I think Doherty wants to talk to you about that."

Her breath froze. "Has he experienced a setback?"

"Nothing like that, ma'am. Just something I was told not to talk about."

She sought any distraction to squelch her fears as they twined through rubble, occasionally turning onto a side street before angling back. She recognized the one leading to the hospital, dwarfed now by leafing trees. The corporal parked the ambulance with two others and pointed to double doors. "Take the emergency entrance, ma'am. The hall will lead you to the nurses' station."

"Thank you, Corporal." She stepped across the gravel drive and through the doors. Her shoes echoed within the hallway, the green conical lights urging her on.

"Miss Serat!" Doherty lifted the glasses from her nose.

"Lieutenant." She nodded and tried to smile. "How is David?"

"Dremmer is doing well, I'm sure. Likely on his feet by now." Doherty drew an envelope from her desk. "Major Marsh put him on a train last Tuesday. He's scheduled to ship out of Le Havre the day after tomorrow on the SS *Argentina*." She extended a letter. "He left this for you."

She shook, held back tears. "Why was he shipped out?"

"To keep him from testifying, I suspect." Doherty pressed her hands against her pleated uniform. "There's something else. A friend is waiting to see you." The lieutenant rose and motioned for her to follow. They reached the nurses' lounge, and the door opened to a table with six chairs. Two nurses leaned against a counter, cigarette smoke rising to the ceiling.

Doherty stepped to a second door. "Mrs. Schneider, Miss Serat has arrived."

A chair scooted across the floor, and Élodie stepped from the anteroom, her face blanched and her eyes red.

Nicole gasped. "Are you all right?"

Élodie stepped close, her arms extended, and rested her head on her shoulder. "I need your help, Nickie."

* * * *

Nicole waited for Lieutenant Franklin to end his conversation with a nodding junior leader in the secretarial pool. He seemed frustrated, was seeking a missing procedural manual, and appeared unable to make the young woman understand the exigence of his request.

She fingered David's message and tried to ignore the young woman's fascination with the handsome advocate. The girl was clearly moonstruck. After several minutes, he dismissed her, turned, and extended his hand. "Miss Serat, I've been expecting you. I'm sorry Lieutenant Dremmer couldn't be here to greet you. I know he is, as well."

She smiled and shook his hand. "It's—"

"You're looking for a way to get in touch with him, I'm sure." His mouth twitched. "Major Marsh is the only one here with connections to the British wireless. He could—"

"Lieutenant. That's not—"

His finger rose. The man was fired up. "I'll get you in to see Tilley first thing in the morning—line up a couple of advocates to go with us. He isn't fond of me, but he's fuming at Marsh for sending his prime witness home. Could be a mess if it were to go to a tribunal, but here's the deal. Captain Schneider believes his former comrades will kill him, so he's denied cooperating with the Resistance. INS would object to any offer of asylum, but I'm working another angle." A grin covered his face. "If we could find an MI6 operative to accompany the Schneiders, that would amount to a British stamp of approval. It would also get the operative to the States so she wouldn't be stuck in England for a year waiting to get married."

He wasn't grasping the gravity... "That's a wonderful plan, Lieutenant. I'm truly grateful, but there is a more pressing matter."

He sobered. "More pressing than getting you and Dremmer together? What is it?"

"May we speak privately?"

"Sure, we can talk on the way to my office."

She gripped the duffle straps and stepped into the empty hall. "Several days ago, a German civilian was detained by your troops along the line. They have now confirmed that he was a Resistance radio operator in Waldheim. He came with a message for Élodie, Herr Hauptmann's wife, but was allowed to see her only this morning. It seems Élodie's brother, Henri, is in grave danger inside Dachau Concentration Camp."

Franklin stepped into his office, pulled her chair out, and moved to the opposite side of the desk. "I'm sorry, but it's not possible for us to do anything in advance of—"

"Wait. Henri is an important asset, Lieutenant. He works under Oberst Schuster at Dachau and has been active in the Resistance for years. He has recorded and photographed a number of executions, several of internationally known dissidents. He is eager to testify against Schuster. However, Herr Oberst is demanding that his staff take their own lives should the Allies reach them, and he is threatening to hang those who try to escape." She paused. "The Americans are quite close, Lieutenant. The suicides and murders may have already begun."

Franklin leaned back. "I see."

She wiped her hands on her skirt. "As you might imagine, Élodie is frantic."

He sat with his hand over his mouth, then stood. "Come with me, please."

"Where are we going?"

"To the officer's club. If my presence doesn't send Tilley into apoplexy, you can tell him what you just told me. I only hope he's sober enough to get you onto Marsh's wireless."

* * *

Nicole sat in the familiar leather chair. It seemed possible that Franklin was more concerned with seizing a prominent case than in saving Henri, but she couldn't object. She'd used just that to entice him, and if Henri were saved in the process, it shouldn't matter. Besides, the lieutenant had been quite brave walking into the officer's club. Certainly, that did nothing to advance his career. And wasn't everyone absorbed in his own battle?

She opened David's note, reread his vow of love, a privilege he said he would miss with every remaining breath. He wrote that he knew their hearts would heal, though life without her would be impossibly long. He then moved on to a list of German operatives that included Henri.

Lieutenant Franklin patted her arm. "Marsh will show up, Miss Serat, and we'll get that call through."

Colonel Tilley glared from across the room, attempted to stand, then sat, his indignation as clear as the redness of his swelling brow. "That was inappropriate, Lieutenant. Enti'ly inappropriate."

Franklin seemed baffled. "Sir?"

"Touching Miss Serat. It was inappropriate."

The door opened, and Marsh surveyed the intruders to his realm. Franklin stood, and Nicole followed suit. Tilley rose unsteadily, the scent of alcohol rising with him. "Major, were you not taught to s'lute a s'perior officer?"

Marsh straightened and offered a salute. "Why do you need my phone, sir?"

"It's advocate business and involves British intelligence. And it isn't just your phone, Major. When the call goes through, you'll need to leave." Tilley spoke deliberately, his slur controlled.

Marsh blossomed a bright red, still waiting for his salute to be returned. "I'm in charge of this post, Colonel. General McBride will hear about any infringement into my area of responsibility."

"He certainly will. I plan to tell him m'self."

* * *

The phone crackled and the operator advised that weather was interfering with the network. Nicole waited, the disturbance in her stomach increasing by the moment, and reminded herself to gather her thoughts and not disclose anything sensitive.

"Miss Serat? Are you there?"

The prime minister's voice never failed to bring a tremor. "I'm here, sir."

A squawk, then "...the unfortunate death of your parents, who assumed responsibility for you?"

"My Tante Marie, sir."

"Good... what do I..." The line crackled and squealed. "...delight of your call?"

"Do you remember my telling you of the hauptmann's wife, my friend from university?"

"Of course. I trust she remains un... by any American..."

She deliberated for a moment. "She is safe, sir. Her brother, however, is not. You remember his role, I'm sure."

"I do, and unless he is present... be imprudent to discuss..."

She covered the receiver and looked frantically at Franklin, who nodded and removed his pad and pen. "He remains in the same frightful place, sir. However, he has records and photographs of atrocities that he wishes to turn over to the Allies. He's also expressed a desire to testify against the individual in charge. With the advance of Allied troops, the chief culprit is now demanding that his staff die either by their own hand or his." The line seemed to go dead. "Have I lost you, sir?"

"No, I am formulating..." The line squawked. "...which I propose... you are willing to leave your lieutenant's bedsi... send a plane. Assuming the hauptmann and... are able, it would be... to bring them."

"Sir, the hauptmann has been charged with war crimes, and I have promised to testify, if needed, at his preliminary inquiry."

"I see." Another protracted wait, then a screech. "...have operatives who could attempt to retrieve your friend's brother... his records and... He must be alerted... at a moment's... impossible to bring him through American lines near your friend... instead across what remains of Germany, if you have... arrange a rendezvous near your present... In the meantime, I would hope the... be concluded quickly, and our agents and your guests..."

She puzzled over what she'd missed and glanced at Tilley. She needed a chance to put it together while it was fresh. "Sir, if you can hear me, I would like for you to speak with Lieutenant Colonel Tilley. He is the highest-ranking officer here. He would be needed to arrange any meeting with officers along the line." She waited for a response, heard only static, and held the phone out.

The colonel stepped forward, swallowed, and took the receiver. "Mr. Prime Minister?" He listened, his face clenched tight. "I can only request such a thing from a CO, sir." He nodded, waiting. "Yes. Yes sir. No sir, I'm with the Judge Advocate General's office."

The man was graying before her.

"Sir, I missed... Oh, yes sir. I will see to it that the preliminary inquiry is expedited, sir." Tilley blanched, turned, covered the receiver with his hand and looked at Franklin. "Write down ev'thing I say, Lieutenant. And ev'thing I've said so far!"

He removed his hand. "That isn't neces'ry, sir. I know Miss Serat 'stremely well and am confident of her integrity."

Franklin continued scribbling and covered his grin.

"The proposed Office of Military Governance, sir? Yes, I'm aware that it will—" Tilley nodded, his face draining what color was left. "Your 'sistance in finding a presiding official would be most appreciated, sir." He nodded. "Yes sir. I will assign someone to this office to await your call. You have the— Oh, yes sir. I understand.

Thank you, sir." He returned the phone to its cradle and looked up. "Franklin, piece that conversation together. Consult with Miss Serat about what Winston told her. Get it on paper for me. I mus' locate the f'cilities."

"Down the hall. Second door on your left, sir." Franklin waited for the door to close, turned to Nicole, and laughed. "Winston? Really?"

Chapter LXXIII

Nicole leaned back in the leather chair Franklin had crowded into his office. If his taunts were any indication, he was as pleased as she at what they had reconstructed from the conversation.

"So, will you ask the prime minister or Tilley to give you away? I'm not trying to intrude, but I think it's unlikely that Tilley will *ever* give you to anyone else."

She snickered. "You're assuming David will still have me."

"I'm assuming nothing, Miss Serat. I saw those sad puppy eyes before he left. The man won't leave you here alone. He'll hitch a ride back, if need be, and send a boat for his cows."

Laughter rose from deep inside. It had been so long. "If he does, I'll take them, too."

"Happiness becomes you, Miss Serat." He raised a finger. "But I have a couple of things left to cover. MI6 will need to verify your credentials for the PI. I assume Tilley's buddy, Winston, will take care of that. And we'll need to confirm that Schneider was complicit in at least a couple of Resistance operations. Was he?"

She nodded. "Certainly. He refused to identify me, and he allowed David to escape prison as well as contacting other operatives, including the hauptmann's brother-in-law. He wanted no more bloodshed. On either side."

Franklin rubbed his hands. "Perfect. I'll ask a question that will provide you an opportunity to include that in your statement. I don't want you leaving for the States until we've extracted all we can from you."

She smiled. "I can't chase David to New York without a promise of marriage, Lieutenant." She tilted her head. "I'm not that kind of girl."

The deep chuckle again. "You're clearly without guile, Miss Serat." He laced fingers behind his neck and leaned back. "You realize your statement will effectively ensure Schneider's case won't get past the preliminary investigation, right?"

* * *

Nicole sat on the third of five pews, all of which had been salvaged from a bombed church. For twenty minutes she'd deliberated on the reason courtrooms were furnished so uncomfortably, and her musings had availed her of only one possibility. Discomfort had to have been shown to encourage brevity.

Observers drifted in, several of them advocates she recognized from her long sessions with Lieutenant Franklin while sifting through kriegies' statements. An auctioneer's podium had also been installed for the investigating officer, a British official flown in for the occasion.

Colonel Tilley strode into the room, caught her glance, and stepped to her pew. "Your contributions to this case were most helpful, Miss Serat. I'm very appreciative."

She smelled alcohol, Beeman's, and not a little blarney. "I only wish to see justice done before returning to London, sir."

"Of course. You're eager to get back to the prime minister." Tilley appeared to sulk.

It seemed unwise to offend him further. "I'm equally concerned that this inquiry render an appropriate outcome, sir. That's why I stayed."

He brightened and moved her over with his elbow. "I'm sure justice will be done. I noted the significant parts of the statements for Mr. Canter." He winked. "He is also an acquaintance of the prime minister, as you might know."

Had the man forgotten she was present when the PM asked to be allowed to help select the presiding official? "I only know he was cleared by the OMG, sir."

Tilley chuckled. "You understand, of course, that the OMG isn't officially in operation yet. But as it is to represent the Allies, British participation did seem crucial." He lifted his chin. "That's why I suggested Canter."

He had forgotten!

A narrow fellow entered the room, strode to the bench, and seated himself. The room quieted. "The preliminary inquiry into the Charge of war crimes, including but not limited to Specifications of enslavement and ill treatment of prisoners of war, purportedly committed by Luftwaffe Hauptmann Heinrich Schneider, is now in session."

"I object!" Marsh rose from the front row. "I'm in charge of this post, sir, and I wasn't allowed a voice in your appointment."

Canter's face reddened. "This is a preliminary inquiry, Major. I am here to present my findings as to the appropriateness of these charges based on evidence gathered by the Judge Advocate General's office. You may hear them so long as you remain silent. Is that clear?"

Marsh leaned back. "But I—"

"My findings will be brief. Please don't interrupt." Canter picked up a ream of narratives and placed them beside an equally impressive stack. His gaze slid past Nicole to settle on Heinrich. "I have read those narratives provided by Judge Advocate Franklin for the accused and Judge Advocate Anderson for the Office of Military Government. In addition, I have reviewed statements made by prisoners confined under Luftwaffe Hauptmann Heinrich Schneider's authority, those made by the Man of Confidence in Special Stammlager 457, Lieutenant David Dremmer, his adjutant, Sergeant Amos Billington, and one offered by Nicole Serat, an operative for MI6. I have also weighed the letter signed and submitted by over two hundred former prisoners of war requesting leniency for the acting commandant."

Tilley nudged her and winked. She slid lower in the pew.

"No evidence presented demonstrates a breach in the rules of war as laid down by the Geneva Convention, nor was an instance cited that indicates any ill treatment of prisoners. Further, Hauptmann Schneider put himself at considerable risk to diminish the privation of prisoners under his authority. Finding his government's positions untenable, the hauptmann reached out to Second Lieutenant David Dremmer, the Man of Confidence, for assistance in turning both prisoners and staff over to American forces. Lieutenant Dremmer was, in turn, aided by Hauptmann Schneider in establishing necessary contacts with known Resistance operatives.

"Whatever loyalties Hauptmann Schneider held at the outset of this war, it is probable he saved the lives of many Allied prisoners." Canter looked at Marsh. "It has therefore been resolved that Luftwaffe Hauptmann Heinrich Schneider shall be remanded to Camp Atterbury in Edinburgh, Indiana where he will remain a prisoner of the United States Government for the duration of the war. Under the terms of an agreement reached between the US government and the Prime Minister's Office, Hauptmann Schneider will be delivered to that facility under the supervision of MI6 operative Serat. While there, the hauptmann has agreed to prepare Luftwaffe troops for reentry into society prior to their repatriation after the conclusion of hostilities.

"Hauptmann Schneider shall be kept in seclusion until such time as he is transported. No additional punitive measures are deemed appropriate. This inquiry is hereby concluded." Canter rose and exited the room.

Nicole felt a weight lift from her shoulders a moment before Tilley's hand captured her arm. She shuddered, caught the colonel's polished smile, and straightened.

"Thank you for all you've done, Colonel."

"I promised, did I not? It's time that we both relax. You'll have a drink with me, surely?"

"I must speak with the hauptmann, Colonel. And with Lieutenant Franklin."

The colonel stared, the huff returning. "Franklin will meet with Mr. Canter regarding the prisoner's extradition. It could take hours to hash out an itinerary."

"But since I am to accompany the prisoner, I should be part of that discussion, sir. I'm sorry." She forced a deep breath and turned.

Tilley grabbed her shoulder. "You owe me something, don't you think?"

She'd not dreamed— "I've expressed my gratitude, Colonel."

"Everyone knows what MI6 expects of their agents. I'm sure you've expressed your gratitude in more profound ways." The smile was gone. "You made it here alive, after all."

"I'm afraid you've entirely misperceived me, sir." She spun and started down the short aisle toward Heinrich who stood silent, his face drained of blood.

He looked up. "It is as David promised."

She nodded, trying to regain her composure. "You're surprised? You will be treated well, I'm sure."

"Please thank him for me. I know he worked hard to accomplish this."

"I believe you'll have the opportunity to thank him yourself when we reach the States." She caught Franklin's grin as he stepped away from Canter. "Others worked hard for you, as well, and Lieutenant Franklin was foremost among them. Some men prize justice,

Heinrich. That is also true of those who have been denied it." She allowed a blunted smile. "I've also been asked to convey Élodie's love. She misses you."

Franklin stepped from behind and offered a perfunctory pat on Heinrich's shoulder, then turned to her. "May I speak with you, Miss Serat?"

"Of course."

He ushered her to the bench. "British agents made it through the lines last night and found the leader of a combat group. Groups up and down the line had been informed of their presence, so they were watching for them." Franklin smiled. "Oberfeldwebel Devillier was among them. He's asked to see you."

"Let's go now, shall we?"

The advocate looked puzzled. "You'll have an opportunity. There's no hurry."

She turned her head toward Tilley. "I'm afraid there is."

She bustled toward the door as Franklin's hand reached over her shoulder to open it. The door closed, and she turned. "And where is Henri, Lieutenant?"

"He's being sheltered near the airfield. You'll have time to talk things over on your flight to London." He looked back at the door. "Is something wrong?"

"I believe I was just propositioned by the Colonel!"

"Just now? The man's slowing down." His expression changed. "The prime minister is sending a plane for you, the Schneiders, and Devillier. It should arrive around fourteen hundred hours. The MPs will get the Schneiders there."

She glanced at the clock over the lieutenant's shoulder. "That gives me just under three hours to hide."

Franklin pointed to the door of the secretarial pool and ushered her inside. "I didn't mean to make light of your situation, Miss Serat. I understand that the colonel's behavior may have been disconcerting."

She smiled. "It's alright, Lieutenant. I'll survive the man's overtures. They were just unexpected."

"It's been a pleasure working with you, Miss Serat. I wish you and Dremmer the very best."

She seized his shoulders and squeezed. "I don't know how to thank you, Lieutenant."

"You could name your first child after me."

"Must I call her 'Lieutenant'? I had hoped for something more endearing."

"It's Charles, Nicole." He laughed. "Give Winston a slap on the back for me, will you? Let me escort you to the room where Devillier is being held."

Chapter LXXIV

Mud spewed from beneath the wings of the Bentley, only to be washed from memory by a pelting rain. Nicole traced the lines of the palace, and a familiar weakness trickled into her limbs. Some of her worst moments had taken place behind those walls, and she fostered a dread that she might always shoulder a warrior's penchant for alarm.

The car splashed over the bridge to advance onto the Principal Approach, which seemed an excessively grand entrance. They stopped, and the driver stepped into the rain, spread an umbrella, and opened her door. "May I assist you to the gate, miss?"

"I hate terribly for you to be forced into the cold. I shall make it on my own." Her words came in a stutter, the chill cutting them short.

"You needn't be concerned. Step to my right, and you shan't be doused."

"Thank you, then." She lengthened her strides, reached the iron gates, and found Alice waiting, her smile as sweet as she remembered. The young woman extended another umbrella.

"Miss Serat, how wonderful to see you again."

"And you, Alice. Truly."

They entered the great door, and Alice hung her umbrella to dry. "Allow me to escort you to the Second State Room, miss. The prime minister is waiting."

She held the young woman's gaze, wished to embrace her for her kindness, but wasn't sure what propriety allowed. "Thank you for all you've done, Alice."

"It's been my pleasure, miss, just as it is today." The assistant checked a curtsy midway.

She trembled as they marched through the Grand Salon and entered the First State Room. Alice opened another door, and the PM rose from his afternoon Johnny Walker. His mouth lifted, and he offered a nod that began near his trouser tops. "I shan't waste what breath the Almighty has lent me to offer a whisky, Miss Serat, but would you care for a drink of another sort?"

She eased at his conviviality. "No, thank you, sir. I'm entirely too wet as it is."

He smiled, re-lit his cigar, and filled the air with smoke. "I understand your friend, Devillier, has provided SOE with a great deal of information. He has, as well, endowed us with documentation regarding the horrid practices these Huns instituted in their prisons, not to mention giving us an account of several good men who dared oppose the little corporal." He seemed exhausted but gathered himself. "And the Schneiders are comfortable? That is, your friend Élodie is comfortable?"

"Both were last evening, sir. Élodie is most grateful to you, and Heinrich was received graciously at Shooters Hill. As I understand, he has promised to teach the guards chess."

"Very good, indeed. I requested he be considered Grade A, and the staff seems always to act commendably in carrying out my requests. That is, except prior to elections. They somehow manage to exasperate me during those awful times." He smiled and straightened. "Well then, let's get down to business, as you Americans are fond of saying."

She laughed. "I hope to grow accustomed to being called that, sir."

He lowered his face and seemed to stray for a moment. "You recall, I suspect, the discussion we had regarding Britons being enticed to exchange their liberties for equity."

"Of course, sir. I assured you that most were apt to believe as you do."

"Yes, well, we shall soon see. Do you remember the missive you left me that day and whom you so aptly quoted?"

Her heart lifted. "I wrote what my Tante Marie often told me, that the light of truth can be hidden for a time, but the pain of bashing our toes will eventually lead us to uncover our lamps."

"And I thereby deduced you to be both virtuous and prudent." The prime minister placed his cigar in a silver tray.

"I hope I've given you no reason to doubt your conclusions, sir."

"Not for a moment." He lifted his head. "I fear I promised to get down to business and immediately strayed." His smile returned. "My staff was most diligent in searching for records that might help locate your Aunt Marie, though they found nothing in the vicinity of Bruges. They also explored Antwerp since many of your countrymen sought safety there." He lifted his chin, and she again saw the weariness in his face. "The results were equally disappointing. No one suspected that she might have had the opportunity to come to London so late in the war. Quite fortuitously, however, one staffer uncovered her name while reviewing cases of Nazi collaborators."

Her heart stuttered. "That can't be!"

He smiled and patted her arm. "You are familiar with Jean-Baptiste Piron, I am sure."

"Colonel Piron, yes." The name brought a shiver of respect.

"After the Huns were driven back September last, your Prince Charles required the colonel to intervene in the disposition of collaborators. Madame Clotiér, your beloved aunt, was at that time aiding refugees, and as several among them were accused of collaboration, she found herself embroiled in a battle to protect those unjustly charged."

She eased as he caught a breath.

"The colonel recruited several workers to assist the accused in London where their cases would be brought before what Belgian jurists remained. Most of those were part of the Pierlot government, and it seems your aunt was among them." He paused and smiled. "It appears that you have both become altogether too familiar with the flaws of European justice."

She drew deeply of the dense air. "And will I be able to see her?"

The prime minister rose, seemed ready to offer an embrace but stopped. "We had hoped to have her here to meet you, dear child. London traffic, however, interfered with our plans. Still, I am in hopes that she will arrive before my return this evening."

She stepped forward, laid her head against his chest, and wrapped her arms around his soft shoulders. "Thank you, sir. You have restored the most treasured parts of my life."

His hand pressed gently between her shoulders. "And this precious island must count you among those to whom it owes her future. Had I known you at the time, I would have been delighted to have had you among our SOE agents. You quite exceeded the cast of characters with whom you acted." He released her slowly and stepped back. "I must address some rather urgent matters, but that will allow you and your aunt time to become reacquainted.

"I very much hope that you will both join me for dinner, however. Clemmie is chairing a meeting of the Young Women's Christian Association. I would otherwise have enjoyed having you meet her." He paused. "You will spare me eating alone, won't you? And your aunt will perhaps enjoy a good whisky?"

She laughed. "I would be most honored, sir. I'm sure my aunt will be, as well."

"Very good, indeed. First, however, it is imperative that you write a missive to your brave lieutenant so that I might send a telegram to his ship. In a few days, we shall arrange for this Nazi fellow and your friend, Élodie, to join you on your flight to the States so that you might meet your lieutenant in New York."

* * *

Gun metal clouds unknotted above an empty sea. David steadied himself against the railing, his leg usable but stiff. He'd stared into a burning dawn, unable to escape the emptiness of a future without Nicole, had rehearsed a thousand iterations of waking alone, and seen himself as an old man calling a young man's sons by their father's name. Each generation would struggle, gather what it could, and rise like sparks swirling above flames before fading to ash.

But he was left without the hope of a momentary climb, the grasping for what was needed before his solitary ember ebbed to gray. Another generation would follow, the names and faces a homologous flurry. And within the ascent, some cancer would overwhelm them, its shadow taking the peace or produce they created, stealing both their lives and property, calling itself by a hundred names—the dictatorship of the proletariat or Lebonsraun; the redistribution of wealth or eminent domain—it would reshape itself from whatever vernacular was fashionable and make a virtue of taking all they'd built.

And if he should regain the ranch? It wouldn't be enough without Nicole. That was the heart of it. That and the end of war. When others' lives hung in the balance, he'd found the strength to endure. Now he had only the dusty repetition of tomorrows and the trust that things would somehow be bearable.

A shadow advanced within the flame—a still, small assurance that had been implanted in his heart on the train to Kassel where he had touched eternity, known its fabric, and been drawn into its peace. The glimpse had not been offered simply to help him bear the intolerable or mitigate the loss of what he treasured. It had been given to provide meaning to the temporal, to supply beauty to the broken, and to offer the promise of perfection within a disintegrating world.

He straightened, vowing to question only the gloom. God would make life more than bearable. Somehow, it would be good. A sea breeze touched his cheek, and he whispered her name, giving her back to the One who'd allowed him to hold her for a while. The offering was final, given without expectation of having it countermanded. He felt the release this time, had done what was essential however often it returned to haunt him.

He glanced above the sea and caught the image of a dove—perfect, white, and frigid—hovering against the breaking sky. The gray relented in a moment cut from time, the crystal clarity suspended in the morning breeze as if it were light itself. It overwhelmed him, cleansing all he was and all he knew, filling him with hope and certainty before withdrawing from sight. It was the perfect dove he'd seen in the field before the war.

Boots slapped the deck behind him, and he turned awkwardly to see Bear running, the sergeant's belt drawn tight against gathers in his new fatigues.

"Did you see it, Bear? The dove?"

"This far out to sea? Couldn'ta been a dove." His friend grinned. "But you got a telegram, Dremmer. From London!" Bear extended a slip of yellow paper. "I looked at it, but I figured you'd forgive me once you read it."

David squinted within a chute of unsullied light.

DELORES FILED FOR ANNULMENT JULY LAST STOP
PAPERS AWAIT YOUR SIGNATURE IN NEW YORK STOP
I WILL MEET YOU THERE IF YOU STILL WANT ME STOP
WILL BE ACCOMPANIED BY THE SCHNEIDERS STOP
FRIEND WC EXTENDS BEST WISHES STOP
PLEASE ADVISE STOP
LOVE NICOLE

His legs went weak, and his throat tightened. "It was a dove, Bear."

Bear's arm came over his shoulder. "WC. Is that who I think it is?

"It isn't Fields." He looked up, his chest boiling with a giddiness he couldn't contain. "I can't believe this is happening, Bear!"

The grin now covered Bear's face. "Believe it, Dremmer."

He laughed, tears edging onto his cheeks. "I've got to word my response just right. What do you think of 'Yes'?"

The dollop of hair lifted in the breeze. "You oughta add 'please.'"

* * *

The bow crashed through a wave, forcing a sodden mist onto the deck. David watched, sought reassurance that they were moving at a pace that would get them to New York before she changed her mind.

A heavy hand fell on his shoulder. "D'you buy this spot, Lieutenant?"

He chuckled. "Paying by the hour, Sergeant. Poker game still going on below?"

Bear nodded. "Can't believe they stay down there when they could be countin' waves with you. You figure out how many we gotta cross before we get to New York?"

He snickered. "First time we get into a drought, you'll beg to see water again."

"Rain in Oklahoma just meant gettin' stuck and sinkin' to my knees in red mud." The sergeant stared over the prow. "So, tell me what you was thinkin' when I come up."

The truth still warmed him. "I believed I had to have Nicole to complete me, Bear. I couldn't see that if I weren't whole without her, it would mean I had nothing to offer. I could only have taken from her. What I needed, I already had. I was God's, and he was mine, and all I need and who I am comes from him. He wanted to bless me, but he couldn't bless what I put above him. I had to stop insisting on having what I wanted long enough to know that with him, I had everything."

Bear lifted his chin, the rigid lips curving upward. "And when did you give her up?"

He shrugged. "The last time? A minute or two before you came with the telegram. Only this time I wasn't expecting him to give her back."

Bear smiled. "Catherine ain't gonna be there to meet me, Dremmer, but I'll have Babs and Irene, and we'll do some healin' together. And we'll all see Catherine again—something to look forward to when we get closer to the end."

"I wish it were different, Bear. I wish Catherine could be waiting, an eleven-week-old girl you could love and wonder over as she turned into a beautiful young woman."

"I know you do, Dremmer, but we both have a lot, and someday we'll have it all."

* * *

David neared the bow, struggling to keep up with Bear. The first trip around the deck had taken seventeen minutes. Ten days ago? With his friend opening the gates beneath the upper decks, he had honed his times, lengthened his stride, and set a ten-minute goal.

Bear raised his watch. "Nine minutes, thirty seconds, Dremmer. You can make it!"

With aspirin his leg wasn't that painful, but it was stiff, and he'd lost coordination. "I'm trying, Bear."

"Twenty seconds. You can do it!"

He stepped to the side, avoiding a cable, stumbled, righted himself, and pushed ahead.

"Ten seconds."

The point of the bow was no more than fifteen yards. He threw the injured leg forward, felt a pop, and grabbed the railing.

Bear gripped his shoulder. "What happened?"

Speakers cracked, and a voice emerged from the trailing squeal. "Attention. Attention. This just in from the New York *Daily News*: 'Adolf Hitler and Paul Joseph Goebbels committed suicide in Berlin before the Reich capital toppled, the official Soviet commander said last night quoting Hans Fritzsche, Goebbels right-hand man, whom Russia captured.'"

A low rumble rose from beneath them, then thundered from the stairs. Men threw their caps and boiled across the decks.

"Why couldn't those two lunatics have done this five years ago, Bear?"

The sergeant shook his head. "It would have saved a lot of lives, but that wasn't what they was after."

He turned from the railing. "No, they couldn't tolerate anyone having more or looking smarter. Better to reign in hell than serve in heaven, I guess."

Bear tilted his head. "That's pretty much it. So, what happened to your leg?"

"I don't know, but it seems okay, now. We're scheduled to reach New York on Saturday. I'll see a doctor then if I need to. The medics in the infirmary have more than they can handle."

* * *

"Just scar tissue, Lieutenant. It may happen again. Keep stretching it. Be a little painful, but it'll increase your range of motion. The sooner you break it loose, the better."

David glanced across the infirmary, saw men with missing limbs, others bandaged for burns, some with IVs. His concerns were trivial, as were Bear's, who had insisted he be checked out. "Sorry to take your time, Doc. You've got more important things to do."

"It's okay, sir. Good to see somebody recovering. Some haven't, you know." The medic scanned the deck. "And some may not." He looked back. "We're six hours out. You have anybody meeting you in New York?"

He smiled. "I do, and I can't wait to see her."

The sergeant grinned. "I thought I smelled aftershave. Better find a place on deck, Lieutenant. The boys'll crowd you out if you don't."

* * *

David stared into a monochromatic sky, dull-edged spires rising through the gray, smoke and steam shrouding their flanks. The men in front cheered at the sight of home, while he shuddered at the thought of not being able to find her. If the crowd were as impenetrable on the docks as it was on board, how could he?

The ship began a slow rotation, the churning roar of tugboats rising on their port. His vision cleared, and he saw a dock filled with people and raised himself to his toes.

A hand clenched his shoulder. "Relax, Dremmer. It'll take hours to deboard. She won't leave without ya."

"Sure, I know." But he'd wondered. "Marsh didn't intend to do us any favors, but some of these boys will likely spend months getting a discharge. I'm hoping we'll be out of here in a day or two. You'll be halfway to Oklahoma before I can resign my commission. So, how long before you'll be ready to come to Texas?"

"Won't be long. Don't want you comin' up with any plans I have to make work."

* * *

She stared at the gangway where the infirm were debarking, her arms wrapped around her as if she were cold. David let himself be taken with the sight of her before moving close. She didn't turn, seemed not to notice his approach, though he'd walked from the gangway near the bow, wishing beyond words that he had a ring in his pocket.

He eased to her side, his heart pounding against his ribs. "Are you lost, miss?"

She turned, her smile widening with delight. It was as thrilling a sight as had ever reached his heart. He searched for words. "It's grand—"

She grabbed his neck, and he slid his arms around her, taken by her trembling sobs. He kissed her and whispered. "Marry me. Please."

"Yes. Yes."

"Today?"

She laughed. "Do you think there might be another draft? A few more months won't matter, will it?"

A chill ran up his spine. "It's the first aftershave I've owned in three years, and it won't last that long." Brilliance ebbed from her eyes, and he grinned. "Besides, I plan to get married as soon as I sign those papers, and I'd really hoped it would be to you."

She pinched his cheek. "All right. We'll try to work it into our schedule, though it's getting a little late to find a minister today."

He drew in the joy he'd not dared hope for and felt the gentle crush of her breasts, her body pressing fiercely into his. He found her lips, was taken by the warmth of her mouth, abandoned and eager. She released him, the crystal blue of her eyes drawing him from the moment. He caught his breath. "Just remember that I was the first to compromise."

"Well done, my love. I'll see to it you get more practice."

Epilogue

Jesse wheeled himself to the tack shed, spinning across the planks old Niedermeyer had laid down for him. Ben had been good, the best friend he'd ever had, really, but he could see the man changing, knew that time had turned against him, and wondered if he might have to make it without him. He hoped, for a moment, that he would go first. Still, Ben showed up offering trips to town or help in rebuilding the wire trap beyond the pens where Dancer could graze and stretch his legs. He would be clear of Morgan, there, who never ventured near the house.

The black nickered against the blushing cheeks of morning, consented to step into the pens as he had in the dead of winter, where he'd again become accustomed to kindness and touch. The horse offered little of the affection he'd given the boy, but David would be home soon to claim it. That was his prayer, at least, though some asinine senator had proposed a plan to hold troops in Europe for a year or longer or send them to the Pacific to keep the job market from collapsing. That and the Japs were still holding out, spilling the blood of countless more every day, including their own. And all for naught.

He scooped oats into the bucket, settled it on his useless legs, and spun the chair around. Light reflected between elm branches, and he felt the warmth of it. Ben had stopped for mail and was coming up the road for coffee.

The two hundred twenty-one cubic inch V-8 settled into silence near the house as Jesse lifted the bucket to the hanger Ben had fashioned on the middle plank. The old cuss had cut a slot to slide the oats through and receive a nuzzle of gratitude or impatience. This morning it seemed more affection, though Jesse was hesitant to believe it. He returned a gentle stroke across the soft muzzle and withdrew, grateful for the grace of the exchange, and turned his chair onto the steady climb to the house.

Ben stepped slow, his sciatica halting his gait. "I'm thinkin' that horse has a surprise coming, Jesse."

He puffed against the grade, worked to keep old Niedermeyer from seeing his eagerness. "That right?" He offered nothing more. Needed his breath.

Ben's grin broke free. "Got a letter for ya. I've seen the writin' before. Stamped in New York City, too. Can you make anything outta that?'"

He glanced at the lone cedar, hope threatening to consume him. "Lotta folks in New York City, Ben, and I don't believe I know a one of them."

"You'll know this one." Niedermeyer extended the envelope. "Open 'er up, old man."

A wave of heat flashed through his chest. "It's the boy's hand!" His breath left him as Ben handed him an open pocketknife. He cut the flap and lifted the pages, his hands trembling as he began mouthing words in breathless silence.

"Well, Jesse, just keep it to yourself. I don't need to know what's goin' on."

"Good gosh, Ben!" He pulled what was left of the morning cool and began again, this time aloud.

>*Dad,*
>
>*I hope you're well. I'm really looking forward to seeing you again as I have so much to tell you. I'll start with the best news of all. I met the woman of my dreams. She worked with the Resistance through the war and played a key role in gaining freedom for me and the other prisoners in my last stalag near Waldheim.*
>
>*I love her more than I can say, Dad, and I believe you will, too. I can't wait for you to meet her. We plan to be married in Indiana where we are being sent on our last assignment. While there, I will resign my commission and receive remuneration for my last year's pay.*
>
>*I'm guessing you're wondering how I'm able to marry. I'll share the whole story when I see you, but you should know that Delores filed for annulment a year ago. With the help of some amazing Brits, that process has now been expedited and will be complete as soon as the papers reach Texas.*

Just so you know, I was wounded a few weeks back, but I'm doing well, and I expect to recover completely. I just received my mail for most of the past year and plan to catch up as I'm able. I did read one letter detailing your attempts to get the ranch back. The Brits contacted an attorney there who is working on our behalf to recover whatever is left of the herd. He looked at the lease-purchase agreement filed with the county clerk and said it shouldn't be a problem getting the title cleared.

I hope Dancer is well. I think of him every day. That horse taught me more than I can say, and I can't wait to roam those hills with him again.

*Love,
David*

Jesse nodded toward the cedar, his eyes crowning with pleasure. "Now, how are we going to enjoy our coffee without you bringing cream every morning, Ben? Did you even think of that when you sold your Jerseys? Didn't keep one for our use, did you? And I suppose you'll be wanting to run home as soon as I start cleaning the house."

Niedermeyer shook his head. "You're gonna clean *this* house? Yeah, I'm leavin'." Ben scraped the bristles beneath his chin. "Tell you what I'll do. I'll bring my wheelbarrow in the mornin', and we'll hitch that horse to it, drag out whatever's inside, and dump it in that lake down yonder. 'At's the onliest way you'll ever get this place clean."

"Well, you do that. And bring some cream with you when you come." Jesse spun around and wheeled himself to the tack shed, had no time for foolish conversation. He had a horse to tend to.